Reverie

Eliza Andrews

Andrews

Copyright © 2018 Eliza Andrews

All rights reserved.

ISBN: 9781976839900

REVERIE

For LT.

Andrews

Table of Contents

Part 1

Chapter 1 7
Chapter 2 15
Chapter 3 26
Chapter 4 33
Chapter 5 45
Chapter 6 56
Chapter 7 70
Chapter 8 83
Chapter 9 90
Chapter 10 99
Chapter 11 106
Chapter 12 114
Chapter 13 121
Chapter 14 129
Chapter 15 139
Chapter 16 151
Chapter 17 161
Chapter 18 174
Chapter 19 186
Chapter 20 198
Chapter 21 207

Part 2
Chapter 22 212
Chapter 23 220
Chapter 24 228
Chapter 25 236
Chapter 26 249
Chapter 27 262
Chapter 28 270
Chapter 29 282
Chapter 30 289
Chapter 31 300
Chapter 32 311
Chapter 33 320
Chapter 34 327
Chapter 35 337
Chapter 36 348
Chapter 37 356
Chapter 38 362
Chapter 39 373
Chapter 40 379
Chapter 41 384
Chapter 42 393
Chapter 43 404
Epilogue 407
Afterword 411

PART 1

LUCINDA HAMILTON

"A heap of broken images, where the sun beats,
And the dead tree gives no shelter, the cricket no relief,
And the dry stone no sound of water. Only
There is shadow under this red rock,
(Come in under the shadow of this red rock),
And I will show you something different from either
Your shadow at morning striding behind you
Or your shadow at evening rising to meet you;
I will show you fear in a handful of dust."

- T. S. Eliot, The Waste Land

Chapter 1

The first day is hard. It's mid-summer and it's hot, the air breezeless and heavy, the kind of day that makes shirts cling to backs and feet swim in shoes within mere seconds of stepping outside the artificial chill of air-conditioning. Lucinda stands in sandals in the sandy front yard, surveying the dilapidated little duplex before her, hands on her hips as she blows out a puff of air.

Cicadas drone in the background. The only other sounds come from her cousin Dan, as he grunts and pants out instructions to his friend.

"Grab it there — no, on the top," Dan says. "Tip it towards me — yeah. I'll hold it while you get down."

Lucinda bends over, picks up the plastic crate she'd set down between her feet. She twists, looking over her shoulder at Dan and his buddy Wheeler.

"Y'all need a hand with that?" she asks, not able to keep the anxiety out of her voice. It's her grandmother's antique dresser, after all.

"We're fine," a distracted Dan answers without turning to look at her. Sweat rolls down his temples, and the tanned muscles of his arms are tight with effort as he holds most of the weight of the dresser.

Wheeler hops down from the open tailgate, making the

truck bed bounce a little as the dresser balances precariously on its edge.

Wheeler glances over at Lucinda, lifts the dingy old baseball cap from his head long enough to run a thick hand through his matted brown curls. Then he puts it back on, adjusting the bill down to block out the sun.

"Don't worry," he drawls to Lucinda. "We got it."

He grins, and Lucinda remembers that she doesn't like the way he looks at her. She never has; it's a crafty, sharkish look that reminds her too much of her ex-husband.

"We ain't gonna drop it," Wheeler says. "Not so long as you open the door for us."

She nods once and climbs up the porch steps with the plastic crate still in her arms, fishing shiny, fresh-cut keys from her shorts pocket and pulling open the squeaky screen door. The corner of the screen is torn, she notes as she fiddles for the right key. And the whole door tilts sideways from the top, like it might be coming off its hinges. She'll have to talk to the landlord about getting it fixed.

She props the door open and waits, the men arguing and cursing as they heft the solid oak dresser up the three weathered, peeling porch steps and through the front door.

#

The second day is easier. It's just her, no Dan, no Wheeler, with only cicadas and classic rock she plays softly from an old radio to drown out the silence. She prefers being alone. Solitude means her thoughts have space to float, form, dissolve, like clouds in an empty sky.

She spends the day unpacking, and at the day's end, she makes herself a simple meal of rice and beans, because she hasn't gone grocery shopping yet and because she unpacked the box with the can opener late in the afternoon.

#

The third day is harder. It starts with her waking from a vivid nightmare, gasping and sweating, and as the day progresses, she jumps at every shadow, flinches at every creak the old duplex emits.

It seems as if Hart's voice follows her out of the dream and into the dawn — *"Lucinda, don't you walk away from me when I'm talkin' to you!"*

The day ends with a fear of sleep, a thought that insomnia and late-night novel reading might be preferable to what awaits her in her dreams.

#

On the fourth day, Dan comes by, because he's as kind and considerate and big-hearted as he was when they were all kids.

"How ya making out?" he asks after accepting the lemonade she offers him. They settle into two rickety old rocking chairs on the front porch.

Lucinda nods thoughtfully. "Alright, I guess." She wipes away the perspiration beading on the back of her neck. "Might be better if this heat would break."

He squints, scans the horizon with bright green eyes as if he expects to find something there. "S'posed to storm on Wednesday. That might help."

He sips his lemonade.

"Might do," Lucinda agrees. She almost asks, *"Is tomorrow Wednesday?"* but that would be embarrassing, as she really should know what day of the week it is. She'll check on her phone when she goes back inside.

"Aggie talked to her friend, the one I told you 'bout," Dan says, sounding pleased with himself.

"The one with the hair salon?"

"Yeah. Her name's Georgie. She's kind of an institution in this town." He adjusts the black-and-garnet Gamecocks hat on his head and lifts the corner of his mouth into a smile, making him look boyish and charming despite his unkempt red-brown beard. "Georgie seems to think you coming on board right now could be really good timing. On account of one of her hairstylists is expecting soon, and gettin' close to that point where she's not going to be able to work for a while. She told Aggie to tell you to drop by and talk to her."

"Thank you, Dan. You've been too good to me — you, and Aggie, too. Please tell her I said thank you."

It hasn't been easy, accepting the charity of her cousin and his wife. But sometimes, life pushes a person into a corner and doesn't give any other choice but to accept a handout.

Dan shrugs and leans back in the rocker, extending his legs out and crossing them at the ankle. Sandy dirt from the front yard cascades off the rubber treads of his work boots and creates a film of dust beneath his feet.

"This is what family's for, Lu. We were real tore up when Harriet called us and told us what happened. When she said you needed a place to be for a while. If I'd known sooner what you were going through with that bastard, I would've — "

"Let's not talk about it," Lucinda says quickly before he can go any further. She's hoping to sleep tonight and doesn't want to tempt the nightmares into bed with her.

"I'm sorry," Dan says, sounding like a child reproached.

Lucinda shrugs. "What's done is done. I'm here now. I'm moving on with my life."

Dan glances sideways, studies her for a long second like he might say something else, ask something else, but then he must think better of it, because all he does is nod and adjust his baseball cap again.

Silence ticks by — almost audible, almost tangible between them. Cicadas drone in the background.

The porch faces west, towards the two-lane highway that runs in front of the duplex. On the other side of the highway is an empty lot filled with kudzu-covered pine trees. Someone's tacked a hand-painted plywood sign onto one of the pines; it reads: "PRIVET PROPERTY. NO TRESPASSING." One day, Lucinda thinks, she'll cross the highway with a tin of black paint and fix the spelling error. From the front porch, though, the letters are barely legible; the error only bothers her when she's waiting for cars to pass so she can pull onto the highway.

A few more minutes go by. Like Lucinda, Dan isn't someone who needs to fill every empty space with meaningless chatter. The sun dips lower in the sky, but it's still strong, bright. It won't set until about the time Lucinda's ready for bed, and she's grateful for that.

Dan drains the rest of his lemonade, hands his empty glass back to Lucinda. He slaps his palms onto the arms of the rocking chair, pushes himself up with a soft grunt. "I should be gettin' on home," he says. "Aggie hates it when dinner gets cold on account of me bein' late." He takes a step towards the porch steps, then stops, turns back to Lucinda. "Oh. Speakin' of dinner, Aggie wanted me to tell you to come over and see us as soon as you get settled in." He chuckles. "Truth be told, I think she's hoping for a free haircut."

Lucinda tries to smile, but aborts the attempt halfway through. She's not ready to smile. Not yet. Maybe soon, though. Maybe by the time she accepts Aggie's invitation and goes to her cousin's house for dinner.

But even though she can't manage the smile, she says as warmly as she can, "I'll bring my scissors."

Dan nods and reaches down, thick fingers headed for

Lucinda's shoulder, and she flinches away automatically. His hand hangs in the air for a moment before dropping to his side.

Confusion washes his face for a moment, quickly replaced by remorse. "I shouldn't have — I guess I keep forgetting that — "

"It's fine," Lucinda says. "You didn't do anything wrong. Honestly. You and Aggie have been nothing but generous to me. And Wheeler, too. Tell him I said thanks next time you see him."

He shifts his weight from one foot to another, looks like he's about to say something but doesn't. Finally he shrugs and says, "Glad we could help. And you've got my number, right? And Aggie's? You just call if you need anything. Anything at all."

She nods but can't look at him anymore. She hates being pitied.

"I will. And I'll go see Georgie tomorrow."

#

But she doesn't venture into town the next day. She stays at home, unpacking, cleaning, weeding the little patch of dried mulch running in front of her half of the duplex that she wants to turn into a garden.

It passes the time. It keeps Hart's voice at bay.

#

The day after that must be Wednesday, because it storms. She smells the rain before she hears the first pattering drops slamming hard against the bare, dusty earth, and she goes out onto the porch to watch the thunderstorm roll in.

She sits in the rocking chair and kicks off her flip flops, pulls both feet up, wraps her arms around her knees as the sky slowly darkens. Leans her head back, watches silver-grey drops pelt the pine trees across the highway, pelt her old red Pontiac, pelt the dried patch of mulch that might one day be a garden.

And from the center of her chest, a memory surfaces — another summer rainstorm, long ago; a woman's hand, gently brushing drenched hair from Lucinda's forehead, and there's warmth in the woman's eyes when she smiles and says, *"I can't tell, Lulu. Are those teardrops or raindrops on your cheeks?"*

The memory fades as quickly as it came, but the twisting pain in Lucinda's heart remains. And for the first time since she arrived, she cries.

She cries hard, and she doesn't try to stop the tears.

Chapter 2

On Thursday, Lucinda heads into town and, after dropping by the post office to mail off a birthday card to a niece in Georgia, she forces herself to go to the hair salon.

The salon is situated on Main Street, with a shoe repair shop on one side of it and a mom 'n pop restaurant called *Linda's* on the other. It's midday, which means Linda's lunch crowd has taken up all the diagonal parking spaces out front, and Lucinda has to park down the street a ways, next to the cemetery. It's an old cemetery, the kind that contains its share of crumbling white gravestones marked "Unknown Confederate Soldier" if a person knows where to look. Lucinda knows where to look; when she was growing up, she spent every summer in this one-horse town with her mother and two sisters. Lucinda, her sisters, Dan, and the rest of her cousins used to play hide 'n seek in this very same cemetery almost every night after dinner and before bedtime.

On the other side of the cemetery, a few blocks up a street lined with old live oaks, is the stately Victorian where her Aunt Sophie, Dan's mother, used to live — the place where Dan and his family live now, Lucinda reminds herself. It's old enough that it might've stood defiantly when Union soldiers marched this way during the War. She stands on the sidewalk next to the cemetery, hands on hips, gazing across gravestones to see if she can remember which direction the house is, the direction they used to ride their bikes from.

Another glimpse of a memory surfaces: Her older sister, Edie, hunching over her bike with a wild grin on her face, pedaling as hard as she could across the tree-lined street towards the cemetery, while Lucinda and her baby sister, Harriet, stood on their pedals, pumping their little scab-kneed legs up and down like pistons, breathless in the attempt to catch up to their big sister. Tiny cousin Dan, who couldn't have been more than five years old at the time, shouting out a forlorn, *"Wait for me!"* from far behind.

"Pedal and pedal as fast as you can," Edie sang. *"You can't catch me, I'm the Gingerbread Man!"*

Even then, ten year-old Lucinda had recognized something in her sister that she didn't quite know how to articulate. The taunt was all wrong. The way Edie would have it, the Gingerbread Man was the superior one, the fast one, the clever one. Had Edie missed the moral of the story? The Gingerbread Man was a villain, a villain who tried to outsmart everyone else but who ended up outsmarted himself when the fox ate him halfway across the river.

Even today, Edie always thinks she's one step ahead, smug in her knowledge that she understands everything about everything, when really, she's riding on the fox's back without realizing it.

"I'm sure he's just stressed about his new job," Edie had told a twenty-two year-old Lucinda over the phone when she'd called her big sister to talk about her new husband's mood swings and angry outbursts. *"And y'all are still gettin' used to livin' with each other. Give him time. I'm sure it'll be fine."*

A car door opens, startling Lucinda out of her memories. She turns away from the cemetery; a man dressed in slacks and a short-sleeve button-down gives her a friendly nod and smile as he climbs into a shiny new pickup and starts the engine.

Lucinda smiles back, walks towards the salon.

How long will it be, she wonders, before the people of Reverie remember who she is? How long before the old men who play cards and hold court outside Linda's restaurant place her? How long before their wives at Georgie's hair salon pass her name from one to the next like a shared box of chocolates?

How long before they ask each other why she's living here now, when she's never seen fit to live here before?

#

Georgie's isn't actually called Georgie's, Lucinda realizes as she approaches the salon, even though that's all she's ever heard anyone call it. The words *Beautiful You* are stenciled on the plate glass window that faces the street in curving, large, orange-red letters, obscuring the row of women within reading magazines while they wait to get their hair "fixed" for the week. The "Y" in "You" is fashioned to resemble a pair of scissors, making Lucinda pause and stumble over the word a few times before her eye recognizes what it's supposed to be.

The bell tinkles pleasantly overhead when she opens the door and steps inside. Georgie's is replete with all the familiar sounds and smells of a hair salon, which makes something inside Lucinda unwind just a bit, a metal coil in her gut loosening that she hadn't known had tightened in the first place.

Stylists have customers in front of the long mirror that takes up one wall, pinning and trimming and clipping as they chatter. One of the stylists is remarkably young, Lucinda notices. The girl, who can't be more than twenty, chews her gum in perfect harmony with the rhythmic string of, *"Uh-huh. Yeah. Mmm... uh-huh,"s* she gives to the woman in her chair. An African American stylist in the rear of the shop leans an older woman back into a hair-washing station, and they both talk over the sound of the water spraying into her long, blonde hair.

On the other wall, an elderly woman sits beneath one of three large hair dryers, her eyes lightly closed as if in meditation or prayer, her wrinkled skin molded around the arms of the chair as she waits for her time to be up.

Four more women sit in a row along what must've once been a church pew but which now serves as the Beautiful

You waiting area. A bookshelf sits in the corner next to the pew, crammed with magazines and Christian self-help books and a beat-up radio crooning out staticky country music. And resting on top of the shelves, next to a dusty fake plant, an old-fashioned electric fan tries but fails to circulate air through the stuffy shop.

Three of the four women sitting on the pew turn to look at Lucinda when she walks in, the fourth remains absorbed in a magazine, flipping pages so quickly that she can't possibly be reading them.

None of the stylists see her, though, so Lucinda takes a few tentative steps forward, standing awkwardly next to a pile of hair clippings until the young stylist with the gum turns to acknowledge her.

"Can I help you?" the girl with the gum drawls. It's clear the girl wants to smile politely, but just as clear that she isn't thrilled about Lucinda interrupting her work. Before Lucinda can respond, she adds, "If you're here for a haircut, you can take a seat with those ladies over there." The girl, whose dyed, platinum blonde head barely reaches past Lucinda's chin, gestures at the pew with her scissors. The stabbing point is near enough to Lucinda's face that she leans backwards on instinct.

"I'm actually here to talk to Georgie," Lucinda says, eyes flitting from the girl to the tall, lean stylist her own age who's bent over a client's head and holding a black comb like a carving knife.

The older stylist straightens, looks Lucinda over with

interest, and Lucinda thinks her guess that this woman is Georgie must've been right.

The young blonde glances at the older stylist expectantly.

"What can I do for you?" asks Georgie, and her accent is every bit as thick as the girl's, but her smile is far more genuine. The necessary warmth of a small-town business owner.

"I'm Lucinda Hamilton, Dan Anderson's cousin? He said y'all might need someone to fill in for one of your girls when she has her baby."

Georgie puts down the comb on the counter, says something in her customer's ear that Lucinda can't hear over the hair dryer, the electric fan, the country music. Then Georgie strides over to Lucinda, offers a firm handshake.

"Lucinda!" she says, smile growing even more broad, showing off teeth too perfect for a woman her age. Her hair is greying but tastefully highlighted with blonde, falling to her shoulders and ending in a neat curl. She still has bangs — a more subdued version of the kind that were popular in the '80s and which some women never saw fit to abandon. In all, Georgie strikes Lucinda as well-put-together and rich. Well, Reverie rich.

"Welcome to Reverie," Georgie says. "We've heard so much about you from Aggie and Dan. How are you finding it here so far? Friendly enough for you? Although Dan says you spent your summers here with him when you were young, so I guess it's not entirely new to you, right? Did Dan tell you that he and Aggie are practically my closest neighbors now?"

The stream of questions overwhelms Lucinda, and she doesn't know how or where to start answering. She chooses the question that came last.

"Yes, ma'am, I do believe Dan said something about you and your husband moving in down the street from him recently."

"Mm-hmm, Walt and I — our children are all out of the house now, can you believe that? They grow up so fast. But Walt and I decided to downsize some after the last one went off to college, didn't need the big ol' farm we'd been living on, and plus we wanted to be closer to town."

Lucinda's mind snags on the word "downsize," because she knows that the houses near Dan's place are all like his — stately old Victorians, and not a one of them small. But, she supposes, maybe it would be easier to maintain one Victorian on a two-acre plot of land than managing an entire farm.

"Anyway," Georgie says, "listen to me rambling on! And I'm sure you have other things you need to get to today. I just love your hair, by the way. Whoever does your color does a real nice job," she adds, interrupting herself to reach out and twirl the chin-length waves of auburn on either side of Lucinda's temples. Georgie brushes it back just behind Lucinda's ears, and Lucinda blushes involuntarily.

"Thank you," Lucinda says, suddenly conscious of the fact that she hasn't had her hair colored since before everything happened back home, and the grey is probably starting to show at the roots again.

"Is this your natural color?" Georgie takes a half-step backward, squints at Lucinda's hair. "Not quite, right? But the curls, that's all you. I bet you were a regular Shirley Temple when you were a girl."

Lucinda's blush deepens as the conversation draws the attention of several other women in the shop, no doubt all of them inspecting her curls for authenticity. Her hair's a little longer than she normally keeps it, so the weight of it has drawn some of the curl out.

"It's... my hair doesn't naturally have this much red in it," she says at last.

"Well, I just love it," Georgie says. She puts her hands on her hips. "You have good taste, Lucinda, even if you didn't color this yourself. You didn't, did you? Tell me you didn't."

"No — of course not. One of the other girls in my shop —"

"Mmm-hmm," Georgie says with a nod. "Good taste and smart enough not to do it yourself, too. A professional, just like Aggie said. How many years did Aggie tell me you'd been cutting hair?"

"Thirteen years at a salon in Georgia before I..." Lucinda trails off before she makes it to the awkward part, wondering what to say about Hart, the divorce, her move.

"My other girl — Kathy's her name, bless her heart — her doctors want her on bedrest for the rest of her pregnancy. And she's only six months along, mind you, which means we have just been *scrambling* to keep up with everyone. Aggie says you're good, and you know how picky that woman can be about her hair! When can you start? Is tomorrow too early? Or do you still need time to settle in?"

"Yes, I suppose I could start tomorrow," Lucinda says, recovering from the shock of suddenly having a job without being asked about her cosmetology license, her salary needs, her references.

But this is Reverie, and Georgie is neighbors with Dan, and does Aggie's hair, and might've even done Aunt Sophie's hair and Aggie's mama's hair, and might've known Lucinda's mama before she moved to Georgia. In other words, Georgie already has Lucinda's references and then some.

"Good," Georgie says, softening with what appears to be sheer relief. She lowers her voice conspiratorially. "I've been covering my clients *and* Kathy's clients for the past two weeks, and girl, pardon my French, but I am as tired as a one-legged man in a butt-kicking contest. You can take over Kathy's schedule tomorrow. First appointment's eight-thirty AM. Is that alright?"

"Yes, ma'am, I can... do I need to bring anything?"

"If you got anything special you like to use, then go right ahead. Otherwise, you can use what we have here."

Georgie smiles broadly again, sweeps her hand out to indicate the counter of scissors and combs and hair dryers. For a moment, Lucinda thinks Georgie looks like a contestant in a beauty pageant, sweeping out an arm before a catwalk turn. She's still in the middle of that thought when Georgie takes one of Lucinda's hands in both of hers and shakes it vigorously, squeezing too hard. "It's good to have you on board, Lucinda. Now, if you don't mind, I really should get back to my customers."

"Thank you," a reeling, practically breathless Lucinda answers after a moment. "I appreciate it. I really do."

#

She drives home in a state of half-shock, still adjusting to the idea that she has a job again, that she'll need to figure out where her best scissors are from amongst the boxes she still hasn't unpacked.

When she pulls into the drive, there's another car in the yard, parked not in her space but in front of the other half of the duplex. It's a newer car, a shiny blue compact, the kind you see more often in cities with crowded roads and a shortage of parking than in a place like Reverie. The car almost looks familiar, like she knows someone with the same model, but she can't place it. When she climbs the porch steps, she sees shadows flitting behind the curtains of the unit next to hers.

Maybe she has a new neighbor?

If so, she should bake them something, just to be friendly. It *is* Reverie, after all, and being a good neighbor here is the rule, not the exception.

Chapter 3

The car's still there in the morning when Lucinda leaves for Georgie's, and there's a light on in the front room on the other side of the duplex. She definitely has a new neighbor. She mentally runs through the contents of her pantry and her refrigerator as she sits across from the "PRIVET PROPERTY. NO TRESPASSING" sign and waits to pull out onto the two-lane highway. She already has eggs and flour and milk and sugar; she'll need to pick up some butter, chocolate chips, and pecans on her way home from the salon.

Her first day of work will be a busy one, and now Lucinda understands why Georgie had wanted her to come on board so quickly. Knowing that their stylist was pregnant and would be out for a while, clients had clambered for a spot on Kathy's schedule while they still had time. No one had expected Georgie would end up taking most of those spots, and definitely no one expected Lucinda.

The African American stylist Lucinda had only seen from behind the day before is the only other person in the shop when she arrives, giving a middle-aged man dressed for work a fade cut with a set of buzzing clippers. Instead of country, the radio on the bookshelf is set to gospel this morning, and except for the clippers and the radio, the shop is quiet. The stylist hums along to the hymn as she tips the man's head forward, looking up at Lucinda when the silver bells above the door announce her entrance.

The stylist greets Lucinda with a smile. "You must be Lucinda," she says. "My name's Rhonda."

"Nice to meet you, Rhonda," Lucinda says, not offering a handshake since the woman's hands are full. "Can you tell me which chair is Kathy's?"

"Mmm-hmm. It's that one right there, on the end," Rhonda says, pointing with an electric blue-painted fingernail patterned with small white flowers.

They chit chat above the head of the silent man while Lucinda settles in and checks the supplies arranged on the counter. She sees a snapshot of a woman and man and two young boys taped to the mirror, and finds out from Rhonda that this is Kathy and her family, and isn't it a shame about how difficult her pregnancy is?

"I been prayin' for her," Rhonda says. "My whole church been prayin' for her." She pauses a moment, glances over at Lucinda curiously. "You got a church family in Reverie yet?"

"No," Lucinda says, "not yet," and given the fact that Rhonda's playing gospel, that she mentioned her prayers for Kathy already, and that Lucinda's learned, in less than ten minutes of conversation, that one of Rhonda's favorite sayings is, "Mmm, God is *good,* sister," Lucinda decides not to mention the fact that she doesn't believe in God. She hasn't believed in a few months. Before that, she was agnostic for many years, not quite willing to dismiss the preachers of her youth, but not quite ready to embrace their easy confidence in the existence of an All-Powerful Almighty Creator, either.

She'll be polite to Rhonda, she decides, because first impressions matter, but Lucinda heard the phrase *You're in my prayers* so many times before leaving Georgia that she'd wanted to scream at everyone by the end.

"It's not your prayers I want, goddammit!" she might've shouted. *"It's Dionne!"*

Dionne, the woman with the soft brown eyes and softer lips. Dionne, who always called her "Lu" or "Lulu." Dionne, youthful and fun, who eventually got good at making even boring, plain-old Lucinda feel youthful and fun. Dionne is the part of Georgia Lucinda misses the most.

But Lucinda's not the kind of woman who shouts or curses.

She's glad no one's said *You're in my prayers* to her so far in Reverie. Not even Dan.

"You should visit my church sometime," Rhonda says. She pauses, then adds, "I gotta be honest, we don't have a lot of white faces in the pews, but there's a few, and everyone would make you feel plenty welcome."

"I'm sure they would," Lucinda agrees pleasantly. "Maybe I can drop by sometime."

The man in the chair makes a noise that sounds halfway

between a cough and a laugh, and he pipes up for the first time. "What church you go to, Rhonda?"

"Mount Zion. Out near the clinic."

"Reverend James still the preacher out there?" asks the man.

Rhonda clucks her tongue and smiles happily. "Now how you know Brother James?" she asks, and the two launch into a conversation about a preacher Lucinda's never heard of and the four main church congregations in Reverie (First Baptist, First Methodist, St. Mark's Lutheran, and, of course, Mount Zion AME). Lucinda is glad to be left out of the conversation, and her first client comes in a few minutes later.

#

Lucinda's second client is already waiting by the time the first one's finished, and by then, Kylah — the young blonde stylist with the gum and the impatience from the day before — has arrived, preparing her space for her own first customer. Georgie doesn't come in at all that morning, and Lucinda learns from Rhonda and Kylah that she usually only cuts hair on Tuesdays and Thursdays; the rest of the week, she only pops by to check up on "her girls" and gather the mail.

When Lucinda shows surprise about this, Kylah grins and chews her gum and says, "You said you used to spend summers here as a kid? Then you prob'ly know who

Georgie's husband is."

Lucinda glances from Rhonda to Kylah, then back down at the head before her. "No. Who's her husband?"

"Walt Brinkmann," says the woman in her chair. When Lucinda doesn't let out a knowing *Ahhh,* the woman adds, "Of Brinkmann's Lumber?"

"Brinkmann…" Lucinda repeats, because now that the women bring it up, the name *does* sound familiar.

"Brinkmann's Lumber's been in Walt's family for generations," says Rhonda's client. "The Brinkmanns must own half of Reverie."

"More like three-quarters of it," says Lucinda's client.

Then Lucinda remembers where she knows the name from. "The duplex I'm living in, it's a Brinkmann who owns it."

Rhonda clucks her tongue against the roof of her mouth. "That'll be *Zeke* Brinkmann. Walt's little brother."

The woman in Lucinda's chair scoffs. "Ne'er-do-well," she says derisively. "How's your duplex, Lucinda? In good shape?"

"Well," Lucinda says carefully, because she's not familiar enough with Reverie's politics and social networks to know who is or isn't kin with the Brinkmanns, who will and won't be offended when she admits what terrible shape the house she's renting actually is. She settles on simply admitting: "It's an older house. All older homes have some… personality."

Each of the women listening laugh, and even one of the

women waiting on the church pew looks up from her spot to see what everyone's talking about and joins in with the laughter when someone says to her simply, "Zeke Brinkmann."

"Personality, huh? That's a polite way of puttin' it," Kylah says.

"Older house, *nothing*," shrills the woman in Lucinda's chair. "I bet it's falling apart, is what it is. You should call up Zeke, get him to fix it up for you. Threaten to move out if he won't. That's all Zeke responds to — threats."

Lucinda shrugs. Yes, the screen door is half off its hinges and won't close properly; the numbers on the stove dials have all been worn off with time; the back stairs leading out of the kitchen are so rotten that she's afraid to put a foot on them. But…

"The rent's low," is all she says in the end.

Rhonda arches an eyebrow. "Mmm, Lord bless, I know *that's* right."

Conversation moves on to high school football, and most of the excitement centers around Rhonda's older son Brandt, who's a senior this year and fully expected to be the team's top running back. Rhonda goes on and on about him, not only about football, but about how college scouts started looking at him last year, and how he's got the brains to match all his brawn.

Lucinda doesn't know anything about the Reverie High School football team, so she keeps quiet, finishes her customer, and sweeps up her station before looking down at the handwritten sheet of notebook paper that Georgie had left for her.

She squints at the next name on the list before looking over at the church pew filled with women.

"Are one of y'all Ardie Brown?" she asks them.

A squarish woman with a thick mop of black hair folds a page corner down in the paperback she's reading and raises her hand halfway.

Lucinda smiles at her. "You're here for the twelve o'clock? C'mon over."

Chapter 4

Ardie Brown stands, hitches up faded blue jeans, walks over to Lucinda's chair with workboot-heavy steps. Lucinda thinks she must be in her forties somewhere; she's no spring chicken, but her dark hair doesn't have enough grey in it to make her any older than about forty-five or forty-six. And Ardie's thick in all the places a person can be thick at — wide hips, broad shoulders, a squat neck that looks like it would fit in on the Reverie High School football team, topped off by a strong, jutting jaw. But Lucinda wouldn't describe Ardie Brown as "fat," per se; she just has one of those big frames that's usually more common in men than in women. Ardie Brown is what Lucinda's father would've called *"a sturdy woman."*

Strong and sturdy. It's something Lucinda can respect.

Ardie's black eyes meet Lucinda's hazel ones in the mirror once she sits down. "What happened to Kathy?" she asks. "I thought she wasn't due for another couple months."

"Apparently the doctor put her on bed rest," Lucinda says, and she notices that Kylah and Rhonda, who've been chatty all morning, have gone oddly quiet.

"Oh. Well, I hope everything's okay with the baby," Ardie says.

"Me, too."

To Lucinda's left, Rhonda gets to talking with her client again, going back to the topic of her son and high school football and the prayers they do with him for an injury-free season. Kylah picks up a conversation about afternoon soap operas with her client, leaving Lucinda to talk with Ardie on her own.

"What are we doing with your hair today?" Lucinda asks.

Ardie laughs. "Whatever you *can* do with it."

Lucinda smiles, because Ardie's hair is that thick, black kind, notorious for cowlicks and refusing to be tamed. "You want the same style, or something new?"

"Just the same is fine. A trim so I don't scare children in dark alleys, I think."

"Then let's get you a shampoo first," Lucinda says, rotating Ardie's chair towards the wash station in the back. "Your hair will be easier to work with if it's damp."

Ardie laughs again. "You sure 'bout that? Kathy once threatened me with sheep shears."

Lucinda laughs with her. "I can see why."

Ardie's quieter than Lucinda's other customers so far. She doesn't talk at all during the wash, holds her paperback in her lap and patiently follows directions when Lucinda begins to work on her hair.

Lucinda doesn't mind the quiet. Hair salons are chatty places, and she's gotten used to it over the years, but she's naturally reserved herself, and never forces a conversation with a client who's not particularly garrulous.

After a few minutes of comfortable silence, though, Ardie's the one who starts talking.

"Do you know Kathy well?" she asks.

"I don't know Kathy at all," Lucinda says. "I just moved to Reverie. My cousin, Dan Anderson, told me that Georgie might need another stylist soon on account of Kathy's pregnancy. But when I came in yesterday to see about it, I sure didn't expect to be cutting hair *today.*"

"I know Dan. He's been a customer at my Daddy's auto shop for years. Like most of the folks in this town." Ardie smiles at her in the mirror, a mischievous twinkle in her dark eyes. It gives her an almost schoolboy charm. "But you moved to Reverie? Now why on Earth would you want to do that?"

Lucinda dodges the question artfully. "What's so bad about Reverie? You live here, don't you?"

"I do, but I don't have a lot of choice in the matter. I was born here. 'Born 'n bred,' as they say."

"If you don't like it, you could've moved away," Lucinda counters.

"I did. For a while. Joined the Marines not long outta high school, wanted to 'see the world' and what-not. Lived in Tucson for a couple years after I got out." Ardie sighs. "But you know how it goes. Aging parents. Dad got sick, then fell and broke a hip. Came back home to help out."

"Mm-hmm," Lucinda says, nodding in agreement. "My mom passed a couple years ago. Alzheimer's. It was a lot to keep up with, those last few years of her life. We kept her at home for as long as we could, but eventually had to put her in a place. Got too hard to take care of her."

"We?" Ardie asks. "Who's 'we'?"

"My husband and I," Lucinda responds automatically. Then she corrects herself. *"Ex*-husband."

"Ah," Ardie says, and falls silent again. A couple minutes later, just as Lucinda's almost finished with the fade she's giving to the sides of Ardie's uncooperative hair, Ardie asks, "Did I hear you say you're living in one of Zeke Brinkmann's places?"

"Yes, ma'am, you heard right."

"I went to high school with Zeke," Ardie says. "We were the same year. He did slipshod work back then and he probably still does slipshod work today."

Lucinda switches out plastic guards on the clippers, leans Ardie's head to buy a moment's time. She's surprised by Ardie's frankness. In a town where most of the people she's met so far hold tightly to the distinctly southern habit of indirectness with all but their most trusted circle, Lucinda both appreciates and also doesn't know how to take Ardie's straightforward honesty.

"I'm pretty handy with most things," Ardie continues. "If you ever want me to come over and fix a few things up, I'd be happy to do it."

"Thank you," Lucinda says, going from surprised to taken aback. "But it's my first day on the job today. And I left Georgia without two pennies to rub together, to be honest. How d'you think I ended up at Zeke Brinkmann's in the first place?"

Ardie chuckles. "Who said anything about charging you? That's how Kathy and I met. I fixed her car for her; she gave me free haircuts for a year."

"Oh-ho," Lucinda says, chuckling. "So *that's* what you're hoping for — come fix my screen door and get a year's worth of free haircuts from the gullible new girl?"

Lucinda's surprising herself, bantering like this with Ardie. She can't really say why she's teasing the stranger in her chair this way, she just knows it feels light and easy. Natural, despite the fact that they don't know each other.

But the reflection of Ardie's face in the mirror develops a hot, red flush. It creeps up Ardie's neck until it reaches her ears, then her cheeks. Lucinda feels both mildly guilty for making her blush and charmed by Ardie's sensitivity at the same time.

"I didn't mean it that way," Ardie corrects. "I didn't say it for a free haircut. Heck, I could go without *any* haircuts."

"Now you know *that's* definitely not true," Lucinda says, pulling a talc-coated brush from its place on the counter.

"Well, I was only trying to say…" Ardie starts again, flustered.

Lucinda winks at Ardie in the mirror. "I know. I was only teasing you."

"I wasn't asking for anything in return," Ardie says,

still red. "I just know what Zeke can be like, is all. And since you're new in town... I was just wanted to be neighborly. Welcoming."

Lucinda takes a clean towel, whisks it across Ardie's still-red ears, the back of her neck, the sides of her neck. She catches the smell of Ardie herself as she leans in, a slurried mix of leather, motor oil, old denim, and men's deodorant. She has to stop herself from leaning further in, taking a deeper whiff.

Lucinda straightens, puts both hands on Ardie's shoulders, gives them a squeeze. She meets her eyes in the mirror. "You're gracious and generous to offer, and I'll keep it in mind."

Then she unsnaps the back of the nylon smock and sweeps it off Ardie with a practiced hand, sending a cascade of black hair to the floor and getting none of it on Ardie. Before she turns the chair around, she pats Ardie's shoulder one last time and says, "Who knows. If you really do want to help, there might even be a couple free haircuts in it for you." And without knowing she's about to do so, she gives Ardie another wink in the mirror.

Ardie stands, brushes her hands down the sides of her jeans in a manner that looks more habitual than purposeful. "Thanks, Lucinda. Do I pay you, or...?"

"Yes, you can just pay me."

Ardie pulls a man's-style leather billfold from her back pocket and opens it, pulling out a twenty and a ten that are both warm and slightly moist from having been sat on for who knows how much of the humid August morning.

"You can keep the change," Ardie says, even though a simple trim is still only eighteen dollars at Beautiful You.

Lucinda looks at the bills, looks at Ardie. "No, Ardie, this is way too much."

Ardie shrugs. "It's your first day on the job. I want you to have a couple extra pennies to rub together." She looks in the mirror, runs a meaty, calloused hand over the shaved back of her head. "Besides, it's the best haircut I've had in a while."

"It didn't look like you'd had *any* haircut in a while," Lucinda says.

Ardie grins crookedly, the twinkle glinting in her dark eyes again. "Guilty as charged."

She walks to the door, pushes it halfway open, turns to wave goodbye to Lucinda. Lucinda smiles, raises her own hand in return, then grabs a broom and dustpan to sweep up.

Rhonda watches Lucinda in the mirror as she sweeps up, then wraps another strand of her client's white hair tightly around a curler.

"Mmmm, *girl,*" Rhonda says to Lucinda. "Looks like you made yourself a little friend. Bet you're glad about that."

"She seems like a very generous person," Lucinda agrees, not catching the sarcasm in Rhonda's tone.

Rhonda snorts through her nose, shakes her head. *"That's* not the kind of generosity I would want, personally.

It's why Kathy cut her hair and the rest of us didn't."

Lucinda looks up from her sweeping, glances at Kylah, who's chewing her gum and nodding, and then at Rhonda, whose lips are pursed and whose eyebrows are raised in the center, forming a little horseshoe of creases on her forehead.

"What do you mean?"

"She was flirting with you!" Kylah barked, then broke into cackling laughter.

"Next time she comes in and offers to come 'fix things up' around your house, you gotta tell her thanks-but-no-thanks, make it clear you're not her kinda girl," Rhonda says.

Lucinda blushes, but not for the reason the other women think. She doesn't blush about Ardie's halfhearted attempt at flirting with her; Lucinda appreciated the attention. Enjoyed it, even. It's the first time since she moved to Reverie that she's felt *awake,* like she wasn't swimming through some kind of foggy dream. And if she'd met Ardie under different circumstances — at a bar, for instance, or by chance on the sidewalk — she might've worked a little harder to show that the interest was mutual. And if Ardie had asked for her phone number, she might've given it.

So no, the reason Lucinda blushes isn't because she'd missed the fact that Ardie is clearly gay and showing some interest in her. The reason Lucinda blushes is that she *hates* to be condescended to. It reminds her of her ex-husband,

and it brings up a complicated mix of feelings that contain both anger and fear.

"That's not your kind of girl," he'd said once, referring to Dionne. *"You can tell her that, next time you see her. Tell her you got better things to do with your time. And if she gives you any trouble 'bout it, you tell her she can talk to me."*

But Rhonda takes Lucinda's blush as further evidence of her naiveté, and keeps going.

"See what I mean?" she says. "Now you understand why I won't put my hands on that woman. If you can call *that* a woman."

On Rhonda's other side, Kylah laughs. "Oh, Rhon. What's wrong, you afraid it's gonna spread? You afraid one day you're gonna show up in motorcycle boots and start offering to fix up my house?"

Rhonda closes her eyes a moment, shivers, opens them again. "It's just not *natural*. A woman like Ardith Brown, that's a sign something's *wrong* inside a person."

"There's nothing 'wrong' with her!" Kylah says with another laugh. "She's just *gay*."

"Like I said," Rhonda says. "Not natural. *God* says it's not natural, right there in black 'n white in the Good Book. It's in the Old Testament, in Leviticus, and Paul says it to the Romans in the New, 'cause apparently they'd forgotten all about Sodom and Gomorrah by then."

"Uh-huh, sure," Kylah says, chomping down on her gum a couple times. "Bein' gay's not natural and the Bible condemns it, but your black magic, that's just perfectly normal?"

Black magic? Lucinda looks from Rhonda to Kylah with curiosity and confusion.

Kylah catches her expression, explains, "Rhonda didn't tell you? Her family's, like, practically hoodoo royalty down 'round Beaufort."

"Hoodoo?" Lucinda repeats, not sure what the word means but also hoping the topic might take Rhonda's attention off Ardie.

"You don't know what you're talkin' 'bout, Kylah," Rhonda says brusquely, reaching for another hair-curler.

"I don't?" Kylah says, clearly enjoying herself. "That's what Brandt told me. Said his great-grandmother called herself the Mother Hen or something, and people used to come from all around for love potions and all sorts of things."

The skeptical horseshoe reappears on Rhonda's forehead, her lips press into a tight line. *"Root* work. It's called root work. You shouldn't talk about that which you clearly do not understand." She scoffs. "Black magic. Anything white people don't understand and get a little scared of, they call it 'black.'"

"See?" Kylah says gleefully, jabbing her scissors in Rhonda's direction. "You can talk about other people being unnatural all you want, but if you ask me, that hoodoo stuff is some pretty creepy shit."

Rhonda bristles, doesn't even look at Kylah when she

says, "There's nothing 'unnatural' about tapping into the energies God Almighty put on this Earth and learning how to use them properly."

"If you say so," Kylah says.

The dueling women fall silent after that, both of them shifting their focus to the customers in their chairs instead of each other. Lucinda uses the silence to make her escape.

"I'm heading out for lunch," she says. "Any of y'all need anything while I'm out?"

They shake their heads, and Lucinda unbuttons her smock, shakes the loose hairs off once, and hangs it on the back of her chair.

She goes next door to Linda's for lunch, deciding she'd better go ahead and get to know the other local businesses on the Main Street strip. When she finishes and heads back to Beautiful You, she catches a glimpse of Ardie down the street, not far from where Lucinda's Pontiac is parked. Ardie looks like she's having an animated, happy discussion with the bearded man in front of her, who's leaning back on his elbows, propped atop the edge of an old pickup truck bed. Ardie's standing next to a motorcycle, a helmet dangling from one hand, the other hand resting on the motorcycle's seat.

Lucinda waves, but Ardie's too engrossed in her conversation to see her.

#

The afternoon is unremarkable. Lucinda has only two more clients to see and leaves for the day by three o'clock. She could've left earlier than three, but Georgie had shown up around two to check in on things and collect the mail, and kept Lucinda talking for a full thirty minutes after her last customer paid and left.

She swings by the grocery store on the way home, picking up the chocolate chips and pecans she plans on using in the cookies she's going to bake for her new neighbor. Maybe the neighbor (or *neighbors?*) will be around when she gets home, and she can meet them.

Chapter 5

Lucinda's a little disappointed when she arrives home to find the compact car missing from the driveway and the unit next to hers dark. She bakes cookies anyway, puts them in a glass casserole dish covered with tinfoil and leaves them on the new welcome mat that's appeared in front of the screen door next to hers.

When she wakes the next morning, the casserole dish is gone, the compact's in the front yard again, and there's definitely a light on inside the unit. She smiles to herself, hoping someone enjoyed her cookies.

Her customer load is even lighter than it had been the day before, and she's finished by lunchtime, and that's even after she'd taken a walk-in. Kylah invites her to lunch at Linda's, but Lucinda opts to go home, pulls back into her yard a little after twelve-fifteen.

The compact is still there, she notes, and as she climbs the porch stairs she thinks she hears music playing in the other unit.

Should she knock on the door? Introduce herself? Lucinda hesitates at the top of stairs, standing in the ambiguous no-man's-land between the two doors.

In the end, the decision is made for her. The music shuts off abruptly, an interior light goes off, the front door swings opens.

A young woman steps out backwards, brunette hair falling in waves to the middle of her back. She wears dark green nurse's scrubs, holds the strap of some kind of lunch cooler in one hand, her keys in the other. Her mouth is stuffed with a bagel, and it waggles up and down a little as she tries to get the door closed without letting the lunch cooler get caught in the closing door.

"Can I hold something for you?" Lucinda asks.

The young woman spins around, bagel flying from her mouth and landing on the porch below. Her eyes widen, then relax when she sees Lucinda.

Her face breaks into a big smile, and Lucinda's breath catches.

This girl. She looks just like Dionne. *Just* like Dionne — especially with that smile. She could be Dionne's sister.

The girl puts a hand over her heart and exhales. "Oh my gosh, you *scared* me."

"I'm so sorry," Lucinda says. "I made you drop your —"

They both reach for the fallen bagel at the same time, bumping crowns in the process. Lucinda lets out a soft, surprised, "Oh!" at the same time the girl says, "Ow!"

They stand again, meet eyes, and both break into laughter. The girl who looks like Dionne bends down and picks up the bagel — which fortunately didn't fall cream-cheese-side-down — and brushes it off.

"Is your head okay?" the girl asks.

"It's fine," Lucinda says. "My mother always told me I was hard-headed anyways."

"Mine, too!" the girl says. She takes a bite of the bagel, says around a mouthful, "I'm a nurse, so if you think you really did hurt your head just now, I could check you out."

"No, no, I'm fine," Lucinda assures her. She holds out a hand. "I'm Lucinda. Or — my friends and family call me 'Lu,' sometimes."

Not many people call her Lu, actually. But Dionne had called her Lu.

The girl brushes the hand that had just been holding the bagel down the side of her scrubs and shakes Lucinda's hand. "Lu. Nice to meet you." Something seems to occur to the girl, because her face suddenly brightens. "Are you the one who left those cookies outside my door this morning?"

Lucinda smiles, nods.

"O. M. G. They were — *are,* I should say *are* instead of were, I haven't eaten *all* of them yet. They're amazing, Lu! Does that mean you're my next door neighbor?"

Lucinda nods again.

"Okay, so are you gonna, like, bake me cookies at least once per week?" The girl doesn't give Lucinda a chance to respond, slaps Lucinda's shoulder playfully with the back of her hand. "I'm just joshin'. Sort of!" She cackles with laughter. As her laughter trails off, she looks down at her bagel, seeming to consider it. "I should get going," she says. "Gotta be at the hospital early today."

"Second shift worker?" Lucinda asks.

"Yep. Down at County," says the girl. She takes another bite of the bagel, is still chewing when she adds, "Some people don't like the second shift, get all uppity about needing to have first shift, like it's some kind of badge of honor to have to be at the hospital by seven in the morning." She swallows her bagel down. "Not me. Doctors go home by five, visiting hours are over by eight, the hospital gets real quiet those last few hours as everyone falls asleep. But you still get home by midnight, so you can get a decent night's sleep." She pulls a cracked cell phone from her breast pocket, makes a face when she sees what time it is. "It was nice to meet you, Lu," she says, reaching out and shaking Lucinda's hand a second time. "I've got to run if I'm going to get there on time."

Without a backwards glance, the girl bounds down the stairs and into the shiny blue compact car, throwing the lunch cooler on the passenger seat and waving at Lucinda when she pulls onto the highway.

It's not until the compact is well out of sight that Lucinda realizes the girl never offered her own name.

Lucinda shakes her head with fresh amusement, smiles to herself as she unlocks her door and steps inside. She hums as she tidies up around the house and finally finds the motivation she'd been missing to unpack the rest of her boxes. A few hours later, she prepares an elaborate dinner for herself even though it's still early, because she never did manage to get a proper lunch. She tries watching a movie on Netflix when she's finished, but the Internet is acting up again and she gives up and retreats to her room before seven.

She reads for a couple hours, thinking she might stay up long enough to hear the nurse come home from her shift at the hospital, but falls asleep long before midnight.

#

Lucinda sleeps in until almost seven the next day, glad that it's Sunday and the salon is closed. Most things are closed in Reverie on Sundays — everything on Main Street is closed, from Linda's on one corner up to the old hardware store on the other. Even the bigger places, chain stores that are either in Reverie or in neighboring Ballast, stay shuttered on Sunday or open late.

A quiet Sunday morning sitting at home suits her. She brews coffee early, steps out onto the dew-dampened front porch in bare feet and curls up into the rocking chair like a coffee-drinking cat, thinking to watch what's left of the sunrise.

Her Pyrex casserole dish, the one she'd filled with fresh-baked cookies for her new neighbor, sits on the round glass table between the two rocking chairs, a Post-It note inside with "THANKS" and a smiley face scrawled in blue ink.

The casserole dish sends Lucinda's gaze to the unit next door, which is dark and quiet. She wonders what time the girl got home from the hospital the night before, wonders what time she usually gets up in the morning, wonders if she takes coffee or tea or neither one.

She turns back towards the lightening sky a moment later, sips coffee, reminds herself to pick up more creamer when she's in town tomorrow.

Even if it weren't for the fact that the neighbor girl looks remarkably similar to the absent Dionne, she's beautiful in her own right. And it's not simply the long, wavy hair that still has the luminosity of youth; it's not the heart-shaped face or the brown doe's eyes. It's not her long, lithe frame. There's something about the girl that *glows,* that bespeaks of an energy bubbling beneath the surface that contains both vibrancy and the potential for tenderness.

Dionne used to glow like that.

Perhaps the girl will become Lucinda's first real friend in Reverie, someone who will talk to her not out of circumstance, like her co-workers and customers do, and not out of pity, like Dan and Aggie. Perhaps she'll talk to Lucinda because that bubbling energy won't contain itself, but will spill over and share itself in the natural, organic way that such energy tends to do.

Perhaps she'll overlook the fact that Lucinda is at least twenty years her senior, and see something beautiful in Lucinda, too.

Lucinda shakes her head at herself. She spoke with this girl all of five minutes the other day, and nothing in those five minutes should've given her any indication that the girl is anything more than a friendly neighbor. She needs to put any other kinds of ideas out of her mind.

She takes another sip of coffee, studies the winding patterns of shadows the kudzu across the street casts upon the pines to give herself something to focus on.

Since across the street is west and behind her is east, it takes time for the sunrise to reach the stand of pines. By the time "PRIVET PROPERTY. NO TRESPASSING." is illuminated by the warm yellow of the rising sun, Lucinda's coffee is down to its dregs. The day seems like it will be hot and humid again; already, the air feels heavy, slow, and soupy.

Lucinda stands with a sigh, stretches, decides she may as well make something of her day while she still has a chance.

#

A palmetto tree grows in the yard, just a few feet from the corner of the porch on Lucinda's side of the duplex, its fronds brushing up gently against the edges of the porch overhang. It's one of the few things in the yard that's actually living, and possibly the *only* thing that's actually thriving, so Lucinda decides that the palmetto is as good a place as any to start the garden.

She doesn't have a plan for the garden, not exactly, but she knows she wants to transform the dry, barren strip of mulch that runs in front of her side of the duplex into something cheerier to look at. Something that doesn't remind her she's living here because she ran, that doesn't remind her of the horror show life in Georgia became before she picked up the phone and called Dan.

She'll build out her new garden at least to the dusty path that leads to the porch steps; and if the girl next door will let her, she'll extend it out further so that it reaches the opposite corner of the porch. If she had a different landlord, if the house was in better shape, she might've thought to ask permission before transforming the yard this way. But Zeke will thank her, if he has any kind of common sense, for improving his property. And if he doesn't thank her… well, she won't feel bad about stating just what kind of condition the duplex is in the next time his name comes up at the salon.

But her landlord's reaction is something to worry about later. For today, she'll focus on simply clearing the ground — removing the dry mulch, pulling up what few weeds have managed to grow in the unforgiving sandy soil, and turning over that same soil to see if there's anything richer worth working with beneath, or if she's going to have to spend more than she can really afford on topsoil at the greenhouse out in Ballast.

Fifteen minutes after she's washed her coffee mug and put it it upside down in the rack to dry, Lucinda is on her hands and knees in the dirt next to the palmetto tree, digging out a stubborn dandelion root with a spade. An hour or two after that, she's made a nice boundary around the tree, and has turned over most of the soil between her boundary and the edge of the porch.

Her attention is somewhere in the earth, dreaming of the clematis she'll train to climb the lattice work, when a voice startles her back into the present.

"Hey, neighbor," the voice says.

Lucinda jumps, drops the spade.

"Oh, sorry — I didn't mean to sneak up on you."

Lucinda turns slowly towards the voice, trying to get her racing heart under control. It's an overreaction, she knows, but she can't help herself; she spooks easily. Often as not, nightmares follow her out of the night and into her morning, then into her afternoon, her evening, only to crawl back into bed with her once again when she turns off the reading lamp at bedtime.

But it's not a nightmare standing a couple yards away, it's Ardie Brown. She gazes down at Lucinda curiously, holding something in one hand that's covered with foil.

Ardie sees Lucinda glance from her to the tinfoil-covered item in her hand. She lifts it a few inches.

"It's a pie," she says. "Peach. My mom made it for you when I told her you'd moved into one of Zeke's places down the way from us."

Lucinda stands up, uses the back of one gloved hand to wipe the beads of sweat from her eyebrows. It sends a little spray of sand and dirt into her eyes, so she takes the glove off, cleans off her stinging eyes with fingers that are mostly clean.

"I called up Georgie to find out where you moved into, because I knew that some of Zeke's places are close to us. I hope you don't mind," Ardie says, sounding self-conscious. Lucinda finds herself wondering how Georgie knew where she's living in the first place. But then again, it's Georgie's, and this is Reverie, and Beautiful You is one of the town's nerve centers.

"Turns out you're neighbors with Mom and Dad and me," Ardie says. She lifts the pie again with a sheepish smile when Lucinda doesn't respond. "Hence the pie. Mama hardly ever makes it out of the house anymore, but she does still like tinkering around the kitchen. Peach is her specialty, and she insisted on making it for you."

Lucinda takes the sight of Ardie in, standing there awkwardly with a pie in her hand, wearing worn-knee blue jeans and a grey t-shirt that strains around her shoulders and her chest. There's a motorcycle next to her, the same motorcycle Lucinda had seen her next to a few days earlier in town. Lucinda realizes that Ardie must have pulled into the yard, parked between Lucinda's Pontiac and the shiny blue compact, and dismounted, all without Lucinda noticing.

Had she really been so lost in her own world to miss all that happening?

"Is this a bad time?" Ardie asks when Lucinda is still silent several seconds later. She gestures with the pie towards the duplex. "I can just leave the pie on your porch and get on back home. My dad needs some help around the house today, anyway."

"No, no, of course not," Lucinda says, snapping out of her fog at last. She walks over to Ardie, taking the pie from her with a smile she hopes is welcoming enough to make up for her earlier lack of responsiveness.

She lifts a corner of the foil covering the pie plate, peers inside at the peach pie. Lattice strips of pie crust criss-cross over the top, and Lucinda catches a whiff of something that smells like nutmeg.

"Is it too early for pie?" she asks Ardie. "Or will you join me for a slice?"

Ardie's face relaxes, breaks into a broad smile that lights up her moon-round face.

Strong and sturdy, Lucinda reminds herself, feeling a spark of affection for Ardie kindle in her heart.

"I don't know what your family's like, but in my family, it's never too early for pie," Ardie answers.

"Good," Lucinda says, "I think I like your family already."

She heads up the porch steps with the pie in her hands, leaving it on the wobbly glass-topped table between the two rocking chairs as she heads inside for saucers, forks, and sweet tea.

Chapter 6

"A little late in the season to be starting a garden," Ardie says a few minutes later, after they've each had their first bite of pie.

Lucinda licks the gummy sweetness from her fork, marveling at the baking abilities of Ardie's mother. "I know," she says. "But I couldn't bear to look at that sad ol' patch of mulch anymore. It was depressing."

Ardie chuckles, seems to think about it for a moment. "You might could still plant some fall vegetables. Probably too late for tomatoes, but maybe collards. Beans, even. Onions."

Lucinda nods. "And spinach, in about a month."

Ardie takes another bite of her pie. "So what brings you to Reverie? Besides the peach pie and the fall spinach? You never did tell me the other day why you moved here."

Lucinda sighs, preparing to deliver the honest-but-not-full answer she's constructed in her head to answer this question she's been anticipating from Reverie townsfolk.

"Came here from Georgia, after some ugliness with my ex-husband."

"I see," Ardie says. "I'm sorry to hear about that."

Lucinda thinks for a moment, trying to figure out how she can signal to Ardie that the sturdy woman isn't the only woman in Reverie who appreciates the beauty of other women. Trying to figure out how to signal her interest in Ardie without having to bring Dionne up.

"I was sorry, too," Lucinda says. "About the ugliness, anyway. I wasn't sorry to leave him."

She almost adds, *The bastard can rot in hell, as far as I'm concerned,* but doesn't say it, of course. Instead, she decides to be brave.

She looks right at Ardie and says, "He didn't seem to much appreciate that, after almost sixteen years of marriage, I realized I was much more interested in the charms of women than of men."

There. She hopes that's clear enough.

If Ardie is shocked by Lucinda's admission, she doesn't let it show on her face. She looks away from Lucinda and gazes out across the yard, eyes tracing some indefinite line in the kudzu on the other side of the highway.

"Yep," she says after a moment. "Women tend to be a good deal more charming than men in general." Then she laughs. "Most of us, anyway. Can't say I passed charm school with flying colors."

Lucinda laughs with Ardie, but then it occurs to her that Ardie might have meant "charm school" as more than just a joke.

"You didn't truly go to charm school, did you?"

Ardie laughs again, and Lucinda likes the sound; it's warm, round, full — like Ardie herself. "Oh, what I had to go through was *much* worse than charm school. I had to go through an entire debutante training. *And* a debutante ball, to top it off. Took etiquette classes, learned the whole cotillion dance-thing, wore white gloves to my elbows, got taught to speak like a proper little southern lady."

The thought of Ardie, whose forearms are streaked with what appears to be motor oil, wearing white gloves to her elbows sets off another bout of laughter in Lucinda. She hopes she's not being offensive, because she laughs so long and so hard that tears stream from the corners of her eyes.

"Hey," Ardie says, and indeed her voice is full of offense, but only mock offense. "Is it really that hard to imagine me in a floor-length white dress, waltzing around in heels?"

"Yes," Lucinda says, wiping her eyes.

Ardie shakes her head sadly. "I s'pose you can put lipstick on a pig, but it's still a pig."

"I *know* you didn't just call yourself a pig," Lucinda admonishes. She looks right at Ardie. "Not every woman is meant for white dresses and white gloves. Doesn't mean she's not beautiful the way she is."

Ardie holds Lucinda's gaze thoughtfully. A moment goes by. "Well, be that as it may," she says, "I was a graceful dancer. Even in heels."

Lucinda chortles.

"What, you don't believe me?"

"I didn't say that."

Ardie stands up. "Do you want me to prove it to you? I still remember the steps to the cotillion — probably won't ever forget them. I'm sure I'll still know 'em even when I'm a drooling old woman who can't remember her own name. They practically brainwashed us." She straightens at the top of the porch stairs, rests one hand delicately upon the corner post. "You ready?"

"You're not really going to waltz."

"Sure I am." Ardie clears her throat and says, in a booming presenter's voice, "Now presenting Miss Ardith Brown, daughter of Grayson Brown and Tiny Brown."

"Your mother's given name is Tiny?"

"Hush," Ardie says over her shoulder. "I'm making my grand entrance."

Her back still facing Lucinda, she lifts an imaginary white dress daintily with her left hand, places one worn motorcycle boot behind the other, and dips into a curtsy.

Continuing to hold her imaginary dress with one hand, running her hand lightly down the porch railing with the other, she walks gingerly down the porch steps. When she reaches the bottom, she turns towards Lucinda and drops into another curtsy.

Her thick black brows furrow. "You're not clapping."

"Oh," Lucinda says. "Was I supposed to clap?"

"Absolutely. That's what high society does when a young lady is introduced to them."

"Sorry," Lucinda says, and she claps half-heartedly, afraid the sound might wake her next door neighbor from a much-deserved slumber.

"That's not very enthusiastic," Ardie chastises.

"I don't want to wake the girl next door."

Ardie's eyes flit to the door beside Lucinda's, a momentary look of confusion crossing her face. "Ahh. Fair enough." When she speaks again, she raises her voice into her imitation of an announcer again, but this time not as loud. "Miss Brown is escorted by Mister Roderick Brown."

"A Brown again? Your escort was a relation?"

Ardie's head cocks to the side as if she's taken aback by the question. "Of course he was," she says. "I wasn't going to be able to get any of the fine young gentlemen of Reverie High School to be my escort. I looked like a linebacker in high heels. My Aunt Doris had to bribe poor cousin Roddy with a gun rack for his truck before he'd agree to do it. He hated having to do it, but a new gun rack was a powerful motivator."

"You'd think he'd do it just to support you," Lucinda says.

Ardie shrugs, a what-can-you-do gesture. "We were teenagers. I think what really bothered him the most was that I was taller than he was, even though I was a sophomore and he was a senior. Anyway. Ready to watch me walk through my cotillion?"

"Oh, definitely," Lucinda smiles.

"Alright, then."

Ardie rolls her shoulders back, stretches her neck from one side and then to the other, looking more like she's about to lift something heavy than dance. She puts one hand behind her back, raises the other as if she's holding the hand of an invisible dance partner. She walks in a slow, deliberate circle. Reverses. Circles in the other direction. Then she pauses, letting the raised hand fall, gaze dropping to the ground.

"Shoot," she says.

"Don't tell me you already forgot what's next," teases Lucinda. "I thought you said it was seared into your memory?"

"It is," Ardie says. "But it's hard to do without a dance partner." She smirks, quirks an eyebrow at Lucinda.

"Oh, no you don't," Lucinda says with a giggle. "I never had a debutante ball. *My* family was not high society."

"And you think mine is? Daddy owns an auto shop. Mama was a schoolteacher. We weren't high society. But Mama's in Junior League — they're the ones who organize the ball every year around here — and she *made* me participate because she'd gotten the idea that somehow getting her daughter into the annual debutante ball would take us one step closer to being upper crust. That, or she thought maybe it would fix whatever had gone horribly wrong with me."

"There's nothing wrong with you at all," Lucinda says.

"You know that and I know that. But look at where we live. I wasn't exactly my mother's ideal daughter." Ardie waves her new neighbor off the porch. "C'mon. Waltz with me."

Lucinda heaves an exaggerated, long-suffering sigh as she rises from the rocking chair and descends the stairs. "Fine, fine. But only because you brought me peach pie."

"Technically, that was also my mother's doing," Ardie says. "I don't bake." She positions Lucinda facing the opposite direction from her, then stands beside her and raises Lucinda's hand between them.

"You don't bake. But you waltz," Lucinda says.

"Shh. I'm concentrating," Ardie says, guiding Lucinda into a small circle. She turns. "Now this way."

Lucinda does as instructed, turning and taking Ardie's other hand.

"What do you do?" she asks Ardie. "Besides waltzing."

"Not too much, really. Ever since I moved back home, life's been pretty quiet," Ardie responds. She lifts Lucinda's hand up higher, twirls her, then puts one hand on her waist as she begins the next portion of the waltz. "I read a lot. Work in Daddy's shop. Tinker with my bike."

"I assume that by 'bike,' you mean the motorcycle, not a pedal bike?"

Ardie chuckles. "Yeah. A girl my size — on a bicycle? That would be almost as funny as a girl like me trying to waltz." She sends Lucinda into another twirl, deftly brings her back into the waltz's next steps.

"But you're good at this," Lucinda says when she comes out of the twirl and puts her hand back on Ardie's hip. Lucinda can feel Ardie's lower back muscles working beneath her hand as they move through the steps of the waltz. She decides her earlier assessment was right — Ardie's got a big frame, but her bulk is as much muscle as it is extra weight.

"Maybe," Ardie says, "but I'm much better at changing out fan belts and radiator hoses."

Lucinda almost says, *But your hands are so soft,* because she'd expect tougher callouses on someone accustomed to working with their hands all day, but she decides that might come across as rude or... or as something else.

"So you read," Lucinda says instead. "You work, mess with your motorcycle. What else do you do?" She hesitates a moment. "Is there a Mrs. Ardie Brown?"

Ardie sighs. "There used to be. But Mrs. Ardie Brown is back in Arizona. With Ardie Brown's cat."

"I guess you lost the custody battle?" Lucinda says, trying to be light about it.

"You might put it that way," Ardie says, but the words are heavy.

After another few minutes of dancing in silence, Ardie stops, wipes the accumulated sweat from her brow with the back of her wrist.

"Whew," she says, squinting skyward. "It's gonna be a mighty hot afternoon. I'd better stop bothering you and let you get back to gardening before it gets too hot to work outside."

"Yes, I guess I ought to get a bit more done on it," Lucinda says with a sigh.

"Enjoy the rest of that peach pie," Ardie says, stepping towards her motorcycle and picking up the helmet. "Oh," she says, setting the helmet back down. "While I'm still here, did you want me to look at anything in the house? At Georgie's the other day, you kinda made it sound like there's a few things about your place that Zeke might've neglected. You were trying to be polite, but I could tell." She grins.

"Ardie," Lucinda says, holding up her hands, "you've already been so kind. Bringing me the peach pie — "

"I told you. That was my mother, not me."

"Well, but you brought it."

"Yeah, and you finally did something with this ragamuffin I call a head of hair," Ardie counters, tussling the top of her black hair with a thick hand.

"Really, I don't want to impose."

"*Really,* it's not imposing if I'm the one who offers. Just let me look."

Lucinda finally acquiesces, takes Ardie on a quick tour of her half of the duplex. She shows Ardie the way the screen door's coming off its hinges, the way she can't manage to get one of the windows in the front room to open more than a few inches, the way the air-conditioning unit in the other window sounds like it might blast off every time she turns the setting higher than "low." Finally, she opens the back door and shows Ardie the rotten, wobbling rear steps.

Ardie listens and nods as she follows Lucinda through

the house, pausing occasionally to ask questions. She sounds like a medical doctor quizzing a patient about symptoms.

"Alright then," Ardie says when the tour ends and they're standing in Lucinda's living room. "Is Sunday the best day for me to come over with my tools? I know Georgie's is closed on Sunday's. And so's my dad's shop, like pretty much everything else in town."

"You don't go to church?"

"Hell no," Ardie responds without skipping a beat. "A town like this, any church that even lets me through the front doors is going to start handing out ex-gay summer camp brochures before I even make it into the sanctuary."

Lucinda hesitates, wonders if she should ask Ardie the next question that's on her mind. It's a personal one, she knows, and she's not sure if it would be polite to ask. But given Ardie's big heart, along with the friendship that seems to be budding between them, Lucinda decides the question's probably okay.

"Does that mean you don't believe in God? If you don't go to church?"

Ardie leans her head back, rolls her neck from side to side, lets out a long breath. "I tell you what, Miss Lucinda. You bring me a couple beers, and we'll sit out on your porch next Sunday and drink 'em after I've finished working on your house. You can ask me about my relationship with the divine again, and we'll see what I have to say then."

Lucinda smiles, happy at the prospect that she'll be seeing Ardie again no later than this time next week. "I like that plan. But do they even sell beer in Reverie?"

"Ha!" Ardie barks. "There are three things you should never try to take away from the fine citizens of Reverie. The first is their guns. The second is their Confederate flags. The third is their beer. So yes, my dear, you can find it at the Shop 'n Go."

A moment of silence falls between them, stretching out like taffy in the sun. Lucinda feels their time together drawing to a close. For now.

"Well..." she says. "I guess I..."

But Ardie's gaze has fallen to a framed snapshot sitting on the corner table.

"Is that her? The woman whose charms convinced you to leave your husband?" she asks, leaning over to pick the photo up. "She's pretty. And she looks young." Ardie looks back to Lucinda, a question in her eyes and the photo in her hands.

It's as if the wind's been knocked out of Lucinda. She opens her mouth to speak, but she can't form words, she can only stare at the grainy photo that Ardie's holding. Dionne's arms are both slung over Lucinda's shoulders; she's squeezing Lucinda to her chest. Even in the stillness of the photo, it's clear that Dionne's in the middle of a hearty laugh. An open-mouthed, full-throated, characteristic laugh. Lucinda's caught in an equally idiosyncratic gesture — she's ducking her head, a shy smile on her face, eyes lightly closed as if she's just tasted something delicate.

It had been a good moment. A stolen reprieve at a friend's lakeside barbecue, a moment when she and Dionne could simply be themselves, without any need to hide or act like they were nothing more than friends.

It had been rare, being able to act like a couple together, because Lucinda had warned Dionne. She'd warned her over and over again, telling her exactly what would happen if they said the wrong thing to the wrong person. But Dionne, so young, so filled with the cheeky invincibility of youth, had always told Lucinda she worried too much.

"He won't find out," Dionne had said. *"He doesn't have the imagination to think you'd be with a woman."*

Maybe Dionne had been right. Maybe Lucinda had worried too much, made their relationship too difficult, too filled with the dark shadows of Lucinda's insecurities and anxieties. Too filled with hiding. Maybe things between her and Dionne would've turned out differently if Lucinda hadn't worried so much, if she'd felt comfortable being more open.

"Lu?" Ardie asks. She uses Lucinda's nickname with casual ease, as if she's just now spontaneously invented it. Hearing it come from Ardie's mouth instead of someone more familiar — someone like one of her sisters, or Dan… or Dionne — jolts Lucinda back to the present.

"Yes," Lucinda says at last. "That's her."

Ardie frowns slightly. "Where is she now? Are you

two still…?"

"Not together," Lucinda says quickly. "We aren't together anymore."

Ardie nods, sets the photo gently back in its spot. "I'm sorry. Maybe I shouldn't have asked."

"No, no," Lucinda says, waving her hand dismissively even though she speaks as if she's gasping for air. "There's nothing wrong with asking. It's all just still a little… raw." She forces a smile. "So. Next Sunday?"

Ardie studies her face for a moment, probably checking to see if Lucinda's actually as alright as her forced smile would lead one to believe.

Ardie smiles softly. "Sure thing. Next Sunday. Say around eleven o'clock?"

"Perfect. I'll have the beer."

Ardie's smile widens. "And I'll bring the power tools."

"Please tell your mother I said thank you for the pie," Lucinda says, opening the door for Ardie.

"I will. She'll be glad to hear our new neighbor's civilized. She's always complaining that Zeke has a habit of only renting to poor white trash." Ardie laughs, shakes her head. "I try to remind her that *we* are poor white trash, but she won't have it. Still thinks being in Junior League makes people forget that we're working people and won't ever be a part of Reverie's upper crust. Not that the upper crust of Reverie, South Carolina, is really all that much to aspire to."

"I think your mother's right," Lucinda says. "Being

poor white trash isn't about how much you have or don't have. It's about how well you take care of what you *do* have, and whether or not you're as ignorant as everyone outside the South thinks you are. Poor white trash is a state of mind."

Ardie raises an interested eyebrow, mouth curling into a crooked half-smile. "You're a regular philosopher, Lucinda Hamilton." Ardie pushes open the screen door. "And I'll tell that to my mother. I'm sure she'll like it."

They wave goodbye, and Lucinda stands on the porch, watching Ardie drive away, motorcycle roaring as it accelerates down the two-lane highway. She stands there even after Ardie's out of sight, hugging herself around the middle.

Dionne. Gone. Dionne is gone. The girl who said she'd love her for the rest of her life is gone. Lucinda tries to fit them together — the words "forever" and "gone" — but she can't make them fit. She just can't.

When Lucinda goes back inside, she turns the photograph face-down on the corner table.

Chapter 7

The rest of Sunday slides by quietly, with the sun burning the back of Lucinda's neck as she kneels in the dirt next to the garden she's trying to form, using her spade to dig up rocks and weeds and turn over dry earth.

She pauses when she realizes she's out of breath, leans back on her heels to look at her progress and wipe away the sweat that's stinging her eyes.

This is stupid, trying to do all this work with a hand spade. To call it slow-going would be a tremendous understatement; it's more like draconian punishment. A penance that someone more devout than Lucinda would force themselves through as a way of atoning for their sins.

It's the kind of thing she can imagine Hart forcing her to do after she'd said something to anger him.

"...Having some snot-nosed kid fifteen years my junior telling me what to do," he'd said at the kitchen table one night between pulls on his beer. *"He acts like he knows the industry better than I do. Like he has some sort of sixth sense that tells him which doctor's going to say what."* Hart shook his head. *"Acting like he knows my job. He doesn't know my job."*

"No," Lucinda said. "No one else could possibly know more than you do."

Hart set his beer down, turned slowly to look at her. Narrowed his eyes.

If only she'd left out the word "possibly." If she'd done that, the sarcastic tone just might've slipped past him, lost as he was in his own sorrows.

"Was that sarcasm? You think you're better than me, too? Even though I support you and you just sit on your ass all day?"

Lucinda didn't respond, didn't bother to remind him that she worked all day long, just like he did, because he couldn't afford to have a stay-at-home wife the way he wanted to. She avoided his gaze. But it was too late. Hart's chair scraped back from the table, he grabbed the front of her shirt, lifted her from her seat…

Lucinda knows she has sins, but she refuses to atone for them. And especially she refuses atoning like this.

She needs real garden tools. A hoe would be a good start. A sturdy rake, a shovel. If she remembers, she'll get some at the Main Street hardware store up the block from Georgie's when she's at work tomorrow.

On second thought, maybe she can just borrow some tools from Ardie. She probably has everything Lucinda needs and would no doubt be more than happy to loan it.

But maybe she shouldn't. Maybe it would be asking too much of a relative stranger.

Lucinda sighs in frustration, stands up and throws her spade into the upturned earth. It sticks, standing up on its point.

"Now c'mon, Lu," says a voice from behind, making her jump. "Surely the dirt didn't do anything to deserve that sort of treatment."

Lucinda turns to see that the girl next door has finally emerged from her side of the duplex. She's standing there, barefoot, on her welcome mat, hands on her hips. Her long dark hair is a little tangled on one side, giving the impression that she might've just rolled out of bed. She's got on a white undershirt whose sleeves have been hacked away, leaving a jagged row of tangled threads. Her plaid boxer shorts are so short that they accentuate the length of her long, lean legs.

"Don't tell me you just woke up," Lucinda says. "It's almost two in the afternoon."

"Naw, I've been up for an hour or so," the girl says, lifting one bare foot to scratch at the opposite bare calf. "Woke up when your friend drove away on her noisy Harley."

Lucinda squints in the direction of the two-lane highway, as if she might catch a glimpse of Ardie driving by. "Is it a Harley?" she says, almost to herself. She honestly hadn't noticed. Or bothered to ask.

The girl gives Lucinda an impatient click of her tongue. "I've never known a woman like that to ride anything other than a Harley."

A woman like that.

Lucinda frowns. She'd hoped that, with this girl being so young, she wouldn't display the same kinds of prejudices that Lucinda had heard at Georgie's salon. But the phrase *A woman like that* rings jarringly in her ears, and she braces herself for the worst when the girl starts to speak again.

"Dated a girl like her once," the girl says wistfully, gazing out in the same direction Lucinda had looked a moment earlier. "Younger than your friend, of course. No offense," she adds with a quick glance towards Lucinda. "But I swear that woman loved her bike more than she ever loved me. Her bike and her two dogs. She practically cried a river when she had to take one of her dogs to the vet when he got sick — and he wasn't even really that sick. Just got into something he shouldn't have and gave himself a stomach ache. That's when I realized she'd never *once* gotten that emotional over me. So I had to leave her." She shrugs, looks down at Lucinda. "See? Girls like your friend, they like to put on a show of being all tough, but they're all a bunch of softies underneath the front. Emotional but damaged, so they love their animals more than they do their women."

"You — you're gay?" Lucinda asks, the question tumbling out of her mouth before she has a chance to think of a more tactful way of putting it. "I'm sorry," she says immediately. "I shouldn't have — "

"Why are you sorry? Nothing wrong with asking." The girl pauses, wrinkles her nose. "But honestly, I don't like labels. Have you ever wondered why everything has to be so black and white? Why everything has to have its own name? Gay, straight, bi, trans. Poly, pan. Butch, femme. It's like, you either have to ride a Harley or have curlers in your hair?" She rolls her eyes. "Why can't we all just *be,* without any names attached to it? And love who we wanna love, when we wanna love them? I don't know why people have to always put what they feel and who they are into neat little boxes all the time." She looks at Lucinda, meeting her eyes. "'Cause ya know what? Most people don't really fit into a box. Even if they're the ones who picked out the box and put themselves into it."

Lucinda blushes under the girl's steady gaze, although she can't say exactly why. Maybe it's because it sounds like she's accusing Lucinda of living in a box, when Lucinda feels like she worked her whole life to get *out* of the box she'd gotten stuck in.

But maybe Lucinda blushes more because there's just something about the way the girl looks at her... It's like she *knows.* Knows how much she reminds Lucinda of Dionne. Knows that Lucinda can't deny the subtle but deep stirrings of desire coming from within. Lucinda hopes the younger woman will assume the redness climbing up her cheeks is just the result of the blistering August sun.

She leans down, picks up her spade from the dirt to have an excuse to break eye contact with the girl.

"Hey," she says when she stands back up, a change of subject occurring to her. "I realized last night that you never told me your name."

A sly grin spreads across the girl's face. "I know I

didn't. You never asked me for it. I started to sign the note to you when I returned your casserole dish last night, but then I thought it would be more fun to make a game out of it."

Lucinda cocks her head to the side. "A game?"

Her neighbor nods, walks forward a few steps and sits down at the top of the porch stairs, absent-mindedly scratching both shins as she talks.

"Rumplestiltskin was always my favorite fairy tale when I was little," she says. "My little brother and I had this big, moldy book of old-fashioned fairy tales that had belonged to my grandmother, and I used to make my dad read it to me over and over again. I loved the idea of being able to spin straw into gold, but I didn't really understand what spinning meant, so I used to go out into the yard in springtime, when my dad was planting his vegetable garden, and take pieces of straw he used for covering the beds, and spin around and around and around hoping they'd turn into gold."

The girl stands up and walks down the porch stairs, demonstrating. She holds both arms out, turns circles on her bare feet. It reminds Lucinda of Ardie's waltzing, but the girl is as lean and lithe as Ardie is square and stocky. After a few seconds, the girl stops twirling, puts her hand on the porch post to steady herself, sits back down on the bottom of the stairs.

Lucinda walks over, sits down across from her. "And did it ever work? Did you turn straw into gold?"

"No," the girl says, an imaginary regret in her tone. "For some reason it never worked. But I did make myself so dizzy once that I threw up my lunch when I was finished. After that, my mom wouldn't let me try again."

Lucinda chuckles.

"Anyway, the other part I love is when the miller's daughter overhears Rumplestiltskin's song, where he gives away his name, and so she ends up outsmarting him." The girl grows still and thoughtful for a moment. "It's like, if the miller's daughter hadn't happened by right at that moment, it would've all been a lot different for her. No happy ending to the story. She'd have to give her baby away and Rumplestiltskin does Lord-only-knows-what with it. I always wondered what he wanted a baby for anyhow."

She looks at Lucinda. "But I liked that part because, I don't know, life's just like that sometimes, isn't it? What happens to us ends up depending on this *one* little accidental moment that winds up changing *everything*. And the crazy thing is, a lot of times we don't even really know which moments are important and which ones aren't until after they've already passed. It makes our whole life seem almost like… one accident after another."

Lucinda thinks about her own life, looking back for the accidental moments that changed everything. Meeting her ex-husband was one such moment. She bumped into him — literally bumped into him — in an elevator, of all places. And there, even though being trapped with him inside that confined, downward-zooming metal box should've been an ill omen, Lucinda had thought she'd met the love of her life. The father of her children. He'd been so sweet in that elevator, all dimpled smiles and good humor, giving no indication of his true, underlying nature.

Lucinda shivers, the kind of involuntary spasm that would've made her mother ask, *"What's wrong? Rabbit run over yer grave?"*

The girl claps her hands together once, her pensive mood having passed like a fickle summer cloud, and the devilish grin returns to her face. "So yeah. I'm going to make you *guess* my name. What do you think about that?"

"I think it sounds like I'm not going to know my next door neighbor's name for a good long while."

The girl chortles and claps her hands a few more times, like a pleased child. "I believe in you, Lu. I've got confidence you'll figure me out." She wags a finger playfully. "But no sneaking into my side of the duplex to listen to me sing some kind of Rumplestiltskin song in the shower, okay?"

Without meaning to, a vision comes to Lucinda of her young neighbor in the shower, naked and singing and covered in gooseflesh as she scrubs sudsy body wash down the front of her breasts, over her nipples…

Lucinda shivers again, pushing the uninvited image away.

"Why do you keep shivering?" asks the girl. "You can't possibly be cold. It's, like, ninety-seven degrees out here."

"It's not that hot," Lucinda counters, telling herself she hadn't actually just imagined the girl in the shower. She studies the girl's smirk, searching for a sign that it's all just a joke, and that her neighbor will reveal her name any moment now. "Are you honestly going to force me to guess your name?"

"Mmm-hmm," the girl says cheerfully.

"That's kind of silly."

The girl waggles her eyebrows. "I'm a silly person."

"Do I get any hints?"

"Nope."

"This is ridiculous," Lucinda says, but the girl's smile and good humor is infectious, and she feels a smile growing on her own face. "Okay, okay, if you're really going to make me do this..." She thinks for a moment, trying to come up with common names in the generations younger than hers. "Is it... Taylor?"

The girl tips her head back and laughs. "No. It's not. You can't just guess *whatever*, Lu. You need a strategy. What kind of name do I *look* like I have?"

You look like you're Dionne, Lucinda thinks, and the name sticks in her head, echoing, repeating itself again and again, like the steady beating of a drum.

Dionne. Dionne. Dionne.

"I don't know," Lucinda says after a moment. "I've never understood that, when people say someone 'looks like' a certain name. Do I look like a Lucinda?"

The girl squints at her for a moment. "Not really. But you *do* kind of look like a Lu. But I probably wouldn't have guessed Lu, to be honest."

"No? What would you have guessed?"

"Mmm, I don't know. One of those old-fashioned, two-name southern lady names."

Lucinda laughs. "Like what?"

"Oh, I don't know. Like Bobbie Jo. Or Emma Jean. Something like that."

"Sounds more country than southern," Lucinda says. "Are you calling me country?"

"What's wrong with being country?" asks her neighbor. *"I'm* country. This town is *definitely* country. That doesn't make it *bad."*

Lucinda raises an eyebrow, unconvinced. "Alright. So not Taylor. What about… what about something that ends in an 'i-e' or a 'y,' like Annie or Vicky?"

The girl wrinkles her nose. "Annie? I really look like an *Annie* to you?"

"I've always liked the name Annie. I had a good friend growing up whose name was Annie."

"Fine, but I don't think I look like an Annie at *all.* And I already told you I'm not giving you any hints. So I'm not telling you if it ends in 'i-e' or not."

"Then how'm I ever s'posed to guess?" Lucinda asks, half-frustrated, half-amused by her young companion. "There are only hundreds of thousands of names to choose from."

"Your accent gets stronger when you get upset, you know that?" the girl says. "I like it. It's cute."

Cute.

This twenty-something girl *can't* be flirting with her. But then... why did she bring up dating women earlier? Why bring it up unless she was sending a subtle signal?

Even if she is flirting with Lucinda, though, it doesn't matter. Nothing can happen between them. She's got to be half Lucinda's age. Lucinda already tried dating a younger woman. And look at what happened.

Besides that, ever since Dionne disappeared from her life, her heart has been an open wound, tender and exposed, writhing in pain at the slightest provocation. As much as she enjoyed Ardie's company this morning, as much as she enjoys this current banter with her nameless next door neighbor, she's not sure she's ready to invite anyone inside the tender space of her heart anytime soon.

So instead of letting her mind wander over the terrain of question marks the comment about her accent being "cute" brings up, Lucinda opts to ignore it. Opts to say, "So you won't even tell me what letters it ends in?"

"No. And you only get three guesses every day. You've already used two of them — I'm not Taylor and I'm not Annie. I'll give you a freebie and not count Vicky — and I'm not Vicky either, by the way. You want to guess one more time today?" She bounces her eyebrows up and down again. "One more roll of the dice?"

"Well..." Lucinda starts.

The girl rises from her spot at the top of the steps, stretches like a lazy cat that's been lying in the sun. "You've only got five minutes," she says. "Then I have to get ready for work."

"On a Sunday?"

The girl shrugs. "I'm a nurse. Sick people don't stop being sick just because it's Sunday."

"Why'd you sleep in so late today, if you have to work at three? You wasted the best part of the day in bed."

"Ugh, Lu, now you sound like my mother." She finger-combs her hair, trying to pull the tangles out of one side. "And if you must know, I was at a party last night. Drank too much, so I didn't come home last night. Ended up waking up around five in the morning beneath some girl on a couch. I was sober enough to drive home by then, so I came home and crashed in my own bed."

"Is this girl someone you're... dating?" Lucinda can't stop herself from feeling disappointed at the thought.

"No, no, it wasn't like that." The girl laughs. "I guess it sounded like that, the way I put it, right? No, I passed out on my friend's couch, and this girl I was under... I guess she passed out on the same couch. On top of me. Ha." She shrugs. "So are you gonna guess my name one more time, or am I going inside to get dressed?"

"Rebecca," Lucinda says. It's a pretty name. She always thought that if she'd had a daughter, she would've named her Rebecca.

The girl's eyes widen with apparent shock, and Lucinda

wonders if her phantom daughter's name was actually the correct guess. "Lucinda. I can't believe it. You guessed… *wrong!*" She breaks into laughter, amused by her own trick. "Anyway, I have to run."

She steps halfway down the porch stairs, leans over Lucinda, kisses her cheek lightly, then disappears inside the duplex.

Lucinda sits there a minute longer, the ghost of the girl's lips still tingling on the side of her face. She finds the energy to get up a few moments later, deciding to shower for the second time that day and relax for a while before she fixes dinner.

Chapter 8

The phone call from Lucinda's divorce lawyer comes early Wednesday morning, right as Lucinda's leaving the house to get to her first haircut appointment of the day. She digs the buzzing cell out of her purse, intending to send the call to voicemail, until she sees who it is. She fumbles with the phone, drops her keys in the process.

She presses the green answer button, wanting to demand of her lawyer, *"Where have you been? Why haven't you called me? Don't you know I've been waiting to hear from you?"*

But instead she simply says, "Hello?"

"Lucinda? Hi, it's Margaret."

Lucinda picks her keys up, dusts them off on her jeans as she stands back up. Margaret seems to be waiting for her to say something, but Lucinda stays silent. Her lawyer is the one who needs to be talking.

A sigh crackles in Lucinda's ear. "I'm sorry I haven't called sooner. There are some things I've needed to fill you in on, and I was delaying the call because — well, because I was hoping everything would resolve itself, but it hasn't, and I know you've been waiting to hear from me, and…"

Lucinda grips her keys in her hands, squeezing her palm around their jagged edges, using the sharp sensation like a smelling salt to keep her on her feet.

"What?" she asks. She leans against the car door, squeezes her keys harder. "Just tell me. What's happened?"

"They can't find Hart."

Lucinda's stomach drops out from under her. The world rolls, and she feels faint. She drops her keys again and reaches behind her, searching for something to hold onto that will keep her upright.

"What do you mean they can't find him? *Who* can't find him?"

"The police. His lawyer. No one can find him."

"But that's… how can they just lose him?" Her heart races; her mind spins with possibilities. Hart… loose somewhere… unfindable… "I told them," Lucinda says. "I told them he shouldn't be out on bail. He could be anywhere."

Another sigh from Margaret. "Lucinda… he hasn't tried to contact you… has he? You would tell me — or the police — if he did?"

Lucinda squeezes her eyes shut, presses two fingers into the spot above the bridge of her nose, rubbing her forehead. "No, of course not. If he had… If he had, we wouldn't be having this conversation right now. How long has he been missing?"

"He failed to make his check-in report to the supervising officer about two weeks ago."

Lucinda thinks back to two weeks earlier. It was the

week she finalized her plans with Dan to move to Reverie. The week she held the big yard sale and sold all but her most essential possessions. Now she wonders if she's known all along these past fourteen days, subconsciously, that her ex-husband's whereabouts have been unknown. She wonders if God or the Universe tried to get her attention with some subtle vibration, some sign that she failed to recognize because she'd been so intent on getting out of Georgia as soon as she could. She wonders if that's why the nightmares haven't subsided but have only intensified since she moved here.

"Why didn't anyone tell me before now?" she asks.

"I'm surprised they haven't, to be honest," Margaret says. "I expected you to call me once they contacted you. That was one of the reasons I was waiting."

"No one's called me."

Margaret sighs. *"Gawd.* You know what I worry? I worry the Calvin police department has its head so far up its ass that he's been gone even longer, and it took them until now to realize it. And I can't believe they called me before they called you. No wonder they were asking me if you'd mentioned anything about him lately."

"You should've told me. You should've called me right away."

"I'm sorry, Lucinda, I really am. I honestly thought they would've told you first thing."

Lucinda turns around, pounds her fist once against the closed driver's side window. Then she covers her mouth, stifling a sob. "I guess that explains why you haven't called me until now about the paperwork," she says.

Margaret manages half of a laugh. "Yeah. Hard to get him to sign anything when no one knows where he is."

A moment passes. Lucinda tries to control her emotions, forcing bile and the threat of tears back down her burning throat.

"What now?" she asks.

"Now... I expect that if they didn't call you, it means they'll be surprising you soon with a search warrant."

Lucinda's heart does another backflip. "A search warrant? Why?"

"Because even if they ask you if you've heard from him and you say no, they'll still want to double-check your place just in case. In case you're hiding him or... otherwise helping him."

"I haven't heard from him," Lucinda snaps defensively. "Don't they think I would've contacted them right away if I'd heard from him?"

"Lucinda, it's not that they think you've done anything wrong," Margaret says gently. "It's just that... sometimes with women who have been in your position before..." She trails off, leaving Lucinda to fill in the implied blanks. "They just like to know that they've searched the premises for him thoroughly, without putting you in a position of telling them whether he's there or not."

Lucinda lets out a ragged breath. She supposes she understands. Hart is terrifying. If he was actually here and the police came knocking… he'd be likely to put a gun to her back and hide behind the door while she opened it. She'd smile to the police politely, tell them that no, she hadn't seen her ex-husband — or the man who *would* be her ex-husband, anyway, if she could ever get the paperwork finalized. It would be hard to send the police away, but it would be even more terrifying not to, if Hart were here.

She understands. But she hates it. A search warrant only makes her feel more powerless, more voiceless than she feels already.

"Lucinda? Are you still there?"

"I'm still here. When should I expect the police?"

"Any day now, I'm sure. Even today, maybe."

Lucinda says nothing.

"Are you alright?"

Is she alright? What kind of question is that? The whereabouts of Hart Hamilton, the man who had dissolved the boundary between one night's nightmare and the next day's terror, is no longer known to police. When he'd accepted the plea bargain with sullen resignation, Lucinda had been pleasantly surprised. She'd thought the nightmare might finally be over — or at least ending. And she'd moved to Reverie thinking she could genuinely have a fresh start.

What a fool she's been. There will be no fresh start for her. Not now. Not ever. She's cursed, paying penance for some sin she doesn't even know about.

"Lucinda?"

"Yes," she manages. "I'm alright. I have to go," she tells Margaret. "I'm late to meet a client."

"Alright," Margaret says. "Stay safe. And let me know if you learn anything."

"Same here — please don't wait to tell me if you hear anything new."

"I won't," Margaret assures her. "Take care, Lucinda."

"You, too." She hangs up the phone, manages to unlock her car door with a shaky hand. The click of the lock triggers another thought, and she turns around, heads back to her front door on unsteady feet. Did she lock the front door? Is the deadbolt in place, too? She did; it is. She turns back around, sees the blue compact car parked next to her Pontiac.

She should tell the girl next door, warn her.

She raises her fist to knock on the door. Hesitates.

What will Lucinda say to her — how will she explain it? And how will the girl look at Lucinda once she knows the truth? Will her smirking grin falter? Will her gaze change? Will she start looking at Lucinda the way Dan does, the way so many of her old friends do — as an object of pity? As a woman who — she's sure they say it behind her back — should've known better, should've seen it coming long ago, should've gotten out of a bad situation much, much sooner?

She drops her fist. Turns towards the car. Nothing to do except go to work. Lose herself in the sounds of hair dryers and snipping scissors, shampoo sinks and lilting country music. Southern accents and the endless banter of women.

Chapter 9

Georgie's makes her forget her problems, for a time. Georgie herself is there today, dyeing an older woman's hair a shade of auburn that looks far from natural.

Georgie is all smiles for Lucinda when she comes in, despite the fact that Lucinda's late and her client's been waiting for ten minutes. Neither Georgie nor the client seem particularly bothered by the delay, but Lucinda apologizes to both of them, anyway.

"I'm so sorry," she says, directing her words at both Georgie and the client. "I had a phone call right when I was on my way out the door this morning that I had to take, and it was a longer conversation than I expected."

"Everything's okay, I hope?" Georgie says, brow crinkling with maternal concern.

Lucinda sighs. "Yes. Just that my lawyer's having trouble making my ex-husband my ex."

"He won't sign the paperwork?" asks the woman with the fake auburn hair.

Lucinda drapes a nylon smock around her own client, grabs a comb and a spray bottle. "No," she says. *That's one way of putting it,* she thinks. "He won't."

"My second husband did that to me," says the woman with the auburn hair. "Refused to sign the paperwork. Said he'd lost it, said he was busy, said he'd get to it later. But he signed it eventually."

"How'd you get him to do it?" Georgie asks. "Sounds like Lucinda might want some tips."

"Threatened to put sugar in his gas tank," the woman says matter-of-factly. "He knew I'd follow through, too. That paperwork got signed with a *quickness* after that, honey, tell you what."

Everyone laughs — even Lucinda chuckles.

On Lucinda's other side, Rhonda shakes her head disdainfully. "Men and their cars. They're like little children, aren't they? The only way to get to them is to threaten to take their toys away, otherwise they will not, *cannot* listen."

"Mmm-hmm," the woman in Georgie's chair agrees. "For months it was, 'Oh, Dolly, I love you so much, don't leave me, I can change.' The moment I threaten his Mustang — " she snaps her fingers " — it's all, 'You're a conniving bitch, I never should've married you.'"

Georgie clucks her tongue like a disappointed parent. "Oh, tell me he *didn't*. He really called you the b-word?"

"He did," the woman confirms, nodding her head so vigorously that Georgie has to stop what she's doing for a moment. "And I say, 'Ex-*cuse* me? I've been trying to divorce you for months, and you won't sign the paperwork, and now *I'm* the bitch?'"

"That man's mama never taught him how to speak properly to a woman," Rhonda says from Lucinda's other side. "If I ever heard one of my boys talk to or about a woman like that…" She swings her hand, miming a slap. "I'd pop 'em upside the head."

"Or you'd hex 'em," Kylah says with a laugh.

Rhonda shoots her a sidelong glance. "Don't you start up with that, now."

Georgie intervenes, changing the subject before Rhonda and Kylah can recuse their weekly debate surrounding Rhonda's unusual spiritual beliefs. "A mother's lessons are important," Georgie says, "but I think men learn how to respect women by watching their fathers. So I guess in part it depends on what kind of role models he had."

All the women but Lucinda *"Mmm-hmm"* at this.

"Your ex-husband didn't call the poh-leese on you for threatening his car?" Rhonda asks the auburn-haired woman.

The woman lifts her eyebrows, grins like a cat with a canary. "Lory Wheeler's my first cousin," she says. "And Sheriff Bronson's married to another one'a my cousins. He knew better than to try."

Lory Wheeler — Dan's best friend since childhood. The same Wheeler who'd helped her move into the duplex. She'd forgotten he'd grown up to be a sheriff's deputy.

Kylah grins at Lucinda. "What about you, Lu? You gonna put sugar in somebody's tank if your ex doesn't cooperate with the lawyer?"

The women laugh. Lucinda offers up a weak smile. *If they only knew,* she thinks, and somewhere deep in the pit of her stomach, shame sparks a fire that threatens to burn her down from inside out.

"Maybe I should," Lucinda says after a moment. "Maybe that's exactly what needs to happen."

The women cackle approvingly.

#

It's a relief to get away from the women's inquiries about Hart when lunchtime finally arrives. Lucinda had planned on heading home to eat, but Georgie asks her to take a client at one-thirty, so she heads to Linda's instead. Being surrounded by people might help take her mind off Hart anyway.

Not that she feels like socializing. But if Hart's on the loose, well, there's safety in numbers.

Lucinda waits at the hostess station in the busy restaurant, trying to slow her racing thoughts, when she hears someone call her name.

She jumps at the sound of it, anxiety ramped so high that for a moment she hears a man's voice instead of a woman's. For a moment she hears Hart, before remembering with a wash of relief that he doesn't have any way of knowing where she is.

Not yet.

"Lu, hey, over here," says the woman's voice again.

Lucinda turns to her right just as Ardie stands up from a booth, a face-down paperback and glass of sweet tea on the table.

She smiles at Lucinda, lifts her hand in an awkward wave. "Here for lunch?"

Lucinda nods.

"Come join me. If you want."

Lucinda hesitates a moment. "You sure? I don't want to interrupt."

"You're not interrupting anything. I'll be glad for the company."

I would, too, Lucinda thinks, and she smiles her thanks at Ardie.

"So? How's your day been so far?" Ardie asks once Lucinda sits down.

Lucinda takes a breath, preparing to say, *Just fine, thanks. How 'bout yourself?*, but then stops herself.

Lucinda doesn't know Ardie well enough to trust her, but she does anyway. She can't say exactly why. Maybe it's the down-home earnestness combined with easy, relaxed humor. Maybe it's Lucinda's sense that Ardie is a sturdy kind of creature, unflappable and soft-hearted at the same time.

Maybe it's because Ardie's the only other lesbian in Reverie, and so Lucinda feels a natural kinship with her. Or something more than kinship.

"It's been… a difficult morning," Lucinda says at last.

Ardie's brow immediately crinkles with concern. "Why? Is Zeke giving you a hard time? Or is it the new job?"

"Neither," says Lucinda. "It's my ex-husband — or, he would be my ex-husband if they could find him to sign the divorce paperwork."

"Find him?"

"He was… I came to Reverie because there was an incident with him. An incident that led to charges filed against him."

"What kind of charges?"

Lucinda hesitates. She might trust Ardie, but that doesn't mean she's ready to reveal the whole truth.

A waitress appears, setting a glass of ice water down in front of Lucinda, which saves her from having to immediately respond to Ardie's question.

"What else can I get you to drink, hon?" the waitress asks Lucinda.

"Sweet tea, please."

"Sure thing. Be right back."

Lucinda wraps a hand around the sweating glass of ice water, the chill seeming to ground her somehow. She feels Ardie's gaze upon her, and it's steady. Patient.

"My ex… He's been charged with assault and battery. And a few other things." Lucinda won't say the other words, and not even because she's trying to hide them fro Ardie.

Saying the other words would make them real, would give them power.

And somehow Ardie seems to intuit the weight of what's happened without knowing the details, because she reaches across the table, touches the back of Lucinda's hand lightly. "Sweet pea. I'm so sorry."

Sweet pea. It's not an unusual phrase to hear from Southerners, any more than it was unusual for the waitress to call Lucinda "hon" or "darlin'." But something shifts inside her heart when Ardie says it. She wants to wrap the words around her like a blanket. She wants to hear Ardie call her *sweet pea* again.

Lucinda shrugs. "It's okay," she says, even though it's not. But *It's okay* is what you say in a situation like this. She certainly wouldn't bring up the nightmares or the tears or the way she jumps at every shadow, every floorboard creak.

The waitress returns with Lucinda's sweet tea, and Ardie withdraws her fingers from Lucinda's hand. Lucinda misses it immediately; the absence is a burn tingling on her skin.

"What'll y'all have?" the waitress asks, oblivious to the mood that hangs like a raincloud above the booth.

They give their orders; Ardie waits until the girl disappears again before returning her attention to Lucinda.

"And now they can't find him?" she asks.

Lucinda shakes her head. "No. I just found out this morning."

"Where do you think he might be?"

"The North Georgia mountains," Lucinda says immediately, and realizes even as the words escape her mouth that this is exactly where Hart is. He'll set up a base of operations in the wilderness somewhere, and then, if he hasn't started already, he'll begin the process of tracking Lucinda down. "But he'll be looking for me."

As if Ardie has heard Lucinda's thoughts, she leans forward a little, lowers her voice when she asks, "Lu, are you in danger? Do you need a safe place to stay until all this blows over?"

"I'm as safe where I'm at now as I would be anywhere."

Which is true. Staying at Ardie's wouldn't make Lucinda more safe; it would just make Ardie less safe.

"I dated a woman once who'd had a boyfriend who beat up on her sometimes," Ardie says. "So I know a thing or two about the anxiety, the paranoia, the double-checking around every corner. Always looking over your shoulder. Nightmares." She looks like she's about to say something else, but closes her mouth again. Then: "I don't want this to come out the wrong way, but if you ever need someone around at night… I'd be happy to sleep on your couch or something. Just so you don't have to be alone."

"That's kind of you, Ardie. Hopefully it won't come to that."

"Let me text you my phone number," Ardie says. "Just in case you ever need it."

They exchange numbers, and their food arrives a moment later. For a minute or two, the women busy themselves with unrolling silverware and settling into their meals.

"Were things always bad with him?" Ardie asks after her first bite. "Or did it escalate with time?"

Lucinda hesitates. "Do you mind if we talk about something else for a while? I kinda came here for lunch so I wouldn't have to think about things for a minute."

"I'm sorry. Of course we can," Ardie says. She smiles at Lucinda. "I'm capable of talking about almost anything, so give me a topic. What do you wanna talk about?"

"Tell me about growing up in Reverie. Maybe we know some people in common."

"Alright then." Ardie drums her fingers against the tabletop for a few seconds, then stops. A broad grin spreads across her face. "So how much do you know about the Brinkmanns?"

Chapter 10

Thanks to Margaret's forewarning, Lucinda's not terribly surprised when she goes home a few hours after lunch and finds two squad cars and an old truck blocking in the neighbor girl's blue compact.

Three men linger between the cars and the house, and they turn as one body when Lucinda's tires crunch against the gravel of her drive.

Lory Wheeler's the first one she sees, wearing a deputy's hat instead of his customary Gamecocks cap over his brown curls. There's another man she doesn't recognize standing next to Wheeler; he's not wearing a uniform but he sure looks like a plain-clothes detective if Lucinda ever saw one. It's something about the man's posture, which is relaxed almost to the point of being smug, his barrel chest, his thick forearms crossed against his chest.

The third man, who awkwardly stands against the truck a few paces apart from the police officers, is as scruffy as the second man is dapper. His face is covered with salt-and-pepper stubble that looks like he's either trying and failing to grow a beard or just hasn't bothered to shave in a few days, his t-shirt's lettering is almost completely worn off, and he's wearing cut-off jean shorts above unlaced, mud-encrusted work boots.

None of the three men approach Lucinda when she parks. They all simply turn back around and continue talking, as if her appearance is nothing particularly noteworthy, and they keep at it that way until Lucinda gets out of the car and begins walking in their direction.

Wheeler's the one to speak first, probably because he's the only one of the three who really knows her.

"Afternoon, Lu," he says genially, tipping his hat towards her.

"Hey, Wheeler," she answers, coming to a stop a few yards from the men.

The bald-headed man turns towards her, his electric blue eyes inspecting her up and down. He nods at her, but says nothing.

"I s'pose you know by now that the 'thorities back in Georgia misplaced your husband?" Wheeler asks Lucinda.

"I heard that this morning, yes."

"Only this morning?" asks the bald man, still with that inspecting look in his eyes. "I'm surprised they didn't say nothing til now."

"The police haven't told me anything at all," Lucinda responds, an edge of defensiveness creeping into her tone. "It was my divorce lawyer who bothered to call me and tell me that he's missing."

The bald man's eyebrows arch in surprise. "Guess they do things differently back in Georgia."

Lucinda says nothing. The drone of summer insects

fills the heavy silence.

"Well, the sheriff's department here's been workin' with them Georgia boys and folks up in Sumter" — Wheeler nods at the bald man — "tryin' to track him down. We're here to give your place a once-over lookin' for him." Wheeler attempts a charming grin. "I don't guess he's here, though, right?"

"If I'd seen him, I either would've called the police," Lucinda says, "or I would've…"

The three men wait, expecting her to finish her sentence. But she doesn't. She puts her hands on both hips and turns her gaze upwards, towards the bright summer sky, blinking and squinting.

If it weren't for the heat, it would be a post-card perfect day. The sky is a perfect, rich azure; cotton ball white clouds roam across it slowly, like lazy animals.

"You would've what?" asked the bald man.

Lucinda brings her gaze back down, looks straight into his scrutinizing blue eyes. "Or I would've died by now."

None of the men seem to know what to do with her statement. The unidentified man by the old truck scuffs the toe of his boot against the ground; the bald man chews his bottom lip; Wheeler momentarily looks away from her.

When he looks back, he says, "I figured you didn't know where he was. Can't imagine you wanting to seek him out, given what happened and all. But we gotta search your place anyway, you know how it goes." He pulls a group of papers from his breast pocket and unfolds them.

"You wanna see the warrant?"

"It's fine," Lucinda says with a wave, her voice flat.

Wheeler hitches a thumb over his shoulder. "That sorry lookin' fella behind us there's Zeke Brinkmann, your landlord. Don't know if you've ever met him or not."

Zeke nods somberly in Lucinda's direction.

She meets his eyes, nods back. "Don't believe I have. We've only ever spoken on the phone."

Zeke clears his throat, points. "Like the garden you're workin' on there. It'll be nice to see some color added to the place."

"Thank you," Lucinda says.

"And this fine gentleman beside me," Wheeler says, indicating the bald man, "is Detective Jack Samuels."

"I didn't know Reverie had any detectives," Lucinda says.

"Oh, we don't," Wheeler says quickly. "He's the one from up in Sumter workin' with the guys in Georgia."

"Do you need me to stay out of the house while you search?" Lucinda asks them. "Or can I make my lunch while you look around."

Detective Samuels speaks before Wheeler can. "Deputy Wheeler will stay out here in the yard, with you. Mr. Brinkmann and I will take a look around the property."

"Both sides of the duplex?" Lucinda asks.

Samuels nods. "Both sides."

"What about — " Lucinda starts, about to ask about the girl next door. But she thinks better of it, given the way

Samuels is still looking at her as if she's harboring a fugitive. She gives a small shake of her head. "Never mind."

There's little she can do but watch and wait while Samuels and Zeke Brinkmann head into her house. She thinks about the underwear she washed by hand and left hanging to dry on top of the shower curtain rod in the bathroom. She hopes she hasn't left anything dirty in the kitchen.

"So," Wheeler says, "I guess you're settlin' in alright? I heard you're working at Georgie's now. That's how we knew you'd be home about now — I called this morning and got your schedule from Georgie. That's how we timed it to be here same time as you got home."

He did? Georgie didn't mention a phone call from Lory Wheeler to Lucinda. Now she feels naked and exposed. But small towns have a way of doing that to people. Laying out their business for everyone to see. She hopes Georgie didn't ask Wheeler any questions about why Lucinda's in Reverie or why the sheriff's department needs to know her work schedule. And if she did ask, Lucinda hopes Georgie will keep the answers to herself.

"Yes, it's my first full week cutting hair for Georgie," Lucinda replies politely.

"Everyone's been friendly enough to you?"

"Oh, yes. Reverie's a friendly place."

Wheeler smiles. "That it is."

"One of your first cousins was at the shop today, getting

her hair colored," Lucinda says, steering the conversation away from herself.

"Oh, yeah? Which one? Since my daddy remarried twice before I was eighteen, I got a whole heap of first cousins and ex-first cousins." He chuckles.

"I don't know which one," Lucinda admits. "Dark red hair, about — "

But Samuels and Zeke Brinkmann walk out the front door of the other side of the duplex, and Lucinda wonders for a second time if they'd let the girl next door know they're coming, and if it's even all that legal for them to go into her space when the warrant is for searching Lucinda's.

Samuels meets Wheeler's eye and shakes his head as he trots down the porch stairs and into the yard.

"Not there," he announces. He strides over to Lucinda, extends a business card towards her. "If you hear anything, if you see anything, if he tries to contact you, call me right away, alright?"

She takes the card, nods. It's not the first detective's card that's been handed to her. She has what amounts to a collection of them in her nightstand drawer, but all of them have Georgia area codes before their phone numbers. She looks down at Detective Jack Samuels' card. This one has a South Carolina area code, and she supposes that should give her a little comfort, but it doesn't.

The truth is that if Hart's decided he doesn't want to be found anymore, he won't be. And if he wants to find Lucinda…

He will.

And there's nothing Detective Jack Samuels, Sheriff's Deputy Lory Wheeler, or Landlord Zeke Brinkmann will be able to do to stop him. Good men always think they can protect women from bad men; the truth is, women have always known that they have to learn to protect themselves.

After another couple minutes of instructions that are meant to make her feel comforted, the men drive away, leaving Lucinda to stand in the yard by herself.

Just as she's about to head inside to make lunch, a hand falls onto her shoulder from behind.

Chapter 11

"Lu?"

Lucinda's heart leaps into her throat as she lets out a strangled half-scream. She spins on her heel, but it's only the girl next door.

The girl chuckles. "Sorry. Didn't mean to startle you."

Lucinda puts her hand over her heart, smiling warmly at the girl as she has a laugh at herself. "It's alright. I've just been a little on edge today."

"You must be," the girl agrees. "And — is it just me, or did I see some cop cars pull away just now?"

Lucinda nods. Then frowns. "You didn't see them searching your half of the duplex?"

The girl's head pulls back and her brow creases. "They *searched* my place?"

"Yeah. You didn't see them?"

"No. I was out. Walking. Found a trail behind the house that goes into the woods, and I followed it to see where it went." She grins and uses a thumb to gesture behind her. "I found some pretty cool shit. You should come see it sometime."

Lucinda lets out a shaky breath. "Sometime."

The girl cocks her head, studying Lucinda's face. "Maybe 'sometime' should be now. No offense, but you kind of look like death warmed over. What did the cops want?"

"It's a long story," Lucinda says, sighing. She glances at her watch. "Wait. What are you doing here?"

"I swapped with a girl. Not going in 'til seven tonight." She ducks her head so that she's even with Lucinda, her brown eyes touching each part of Lucinda's face, as if to check that she's alright. "Is that your way of changing the subject? Avoiding my question?"

It's a gaze every bit as intent and inspecting as Detective Samuels' was. And yet it's infinitely softer, more compassionate.

The girl puts both her hands on Lucinda's upper arms, squeezes them. "You know what? Never mind. Don't tell me if you don't want to. Just come and take a walk with me. You know they're calling it 'forest bathing' these days."

"Forest bathing?"

"Yeah. A fancy way for saying that taking a long walk outside, with sun and trees and birds, makes us feel a hell of a lot better." She takes Lucinda's hand, tugs. "C'mon."

Lucinda looks down at the hand holding her own. The nurse's fingers are built like the rest of her — slender, long, graceful, smooth. The warmth of those fingers, the pressure of them… it's reassuring, somehow.

Lucinda draws in a deep breath. "Okay. Show me what you found."

Lucinda has never heard of forest bathing before, but she understands the concept intuitively.

"I used to play in the woods behind my Aunt Sophie's house around here when I was a kid," she tells the girl, who walks a few paces ahead of her on the narrow dirt path.

"Oh, yeah? By 'here,' you mean here in Reverie?"

"Yeah."

"But I thought you were from Georgia?"

"I was," Lucinda says, then corrects herself. "Am, I mean. But my Aunt Sophie and most of the rest of my mom's side of the family lives in or near Reverie. So I used to come here every summer growing up with my mom and my sisters."

"How many sisters do you have?"

"Two. One older — Edie. And one younger. Harriet."

"Sisters," the girl says with a sigh. "I always wanted sisters. Or at least one sister. All I had was my little brother growing up — and Lord, he was obnoxious when he was little. Truthfully, he's still obnoxious now, but he's gotten better with age."

"What's his name?" Lucinda asks.

"Derrick."

Lucinda chuckles. "I'm surprised you didn't make me guess it."

The girl stops, turns to face Lucinda. The sunlight filtering through the trees brings out red highlights in her long brown hair that Lucinda hadn't noticed before. The girl smiles, and the effect is nearly angelic. "Did you come up with any new names? Or at least a strategy for guessing?"

"What have I guessed so far?" Lucinda says, posing the question half to herself and half to the girl. "You said you're not Rebecca. Not Taylor…"

"Not Annie and not Vicky, either," the girl adds, making a sour face.

"And you didn't like Annie because it's too… plain? Or old-fashioned?"

"Both!"

Lucinda laughs — something she didn't think she'd be able to do after a morning of finding out that Hart's on the loose, and having a sheriff's deputy serve a search warrant on her house.

"Alright," Lucinda says. "So a name not so old-fashioned… and not too plain… hmm…"

They walk on in silence, Lucinda poring over girls' names in her head.

It's cooler on the shady trail than it was on the sun-saturated yard in front of the duplex. Back here in the woods, the sun is warming but not unpleasant, seeming to coax from the land a subtle fragrance of pine straw and earth. Birds flit amongst the trees, calling to each other with songs of love and songs of territory. Every step Lucinda takes further from the house seems to ease her mind and soothe her frayed nerves a degree more.

But then it strikes her, and she shivers. "He's probably in the woods somewhere. Up in the mountains."

The girl stops, turns. She puts a hand out and slouches sideways against a pine tree, gazing back at Lucinda with narrowing eyes. "Who's in the woods somewhere?"

"My ex-husband. That's why the police were here. He's out on bail waiting for his court date, but he missed a call-in with his probation officer, and now they can't find him." Once the words are out, Lucinda's chest spasms, squeezing shut like a fist is closing around her heart.

She'd managed to contain herself earlier — at work, at lunch with Ardie, while talking to the police. But now a sob escapes. She balls both hands into fists, bites down hard on the knuckle of one hand.

"They shouldn't have let him out on bail at all," she says, her voice high-pitched and trembling, half-muffled by her fist. "I told them. I *told* them not to. I *warned* them. But they wouldn't listen to me." She shakes her head bitterly. "What do I know? I'm just a stupid, overreactive *woman.*"

She doubles over, hands dropping to her knees as if her back can no longer support the weight of her shoulders and head. She's embarrassing herself now — crying so freely in front of this young woman she hardly knows — this woman whose *name* she doesn't even know. And yet once the tears begin, they don't seem like they'll ever stop again. It's like the fragile peace she's managed to construct since moving to Reverie two weeks ago has shattered, and now fragments of her will ooze out, spilling all over the forest floor, with only a nameless girl left behind to pick the pieces up again.

"Hey," the girl says. Long, lithe hands grip Lucinda's shoulders, straightening her. Long, lithe hands pull her forward, wrap her into an embrace. "Hey, it's okay. Whatever's going on, it's okay. *You're* okay. You're going to *be* okay. Alright? Lu?"

Lucinda looks up, tries to make the young face in front of her come into focus through a curtain of tears. "It's not okay," she says. "It was *never* okay. It's never going to be okay again."

The girl strokes Lucinda's cheek with the back of her long fingers. "No, Lu, you're wrong about that. I know you're wrong."

"How can you know?" she asks, and her words are sharper, hotter than she intends. "You don't know Hart. You don't know what he's capable of. You don't know what — "

The girl silences Lucinda with a sudden, impulsive kiss. It lasts only a second or two, but the press of full, soft lips against her own is enough to stun Lucinda into stillness.

The girl pulls back. Her brown eyes are wide now, careful, studying Lucinda again but with a whole new question on her face. When Lucinda doesn't move, doesn't say a word, the girl leans forward and kisses her again.

The second kiss has none of the forceful urgency of the first. This one is probing, exploratory, a tongue slipping between Lucinda's lips with a caution that's almost shy.

Without thinking about what she's doing, Lucinda's eyes fall closed, and she sinks into the kiss, senses tingling as she becomes aware of the press of the girl's warm frame against her own, of long, lithe fingers finding their way to the nape of her neck, winding themselves into Lucinda's hair.

Lucinda would be happy for the kiss to last forever, she would be happy to lose herself in a moment that seems as if it's outside time, outside consequences. But after a while — a while that is somehow both deliciously long and far too short at the same time — the girl ends it, pulling back a second time.

Lucinda opens her eyes, and she mentally prepares herself for the inevitable apology the girl will give her, saying something like, *"I don't know what came over me. I never should've done that."*

But an apology doesn't come. Instead, the girl is statue-like in her stillness, gazing at a point somewhere behind Lucinda.

"What — " Lucinda starts, but the girl cuts her off.

"Shhh," she says quietly, keeping her gaze over Lucinda's shoulder. "Turn your head very, very slowly," she whispers.

Lucinda turns as she's been told, cold fear gripping her stomach. What will she see behind her? Hart? Or worse?

What could be worse than Hart?

But it is not the stuff of her nightmares; it is a doe. She

stands halfway between the forest's edge and the path, her dark, enormous eyes taking in Lucinda with nearly the same wonderment as Lucinda has for her. A single tear forms in the corner of Lucinda's eye, but it's not a tear made of fear or pain this time. Not the kind of tears she has in the mornings, when she wakes from a sleep filled with nightmares.

"She's beautiful," Lucinda whispers.

The doe's ears twitch around the sound of Lucinda's voice, her tail flicks. Lucinda holds her breath; deer and human regard one another a moment longer. Then the doe bounds across the path, disappears into the shadows of the woods beyond.

Long fingers cup her chin, turn her face back around again.

"She is. But you're so much more beautiful," the girl says, and she kisses Lucinda once more.

Chapter 12

It seems to Lucinda that romance, like a viper, always strikes when one least expects it, while one has been busy focusing on almost everything else besides love.

That was how it was when Lucinda met Hart. She'd been twenty-two, still wobbling on the unsteady legs of a new adult, the way a fawn wobbles uncertainly once out of the womb. Except that newborn fawns tend to wobble towards their mothers; in Lucinda's case, she was wobbling away from hers.

Her older sister, Edie, had seemed not to wobble at all; the first in the family to go to college, she left home less like a fawn and more like a lioness, striding into Georgia Tech with the same confidence she'd always had, striding into her first job after that as if she had graced them with employment and not the other way around. Lucinda's younger sister, Harriet, took a more circuitous route. When she got pregnant at seventeen, it seemed as if Lucinda's place as second-best daughter would finally be cemented, but instead, Harriet managed to both mother and finish her high school degree before going on to vocational school and landing a respectable job. First the respectable job, then the respectable man; Harriet married a rich second son who made Lucinda's mother blush every time he dropped by the house.

Somehow her wild baby sister managed to nudge Lucinda out of second place despite it all, and at twenty-one, Lucinda was the one still living at home, bemoaning an overcast future.

"You've always wanted to be a hairdresser," Harriet had said. "I bet you'd be good. You should just go for it."

But Lucinda didn't. She'd never been the type to "just go for" anything. And so she lived at home for another year after that conversation with her sister, dutifully sticking to the same grocery store cashier's job that she'd had since the middle of high school.

"My middle daughter is my timid one," her mother liked to say, and the words had always been a confusing mix of disdain and affection.

Timid was one way of putting it; perpetually anxious might've been more accurate. Because as long as Lucinda could remember, she'd traveled through life with a cloud of worry hanging over her head. Thunderheads that would occasionally unleash paralyzing storms of nerves and indecision so strong that sometimes she couldn't even bring herself to decide which clothes to wear in the morning, let alone what to do with her life.

It was the anxiety, in the end, that sealed her fate. The anxiety led her into a doctor's office one day for a prescription; outside of that office there was an elevator; and inside of that elevator, there was a smiling Hart Hamilton.

"Hi," he'd said with a kind smile when she stepped on. A dark grey suit jacket strained to cover a broad chest; a powder blue shirt accented by a dark blue tie peeked out underneath. The elevator smelled of his aftershave.

Lucinda only nodded.

The elevator went down a floor; the doors opened; no one got on; the doors closed again.

"I hope you don't mind me saying so," Hart said, "but you're the most beautiful woman I've seen so far today."

Lucinda's eyes flitted over to Hart, then away from him, landing on the elevator's glowing pad of floor numbers. Heat surged up into her face, her heart sped up as the elevator plunged down, and she knew she was turning red, which only made the heat worse.

She managed a smile anyway.

"Thank you," she said.

"Aww, you're blushing. I didn't mean to embarrass you."

"It's alright," Lucinda said. "My fault, not yours. You were just being nice."

Hart gestured at the number pad. Only "P1" was still illuminated. "Going to your car?" he asked. "Would it be alright if I walked you to it?"

His confidence.

In retrospect, it was his confidence that Lucinda remembers the most from that first encounter. That easy boldness which had always been out of reach for Lucinda herself. That confidence led Hart to walk her to her car that day, to ask for her number, to take her out for the first time. It was flattering, and she said yes because no one had ever pursued her like that. Meeting a handsome, charming man in an elevator seemed like the type of thing that happened to other people, not to her.

She followed the breadcrumb trail of his confidence to see where it would lead. His confidence made Lucinda feel safe when she was with him; his confidence, at least in the beginning, kept the dark clouds of her anxiety at bay. Hart could be self-assured on her behalf; Hart could make decisions for her. All she needed to do was follow along.

She never went back to the doctor's office for her follow-up visit after she started on the anti-anxiety medication; Hart said she didn't need to go. After a while, she stopped taking the medication altogether; Hart said she didn't need them anymore.

"You're with me now," he'd said. "You have nothing left to be anxious about."

She'd believed him. He was a pharmaceutical representative, after all — if anyone would know things about drugs that the doctors didn't, it would be him. He'd told her as much. She took his suggestion about stopping her anxiety medication. And when they married, she also took his suggestion to stay at home and let him do the work. Cosmetology school could wait.

"A woman's place is in the home," Hart had said.

She would be having babies soon, he said, raising his children. Keeping house, cooking, raising his sons: That would be her job. Hart's job would be to bring home the bacon. That was what he said every day when he came home and collapsed onto the couch, draping his suit jacket behind him and loosening his tie.

"How was work today, sweetheart?" Lucinda would ask, bringing him his first tumbler of scotch on the rocks for the night.

He would heave a deep sigh. The sigh of a frustrated man.

"Bringing home the bacon, darlin.' You should be glad you don't have to do it."

And she *was* glad. She knew it was stressful; he told her how stressful it was all the time. She even understood why sometimes he would lose his temper and yell at her — it wasn't really about her, Lucinda knew. It was about work — about supervisors who patronized him and failed to recognize his talent, about underlings who would love to stab him in the back, about equals who thought their fancy college degrees made them better than he was. He couldn't really help himself from taking all that stress out on her.

That was what she told herself, too, the first time he hit her. She should've known better. He'd had a hard day. It wasn't the time or the place for a sarcastic joke at his expense. Her attempt at humor had fallen flat; it had been insensitive. She recognized that; the raised welt on her cheek that she saw in the mirror the next morning reminded her of her mistake.

Ten years passed before Lucinda finally realized she'd

married a monster. Her Prince Charming had actually been the Big Bad Wolf wearing a clever disguise. Another five years passed after that before things got bad enough that she began to wonder if he'd kill her faster if she stayed, or kill her faster if she left.

That was the question on her mind when she fell in love the second time.

She hadn't been looking for romance; once again she'd been focused on everything in her life *except* romance. Nevertheless, she'd found herself in another doctor's office, having stitches removed by a kind-hearted nurse — a young nurse with brown hair and brown eyes and a twinkle in her eye that bespoke of mischief.

"How'd you manage to gash your eye like that?" the nurse asked as she pulled out Lucinda's first stitch. "It's a funny place to cut yourself."

"I fell," Lucinda said, which was true enough. She'd fallen when Hart pushed her. She'd stumbled clumsily backwards, reaching for the kitchen counter but missing, slicing her face on its corner instead on her trip to the ground. An inch or two to the right and she might've lost her eye.

"Really?" the nurse said, but there was something about her tone that made it less of a question and more of an expression of skepticism. She pulled the next stitch out, holding Lucinda's head still with one hand, artfully dancing tweezers across the stitches with the other. "I had a cousin who used to fall all the time. Always thought she was just a big klutz, you know? Took me a while, but eventually I figured out her boyfriend was using her as a punching bag. Actually knocked out all her teeth at one point when he was high on something-or-other."

Lucinda's heart sped up; she was sure the nurse could see the pulse fluttering in her throat.

The nurse sighed, shook her head, started on the next stitch. "I woulda beat the hell outta that man if he hadn't fled the state before I got the chance. My cousin is like a sister to me. And the man who messes with my sister messes with me." She straightened on her rolling stool, cupped Lucinda's chin in her hand and turned her head gently to the side. She was so close that Lucinda could feel the warmth of her breath upon her cheek.

"Almost done," the nurse said. "And once these stitches come out, I don't want to see you back in our office ever again, got it? No more falls. Your face is much too beautiful for you to keep getting stitches in it."

She smiled at Lucinda, and something about the way her eyes sparkled woke something up inside Lucinda that she thought she'd lost long ago — hope.

Wheels whined against the tile floor as the nurse scooted forward again, lifting the tweezers towards Lucinda's temple. "Three down, one to go."

Lucinda let her gaze drop to the name tag hanging from the nurse's breast pocket. *Dionne Summers,* it read.

No, love never arrives at a convenient time.

Chapter 13

After the third lovely kiss from the nameless neighbor girl finally ends, Lucinda follows the girl back down the trail in contented silence, happy to simply listen to the musical quality of the girl's words as they babble out of her, meandering like a stream over topics ranging from the people she dislikes at the hospital, to the many reasons why she thinks her brother needs to change his life, to her newfound appreciation for poetry.

"I was never good at English in school, you know?" she says when she gets to the poetry. "Probably because I never got along with any of my English teachers. I was kind of a bad kid." She chuckles. "So my grades were always pretty crappy. But I have to admit I never tried very hard." She glances over her shoulder at Lucinda. "Are you still listening back there?"

"I'm still listening," Lucinda says, amused smile creasing her face.

"You're so quiet. Sometimes I'm not even sure if you're even walking behind me, or if I just dreamed you up."

The girl stops, turns halfway towards Lucinda, waits for the older woman to catch up with her. When she does, the girl hooks a hand through Lucinda's arm.

"There. Now I can see you as I talk. And you can't get away." She grins, squeezes Lucinda's arm to her side.

The two continue to walk up the narrow trail this way, side by side, shoulder against shoulder, with the girl turning every so often to avoid hanging vines, low branches, blackberry brambles.

"So anyway, I was really surprised when my friend gave me a book of poems, and it turned out I actually liked it." She hesitates, then sounds almost shy when she says, "I memorized a few of them. Do you want to hear one?"

"Of course," Lucinda answers, the smile still on her face.

"*'Tell me it was for the hunger,'*" the girl recites from memory, her eyes taking on a far-away look:

*"'& nothing less. For hunger is to give
the body what it knows*

*it cannot keep. That this amber light
whittled down by another war
is all that pins my hand to your chest.' (*)"*

Lucinda waits, but the girl glances at her hopefully, apparently done.

"What do you think?" she asks Lucinda.

"I don't know," Lucinda says. "What am I supposed to think?"

The girl chortles. "I'm not going to tell you what

you're supposed to think, silly. It's poetry. You think whatever you think."

Lucinda tries to remember the words. Hunger. Amber light. What the body cannot keep. A hand, pinned to a chest.

"I wasn't that good at poetry in school either," she says at last. "I don't think I'm smart enough to figure it out."

The girl shakes her head. "See, that's what I used to think. But it's not about brains. Or about figuring something out. Poetry is just supposed to make you *feel* something. That's why I've gotten so into it lately."

Lucinda considers this, reciting to herself the words that she can remember.

Hunger.
Bodies.
Hands.
Light.

"What does it make *you* feel?" she asks the girl.

The girl lets go of Lucinda's arm for a moment to lift a branch out of the way, and Lucinda immediately feels the absence of her, feels the little *whoosh* of cooler air against the bare arm the girl's skin had covered. But she says nothing about it, ducks beneath the branch, and enjoys her relief in silence when the hand comes back to the crook of her elbow, shoulder pressing against shoulder as they continue down the trail.

"It feels like a poem about loneliness to me," the girl says after she takes Lucinda's arm again. "But not just any loneliness. I think it's about being lonely in the way that only sex can make you lonely."

Lonely in the way that only sex can make you lonely.

Lucinda turns the statement over with the invisible hands of her mind, touching it, probing it, examining it the way she might explore a woman's hair before making the first cut.

When her exploration is over, she blurts without thinking, "Sex made me lonely most of my life." And then, also without thinking, she asks the girl, "What if he finds me? What if he finds me, and he forces me to go back with him, and this time I can't get away?"

The girl stops walking, steps in front of Lucinda. "I won't let that happen," she says softly. "I promise I won't." She strokes Lucinda's cheek with her thumb, swiping away a tear Lucinda hadn't realized had fallen.

"You can't say that," Lucinda says. "You don't know him. You don't know what he's capable of."

The girl's expression goes from soft to hard. "I've known men like your ex-husband, Lucinda. I've known them and I won't tolerate them."

Despondent, Lucinda shakes her head miserably. "Brave words. You don't understand — he's capable of anything."

The girl stops, tugs on Lucinda's arm until she stops, too. "Do you care that I kissed you back there?" she asks. "Does it bother you?"

"No." Lucinda's reply is quiet, as if the girl were

another doe who might be frightened away by any sound too loud, too discordant.

"I've wanted to kiss you from the first moment I saw you."

Lucinda hesitates. "But why?"

The girl shrugs. "Do I have to give a reason? I saw you. I wanted you. Sometimes it's just like that."

"But we hardly know each other. And I... I'm so much older than you."

"I don't pay attention to age any more than I pay attention to gender," the girl says dismissively. "I've dated people older than me. I've dated people younger than me. And as for us not knowing each other all that well, do you really think you have to know someone a long time to know that you care for them?"

Lucinda thinks back, remembers the day she met Hart, the day she met Dionne. Both times, she knew the very same day something would develop between them. She couldn't have predicted *what* would develop, exactly, not in either case, but she knew that *something* would. She knew she wanted them. The same way the girl now says she wanted Lucinda.

The same way Lucinda has always wanted the girl. From the moment she'd recognized her striking resemblance to Dionne.

"No," Lucinda says at last. "I don't guess you do."

"Sometimes... What I'm trying to say is, it's like poetry, Lu. Sometimes we overthink things, make everything complicated. But it doesn't always have to be about thinking, figuring stuff out up here." She taps the side of her head with an index finger. "We just get a certain feeling, and it's not important to be able to explain why." She steps closer, cups Lucinda's face in her hands. "I may not have known you long, but I know I feel something for you. I care about you. And when somebody threatens a person I care about, I'll do anything to protect them. *Anything.*" Her voice goes low and fierce. "Your ex-husband thinks he's a tough motherfucker? Well, goddamn, I'm a tough motherfucker, too. When I say he won't touch you again, I mean it, Lu. Do you believe me?"

Lucinda studies the girl's face. The adamant overconfidence of youth is there, and yet... and yet, Lucinda believes her anyway. Trusts her anyway.

"Yes. I believe you."

The girl slides her hands from Lucinda's face down her shoulders, down her sides and into the small of Lucinda's back. She laces her fingers, pulls Lucinda closer. "Good. You're with me now. And I'm going to protect you."

"He's a monster."

"Yeah? So am I."

They return to the duplex in silence, and Lucinda doesn't argue when the girl follows her inside, pushes her gently down to the couch, straddles her waist while she kisses her. Lucinda feels the pads of the girl's fingers everywhere along her body — brushing across her throat, kneading her breasts, tracing lines along the bare skin between the hem of her shirt and the waistband of her jeans. The girl starts to move her hand below the waistband, but Lucinda stops her.

"No," Lucinda says. "Not yet."

The girl only nods, returns to kissing her, touching her.

It seems like hours pass while she lies beneath the girl's warmth, but it can't be that long. When Lucinda finally catches a glimpse of the clock upon the wall, though, she puts her hands on the girl's shoulders, pushes her back.

"Didn't you have to be at the hospital by seven?"

The girl groans. "Yes. Maybe I'll call in sick." She dips her head, begins dropping sweet, bird-like pecking kisses onto Lucinda's face.

"You can't call in sick just to make out with me," Lucinda says, smiling. "You need to get ready."

"Unh-uh, no," says the girl. "They'll have to make do without me."

Lucinda giggles. "You know I'd love it if you could stay, but…"

"Oh, fine, fine," the girl says, sitting up and straightening her shirt. But then she promptly returns to kissing Lucinda.

"All I want you to do is stay," Lucinda says between the kisses. "But you — "

The girl pulls back. "You're right, you're right," she says with a grin. "One of us has to be responsible. If you weren't… I could do this all night."

She stands with a sigh, uses a mirror on Lucinda's wall

to rearrange her hair and smooth her rumpled nurse's uniform.

"I guess we won't see each other 'til tomorrow afternoon," the girl says without turning around. "Maybe even the day after that. It's a shame."

Lucinda frowns, realizing that the prospect of having to wait so long to see the girl feels suddenly heavy. She wonders if she should've let the girl call in sick after all. Because all Lucinda wants to do is stay pressed together, shoulder-to-shoulder, lips-to-lips, listening to her nameless neighbor carry on about poetry and family members and hospitals.

But there will be time enough later. There will be time, and finally, for the first time since Dionne left, Lucinda has something to look forward to.

The girl leaves a few minutes later, leaving behind a lingering smell of her sunlight-warmed skin. A scent that contains nearly enough sunlight to drive out the nagging thought that Hart is loose somewhere, and probably looking for her.

...For hunger is to give
the body what it knows

it cannot keep.

Chapter 14

For a few hours, while the sun is still up, Lucinda surprises herself by feeling happy. She putters around the kitchen, fixing a light dinner while she replays lines of poetry in her head, replays the sensation of the girl's mouth against her own. She touches her fingers to her lips. Someone else's lips had been in this same spot not long ago. Perhaps with luck, the same someone's lips will be there again soon. She smiles.

A beautiful girl kissed her today. In this very duplex.

Who would've ever thought it possible? Certainly not Lucinda. She's acutely aware that she's now closer to fifty than she is to forty, also aware that the time to dye the silver out of her roots seems to come faster and faster. Lucinda tells herself she's aged well — and it's true. She's maintained her slight frame; the most prominent wrinkles on her face are laugh lines. Nothing droops too much. She was always petite and her chest wasn't that big to begin with, so the sagging isn't as noticeable as it is on some women.

Despite all this, Lucinda knows she's not young anymore. She knows the girl next door could easily find someone more attractive and funny and charming her own age. The thought makes Lucinda sigh. Perhaps the charmed afternoon had been just that — a single, charmed afternoon. A momentary lapse in judgment that the girl will come to regret later.

The more she thinks about it, the more Lucinda realizes she needs to prepare herself for that inevitability. After all, the girl is impulsive. She's shown that. She could impulsively end something as quickly as she impulsively began it.

Perhaps Lucinda should be the one to stop it. Before it really starts. Then at least she could have some control over the process, not get blind-sided when her young neighbor suddenly loses interest.

Lucinda should tell the girl she made a mistake, let her go before either of them have a chance to get invested and therefore hurt. Yes. That's what she should do. Because right now, Lucinda doesn't think she'll survive another broken heart. Not after what happened with Dionne.

Dionne. How she misses Dionne. And with a single name, with two simple syllables, Lucinda's good mood dissipates, evaporating the way mist above a river disappears in the light of the morning sun.

Dionne had been her morning sun. Without her, Lucinda lives in a perpetual night. Why had she been stupid to believe that a few kisses from a stranger would change that?

Outside, the sun finally sets, the light in the living room marching from soft orange to dim to gone. Darkness descends upon the duplex, and Lucinda feels her aloneness more acutely than ever.

"Stop feeling sorry for yourself and just go to sleep," she says out loud.

But sleeping means dreaming. Dreaming means nightmares. Nightmares mean Hart.

She'll read, she decides. Something light and fun and romantic. And when her eyes drift closed and the book flops down onto her chest, she won't bother to turn the lamp off or shift from half-sitting to lying down. She'll just drift off, head filled with visions of romance and kisses.

But two and a half hours after Lucinda falls asleep, she wakes herself again with a strangled cry. In her dream, Hart had found her. He waited right outside the bedroom window of the duplex, shining a flashlight into her room.

"Let me in, Lucinda," he said when he saw her.

He was the Big Bad Wolf. Lucinda was one of the Three Little Pigs. But which one? Was the duplex made of straw, sticks, or stones?

He tapped the flashlight on the glass. *"Let me in, if you know what's good for you."*

She trembled from head to foot but made no move towards the window.

"No," she said.

"Goddammit, let me in!" He pounded on the glass, and it made a splintering sound. A crack appeared, dancing up the windowpane, then into the wall itself, sending a little puff of plaster dust into Lucinda's bedroom. Hart pounded harder; the crack grew, spiderweb arms growing in every

direction. *"Let me in!"*

The window broke, shattering inward, spraying the room with glass. The walls cracked, and with a mighty boom, collapsed all around her.

Lucinda screamed.

And wakes up.

She takes a moment to catch her breath, eyes darting furtively around the room, looking for glass, waiting for the walls to crumble, but it was only a dream. She's glad she had the foresight to leave the light on.

She turns to the side, gaze falling on the cell phone that's plugged in and sitting on her nightstand. Her instinct is to call the girl, but she doesn't have her number. And if she called the hospital, whom would she ask for? The girl still doesn't have a name. Lucinda reaches for her phone, turns it over in her hands a few times before coming to a decision. She opens her contacts and scrolls through until she finds the number she's looking for.

It only rings once before someone picks up. "Hello?" The voice doesn't sound sleepy at all; Lucinda hopes she didn't wake the woman on the other end.

"Ardie? This is embarrassing, but… do you remember the other day at lunch, you said you'd come over, sleep on my couch if I needed you to?"

"I'll be there in five minutes."

#

By way of explanation, Lucinda recounts the dream about Hart when Ardie arrives. With another person there to push back the gloom of the little duplex, it all sounds a little silly. A little melodramatic. Lucinda stands in the center of the living room as she explains, hugging herself slightly as if she's cold.

"And that's when I called you," she concludes.

Ardie is sitting on the couch, leaning forward with her forearms on her knees, hands clasped, listening attentively.

"I'm being ridiculous," Lucinda says.

Ardie shakes her head. "No, you're not. I know a thing or two about nightmares. After I got out of the service, I used to relive the worst things I'd seen overseas almost every night for a while. And like I told you when we had lunch, I've seen what it's like to live with aftermath of abuse." She pats the couch next to her. "So relax. As my mama would say, sit down and stay a while."

Lucinda sits beside Ardie. She brings her knees up to her chest and rotates so she can look at Ardie as she talks. "What was her name? The girl you dated whose boyfriend abused her?"

"Amanda. It was a long time ago, before I joined the military. I was just a kid; Amanda was nine years older than me. Twenty-eight." Ardie chuckles. "Made me feel sophisticated, at the time. To be dating an older woman. Now when I look back, all I can see is how young we both were."

"Did you date her long?"

"No. She was a handful," Ardie says, then quickly adds, "Not because she'd been abused by her boyfriend. Just because she was... Amanda."

Lucinda smiles, thinking about what Ardie might've been like in her late teens and early twenties. "I bet all the girls chased you."

Ardie chuckles. "Not hardly, darlin.' I was too shy back then to encourage any chasing."

"I don't know about that. I bet you were charming without meaning to be. Like you are now." Lucinda feels her cheeks pink as soon as she says it, thinking that she's probably being too bold. She decides to change the subject before Ardie can answer. "Did you always know you were attracted to women?"

"Oh, yeah. Never even occurred to me that I could be any other way."

"Must've been hard on you. Growing up in a place like this."

Ardie shrugs. "It's a lot worse other places. Still plenty of countries where you can go to jail for who you love, ya know. I try to remember that when I get to feeling sorry for myself." She pauses. "What about you? Was the girl in the photo your first... ?"

"Not exactly," Lucinda says. "I had a friend in high school who was — well, we did a little bit more than each others' hair when she came over. But it was confusing, and... and in the end, I guess I just wasn't as brave as you."

"Bravery didn't have anything to do with it," Ardie

says. "I couldn't have been straight anymore than I could've been the proper little debutante my mom wanted me to be." She leans back on the couch, stretches her legs out before her. "Anyhow. If you want to head back to sleep, I'm fine here on my own. Brought a book to read and everything."

Lucinda shakes her head. "I don't think I'll be able to sleep for a while. Actually… would you want to watch a movie?"

It takes them a few minutes to get Netflix working — the Internet connection in Reverie proper isn't great, which means that on the outskirts where Lucinda lives, it's hardly functional half the time — but they finally manage to pull up a list of movies and settle on a romantic comedy.

They sit side-by-side, feet resting on the coffee table as the movie begins. Lucinda isn't sure when it happens, but at some point, she finds her shoulder brushing against Ardie's. But she doesn't move away, and neither does Ardie. By the time the movie finishes, their legs are touching, too. Lucinda knows she should move this time, but still she doesn't.

What would the girl next door say, if she saw what was happening right now? Would she be hurt? Did the kisses this afternoon mean anything to her? They probably didn't. They probably won't ever happen again. The pleasant late afternoon with the girl has already taken on a dream-like quality, seeming almost unreal compared with the warm, present solidity of Ardie next to her.

#

Lucinda falls asleep without meaning to about halfway through the second movie. She wakes up just as the credits roll, her head on Ardie's shoulder, bobbing up and down to the rhythm of the bigger woman's breath. Lucinda finds that she has half-turned, curled in like a cat against Ardie's side.

"You woke up on your own," Ardie says. "That's good. I was sitting here, trying to figure out how I was going to move you without waking you."

Lucinda sits up quickly. "I'm so sorry. I didn't mean to fall asleep on you."

Ardie chuckles. "It's fine. Truth be told, it's been a while since I had a beautiful woman asleep on my shoulder."

Lucinda meets her eyes, unsure how to respond. Their faces are still close. Close enough that if Lucinda wanted to, she could lean forward just a little, allow her lips to find Ardie's. It would be so easy. And Ardie probably wouldn't resist.

She doesn't know if Ardie is thinking the same thing, but it seems like the woman is holding her breath, waiting for Lucinda to do something.

Lucinda straightens, leans away. Out of kissing distance. "When did I fall asleep?"

"Around the time the heroine got sent off to see her

step-mother."

"Step-mother? There was a step-mother?"

Ardie grins. "Maybe you fell asleep sooner than I thought. It's good, though, that you slept."

"But I'm keeping you awake."

"You're not. I'm fine."

"Ardie... I really appreciate you coming over tonight."

Ardie's grin fades; her face grows somber. "I'm glad I could help. Don't ever hesitate to call, Lu. I'm serious. Whatever you're going through, you don't have to do it alone."

The kind words nearly bring tears to Lucinda's eyes. She puts a hand on Ardie's bare forearm, feels its warmth, its understated strength. "Thank you," she says. That same, strange urge to lean into Ardie and kiss her returns, and this time Lucinda gives into it.

But only to peck Ardie lightly on the cheek.

Lucinda stands with a groan and a stretch. "Two movies might've actually done the trick. I think I'm going to head on to bed now. But let me find you some sheets and a proper pillow first."

"Oh, no, you don't need to do that," Ardie says. "It's too hot tonight for sheets or blankets. And your couch pillows'll do me just fine." As if to prove it, Ardie kicks off her boots, reclines in the spot Lucinda had occupied a moment earlier, pushing a pillow beneath her head. "See? I'm perfect. Now you go on and get a good night's sleep."

Lucinda stands above her, hesitating. For a brief

second, she imagines inviting Ardie into bed with her, imagines how the woman's warm skin would feel against her own. But no. That's not why Ardie's here. And besides, there's the girl. What would the girl say if Lucinda took Ardie to bed on the same day that her neighbor kissed her?

"You sure you're alright like this?" Lucinda asks.

"I'm right as rain, Lu."

Lucinda hovers a moment longer. "Alright," she says, and reluctantly, she heads to her bedroom alone.

Chapter 15

The rest of the week passes by slowly, with a sort of timeless meandering, like a broad, rain-swollen river wandering its way through the sun-drenched summer landscape. One day runs into the next, one perm into the next, one afternoon into the next. Hot, listless afternoons of sitting on the porch, listening to the girl read lines of poetry between a ministry of kisses.

The girl (and Lucinda has given up trying to guess her name for now, is happy just to think of her as "the girl" — *her* girl, her lovely girl) has gotten into the habit of waking up early enough to take a long lunch with Lucinda each day between Lucinda's afternoon appointments at Georgie's. Some lunches are longer than others; some lunches include a walk down the pine forest trail, going a little further each time, keeping their eyes out for does and fawns and the occasional young buck. Some lunches are brief, with only enough time to share a glass of lemonade or sweet tea before Lucinda has to head back.

But each afternoon is sweet, like a ripe strawberry on the lips. And Lucinda was wrong about the girl's interest in her being a one-time thing. Like teenagers exploring each others' bodies for the first time, every afternoon includes a make-out session a little longer than the one before.

Lucinda hasn't slept with the girl yet, because she's just not the type to rush things, but each day brings them a little closer to the line that can't ever be uncrossed.

But the sun-filled summer afternoons with the girl make the evenings, after the young nurse has left for work, all the more lonely. All the more ripe for Lucinda's thoughts to turn to Hart, to wonder which part of the Georgia mountains he's holed up in, to wonder how long it will be before she comes home one day to find him waiting for her. She calls Ardie sometimes for comfort, but she doesn't invite her over again. It no longer seems right, given what's happening with the girl next door.

When Lucinda isn't talking to Ardie, she calls her lawyer Margaret — mainly because she prefers calling Margaret to calling Detective Samuels or Lory Wheeler. And every time they speak, Margaret says that there's still no news about Lucinda's missing ex-husband.

And so the days tick by — Wednesday into Thursday, Thursday into Friday, Friday into Saturday.

#

On Sunday, the girl has the day off, too, and all morning Lucinda plans in her head what they might do with the entire afternoon and evening they'll have together. Lucinda might take her into town, she thinks, point out the places she knew as a child, point out other places that have since changed — although only a few places have changed;

Reverie is one of those small towns that has fallen outside of the passage of years.

Like herself, the girl is a transplant into Reverie, landing here as she's worked her way west from Florence. She'd meant to keep going west until she'd hit Atlanta, but somehow she stalled out before even making it past Columbia. That means she and Lucinda are both outsiders in Reverie, but at least Lucinda has some claim to the place, which is why she feels it's incumbent upon her to serve as tour guide.

But on the other hand, maybe that's just another excuse to spend as much time with the girl as she can.

Lucinda wakes up at her normal early hour, brews her normal pot of coffee, sits on the porch and watches sunlight filter in between the pine boughs across the road. She'll garden today, she decides, continuing to work good soil in and pull out rocks and weeds from the plot she's outlined. There's not much she can plant; it's too late for most of the things she loves to grow — watermelon and okra, asparagus and cantaloupe, too early for things like cucumbers, collards, carrots. But she figures she might could eke out a few homegrown tomatoes from her new garden if she goes to the nursery today, and although she's never tried to grow eggplant before, the girl mentioned a love for eggplant parmesan.

She watches the sunrise from the rocking chair on the front porch, sipping coffee and daydreaming of vegetable gardens and feeding the girl eggplant parmesan, one forkful at a time.

The day goes as planned, for once: She finishes her coffee before seven-thirty, makes her way to the nursery and back, and finishes putting a scraggly tomato plant in the ground, all before the clock strikes ten.

It's not until she hears the sound of the motorcycle, still too far down the two-lane highway to be seen, that she remembers in a flash that Ardie had arranged to come by today to work on the duplex. Lucinda's embarrassed that Ardie's about to find her mud-streaked and sweaty for a second Sunday in a row, so she stands up promptly the moment she hears the rumbling motorcycle engine and hustles inside.

She manages to get most of the dirt off her hands and out from under her fingernails by the time she hears the heavy work boots on the porch stairs and a rattling banging on the screen door.

"C'mon in," she calls, shutting the water off and reaching for a dishtowel. The door opens and bounces closed again, but after a few steps, the sound of work boots stops. Lucinda frowns, wondering why Ardie's stopped in the living room instead of coming on back to the kitchen.

Then her heart quakes with sudden fear.

What if it's not Ardie at all? What if it was someone else's heavy footsteps?

What if it's Hart?

He wears work boots, too. His step is heavy, like the one she'd just heard.

He's missing. He said he would find her. He said he would finish what he started. And maybe he would do that... now.

Pulse echoing with tidal intensity in her ears, Lucinda inches forward, grabbing a butcher knife from the holder next to the sink as she edges around the refrigerator.

She lets out a breath when she sees Ardie, standing on the mat by the front door, holding some kind of plastic case and gazing down at her feet. Ardie looks up when she hears Lucinda, barks out a half-laugh.

"Well, man alive, you're not planning on stabbing me, are ya?"

Lucinda glances at the knife in her hand, feels the wave of adrenaline subside. "S-sorry," she says, stumbling over the word. "I — you caught me chopping vegetables."

"I knew you were back in the kitchen," Ardie says, smile turning sheepish. "But I didn't want to track mud through your house."

Lucinda waves her hand dismissively and manages to return Ardie's smile. "Oh, it's fine. I need to clean later today anyhow."

"Naw, what would my mama say if I walked through your house like this?" Ardie says, pointing down at the mud-caked boots.

"Ardie, it's fine. Honestly."

Ardie narrows her eyes skeptically. "You sure? I could take 'em off, or..."

"Oh, *please,*" Lucinda says, waving a hand. "I'm not

that particular. You see what a mess my place is. I just came in from the garden and tracked in half of it with me, anyway."

Ardie hesitates for one more second, then walks through the living room and into the kitchen. "Okay. But your place *isn't* a mess."

Lucinda puts the butcher knife back in its holder.

"Where are your vegetables?" Ardie asks.

"What?"

"Your vegetables. You said you had a big ol' kitchen knife in your hand because you were chopping vegetables."

Lucinda shrugs. "I was just finishing up when you knocked."

Ardie looks like she's about to say something else, but thinks better of it. She holds up the plastic case. "Brought a drill. Got some more tools by my bike. I figured I could work on the screen door today, try to fix the window, maybe come back next week to work on the back stairs? My dad's got some scrap wood from a deck project he never finished laying around; I figure I could use that to shore up your stairs."

"You sure you wanna do all this?" Lucinda says, putting her hands on her hips. "It's an awful lot of work."

"Just being a good neighbor," Ardie says. "Besides, what else do I have to do on a Sunday afternoon except read or watch my parents watching TV?"

"Alright," Lucinda says. "If you say so. I guess I'm not really in a position to turn down help."

Ardie sets herself to work on the screen door while Lucinda starts on a second batch of cookies. During her time with the girl next door this week, she's learned that her neighbor has an irrepressible sweet tooth — that, and a constant craving for peanut butter. So this week, she's making her peanut butter and M&M cookies, hoping to share them with her once Ardie leaves.

Ardie.

Lucinda glances over her shoulder, watching Ardie work. She's pretty sure Ardie's developing an interest in her as something more than just a friend. Which she can understand; Reverie isn't a big town, so dating options aren't particularly wide-ranging even for its straight inhabitants, let alone for what must be one of its only lesbians. Maybe the *only* lesbian in town, if not for Lucinda.

And truthfully, if not for the girl next door, Lucinda might've been happy for Ardie to pursue her. Ardie's generous and charming, Lucinda's generation and probably too old for head games. But with the girl in the picture… It never hurts to make a few friends, but she needs to be clear with Ardie that they can't have anything more than friendship.

Lucinda turns back to her cookie batter, stirring. Through the thin walls dividing her half of the duplex from the girl's, she hears music turn on. Her nameless girl is waking up. Lucinda smiles to herself.

She's just opening the oven to put the cookies in to

bake when she hears the screen door open and close without rattling on its hinges. Heavy work boots creak against the floorboards as Ardie joins Lucinda in the kitchen.

"Well, screen door's fixed," Ardie announces. She smiles in a way that's unmistakably pleased with herself, and Lucinda finds it both sweet and endearing.

"Thank you so much, Ardie. You've been too good to me."

Ardie sniffs the air. "And you've been baking."

"My next door neighbor has a sweet tooth. I've been bribing her with baked goods," Lucinda says.

"Next door neighbor? I didn't know there was anyone in that unit."

Lucinda nods. "Yeah. She works second shift at the hospital, though, so she's rarely up and about before early afternoon. You don't hear her music playing?" Lucinda asks, pointing towards the kitchen wall that separates her space from the girl's.

Ardie cocks her head to the side, listening. After a moment she frowns and shakes her head. "Between the Marines and my dad's shop, I'm afraid my hearing isn't what it used to be." She points towards the front. "Lemme show you the screen door. And then you can remind me which window you're having trouble with."

Lucinda trails behind Ardie to the screen door, where she half listens to Ardie explaining how it had come loose in the first place and which hinges she repaired.

While Ardie's demonstrating, the door to the other half of the duplex squeaks open, and the girl next door appears, obscured in shadow. When she sees Ardie, her eyes darken, her face clouds over with… something Lucinda doesn't recognize. Before Lucinda can catch her attention, though, the door quietly shuts again.

"…so if it comes loose again, your problem's probably right here," Ardie's saying. She looks at Lucinda. Waiting. Her brows dip, painting a curious expression on her face. "Lu? You okay?"

"I'm sorry. I got distracted for a moment. Could you say that last bit again?"

"Sure." She taps a thick, grease-stained finger on the hinge again, and tells Lucinda for the second time how the screen door had gotten loose, along with how to fix it.

Lucinda smiles when Ardie finishes, nodding in understanding this time. "Got it," she says. "Although as long as I've got you around, doesn't seem like I'm gonna need to know how to fix all that much by myself."

An instant too late, Lucinda catches the potential double-meaning to her words, realizing that she might've just sent exactly the opposite of a "let's just be friends" signal.

Ardie grins broadly. "I *am* pretty handy to have around," she agrees. "Being a mechanic, and all. Personally, I'd be extra nice to me." She winks.

Lucinda tries to keep smiling but falters. "I should, uh, check on the cookies."

"Wanna show me which window's sticking before you get too busy in the kitchen?" Ardie asks.

Lucinda directs Ardie to the stuck window, describing the problem in a series of mumbles, then bustles back to the kitchen.

She's chastising herself as she opens the oven door, slides the cookie sheet halfway out with a towel. Why did she have to say that bit about having Ardie around? Why'd she'd have to give the big-hearted woman false hope? If Lucinda isn't careful, she'll end up hurting her only other friend in town besides the girl.

And speaking of the girl… What did that sullen expression on her face mean? Why had she disappeared back into her side of the duplex, instead of coming out and being her normal, gregarious self? Had she decided she didn't like Ardie, based on what precious little Lucinda had said about the kind, just-up-the-road neighbor?

She's startled out of her worries when she hears Ardie's voice, closer to her than expected.

"I think your window's fixed. Not anything that a little bar soap and a wooden mallet couldn't solve."

Lucinda jumps, puts her hand on her heart. "Oh my goodness, you scared me. I didn't realize you were right there."

Ardie answers with an amused smile. "Sorry. Seems like I have quite the effect on you. First you're grabbing butcher knives to defend yourself from me, now I've got you having heart attacks in the kitchen. Sounds like I just make you nervous."

Lucinda tries a laugh, but it comes out sounding as forced as it feels. "Oh, I get nervous about everything, Ardie. My mama used to call me her 'nervous Nelly.' It's just how I am."

Ardie sniffs the air. "Your cookies smell wonderful. Is that peanut butter?"

"Sure is."

Ardie stands uncertainly in the kitchen for a moment, shifting her weight from one foot to the other. She starts to say something, stops herself. Starts again. "Well. I guess I should be heading back. Let you finish your baking in peace."

Lucinda thinks about the girl next door, about her hopes that they would spend most of the afternoon and evening together. Part of her wants to rush Ardie out the door. But Ardie's been nothing but nice to her, and rushing a person out who just helped her isn't the way Lucinda was brought up.

"Why don't you stay for a bit, if you have time?" Lucinda says, half-regretting her words even as she says them. "I've got plans for later this afternoon, but you should help me taste-test these cookies first. Make sure I didn't ruin them. And didn't you say you'd tell me about your relationship with the Almighty if I bribed you with a beer first?"

"If you're going to bribe me with beer *and* cookies," Ardie says with a lopsided smirk, "I might tell you just about anything you wanna know about me, Miss Lucinda."

Chapter 16

Ardie has settled into one of the rockers by the time Lucinda comes back out with two beers and a plate of peanut butter M&M cookies. Ardie's made herself comfortable — her hands are laced behind her head, her feet extend in front of her, crossed at the ankles.

She straightens when she sees Lucinda, accepts the beer with a gracious smile. "Thank you. You're too good to me."

"You're the one who's been too good to *me*," Lucinda says, settling into the other rocker. She reaches across the round table between them, bottle opener in her hand, but Ardie shakes her head.

"Naw, I got it," she says, and her face tightens with effort as she twists the bottle cap off. It gives a satisfying pop and releases a hiss of air.

"I can't believe you just did that," Lucinda says, shaking her head. "If I did that, I'd tear my hand up."

Ardie holds up her hand. There's a red imprint of the bottle cap teeth on her palm, but no other sign that she just took a non-twist-off cap with her bare hand.

"Advantage of working with your hands a lot, I guess," she says. "They get tough."

Lucinda uses the bottle opener to take off her own cap,

and takes a small sip before putting her beer on the table between them.

"Didn't peg you for much of a beer drinker," Ardie comments.

"I'm not, really," Lucinda says. The beers they're drinking are two of the four beers left over from the six pack the girl next door had shared with her the day before, when Lucinda'd had an early end to her afternoon at Georgie's.

"It's Saturday," the girl had said when Lucinda said she didn't much care for beer. *"Just because you worked today and I've got to go in an hour doesn't mean we shouldn't act like it's the weekend. Besides, this is a really good beer. I think you're going to like it."*

"Should you be drinking before you go to work?" Lucinda had asked her.

"I'm only going to have one," she says. *"And it's beer, not hard liquor. My liver's still young and healthy and fully capable of dealing with a single beer."*

The girl had been right about Lucinda liking the beer — though whether she actually liked it for the taste or liked it because the girl had given it to her was hard to say.

The thought of the neighbor girl makes Lucinda wonder about her again, and she glances over her shoulder at the door to the other half of the duplex, debating whether or not she should get up and knock.

She realizes too late that Ardie's watching her. "You okay?"

Lucinda pulls her gaze away from the other door. "Hmm? Oh — yeah. I'm fine." She smiles to prove it.

Ardie takes a pull from her beer. After she swallows, she holds it out to get a better look at it, reading the label. "This is good. I'm impressed by your taste. Not just a beer, but an artisan microbrew. Pretty hard to find at the Shop 'n Go."

"Well, I wish I could take credit for it," Lucinda says. "The girl next door actually brought it home, shared it with me."

Ardie's gaze moves over Lucinda's shoulder, studying the other half of the duplex for a moment.

"Her side looks worse than yours," she says. "If she decides she needs help fixing things up, too, you can give her my number."

"Alright. I'll tell her next time I see her."

"What's your neighbor's name? Maybe I already know her."

"She's not from around here. She's from Florence." Lucinda smiles. "And a funny thing about her name: She won't tell it to me."

Ardie raises an eyebrow, gives Lucinda an incredulous look. "Won't tell you her name? Why on Earth not?"

Lucinda shrugs. Chuckles. "She's young. Decided she'd make a game out of it, force me to guess. So I've just come to think of her as 'the girl next door.'" She pauses, listening. The music coming from next door is still audible. "You really can't hear her music?"

Ardie squints, trying to listen. "Nope. But all it takes is being too close to a couple of mortar rounds going off and your hearing takes a more-or-less permanent hit."

"Where were you serving that you were close to mortar rounds? Iraq?"

"Iraq. Afghanistan before that, and Afghanistan again after that." She takes another long swallow of beer.

"What did you do in the Marines?"

"Mechanic," Ardie says. "Most of the time I was overseas, I stayed on the bigger bases, supervised the grunts who repaired Humvees."

"Was it… were there a lot of female mechanics?"

"A few. More than you might think. But, yeah, the military is still mostly a boys' club," Ardie says.

"So most of the people you supervised were men?"

Ardie nods.

Lucinda imagines what that would be like — telling a bunch of men what to do all the time. She can imagine Ardie doing it; she has a hard time imagine doing it herself. "Did they… listen to you? Treat you with respect?"

Ardie seems to think about this for a moment, takes a drink from her beer again. "Most of the time. That's the thing about the military that civilians don't understand. There's a lot of guys who join up because they want to prove how tough and macho they are, that's true, but at the end of the day, what gets you promoted is how well you do your job. And if you're good at your job… most people, most of the time, they treat you with respect. And if you know more than they do, they listen when you've got something to say."

"I bet you were especially good at your job — having grown up around your daddy's shop and all."

Ardie gives a casual shrug. "I know my way around a machine or two."

"Listen to you, pretending to be modest." Lucinda laughs lightly. She pauses, considering the change of subject she's about to make. "Last time you were here, you said that if I got a couple beers into you, you'd tell me about your… I don't know how to put it, your relationship with the Almighty is what you said."

Ardie nods, her eyes glazing with a far away expression. "So I did," she says. She straightens a bit, glances at Lucinda with her usual good-natured smile, shakes her beer to show how little is left. "But this is only one beer. Usually, 'a couple' means two."

"Is that your way of asking for another?"

"Well, only if you're offering."

Lucinda stands. "I'll be right back," she says, and returns a moment later with two more beers.

Ardie opens her second beer in the same way that she opened her first, face screwing in concentration as she wrestles the cap off the bottle. She takes a long drink, wipes her mouth with the back of her hand, sets the bottle down on the round table between them.

Without looking at Lucinda, she says, "The second time I was in Afghanistan, there was this kid, Lucas Koch, couldn't have been more than nineteen or twenty years old — I put in a full twenty years in the Marines before I retired, so by the time I was on my second deployment, I was practically old enough to be this kid's mother. We used to play poker together in between his patrols." She takes another drink. "He was from the Midwest somewhere, I can't remember where — Nebraska or Kansas or something. One of the big, flat states in the middle. Had all the energy of a puppy, complete with the big, floppy ears to match. And he was a dog handler, too — one of those guys who searches for bombs with a German Shepherd — and I swear the kid kinda looked like his dog. I mean, he was a good-enough looking kid, don't get me wrong, but... I guess it was those floppy ears." Ardie stops for a second, chuckles to herself before continuing. "Anyhow, he used to constantly tell me about all his business ideas, how he was gonna make himself rich one day. Seemed like he came up with a new hair-brained scheme every day. He'd come running all, 'Staff Sergeant, Staff Sergeant! I got another one!'" She takes a breath, raises her eyes to meet Lucinda's. "You sure you wanna hear the rest of this story?"

Lucinda nods, squeezes Ardie's knee reassuringly.

Ardie sighs heavily. "One day, Lucas went out on patrol, stepped on an IED his dog didn't catch in time, got blown to bits. The dog died, too. All his mother got back of him was a shoebox." She drinks again, glances at the hand on her knee before continuing. "I hadn't really believed in God for a long time before that happened, but when I heard the news about Lucas, that was it for me. I knew then God can't really exist, because if He did exist, then He was just a heartless bastard, and that was a God I refused to believe in."

Lucinda is silent for a few seconds, giving Ardie some space, giving time for the story to sink in. "Is that what you still believe now?" she asks after a moment. "If not God… where'd the universe come from? And… Why are we all here? Why does anything happen at all? Is it all just random?"

Ardie shrugs and sets her beer down. "I'm a mechanic, Lu. The way I see it, we're just all parts in a big ol' engine, turning round and round and round *ad infinitum*. Because that's what we're designed to be doing."

"But then, who did the designing?"

"Other engine parts, maybe. I dunno." She leans forward, resting both forearms on her knees. Glances at Lucinda. "What about you? Do you believe in God?"

"No," Lucinda answers automatically. Then she draws in a breath and holds it a moment before giving Ardie a more honest answer. "Some days I don't know if it's that I don't believe in God, or if it's just that I'm really, really angry with Him."

"Yeah? What are you angry about?"

Lucinda looks away, gaze falling on the PRIVET PROPERTY sign across the road. "Everything, I suppose."

"And what's 'everything' include?"

"I don't know," Lucinda says with a sigh. "The kinds of things that happened to your friend Lucas. The way an earthquake or a mudslide hits some poor village in the middle of nowhere and kills hundreds of innocent people. And…" She thinks about Hart, wonders for a brief moment what he might be doing today. Looking for her, probably. "And how bad people get ahead while good people keep getting pushed around by the world."

Ardie nods, scrapes at the sweating label around the neck of her beer with a short fingernail. The label comes off easily, and she rolls it back and forth between thumb and forefinger.

The two women nurse their beers in comfortable silence.

Ardie sets her empty bottle back on the table with a *clink* when she's finished. "Next time we get together, we have to make sure our conversation's serious," she says, grinning. "All this light-hearted, superficial gossip gets old real quick for me."

"Alright," Lucinda says, returning the smile. "I'll be sure to be ready with more beer."

Ardie rises with a prolonged groan, stretches her arms in front of her before saying, "Whew, I tell you what. If someone would've told me twenty years ago what all that squatting and kneeling was going to do to my joints, I might've taken up yoga or something."

"You're going home?" Lucinda says skeptically. She points at the empty bottles. "Are you okay to drive?"

Ardie pats her stomach. "I'm a little bigger than you are, Miss Lucinda. My tolerance for alcohol isn't what it was when I was in the Marines, but believe me, two beers isn't going to slow me down. Besides, I only live a tick up the road."

Lucinda stands, collects the empty bottles. "Well, if you say so."

"I do."

"Thanks so much for dropping by, helping me work on the house."

"Thanks for the beers," Ardie says. "Which reminds me — neither of us had any of those cookies."

There are three of them on the plate, and Lucinda scoops them up and extends all three to Ardie. "Take them home. Share them with your parents."

Ardie accepts the cookies into her hand, takes a bite of one of them. "Mmm," she says. "These might not last long enough to share with my parents."

"Hold on a second," Lucinda says, and she disappears inside the house, returning a few seconds later with a Ziplock bag. "Here. Put them in this."

Ardie does as instructed, tucks the plastic bag into her shirt pocket. "Okay, well… see you about the same time next week? I'll be in my dad's truck instead of on the bike — easier to haul the wood I'll need for the back stairs."

"That would be great, Ardie, really. I'll keep an eye out for you. And thank you so much."

"Oh, it's nothing," Ardie says. "Just glad I can help."

They both stand there for a moment, looking at each other.

Lucinda thinks to hug Ardie, but remembers that she's trying not to send the wrong message. "See you next week."

Chapter 17

They agree on a time for the following Sunday. Lucinda leans on the porch railing, watches Ardie disappear down the road, listens to the bass of the motorcycle's engine until she can't hear it anymore. She likes how the engine sounds against her skin, a tingling sort of sensation that seems to cover her whole body.

Lucinda straightens, turns to go back inside, and nearly jumps out of her skin when she sees the girl standing in front of her, arms crossed against her chest.

"There you are," Lucinda says happily. "I was starting to think you were planning to avoid me the whole day."

"Me?" the girl says. There's none of the normal good humor twinkling in her brown eyes. *"You* were the one who spent practically all afternoon with... that *woman* again."

"You could've come out and joined us," Lucinda says, hurt.

"You could've knocked on my door and invited me," she retorts.

"You're right," Lucinda says. "I should've. I'm sorry."

The girl sighs deeply and flops into one of the rocking chairs. She's still in her usual sleep clothes — a white undershirt above short, plaid boxers. Lucinda notices that she's not wearing a bra. "I thought we were spending the day together. Instead you gave your whole day to *her.*"

Lucinda doesn't know what to say; the girl's reaction has completely caught her off guard.

The girl sticks a finger in her mouth, gnaws on a hangnail.

"I'm sorry," Lucinda says again. "I didn't know you'd get this upset."

The girl pulls her finger out, considers it, turning it in the light. "You're attracted to her," she states without looking at Lucinda.

"I'm not. She just came by to help me with some minor repairs."

"You gave her beer." She sniffs the air. "And cookies. I could smell them baking. They smelled so good, I thought to myself, 'Aww, that's so sweet, my Lulu baked me cookies.' Then I heard you out here, and I came out to talk to you, and you were busy *ogling* her."

She meets Lucinda's gaze, a challenge in her eyes.

"I wasn't ogling her."

"Just admit that you're attracted to her, Lu. You can't fool me, so don't try."

"If you hadn't kissed me last week, I might've been…" Lucinda hesitates, choosing her next words carefully. "I might've been open to dating Ardie."

The girl snorts and looks away, brown eyes going glassy with tears. "That's what I thought."

Lucinda falls to one knee in front of the girl's rocker,

places her hands on the girl's bare thighs. "I said *if* you hadn't kissed me. But you did. I never even thought…"

The girl looks down when Lucinda trails off. "Never thought what?"

Lucinda kisses one of the girl's knees, then the other, letting her lips linger a moment on the smooth flesh. "I never thought that someone as young" — she kisses the inside of one thigh — "and as beautiful" — she kisses the inside of the other thigh — "would be interested in an old lady like me."

Lucinda runs her hands up the girl's legs, the tips of her fingers coming to rest just under the line of the plaid boxers. She's pleased when she feels the legs break into gooseflesh beneath her palms. She glances up; the girl is watching her, mouth hanging halfway open, chest rising and falling with her breath.

"You're not *old,* Lucinda," the girl manages to say. "Old women don't do what you're doing now."

Lucinda's hands move further inside the boxers, stopping when she encounters the warm, damp patch of wiry hair. The girl shifts slightly in the rocker, opening her legs a few inches wider. Lucinda drops her mouth back to the girl's legs, fingertips digging into the soft flesh between the girl's thighs while her lips walk a slow progression up the inside of the girl's legs. When Lucinda's lips reach the seam running down the center of the boxer shorts, she only hesitates a moment before kissing the girl there — lightly, but ending with a nip of her teeth.

Hands press down gently on the back of Lucinda's head, trapping her mouth against the girl's crotch. "Oh, God, baby," the girl says, and the word "baby" sends a thrill of excitement and desire down Lucinda's spine. "Your place? Or mine?"

Without a word, Lucinda stands up, takes the girl's hand, and leads the girl into her bedroom.

#

The girl has all the energy and eagerness Lucinda would expect from someone still in their twenties. She wastes no time at all in stripping Lucinda's shirt, bra, jeans, underwear. Once Lucinda is bare, the girl lays her back on top of the bedspread, straddling her at the waist. Somewhere along the line, her boxer shorts have gone missing, and Lucinda feels the texture of soft, wet flesh and coarse hair just below her belly button. The girl lifts her white undershirt over her head, throws it to the side, tosses her long brown hair out of the way.

Beneath the undershirt, the girl is everything Lucinda had dreamed of and more. Milk-white skin, smooth and unmarred by genetics or age; perfect breasts tipped with large, dark pink nipples. Lucinda reaches up, traces the girl's barely visible ribs with the pads of her fingers, runs a thumb over each nipple. The girl shivers. Lucinda cups the girl's breasts.

The girl drops her mouth to Lucinda's neck, rubbing her

wet clit down Lucinda's belly at the same time. She nips at Lucinda's neck, jaw, earlobe. Hair falls in a long, brown curtain around Lucinda's face, narrowing Lucinda's world to nothing but the girl's hair and the side of her face.

Into Lucinda's ear, the girl whispers, "I'm going to make love to you now. Like no one ever has before. Are you alright with that?"

Lucinda has forgotten how to speak; only a moan comes out.

The girl's tongue darts into Lucinda's ear; Lucinda moans louder.

"Is that a word, Lu? Is that a yes?"

"Yes," Lucinda manages. "Yes… please…"

Hair tickles Lucinda's neck and face as the girl goes back to landing light, biting kisses along Lucinda's neck and ears. She works her way around to Lucinda's mouth, taking Lucinda's bottom lip between her teeth and pulling before kissing her passionately. There's something about the girl that's wild, untamed, like a jungle animal or a mythical creature.

Tigress is the word that comes to Lucinda's mind.

Tigress. Viper. Eagle. Jaguar. Lucinda's lovers always seem to come with fangs.

Nails scrape against Lucinda's sides, just hard enough to make her moan again, not hard enough to hurt. The girl's mouth follows her hands now, moving down her body, stopping at each breast, sucking each nipple into her mouth, teasing each nipple with her teeth. More teeth against Lucinda's stomach, against her ribs — ribs which used to be prominent, like the girl's, but which are now soft with age. Lucinda sits halfway up, trying to see what's happening, but brown hair obscures the girl's face; all she can see is the crown of her head.

The girl must feel Lucinda shift beneath her; she looks up with smoky eyes, lifts her face enough that Lucinda can see her again. "Lay back," she says. "Just relax and let me do this for you."

She runs her palms up Lucinda's torso, over her breasts, pushes gently on her shoulders.

"Let me," she says again.

Lucinda obeys. She eases herself down onto the bed, closes her eyes when the girl's kisses begin landing on her hips, her thighs. She gasps when a tongue meets her lower lips, drawing a light circle around the wettest part of her. She stops breathing for a moment when the same tongue presses hard against her, sliding through the wet. The tongue finds a rhythm, and Lucinda squirms below the girl, pressing her forearm against her mouth to silence any noises she might be making.

The licking stops a moment later; a hand grasps the forearm draped across her face and tugs it off.

"Who's going to hear you?" the girl asks. "No one will hear you scream. Not even your motorcycle dyke up the road. Be loud."

"I can't," Lucinda says between shallow breaths.

"You can."

Lucinda shakes her head. "No. You don't understand — I can't. It's too... I can't."

"You can," the girl says, coming up to her knees beside Lucinda. "You will. I'm going to make you scream, Lulu."

Miserable, not able to explain it to the girl, wishing for the tongue to make its way back to her hungry clit, all Lucinda can do is shake her head again.

The girl rolls off the bed, naked hips swaying as she walks across the room and opens the first drawer of Lucinda's dresser.

Lucinda sits up. "What are you doing?"

"Looking for something."

"For what?"

"I'll know it when I — ah. This should work."

She turns back around, dangling one of Lucinda's few scarves in front of her. This one is her longest, a decorative pink-and-blue plaid scarf made of lamb's wool that Lucinda bought years ago and only wore once.

"How much money did you spend on this?" Hart had demanded, throwing it at her when he found it in the drawer. *"It's not even pretty,"* he sneered. *"An expensive piece of trash. Just like you. I don't want to see it again."*

She should've gotten rid of it. But she liked it. She hid it at the bottom of her underwear drawer, occasionally fingering its softness before putting it away again, but she never wore it again.

So it's fitting, somehow, that the girl would pick that scarf, of all Lucinda's things, out of the drawer. The girl comes back to the foot of the bed with it dangling from one hand, climbs up, straddles Lucinda's waist again before she drops to hands and knees and crawls forward, deliberately dragging her damp center up Lucinda's body as she makes her way to the head of the bed.

"What are you doing?" Lucinda asks.

"Fixing it so you can't hide your screams," the girl answers. "You'll see."

She takes one of Lucinda's wrists, loops the scarf around it, places Lucinda's other wrist on top and covers it in a few more loops before reaching behind Lucinda.

Lucinda can feel the girl tying the other end of the scarf to the headboard behind her. The girl's breasts dangle inches from Lucinda's face. Looking down the line of the girl's body, Lucinda can see the wiry patch of dark hair. She's struck with a sudden desire — a need — to hold the girl in her mouth the way the girl had been about to hold her.

Lucinda lifts her head, manages to kiss the breast that's closest. "I want to taste you," she whispers. "Please. Please let me taste you."

The girl chuckles. "Not yet," she says. "Not until I'm done with you."

"I don't scream," Lucinda says. "I never have. I… can't."

"We'll see about that," the girl says.

Her face reappears as she sits back, apparently satisfied with her work. Lucinda feels the scarf binding her hands together. She tugs against the headboard experimentally. It's loose enough that she could probably pull it off if she really wanted to.

The girl watches her.

"Are you alright?" she asks. "Is this okay?"

"It's... I guess it's alright."

The girl smirks. "No one's ever tied you up before, have they?"

Lucinda shakes her head.

"Good," the girl says. "You should try everything at least once in your life. Except for heroin."

The girl's face disappears from sight again as she presses a soft kiss against Lucinda's stomach, just above her belly button. Brown hair once again tickles Lucinda's sides as the girl slides down her body, taking Lucinda's clit into her mouth.

"Oh," Lucinda squeaks, the word as unexpected as the sensation. She feels, rather than hears, the girl's laugh vibrating against her.

More pressure; more tongue. Lucinda lifts her hips, holds them, then begins to rock them gently, in time with the ministrations of the girl's tongue.

Lucinda's holding her breath, she realizes. She lets out a long, ragged breath, squeezes her eyes closed, remembers to inhale. The girl adds the tip of a finger, sliding it just inside.

"Ohhh," Lucinda says again, louder this time, surprising herself a second time with a sound that is both word and moan.

The finger inside her presses deeper inside. Lucinda's hips jerk up, their rhythm broken. She's holding her breath again.

The girl lifts her face, watching Lucinda as she curls the single, long finger against Lucinda's front. If Lucinda's hands were free, she would put them both on that brown head of hair and push the girl back down. But her hands aren't free. She closes her eyes and forces an exhale.

A second finger joins the first inside Lucinda.

"Uhh," Lucinda utters softly, not even managing a word this time. A tongue lands on her clit. "Mmmm… uh," Lucinda gasps.

"Let go," the girl says. She thrusts hard inside Lucinda at the same time she drops her mouth back down.

Fingers, tongue, hips work together, all conspiring against Lucinda's silence, her aching lungs.

"Let go, Lu," the girl repeats. "Let go, let go, let go…"

She says it like a mantra. She says it in between her tongue flicking against Lucinda's clit, in between kisses traveling up Lucinda's hips and ribs, in between nibbles on Lucinda's nipples. She says it after she draws a line with her tongue up Lucinda's throat. She whispers it into Lucinda's ear a moment before she takes Lucinda's earlobe into her mouth. And all the while, the two fingers move up and down inside Lucinda.

The girl's own wetness begins rubbing against Lucinda's thigh, and Lucinda lifts her leg to add to the friction. The girl comes up on her knees, sitting back against Lucinda's leg, sweeping her hair from her face with her free hand. Her eyes are halfway closed, a beautiful smile takes over her face for a moment.

Then she leans forward again, kissing Lucinda hard at the same moment she drives her fingers deeper inside Lucinda.

Lucinda tries to return the kiss, but only manages it for a moment — she's breathing too hard now to kiss.

Another moan escapes her — timid, like a small animal trying to stay hidden.

"Let go," the girl says, and she adds a third finger.

Lucinda moans — louder this time.

"Let go, Lucinda!" the girl shouts.

And Lucinda does. A scream that begins as a tight coil below her belly unwinds just as Lucinda reaches the edge. It spreads up, into her lungs, energizing itself as her mouth falls open.

Its opening salvo begins with, "Oh, God. God, uhhh, God — " and then it devolves into something more guttural, long and loud and drawn-out. Her hips jerk and then fall, her toes curl, her thighs clench around the girl's hand.

The girl drives her fingers into Lucinda one last time, then still, riding out Lucinda's orgasm with her.

When Lucinda's done, silent again except for a series of shallow, breathless pants, the girl drops down against Lucinda's side, resting her head on Lucinda's shoulder.

She traces a wet fingertip over Lucinda's breast, down her side, back up. "See?" she says. "You screamed for me. I knew you would."

Lucinda pulls at the scarf holding her hands behind her, wiggles it until it comes loose from the headboard. The girl sees what she's doing, sits halfway up to help, unfurling the scarf from Lucinda's wrists.

Unbound at last, Lucinda wraps her arms around the naked girl, sighing deeply. The girl returns the embrace, throwing a long arm and a long leg over Lucinda as she nestles back down onto her shoulder.

Lucinda might be more relaxed in this moment than she ever has been before in her life — a strange feat considering all the uncertainty that looms around Hart.

She hesitates for a moment, then kisses the girl's crown. "I think I'm falling for you."

The girl snorts out a laugh against Lucinda's chest. "After that? Hell, I think *I'm* falling for me right now."

Lucinda slaps her arm playfully. "Oh, Dee — " she starts, but stops herself just before the name *Dionne* can come out. This isn't Dionne, she reminds herself. Dionne is gone. "You're silly," she says quickly, hoping the girl didn't notice what almost happened.

Lucinda disentangles herself from the girl, leans over her, gives her a slow, gentle kiss. "If I make you scream," she whispers, "will you tell me your name?"

"Oh, I'll definitely scream," the girl says. "I'll put your scream to shame — I'll show you how it's *really* done."

She doesn't resist as Lucinda rolls her onto her back, slides down to her chest, takes a nipple in her mouth. Lucinda is every bit as methodical and tender as the girl was unpredictable and wild.

The girl sucks in a breath when Lucinda's mouth reaches the top of her slit.

"I'll scream," the girl says. "But I already told you: You have to guess my name."

Lucinda's tongue dips into the girl, and they begin again, this time with Lucinda on top.

Chapter 18

Lucinda sleeps without nightmares that night, wakes to find the girl still lying in bed the next morning, her chest rising and falling with the gentle rhythm of sleep. Lucinda gets out of bed without waking her, brews extra coffee in case the girl wants any, leaves a peanut butter and M&M cookie on a napkin on the nightstand beside her soundly sleeping girl.

She hums to herself as she putters around the kitchen, waiting for the coffee to finish brewing. Ardie had been right; her work boots did indeed track mud across the floor, and Lucinda almost smiles to herself over it — until she remembers how upset the girl had been to see Ardie and Lucinda sitting together on the porch.

Lucinda stops humming, sweeps up the dried mud from Ardie's boots with a small, troubled "V" folded between her eyebrows.

How could the girl get so jealous of Ardie? And isn't any jealousy unfair, given that the girl won't even tell Lucinda her name?

Lucinda should be upset about the mystery of the girl's name. She really should be. It might have been funny at first, but at this point? When she still doesn't know the girl's name even after sleeping with her? It's gotten ridiculous.

Granted, Lucinda has come to know many other things about the girl — her brother's name, for example, which is Derrick, along with the names of her parents (Rose, who still works as a kindergarten teacher even though she is past the age of retirement, and Bill, who died of a heart attack when he was driving home from work one night when the girl was just fourteen). She knows where the girl went to high school (one of the bigger schools in Florence); she knows that her first kiss was with a boy named Tim at age thirteen, and that her first kiss with a woman was at the age of seventeen. She'd kissed her tennis coach, who was also her history teacher.

Lucinda knows the girl dropped out of college the first time around because she'd gotten pregnant, but then miscarried; she knows that the girl went back to college two years later to become a nurse because it seemed practical and because she wanted a job where she could help people.

Lucinda knows the girl loves smooth peanut butter, not chunky, and that she likes cats more than dogs, and that she plans to have children one day, but wants to wait until she saves up enough money to buy her own house.

The "V" between Lucinda's brow begins to soften, then smoothes. She knows many things about the girl already. Is a name really so important? Maybe it will be something that, years from now, they will laugh about. It will make a good story, at least.

A name might not be that important, after all. What *is* important to Lucinda is that, perhaps more than anything else in her life, the girl makes Lucinda feel hopeful again, young again, as if all the girl's dreams and plans — plans about children and houses, cats and careers — are Lucinda's, too. As if, maybe, alongside the girl, she might be able to construct fresh dreams of her own.

Fresh dreams instead of nightmares would be a welcome relief. Lucinda has grown tired of the sound of phantom gunshots ringing out each night, of screams echoing in her ears, of the hot, searing pain the bullet left behind when it exited her.

She puts her hand on her side there now, where the scar is, and wonders if the girl felt or saw the scar last night when they made love. They'd started their love-making early enough in the evening that the room had still been filled with the warm yellow light of the late afternoon, so the girl had probably seen. And if she didn't see it while the sun was up, she still could've easily felt it as the light faded and they continued into the night.

Will she ask about it?

And if she had noticed it, what will she think about it? She's a nurse, after all; she might be familiar with what a bullet scar looks like. She might have already put two and two together. She might start asking Lucinda questions, questions that Lucinda doesn't want to hear, let alone answer. She might —

"Good Lord, Lulu, do you always get up this early?"

Lucinda takes her hand off her side quickly, as if she's been caught touching something she shouldn't have.

The girl is standing at the edge of the kitchen, completely naked and as beautiful as ever. She yawns, pushes tangled brown hair from her face, rubs bleary eyes with her fist like a child. She leans back languidly against the door frame.

Lucinda smiles at her. She rests the broom against the refrigerator and walks over to her, running her palms over the girl's bare hips.

"You wore me out last night," the girl says. "How can you possibly already be up and dressed?"

Lucinda shrugs. "I wake up before five every day. I always have. Doesn't seem to matter when I've gone to bed, or — or what I was doing the night before."

"Or *who* you were doing the night before?"

"Or who I was doing."

The girl reaches up, laces her fingers behind Lucinda's neck, and Lucinda lets out a contented sigh. She tugs Lucinda closer, kisses her.

"Mmm," the girl says. "You taste like coffee. Did you save any for me?"

"I did. And did you find the cookie I left for you?"

The girl's eyes light up. "You left me a cookie?"

"It's on the nightstand; go back and look."

The girl immediately lets go of Lucinda, turns, and pads out of the kitchen. Lucinda chuckles as she watches her go; the chuckle turns into a full-fledged laugh when the girl calls out, "Oh-my-God, Lu, this is the best thing I've ever put in my mouth!"

Lucinda follows her into the bedroom. She embraces the girl from behind, toying with her bare nipples as she plants a kiss between her shoulder blades.

"The *best* thing you ever put in your mouth?" she teases the girl.

The girl shifts backward suddenly, catching Lucinda off balance. Lucinda lets out a little yelp of surprise as the girl twirls and shoves her onto the bed. She pins Lucinda's arms to her side and leans down for a lengthy kiss.

"Are you always going to bake for me?" the girl asks. "I'll get fat, you know." Lucinda starts to reply, but the girl cuts her off with another kiss, then moves her mouth from Lucinda's lips to her throat. "But maybe," she says between kisses, "that cookie" (kiss) "is actually" (kiss) "the second best" (kiss) "thing I've put" (kiss) "in my" (kiss) "mouth."

She lets go of Lucinda's arms and drops her deft fingers to the button on Lucinda's skirt. The button comes undone; the skirt slides down and over Lucinda's hips.

"You should've known better than to get dressed for work already."

"I've already showered and fixed my hair," Lucinda protests.

The girl pushes up Lucinda's blouse, kisses her bare stomach while her hands work on pulling down Lucinda's panties.

"I don't know why you would do such a thing," the girl says. Panties off, the girl's mouth drops lower. "I hope you're ready to scream for me again."

#

There's no time to go home for a long lunch break that day; Lucinda has clients back-to-back-to-back until four o'clock. She'll miss her opportunity to say goodbye to the girl, but yesterday they'd surely gotten enough time together.

Lucinda's still working off the pregnant girl's schedule, but she's also started to add her own clients as she takes walk-ins and then adds them to her roster of regulars. But today, when she looks down at the list, she does a double-take to see the last name on it.

"Hey, Lu," Dan's wife Aggie says to her just as she looks up. "You ready for me?" But she doesn't wait for an answer; Aggie's already walking over to Lucinda from the waiting area at the front of the salon.

"Of course, c'mon and sit down," Lucinda says, brushing the last customer's hair off the black vinyl seat. "I can't believe I didn't realize you were on my schedule today. How've you been? How's Dan? How are the kids?"

Aggie settles into the chair, meets Lucinda's eye in the mirror. "Now see, you wouldn't have to ask me all that if you'd come on over for dinner when you'd first moved here."

Lucinda's gaze drops. "I know. I just… wasn't really ready to see anyone when I first moved."

Aggie nods. "I can understand that. You had a really rough few months before you came to us."

A rough few months.

A rough few decades with a few smooth months would be more like it. But Lucinda wouldn't ever say such a thing.

"So I did," she says instead. "What are we doing for you today? Keeping it the same? Or trying something new?"

"Oh, just the same is good. And Kathy usually helps me with my roots. Grey hair shows up so easily when your hair's as dark as mine."

"Tell me about it," Lucinda agrees. "We'll start with a shampoo, then, if that's alright?"

"Perfect," Aggie says, and they head to the line of sinks in the back, chatting about Dan and Aggie's kids, trying to figure out what kind of relation the children of one's first cousins are to Lucinda.

"Second cousin," Rhonda puts in, apparently overhearing the discussion.

"Second cousin what?" asks Kylah.

"The child of your first cousin is your second cousin," Rhonda says.

"Nuh-uh," says Kylah. "Your second cousin's the kid of your mom or dad's first cousin."

"That don't sound right," Rhonda argues.

"It is right. My mom's into all that genealogy stuff."

"Then what's the child of your first cousin?" Lucinda asks Kylah.

"That's your first cousin once removed," Kylah says.

"If you say so," Rhonda says skeptically.

"I do say so."

Aggie and Lucinda leave the other two women to their debate about cousins; Lucinda washes her cousin-in-law's hair in peaceful silence, toweling it off before leading her back to the chair.

Kylah and Rhonda are still talking about cousins when Aggie settles back down into the chair, but they're off of second cousins and first cousins once removed and have moved onto third cousins, fourth cousins, and kissing cousins. Lucinda half listens as she combs out Aggie's damp hair.

"But if you're not related to them any more than as a fourth cousin, then all you share is, like, a great-great-great-grandparent," Kylah's saying, her tone high and argumentative. "And you probably share a great-great-great grandparent with, I don't know, like five hundred other people. So why *shouldn't* you date them?"

"Mmm, see, no," Rhonda says. "If they still have the word 'cousin' attached to their name, you don't date 'em."

"Saw Lory Wheeler at church yesterday," Aggie says.

"What's that?" Lucinda asks, pulling her attention away from the cousin debate.

"I said, Dan and I saw Lory Wheeler at church yesterday." Aggie waits for Lucinda to say something, but she doesn't. "Terrible thing, about them not knowing where Hart's gone off to."

"Yes. It is."

"Wheeler told us he and a detective from Sumter had to serve a search warrant on your place," Aggie continues. "That must've been hard for you."

"It wasn't that hard," Lucinda says, trying to keep her tone light. "My lawyer called me ahead of time, warned me that it was probably gonna be coming." She sighs. "So it was fine, really. Wheeler and Detective Samuels were both nice enough about it. And Zeke Brinkmann says he approves of the garden I've been working on."

Aggie chuckles. "That Zeke. He's a card, ain't he?"

"He's something," Lucinda agrees, even though she really doesn't know much about him other than the gossip she's heard.

Aggie thinks for a moment. "Well, still. Just to know Hart's out there somewhere… After everything you've had to go through with him already… I just worry about you so much, Lu."

"I'm not doing all that bad," Lucinda says, her mind going to the girl, their walks in the woods, to the doe, to poetry, to love-making. She looks at Aggie in the mirror, meeting her cousin's eyes before tilting her head and pinning up another few strands of hair. "Honestly. It's gotten a lot easier since I moved out here."

"Really? It warms my heart to hear you say that, hon. I told Dan you'd be okay out here."

"Really, I am," Lucinda says. "And thanks again for helping me with Georgie, by the way. I needed this job."

Aggie flicks her wrist dismissively. "Oh, girl, you woulda gotten a job here just fine without me. Someone with your experience, coming out from the big city and all. You coulda gotten a job anywhere around here with no problem."

"Calvin wasn't exactly the 'big city.' It was a good ways from Atlanta."

"I've lived in Reverie all my life. *Sumter* seems like a big city to me."

They share a laugh. The laughter dies after a moment; Aggie studies Lucinda in the mirror.

"You making friends?" Aggie asks. "Meeting people?"

"A few," Lucinda says. "I've gotten to know the neighbor girl on the other side of my duplex a little."

Aggie makes a face. "Dan said there wasn't anyone else in that duplex."

"There wasn't. She moved in a few days after I did."

"Ah."

A few minutes pass in silence. Lucinda loses herself in the rhythm of snipping, combing, pinning; snipping, combing, pinning.

"You doing anything tomorrow night?" Aggie says. "Dan an' me still wanted to have you out for dinner. It's been a long time since you've seen the girls. They're so big now; you won't believe it."

Lucinda thinks for a moment, mentally reviewing her schedule for the next day. "Tomorrow's going to be busy; what about Wednesday?"

"Girls both have piano lessons on Wednesday."

"Thursday?"

"No, we're going to my mom and dad's for the weekend and leave on Thursday afternoon." Aggie's eyes flit up to Lucinda's in the mirror. "But Sunday night would be good, how about then?"

Lucinda doesn't know the girl's schedule, but she knows she had off yesterday, and she's hoping the girl might work it to where she's got next Sunday off, too. "I might have plans on Sunday," she says.

Aggie laughs. "Between the two of us, you'd think we're regular social butterflies. Alright, then, what about next Monday?"

"I'll double-check," Lucinda says, "but I think next Monday would be just fine."

"Good," Aggie says. "It's a date."

#

Lucinda knows better than to look for the blue compact when she gets home, but she looks anyway. It's almost six — a long day for her, since she left before seven — and of course the girl would've left for the hospital over four hours ago. She hopes the girl's evening is going well.

She finds a note on the kitchen table when she gets inside, right next to a clean, empty casserole dish that had held about a dozen cookies in the morning.

Ate all but three of the cookies. They were sooooooo good. Took the last few to work because I want my coworkers to try them — hope that was okay? You're da best. See you tomorrow? Gonna miss you tonight.

Lucinda smiles, carrying the note with her from the kitchen and into her bedroom, where she places it on the nightstand. She reads the note again after dinner, just as she's getting ready for bed.

For a second night in a row, she sleeps without nightmares.

Chapter 19

Lucinda's sitting in the rocker two nights later, willing herself to stay awake long enough to greet the girl when she gets home from the hospital, when her phone rings and jars her out of her doze. She glances at the caller ID, fearing the worst, but it's only her sister Harriet.

"Harrie?" Lucinda says when she picks up. "Is everything okay?"

"Yes, everything's fine, why wouldn't it be?"

"I don't know. I just… you're calling so late, and I — "

"Late?" Harriet scoffs. "Only you would think this is late, Lu. It's not even nine o'clock."

"I get up between — "

"Four and five. I know. But I hadn't heard from you since you moved, and I wanted to catch up. How's everything?"

Lucinda leans back in the rocker, stretching. "It's alright. It's Reverie, so it's… I don't know…"

"Boring as shit?"

Lucinda snickers. "Something like that. But I've got a job cutting hair at the local salon, and…" She considers telling Harriet about the girl next door — Harriet was one of the few people Lucinda had trusted when it came to revealing the true nature of her relationship with Dionne — but she changes her mind at the last moment, decides to stay vague. "Things are alright. How've you been? How's Greg?"

"Oh, *Greg,*" Harriet says, heaving a long-suffering sigh. "Boys and their toys." She proceeds to tell Lucinda a long-winded story about her husband and his new speedboat. Lucinda listens, laughs along with Harriet at the appropriate moments, takes her sister's side when Harriet complains about how much time, money, and love Greg has been doling out on his new boat. "A mid-life crisis boat if I've ever seen one," Harriet concludes.

If Edie once tried to fashion herself as the Gingerbread Man, Harriet might be said to have modeled her life after Puss in Boots. Harriet's the clever one of the three sisters, the street-smart one, the extraverted charmer. Where the cat in Puss in Boots convinced a king that his poor miller's son of an owner was actually a rich lord, Harriet somehow managed to disguise her poor, working class roots, hide her checkered past, then lose her accent and marry rich. Greg is certainly a modern-day Prince Charming, a handsome, successful man from a family where success is an expectation rather than an exception. He's been a fairy tale son-in-law for Lucinda's parents, a Happily Ever After for Harriet. And Greg and Harriet and the children are happy. Mostly.

Lucinda's glad for her baby sister — glad, and not jealous as she once was, when all she had was Hart. Brutal, angry Hart. A fairy-tale villain instead of a hero.

Lucinda never has been the heroine of a fairy tale; she's

always been the unfortunate, nameless side-character, doomed early on in the story.

"But listen to me, going on about all this," Harriet says when she comes to the end of the boat story. "Tell me the truth, Lu. Are you honestly doing okay?" Her voice lowers. "Are you missing her?"

Phantom gunshots. Screaming, blood. A searing pain in her side.

"Missing… who? You mean Dionne?"

There's a pause that lasts a little too long on the other end. "Of course I mean Dionne. Who else would I be talking about?"

"I don't… I try not to think about Dionne too much," Lucinda says.

"Sweetie. Are you sure that's the healthiest way to cope with everything?" Another pause. "Have you thought any more about grief counseling? You know Greg and I would be happy to pay for it."

"I know, but I… I have a really hard time imagining going into an office to talk to a stranger about her. About her and about… everything that happened," Lucinda says. Tears well in her eyes; she wipes them hastily away, even though there's no one around to see her cry.

Harriet sighs. "I understand. Everyone's gotta process things in their own time, in their own way. Right?"

"Yes," Lucinda says, glad that her sister seems ready to let it go. "Thank you for understanding."

A beat passes.

"Richie just started up cross-country practice this week. The course they run on is across the way from where she's buried," Harriet says.

She pities me, Lucinda thinks.

When Lucinda doesn't comment on Dionne's burial site, Harriet keeps going. "I think about her — and about you, and about what happened — every time I go pick Rich up from practice. Sometimes I still shed a few tears when I see them putting in a fresh grave."

At the mention of a fresh grave, Lucinda's mind yanks her backward, pulling her into the past, into that awful day of Dionne's funeral. She can still smell the newly cut grass, the rain-soaked red Georgia clay piled next to the open hole of the grave. She can hear Dionne's mother, sobbing against Dionne's brother, the latter holding a stoic, stiff jaw while his eyes threatened to spill tears.

And what could she, Lucinda, do at that funeral? She couldn't comfort them. Her love affair with Dionne had been kept secret from almost everyone other than a small, select circle of trusted friends. Dionne's mother hadn't known about Lucinda any more than Lucinda's mother knew what Dionne had really been to her.

She couldn't comfort them; they didn't know her. She couldn't share in their grief. And even if she could have, she wouldn't have.

Because the bullet that ended Dionne's life had been meant for her.

"I'm sorry," Harriet says softly, and Lucinda's mind

rockets back to the present, skimming forward through the past and landing, dizzily, back into the current moment.

Dionne is gone. Harriet is here.

"Maybe I shouldn't have brought it up."

"It's alright," Lucinda says. She lets out a ragged, exhausted breath. "I'm moving on. I think I…" Her exhausted sigh turns into what's almost a giggle. "I think I might actually be seeing someone."

"Oh?" Harriet says, surprise evident in her voice. "I didn't think — I mean I just assumed that after Dionne, you might not be ready to see anyone for a while."

"I thought the same thing," Lucinda says. "And I didn't seek this out. It just sort of, well, happened."

"Alright. Dish," Harriet commands. "Who's the lucky… well, is it a guy or girl?"

"A woman. Or… You're right, 'girl' might be a better word." She smiles, her mind's eye filled with visions of brown hair, smooth skin, perfect nipples. "She can't even be thirty yet. I'm old enough to be her mother. Almost, anyhow."

Harriet clucks. "You *cougar*. What is it with you and younger women? I didn't know you had it in you."

"I didn't, either. It caught me completely by surprise."

Harriet waits a moment. "So?"

"So what?"

"So, tell me about her. What's her name? What's she do? How'd you meet her?"

Lucinda decides she should answer the questions in

reverse, saving her explanation for why she doesn't know the girl's name yet — not even her first name, even though they've already slept together — for last.

"She's my neighbor — lives in the other half of the duplex Dan found for me, moved in just a couple days after I did," she says. "And she's a nurse, an RN in the emergency room at the county hospital."

"A nurse?" Harriet says, laughing. "Again?"

"It's a little surreal, isn't it?"

"It is." Harriet hesitates. "Have you told her about Dionne? About Hart?"

"I... a little. Not anything about Dionne, not much about Hart. But she knows..." Lucinda swallows, and the air around her suddenly seems to grow colder. "They can't find Hart," she says in a small voice.

"They can't — wait, Lu, what do you *mean* they can't find Hart?"

"They can't find him," Lucinda repeats. "He missed one of his phone check ins with — I don't know, whatever police officer was supposed to be keeping track of him, I guess — and he... he's gone. They don't know where he is."

"God*dammit.*" Lucinda hears something bang on the other end of the phone; she assumes it's Harriet's fist, hitting whatever's nearby. "They never should've let him out on bail in the first place."

"I know. I said that from the very beginning, but nobody wanted to listen." Lucinda sniffs, pulls her feet up into the rocker so that her knees are protectively in front of her. "I don't think they believed me. About all the years of abuse," she says quietly, barely loud enough for Harriet to hear. "He was an upstanding citizen. He didn't have a record. He denied everything. And since I never called the police before to tell them… to say what Hart was doing to me, I think they just assumed I was lying, trying to make Hart look bad to draw attention away from… Dionne and me."

"Oh, honey. Why didn't you tell me sooner?"

"I only found out a few days ago myself," Lucinda says. "I guess I've just been trying to… not think about it so much. Just live my life."

"Why don't you come to Alpharetta? Stay with us until they find him?"

"No," Lucinda says immediately. "He's been to your house before; I wouldn't be surprised if he's already checked to see if I'm there with y'all. I bet he's checked Edie's, too." She rubs her forehead, troubled by the thought of Hart scoping out her sisters' homes, her mother's. "I'm probably safest here. He never came to Reverie and probably forgot it exists. Reverie's forgettable — it's why I picked it."

"Then I'm coming to you," Harriet says decisively. "I'll come and stay with you until they find the bastard and lock him up for good."

"Please don't," Lucinda says quickly. "He might be watching you. Waiting for you to break your normal routine. He's smart, Harrie. Way too smart."

"Don't be silly, Lu," Harriet says, but for all Harriet's perpetual, sunny self-confidence, Lucinda knows when her little sister is trying to hide her uncertainty. Puss in Boots might have been bold, but even his tremble didn't need to be faked when faced with the ogre.

"It's not silly. You know Hart. Please don't do anything that might give him any clues about where I am. Or that would put you or your family in danger. Please."

"Okay," Harriet says, and Lucinda suspects she is probably happy to give in. "But I'm calling you every day from now on. And you'd better pick up the phone. If you don't, I'm calling Dan and Aggie."

#

The nightmares find her, even in the rocker on the front porch. She dreams that Hart kidnaps Harriet's teenage son Richie, takes him deep into the woods where he's hiding out. Lucinda's running through the woods, calling Richie's name, when a hand reaches out from the bushes, grabs her wrist.

The hand is Dionne's, and she pulls Lucinda towards her, into the bushes. It's not Dionne as she lived, vibrant and full of laughter, but a ghoulish version, an animated corpse Dionne, with black, sunken eyes and cold white skin.

"Dionne," Lucinda says with a breath of relief. "Thank

God you're here. I thought you were dead."

"I am," the ghoul says. "Why? Why'd this happen to me, Lu? Tell me why you let it happen."

"I didn't mean for it to happen. I swear I didn't."

"But it did," Dionne says. "If you'd been a nurse instead of a hairdresser, you could've saved me."

"I'm sorry," Lucinda says, breath hitching in her throat. "It never should've happened. You never should've met me. If you'd never met me, you'd still be alive." She begins to sob, burying her face in her hands, shoulders heaving.

"You *should* be sorry," Dionne says. Then her voice deepens, grows in volume. "You're so stupid, Lucinda. You can never manage to get anything right."

Lucinda takes her hands away from her face, looks up. It's not Dionne standing there anymore but Hart. His skin is white; his eyes are black and terrifying and smoldering with hatred.

"You got your girlfriend killed," he says to Lucinda. "Now you've gone and gotten your nephew killed. Stupid, stupid, stupid."

She fears him; she wants to run. But she straightens, widens her stance — because she's found that when her stance is wide, she's less likely to stumble when he hits her.

"Where's Richie? What did you do to him?"

Hart laughs — a hollow, merciless sound.

"I told you already. He's dead."

He lunges for Lucinda; she steps back too slowly. A

hand grips her shoulder, shakes her.

"Lucinda!" he shouts at her. "Lucinda, Lucinda, Lucinda…"

He says her name over and over again, and she is falling, tumbling headlong through darkness, headed to meet Dionne, to meet Richie, weighed down forever by the knowledge that this is all her —

"Lucinda!"

She starts awake, gasps for breath as if she's been trapped underwater. A hand is on her shoulder, and she tries to get away from it, but she can't, she's stuck.

"Lulu?" says the voice — feminine, concerned. Not Hart.

She blinks, realizes where she is, what's happening. Richie is alive, even if Dionne is still dead. It's the girl who's standing over her, hand on her shoulder, shaking her and calling her name.

"It's okay," the girl says, dropping her bag and her lunch cooler to the porch. She puts both hands on Lucinda's shoulders. "It's okay. It was just a dream." She rubs Lucinda's arms. "It's over now, Lulu."

Lucinda's breathing slows; some of the tension drains from her body, which is stiff from falling asleep in the wooden rocker.

"I dreamed he found me. He kidnapped my nephew," Lucinda says, words still thick and slow with sleep. The tears that have been threatening since her conversation with Harriet finally spill out, rolling freely down both cheeks.

"He's not here," the girl says. She crouches in front of Lucinda, moving her hands from Lucinda's shoulders to her thighs. "I'm here. He's not. Just me. Okay?"

A sudden, horrible thought occurs to Lucinda. "You have to run. You have to leave Reverie, and find some place safe. Otherwise, he'll find you."

"He's not going to find me," the girl says, using the gentle tone one might reserve for a child frightened over a monster hiding in the closet. "He's not going to find me, and he's not going to find you, either."

"You don't know that — you don't know *him*." Lucinda swallows, pinches the bridge of her nose. "He wants to kill me. I know he does. And he'll do it, too. He will."

The girl puts her hands on the rocker's arms, pushes to her feet, and leans in close to Lucinda's face. She pulls Lucinda's hand from her face.

"Look at me, Lu," she whispers.

Lucinda looks. The girl's brown eyes are round, earnest, and warm, filled with affection. They are the opposite of ghoul-Dionne's hollow black eyes, the opposite of dream-Hart's hateful eyes.

She leans in further, gives Lucinda a tender, gentle kiss. "I told you already," she says when she pulls away. "I protect the people I care about. No one's getting close to you. No one's going to touch you. Not him, not anyone else."

"I want to believe you. But…"

"You don't believe me?" The girl tugs on Lucinda's hands, pulling her to her feet. "I'm taking you to bed," she says. "And when I'm done with you, you'll know I mean it when I say no one's touching you. Well — unless you count me."

Chapter 20

Lucinda wakes as the first hints of dawn begin to filter in through her bedroom window. The clock on her nightstand reads five thirty-six AM, and her eyebrows arch in surprise. She can't remember the last time she's slept so late.

The girl is still in bed beside her, back pointing towards Lucinda, sleeping deeply. Lucinda turns onto her side, runs her fingers lightly down the girl's spine, feeling the ridges of each vertebra, keeping her touch soft enough that she won't wake the sleeping beauty.

Their night together has already taken on a dream-like quality in Lucinda's mind; already, the memory of the girl's touch feels like a memory from another life, a memory that belongs to a different Lucinda.

Because surely, the Lucinda who is now waking up cannot be the Lucinda who fell asleep cradled in the girl's arms last night.

#

She'd been so gentle with Lucinda last night. She'd tamed the restless energy of her youth for once; each touch, each kiss had been deliberate, measured, a quiet language that said more than any words could have said.

She'd led Lucinda by the hand into the house, past the yard sale furniture in the living room, where the photo of Lucinda and Dionne still sat face-down on the corner table; she'd led her down the hallway, past the photo on the wall of Lucinda with her mother and two sisters at their grandmother's funeral, and into the only bedroom.

She'd laid Lucinda down on the bed gingerly, as if she was something fragile that could only be handled with care, and she'd undressed her just as carefully.

Unbuttoning Lucinda's pajama top, she'd placed her lips on one of Lucinda's nipples, sucking until it puckered, then moving to the next one and doing the same thing. Lucinda reached down, twining her fingers in the girl's brown hair.

"I only want to dream of you from now on," she told the girl.

"You already are."

Lucinda giggled. "So I'm dreaming all of this right now?"

"In a manner of speaking," the girl said. She dragged the tip of her tongue down Lucinda's chest, between her breasts, down her stomach, into her belly button. She looked up. "Life is but a dream, Lulu."

Her mouth continued its journey south, pausing to kiss Lucinda's wet core as if it were her mouth.

Lucinda moaned.

The girl traveled back up Lucinda's body the same way, the tip of her tongue making long lines over Lucinda's skin.

"You're so beautiful," the girl murmured. "I could kiss you like this all night."

"I'm not beautiful," Lucinda said. "But if you want to kiss me for the rest of the night, I won't stop you."

The girl sat halfway up, her expression stern. "Never, ever, ever tell me again that you're not beautiful," she said. "You're perfect. Magnificent."

"I'm not. I'm a wallflower. A plain Jane."

The girl's face came close to Lucinda, she traced Lucinda's face with a fingertip before kissing her. "You're a hidden gem," the girl said. "A secret treasure. A mystery only I get to discover."

One of the girl's hands wanders down, her fingers walking over Lucinda's bare hip.

"You can't mean it," Lucinda argued. "You'll find some woman your own age soon, someone younger and more beautiful than I could ever be, and you'll leave me behind before I can even— "

"Shhh," the girl said. She kissed Lucinda, her lips and tongue adding more pressure this time, more insistence. The hand on Lucinda's hip skimmed along the top of Lucinda's thigh, came to rest between Lucinda's legs, cupping her. Lucinda wiggled her other leg between the girl's legs, lifting her thigh until it made contact with something soft and wet.

The girl's fingers began to work against Lucinda, the tip

of her index finger drawing a line through the moisture between Lucinda's legs in the same way that her tongue had drawn lines down Lucinda's stomach a moment before.

The light, teasing pressure was almost too much for Lucinda to bear, and she reached down with her own hand, pushing against the back of the girl's fingers.

"I want you," Lucinda whispered in the girl's ear. She pressed on the girl's fingers harder. "Please, Dionne, I want —"

But she stiffened, realizing her mistake. Her eyes flew open as the girl stopped kissing her and came up on her elbow, studying Lucinda's face.

"Oh, God, I'm sorry," Lucinda said, mortified beyond words. "I can't believe I… I'm so sorry."

The girl only smiled. "You're sorry for what? For finally guessing my name? I guess I won't have to take your firstborn away, after all." She kissed Lucinda's brow.

Lucinda lay motionless, head spinning.

"Dionne?" Lucinda said, her voice thin, like something delicate about to crack.

"Yes, baby?" Dionne drew back a few inches, studying Lucinda's face.

"You came back to me?"

"I never left you, silly."

It all made sense now. Everything. The long, brown hair that hung almost to her waist. The big, doe-like brown eyes. The brother named Derrick. The mother named Rose, the father who'd passed early — Bill. Working second shift as an RN in the emergency room.

The girl didn't just look like Dionne, she didn't just have some similarities to Dionne; the girl *was* Dionne. She always had been.

"But… how?" Lucinda asked. "You can't be — you're dead. We buried you. In your family plot, right next to your grandparents, your great-grandparents, your — "

"Shhh, Lu," Dionne said. "It's okay if you don't understand everything right now. All you need to know is that I told you I would always be here to protect you, and I am."

Lucinda opened her mouth to ask another question, to wonder again out-loud how any of this could be possible, but the girl — could it really be Dionne? — cut her off with another kiss. She captured Lucinda's tongue lightly with her teeth; her fingers slid between Lucinda's legs, finding their path into the source of Lucinda's wetness.

"Dionne," Lucinda mumbled between kisses. "Dee…"

"Lulu. I'm here."

"You're here," Lucinda said, feeling the tears fall onto her cheeks. "You're back."

Dionne kissed the tears from both her cheeks, reached inside her with a long, lithe finger. "No, I told you: I never left. I promised I wouldn't. I didn't." Another finger entered Lucinda; she gasped. "I'm here," Dionne said, sucking the hollow of Lucinda's throat. "I'm here," she said again, rocking her hips, grinding her own dampness against Lucinda's leg. "I'm here," she said, and the fingers inside Lucinda thrust deeper.

Everything began to blend together, past and present layering one on top of the other like double-exposed film. Dionne breathed hard against Lucinda; Lucinda remembered their first time together — not when Dionne was merely "the neighbor girl," but the real first time. It had rained that night; she had been walking away from Dionne, but Dionne had reached out, grabbed her wrist. *"Wait, Lu,"* she'd said.

"God, Lu, oh *Godddddd...*" the Dionne of the present said.

The Dionne of the past gently brushed drenched hair from Lucinda's forehead. *"I can't tell, Lulu. Are those teardrops or raindrops on your cheeks?"*

The Dionne of the present was moving faster, harder. "God," she said. And again: "God, oh God, oh *Jesus* God..."

Her arousal only heightened Lucinda's arousal, and she dug her fingers into Dionne's bare back, trying to lift her entire body towards her lover, as if perhaps she might have been able to levitate off the mattress, merge her body with Dionne's.

"Yes, baby," she whispered, but time was spinning out of control now, the hands on the clock corkscrewing backwards, a runaway train that no one could stop, and she didn't know where she was. Was this Georgia, three years ago, when she met Dionne and they laid together for the first time? Was this South Carolina, now, when the neighbor girl suddenly transformed into her missing lover before her very eyes? Was it possible that she was in both places at once, experiencing —

"Yes — fuck — yes, yes, *unnnnh...*"

— both Dionnes, both places, both times simultaneously?

Lucinda came just a moment after Dionne did, and the girl collapsed on top of her, both women breathless, sweaty, exhausted, pleased.

#

Now, with dawn lighting up the front yard and songbirds calling to one another, a troubled Lucinda continues to trace Dionne's backbone with her fingers. Up... and down. Up... and down. She is here — isn't she? She is warm. She is soft. Her skin smells the same way it always has — like bar soap and vanilla lotion, along with an underlying musk that is all her own beneath those layers of sweetness.

This isn't a nightmare. It can't be a dream. If it is a dream, how could it be so persistent? How could the sheets still carry the damp traces of last night's love-making? How could Lucinda see Dionne's side rising and falling with her breath, how could she trace her backbone with her fingers, if this is all just a dream?

No: She's here. Dionne has come back to her, just as she always said she would.

"I thought you'd gone," a Lucinda of the past said. *A Lucinda soaked by rain.*

"Gone? I'll never leave you, Lu. Not ever."

"You can't say that. You don't know what the future might bring. No one can. For all we know, I could die tomorrow. Or you could."

A Dionne of the past stroked Lucinda's cheek again. Her brown hair hung in long, wet ropes around her face. Like Lucinda's face, raindrops mixed with teardrops, making it hard to tell one from the other.

"Don't say that," Dionne said. *"Even if I died tomorrow, I'd find my way back to you."*

Lucinda's phone rings. She scoops it up and patters out of the room, not wanting the sound to wake her Sleeping Beauty. It's a number that she doesn't recognize, but it's a Georgia area code, so she decides that she should pick it up.

"Hello?"

Silence on the other end of the line. She thinks she hears the rasp of breath.

"Hello? Anyone there?"

"You're a dumb bitch, you know that?"

Lucinda's blood freezes. Time is spinning neither forward nor backward now; it has simply stopped altogether. "Hart?" she whispers, even though she'd recognize his voice anywhere, anytime.

"That's right, Lucinda. It's me. Your *husband.*" He practically spits the last word, like it has a foul taste that he needs to expel from his mouth.

"How… how did you get this number?"

"What's it matter? I found you. Just like I told you I would. You should've known better than to try to run away from me."

"You shouldn't have called me," Lucinda says boldly. "The police are monitoring all my phone calls."

There's a low chuckle that descends into a hoarse coughing. "Bullshit."

Silence on the other end again. The phone jiggles against Lucinda's ear — her hand is shaking.

"I'm coming for you, Lucinda," Hart says, and there's no mistaking the menace in his voice. "I'm coming for you, and I'm gonna finish what I started."

Chapter 21

RHONDA WHITBY
Two weeks later

It's a Sunday afternoon, not long after church. Rhonda realized halfway through Brother James's sermon that she knows *exactly* where she's left her cell phone: It's sitting right in front of her chair at work, just left of the pomade. She can see it in her mind's eye and — may the Lord forgive her — it's all she could think about the rest of the sermon. Fortunately, she and her husband took two separate cars to church that morning, because she'd gone early for Bible study and he hadn't, and wasn't too much of a trek to head on into town and swing by the salon.

She's already retrieved her phone, locked Georgie's back up, and is on her way back to her car when she spots Lucinda. She starts to wave and holler to catch her mousey coworker's attention, but she thinks better of it when she sees what Lucinda's doing.

Lucinda Hamilton is walking — well, *sauntering,* more like — through the old, sun-dappled town graveyard a block down the road, and she's chattering away, happy as you like… except no one else is there.

Is she on the phone? Does she have earbuds in?

Rhonda squints, lifting a hand to shade her eyes from the sun.

No. No earbuds that she can see. Not one of those bluetooth thing-a-jiggies, either. As far as Rhonda can tell, Lucinda is completely alone.

It's not the first time Rhonda's seen the woman talking to herself, either. She's had her suspicions before, but now? It's clear that Dan and Aggie McPherson's cousin is just plain-old batshit crazy.

That, or…

Rhonda shivers, and her hand flits to her wrist, fingers brushing against the prayer beads there. To the uninitiated, the beads wrapped tightly around her wrist look like an ordinary rosary, complete with a pewter cross, which is dingy with black tarnish and dangles just below her pulse. Nothing but ordinary blue-green glass beads, their pattern broken with an occasional seashell. Yes, it looks like an ordinary rosary, which is why Rhonda likes it.

Few people outside her family know it was given to her when she was still a baby by her great-grandmother, the revered Gullah root doctor, Mother Izzie. According to family legend, the rosary was the most powerful talisman Mother Izzie possessed, granted to her as it was by an actual angel of God who came to Mother Izzie in her sleep.

Everyone in Rhonda's family wanted that rosary when Mother Izzie died, but it was little baby Rhonda she gave it to, and so the whispers have circulated around Rhonda ever since childhood, weaving strands of words around her like the baskets her ancestors were known for.

"She'll be the next one," they'd said. *"The next root doctor, the next Mother Izzie."*

But Rhonda fell in love with a man who wasn't from the low country, followed him away from the coast, settled here in Reverie, raised up two sons to be good, God-fearing young men. The only root work of Mother Izzie's that lives on with Rhonda is the rosary, which never comes off her wrist except to sleep and to shower. When she sleeps, it sits on the nightstand within easy reach; when she showers, it sits on the counter beside the sink.

All her life, Rhonda's wondered why Mother Izzie gave her, of everyone in the family, the magical talisman of the rosary. Is there something she's supposed to do with it? Some moment in her life when, with sudden clarity, she will think, *"Now,"* and in that instant, will know why the rosary was gifted to her?

She doesn't know if the rosary wards off evil, the way her kinfolk always said it did. She doesn't know if it has hidden powers. She only knows that it comforts her, to have something with so many unknown mystical properties wrapped tightly around her wrist.

She goes back to watching the oblivious Lucinda Hamilton, runs her fingers over Mother Izzie's glass beads in a kind of quiet trance, feeling each bead give way to the familiar comfort of the rough metal links that bind them together, interspersed with the shells.

And when she begins to whisper under her breath, the

prayer that escapes her lips is — and she is embarrassed to admit it — directed more to Mother Izzie than it is to God the Father.

"Protect us from evil, Mother," Rhonda says. Many yards away, Lucinda's lips bubble into words, words directed to her invisible companion. "Protect your innocent children. They know not what they do."

It occurs to her that she *hopes* Lucinda Hamilton is simply batshit crazy. Because if she isn't, if she's got one foot in this world, one foot in the spirit world, well, then may Mother Izzie help them all.

PART 2

ARDIE BROWN

"I am hopelessly in love with a memory.
An echo from another time, another place."

- Michel Foucault

"In that book which is my memory,
On the first page of the chapter that is the day when I first met you,
Appear the words, 'Here begins a new life.'"

- Dante Alighieri

Chapter 22

It hasn't been the case that Ardie Brown has wanted to date someone. She hasn't been actively looking. When she and Sandra split, Ardie left everything behind in a hurried flurry of bad decisions, taking no possessions with her except an old Harley in need of tuning, a set of saddlebags, and a change of clothes. And until recently, she'd assumed that she's just too old to date. Past her prime. Too old for another romance.

But at the same time, Ardie's always had a flare for the dramatic, a tendency to, as her mother might say, have a head that's "hotter'n the devil's house cat." When she left Tucson — and Sandra — behind, it took her until she was halfway across Texas before it occurred to her that she'd left… hastily.

She should've taken with her more than just the Harley. She should've taken her old Marines dress blues, at least. Some of her favorite paperbacks. Maybe her guns — she rarely uses them, but she misses the ritual of cleaning them. She could've at least sold them for some extra cash. But in her haze of grief and anger, she'd left on the spur of the moment, in the middle of the night, barely even remembering to shove her wallet into her back pocket before sending a stream of sand and gravel in Sandra's direction as she spun away.

These days, it's not the dress blues that she misses most, not her old, basement-smelling copy of *Native Son*, not the well-oiled Glock 19. It's the cat she misses. The cat named Omar that she and Sandra found together in a dumpster behind the Walmart. Omar had gotten tangled and stuck in there, and mewled like the world was ending, but when Ardie reached into the sticky heap of broken crates and rotten fruit and spoiled milk to get the tiny kitten out, she got a series of claw marks down her forearm and across the back of her hand as thanks.

"Sweetie, just leave it," Sandra had said at the time.

"We can't just leave him in there," Ardie said. "He'll die in there. He's too little. And he's all alone."

"You don't know it's all alone. What if the mama cat comes back, looking for it?"

Ardie shook her head. "If I leave him here, I'm going to have nightmares about him for a month."

Sandra huffed and put her hands on her hips, but Ardie knew her girl: Sandra wouldn't be able to resist the skinny, flea-bitten, black and white kitten once he was out of the dumpster. She'd fall in love. Just like Ardie already had.

She named him "Omar" on a whim, even though they found out a week later, upon taking Omar to the vet, that he was actually a she.

Sandra said they should change the name, but Ardie was already attached to *Omar*. The name had a ring to it.

"So she'll be a trans cat," Ardie argued. "Nothing

wrong with two lesbians having a gender-bender kitten."

Sandra argued for another five days over the name, but even she gave in after a week, and the spunky little transman was officially Omar.

Omar became more than their cat; she was their mascot. She was the symbol of the love between Ardie and Sandra, the flagship of their domesticity, the banner of their commitment to one another.

Or so Ardie had thought at the time.

To this day, Ardie still can't believe she let Sandra keep Omar. What had she been thinking?

She hadn't been, that's what. Her head had been "hotter'n the devil's house cat," and so she'd left her own cat behind.

Although she'd never be able to admit it out loud, Ardie still lies awake, tossing and turning, unable to sleep, her anguish over that misbehaving, good-for-nothing cat smothering her like an airless, humid night. She wonders if Omar misses her other mother, wonders where she went, or if the cat's already forgotten Ardie, vaguely recognizing but unable to place the lingering scent of a woman who once rescued her from a Walmart dumpster.

Two years have passed since Ardie rode off on her bike in the middle of the night. Two years since she coaxed the decrepit motorcycle all the way across the country, back to South Carolina. And in two years (if it's only been two years, why does it feel like five?), she's barely socialized outside her small circle of family and acquaintances. She spends most her time at the shop, where she usually eats her lunches with her father's favorite and most senior mechanic, Jim. The best thing about Jim is how much he talks, mainly enumerating the thousand-and-one ways that people fail to take care of their cars, his latest complaints over Carolina football, and why his wife's shopping habits are going to lead him into an early grave. Jim also, in his own words, doesn't give a "rat's patootie" about the fact that Ardie's ex is a Sandy and not a Randy — an absence of homophobia that's as rare as it is refreshing in Reverie.

Other than Jim, her other socializing primarily consists of watching television with her parents each evening until she grows bored of their penchant for game shows and reality TV and retires to her room to read. About once per month, sometimes less, she makes the drive to Columbia or Charleston to have lunch or dinner or coffee with old Marine buddies. And once last summer, she made it as far as Asheville for the Gay Pride parade.

It's a quiet life. A steady rhythm of changing oil and air filters, of tinkering with a bike that should've been retired to a scrap heap years ago, of running errands for aging parents who aren't quite ready to admit how much they've come to rely upon Ardie for help.

And she definitely didn't even think about dating again. Not after Sandra. Not after shedding tears on sleepless nights for Omar. Ardie's come to accept that Sandra was probably the last woman she'll ever be with. Ardie was only ever attractive to a slim subset of the population in the first place, and now, with her extra pounds and her greying hair, she suspects that subset is slimmer than it ever was. And it's all okay — she's been content with her quiet life.

Then she met Lucinda Hamilton.

It's as if Ardie had been sitting in a darkened room, straining to read with no light to aid her, and then someone had walked in and thrown back the curtains with one mighty sweep of the arms.

Sunlight floods the room, chasing away shadows, revealing swirling clouds of dust and dank that's been collecting there for who-knows-how-long, and Ardie, once her eyes adjust, realizes that she should've pulled the curtains back long ago. What had been stopping her? Why had she forgotten the curtains were there?

"Shouldn't read in the dark," a quiet, female voice says. "You'll strain your eyes."

Ardie turns, blinking as her eyes adjust, and in the crisp freshness of sunlight, she sees Lucinda standing there, haloed in soft yellow, smiling at Ardie like she has a secret, like she —

#

Pounding. Fist on wood.

A pause.

Then pounding again. Ardie opens her eyes, surprised to find the sunlight streaming in through her bedroom window.

"Ardie?" booms her father's voice on the other side of the door. More pounding. "Ardie, wake up already. Daylight's wasting."

Another voice, words indecipherable, plays a warm, high-pitched counterpoint to her father's baritone. Her mother, Ardie guesses.

"Oh, c'mon now," her father says, cutting the other voice short. "She prolly jus' forgot to set the alarm again. She'll be glad I woke her up."

Ardie glances at the digital clock on her nightstand, blinks at it twice when she sees that it reads eight o'clock. Eight? She sits up — too fast — a head rush threatening to force her back to the bed. She clasps the headboard with one hand, steadies herself.

It's Saturday, she realizes with relief. She's not late yet; the shop doesn't open until ten thirty today.

"Ardie, you — "

"I'm up, I'm up," she says to the closed door as she stands. "You're right, I stayed up late reading and forgot to set the alarm again. I'll be out in a bit."

"Good," he answers gruffly. "You still helpin' me fix the John Deere this mornin'?"

"I am," Ardie says. *The John Deere* is what Daddy calls the riding lawnmower — an absolute necessity on their three-acre plot of land. Truthfully, she wishes he'd let her fix it on her own, as her mechanical skill has surpassed his now, and when they work on projects together, he still defaults into the position of superior and teacher, which only makes Ardie want to wring his flabby old neck.

She makes her way around the bed to her dresser, pulling on a fresh undershirt and a t-shirt before she hikes a pair of worn, motor oil-stained blue jeans up and over her hips. She sits down in the rocker in the corner to lace up her boots.

Lucinda, she thinks, the name coming into her mind unbidden, possibly the last remnant of a dream she can barely remember anymore. A dream of sunlight and kittens and…

Lucinda.

She stands, inspecting herself in the full-length mirror. Maybe it's time for another haircut? She finger-combs thick black hair into place.

Don't be ridiculous, she tells herself. *You're not spending twenty-some-odd bucks on a haircut you don't really need just because you want to see Lucinda again.*

Almost a week has passed since she finished the work on Lucinda's duplex. They'd had a nice enough conversation, but Lucinda seemed… off, somehow. More distant than she had been on previous occasions. And she kept looking at the door to the other half of the duplex as if it might burst open any time.

If you want to see her again, Ardie tells herself, *go to her place. Or call her. Ask her out.*

Pounding. Fist on wood.

"Ya ever coming on up outta there?" her father calls.

"Yessir, I'm coming."

She fixes the John Deere (with very little help from her father) not long after a breakfast of black coffee, then finds herself on her bike, heading towards the shop earlier than she really needs to. Finds herself parking in front of Georgie's. Finds herself hoping she can get a haircut before it's time to open up the shop.

Finds herself hoping Lucinda will be there.

Chapter 23

When the bell above the door cheerily announces Ardie's entrance, Lucinda looks up from the broom she's pushing across the floor.

"Ardie?" she says, sounding surprised. The expression on her face isn't exactly welcoming. It's the same "off" expression she wore Sunday, when Ardie fixed the stairs leading away from Lucinda's kitchen. "You're not on my schedule today."

"I know," Ardie says. "Sorry. I really did mean to call a couple weeks ago. You got time for me?"

Lucinda holds the push broom like it's a staff, her other hand resting on her hip. It's a bold sort of stance, bolder than the Lucinda who first gave Ardie a haircut over a month ago. Reverie seems to be changing her. Maybe in a good way.

Lucinda sucks in a breath, lips pursing, and Ardie knows what she's going to say before she says it. "I'm sorry, Ardie. I just don't have any room in the schedule this morning. Or this afternoon, for that matter."

"How 'bout Monday?"

"Monday's jammed packed. I'm barely even going to have a lunch break."

"Tuesday?" Ardie asks hopefully.

"Tuesday... Let me look at my schedule." Lucinda picks up a pocket diary from her counter, flips through it. She looks back up. "I'm real sorry about this, but I don't have any space for you next week at all."

"I s'pose that's a good thing," Ardie says, trying to smile. "Sounds like you're building up your clients. Getting popular. Doesn't surprise me. You're like a magician with those scissors."

Ardie kicks herself as soon as she says it. What is she even talking about? A magician? Could she be any more obvious about it? She's practically *begging* Lucinda. *"Nobody likes a beggar,"* her father is fond of saying.

"Maybe week after next?" Lucinda says. "How's Thursday work for you?"

Ardie's hand flits to the back of her neck automatically, as if she might be able to tell simply by touch how long her hair will get by next Thursday. It's already gotten a little ragged; she hates the idea of putting it off a whole extra week.

"Well," she says. "I guess that's just what I get for not calling ahead of time, right?"

Lucinda smiles at her, and for just a moment, Ardie thinks she detects warmth in her smile again — the Lucinda she first met, the Lucinda who banters with her playfully. The Lucinda she thought she just might have a chance with.

"What time next Thursday?" Ardie asks.

They arrange a time; Ardie heads to the shop. At least she'll have the time to do some of the cleaning and organizing she's been putting off.

#

"And so I said to her, 'Woman, do you think we are *made* of money? You think it *grows* out there in the backyard, next to your *prize* watermelons?'"

Jim trails a few feet behind Ardie as he talks, sharing his latest marital woes as Ardie puts the first car of the day onto the rack.

"Uh-huh," Ardie says to show that she's listening. She picks up a socket wrench.

"And she said" — Jim pitches his voice high in imitation of his wife — "'But they were thirty-percent off, honey.' And I told her, 'Only way you're keeping them shoes is if they're a *hunnert* percent off. *Honey.*'"

"Did she take 'em back?" Ardie asks, even though she isn't all that interested in the story or its conclusion. Truth be told, it bothers her how much Jim complains about his wife. She knows he loves her, but his way of showing it is… well, cantankerous at best.

"Sure 'nuff did," Jim says, nodding triumphantly. "Took them shoes back that very day and managed not to buy *nuthin'* else when she went to return 'em."

The bell above the door in the office rings, and Jim turns towards it automatically.

"Want me to get that?" he asks.

Ardie glances into the office, leaning around the car

she's working on to get a better look at who just walked in. It's an older woman, her parents' age, and Ardie recognizes her immediately.

She hands the socket wrench to Jim. "Naw," she says. "I got this one. You finish the oil change." Ardie turns back to him as her hand lands on the office door knob. "And change out the wiper blades, too. The one on the left's looking ratty."

Jim gives her a mock salute. "Yes, Sarge."

She nods. She hates it when he calls her "Sarge."

Ardie opens the door to the office and steps inside, and the old woman's face lights up as soon as she sees who it is.

"Well, *hey there,* Ardie, I didn't know I'd be seein' you in here today," the woman croons.

Ardie steps around the counter, embraces Erna Winchester. The woman is old friends with Ardie's mother. On top of that, decades ago Mrs. Winchester was Ardie's fourth grade teacher. Mrs. Winchester has a tendency to talk to Ardie like she's still nine years old, but if she'd sent Jim in to deal with her, Ardie knows she'd get an earful from her mother by the time she got home:

"Erna Winchester called me. She said she went by the shop today and you sent Jim *to wait on her."*

"Hey, Mrs. Winchester," Ardie says when the tiny old woman lets her go.

"How's your mama and daddy?"

"They're alright. Daddy should be here sometime in the next hour or two. He's been having some trouble with his hip lately, doesn't get around to the shop as much as he used to."

Mrs. Winchester's weathered face breaks into a wrinkled grin. She moves her lips up and down over her dentures a few times, maybe trying to make sure they stay in place. "I tell you, Ardie, you get to be our age, an' you'll be hopin' you have some young'un to open up the shop for you, too. Folks me and your daddy's age, we jus' don't move as fast as we used to."

Ardie chuckles. "Yes, ma'am, I s'pose that's true."

"You still livin' with your folks? Takin' good care of them?" Mrs. Winchester asks.

"Yes, ma'am, sure am."

"That's a good thing, a real good thing." Her lips work across her dentures again. "All my brood, they all grew up and done moved away." She names each of them one by one, details what's happening in their lives. "...and Barry's going through *another* divorce," she says by way of conclusion. "Can you believe that?"

"I s'pose some people... just take a while to settle down," Ardie says diplomatically.

"How 'bout you, Ardie? You got anyone special in your life?"

Ardie thinks of Sandra, of Omar the cat, of how she wants to get her dress blues back from Tucson. She thinks of Lucinda.

"No, ma'am," she says after a moment's hesitation. "It's enough work to keep up with running Daddy's shop and looking after my folks. Don't even know if I'd have time for someone special in my life if I had them."

All bald-faced lies, of course.

"How old are you now, Ardie?"

"Forty-three."

"Aw, you still got time, girl!" Mrs. Winchester puts her hand on Ardie's forearm, squeezes. "Some man'll scoop you up one day, will be happy to have a woman who can change her own tires. Some man, or…" A troubled look crosses Mrs. Winchester's face for a moment, but it passes quickly. "Or I don't know what. I'm an old lady, Ardie. I can't keep up with the changing times. Perfectly handsome young men with other men, women having surgery to become men… I don't know, it's all jus' too much for me."

"Yes, ma'am, I s'pose it *is* a lot to keep up with," Ardie agrees. "Anyway," she says, stepping behind the counter and logging into the computer, "what can I do for you today? You still driving that same old Buick?"

Mrs. Winchester cackles. "It still runs, don't it? As long as it still runs, I'll still drive it."

#

Jim makes the rare decision to go home for lunch an hour later, joining his wife, perhaps rewarding her for returning the thirty-percent-off shoes, which means that Ardie's on her own for lunch. She walks up the block, taking the tuna sandwich and bag of potato chips she brought with her to a bench on the edge of the old graveyard near the center of town.

She's brought a paperback with her, and she finds she doesn't miss Jim's company, is glad to have thirty quiet minutes to herself to read. But the paperback stays sitting next to her while she eats her sandwich. She gazes up the street towards the Main Street shops. Linda's is doing a brisk business today; all the spaces in front of the restaurant are full. Georgie's is next to it, but they seem to be slower. Lucinda's Pontiac is gone, which makes Ardie wonder if she's in the habit of going home for lunch. Maybe she could join her for lunch one day.

I need to just do it, she tells herself with a bit of disgust. *What's the worst that can happen? She says no. That's the worst that can happen.*

Mrs. Winchester's words ring in her ears: *"You still got time, girl!"*

Time.

Time's a funny thing. It goes by too fast when you want to stop and savor something; it comes to an absolute standstill when you're waiting.

The last two years being back in Reverie, time's practically stood still for Ardie. Each day has been the same, with nothing coming to be anxious about and nothing coming to be excited about. It's almost like these past two years have been a sort of purgatory, a weigh station where she sits and waits but doesn't know what she's waiting for.

For life to begin again, maybe.

She sighs, picks up her phone. She thumbs through the contacts until she finds Lucinda's name. Hesitates a moment longer, calls.

The phone rings three times without an answer. On the fourth ring, Ardie thinks about just hanging up and forgetting about it; on the fifth ring, she decides she'll leave a message.

"Hey, Lucinda, it's Ardie. Listen, uh, I was wondering if — I mean, one of the reasons I came by today, besides the haircut, I was wondering if you might want to go to dinner with me one night this week. Any night you're free. I'm flexible. I don't know if you've been to the Italian place in Manning, but it's actually not half bad and… well, anyway, if you think you might have a free night, let me know. Um, yeah. I think you've got my number — or, actually, if you don't have my number, it's eight-six-four —"

But the voicemail beeps, and the phone call ends.

Ardie looks at the phone, wonders if her message was really recorded, wonders if she should call back and leave her number just in case. But then she remembers that she doesn't need to do that; her number will show up on the recent calls list anyway. And Lucinda has it already — doesn't she? Didn't they exchange numbers back when Ardie was fixing up the duplex?

Not that Lucinda has ever called, but yes. She's got it.

Chapter 24

The afternoon goes by without a return phone call or text message from Lucinda. Ardie thinks she hears her phone ring once, over the sound of the winch in the shop, but it turns out to be Jim's. She arrives home tired and demoralized. She'd had some nice moments with Lucinda, but she must've read everything all wrong. That first time she went by with her mother's peach pie, and they'd waltzed in Lucinda's yard…

Well, it had seemed like maybe something was there. But it won't be the first time that Ardie's been wrong about a woman's interest. Lord knows that's right.

She should probably just leave Lucinda Hamilton well enough alone.

"Hey, sweet pea," her mother says when she comes in and kicks her work boots off.

"Hey, mama." Ardie walks into the living room, where her mother's watching the evening news in her easy chair, drops a kiss onto the woman's forehead.

"How was the shop?"

"Good. Daddy never came in, though." Ardie plops down on the couch adjacent to the easy chair, stretching out her legs and rubbing her arm, the arm that was hit by shrapnel in Iraq in 2003. It still bothers her sometimes, usually at the end of a particularly long day.

"I know," her mother says. "He wasn't feeling good today." She lowers her voice conspiratorially. "I keep telling him he needs to go to the doctor and get his blood pressure medication adjusted, but you know your daddy and doctors."

Ardie nods and decides to change the subject before her mother gets going on a rant about her father. "What's the news have to say?"

"Oh, the same old. Police in Sumter's looking for a man who's been holding up convenience stores. A woman in Florence let her child fall into a pool and drown." She shakes her head sadly. "Folks these days, Ardie. Just not the same as when I was coming up. Oh," she adds, eyes lighting up as she uses the remote to point at the TV. "And they're talkin' 'bout a hurricane coming our way." She turns up the volume just as the well-groomed weatherman points at an imperfect circle of orange and purple on the satellite map.

"And we're keeping an eye on Hurricane Amber, first Atlantic hurricane of the season. She's a category three right now, with sustained winds of one hundred twenty-eight miles per hour — almost a category four." A map of the hurricane's projected path comes onto the screen, with the meteorologist pointing at the Georgia coastline. *"Right now, Amber's projected to make landfall somewhere around Savannah, but it's still too early to make any firm predictions. There's certainly a chance she could turn to*

the north and land closer to Charleston. We'll be keeping an eye on her, and we'll certainly update you as she gets closer to land. Back to you, Jeff and Rita."

Jeff and Rita look appropriately concerned over the news of the hurricane.

"That's a dangerous looking storm," Jeff says. *"Certainly brings back memories of Hurricane Hugo coming through our state back in 1989, doesn't it?"*

Rita nods and says something else, but Ardie's mother talks over her.

"You remember Hugo, don't you?"

"How could I forget?" Ardie says. "We were without power for almost three weeks. And still hauling fallen trees for another month or two after that."

Located halfway between Charleston and Sumter, Reverie had gotten walloped by Hugo. Parts of the town never recovered. And the already small population shrank further after the storm; hundreds of people who lost their homes and trailers left and simply never came back again.

"I thought we were all gonna die that night," Ardie's mother says dramatically while a pharmaceutical commercial plays in the background. "D'you remember? I *told* your father we should evacuate. But that stubborn old mule wasn't having any of it."

"I remember," Ardie says. They talk a while longer about Hurricane Hugo — it's strange to think it's been almost thirty years already since the massive storm hit — and eventually Ardie excuses herself to her room for the evening, pulling her phone from her pocket as she goes.

No texts, no missed calls. Not from Lucinda and not from anyone else.

#

A week goes by in dull routine; as usual, Ardie ends up spending more time with ignitions and fan belts, alternators and radiators, than she does with any human companions.

There's finally a text message from Lucinda, the Tuesday before Ardie's scheduled to go in and get her haircut.

I'll have to check my schedule.

is all it says. It makes Ardie raise an eyebrow, because as far as she knows, Lucinda doesn't have much of a schedule to check. She works a light schedule at Georgie's; she lives by herself. She says she spends time with the girl living in the other half of the duplex, but Ardie's never seen any evidence of anyone else living there. Every time she's been to Lucinda's place, the other half of the duplex has been dark, the door's been closed and the windows have been shuttered, and all Lucinda's been doing is puttering around in that dry mess of earth she calls a garden.

But who knows. Maybe there are things going on in Lucinda's life that Ardie doesn't know about.

#

"Ardie? Why are you calling?" Sandra says by way of greeting.

Ardie bristles. "Well, hello to you, too."

"I'm sorry," Sandra says, even though it's obvious that she's not. "I was just surprised to see your name on my caller ID, that's all."

"You been doing okay?"

"I have been."

"And Omar?" Ardie asks, doing her best to keep her tone neutral and not as needy as she feels for that obnoxious cat.

"As terrible as ever," Sandra says, her voice softening. "So… what can I do for you?"

"I'm calling about my stuff," Ardie says. "Do you still have it?"

There's a moment of silence on the other end of the line. "It's been two years, Ardie. I kept all your things for a while, but you never called, you never emailed, you never asked for anything back, so I — "

There's a noise in the background, a voice, Ardie thinks. A woman's voice.

"Hold on a second," Sandra says. "…Yes," she says to the other voice. Sweetening her tone, she says, "I didn't, but I did take the garbage out. Mmm-hmm." Sandra chuckles. "Alright… Lemme just get off the phone and… Ardie. Yes, *that* Ardie… Okay." The other voice fades.

"Ardie? You still there?"

So. Sandra's apparently seeing someone new. That's good, Ardie supposes. She hopes they're happy. Then, more cynically, she wonders: How long did it take for Sandra to get her hooks into her next hapless victim?

"Yeah. I'm still here," she says.

"You were asking about all the things you left here?"

"I was."

"You left *a lot* of stuff," Sandra says. "I sold some of it. Donated most of your clothes."

"What about my handguns? And my dress blues?"

"You left your guns here?" Sandra asks. "I don't remember seeing them."

"They were in a locked box at the top of the hall closet," Ardie says. She's not really surprised Sandra hasn't found them; Sandy's not much of a cleaner, and the hall closet was always Ardie's closet — the one corner of storage space that Sandra afforded her. "I'll pay for you to ship them. And the insurance, too. What about the dress blues?"

"Hold on," Sandra says. "Let me go look in the closet and see if they're in there — oh, your uniforms *are* in here." Something shuffles and clangs. "God, how long has it been since I've cleaned this closet out?"

"I'd like those, too."

"The uniforms? Why? You've been retired for years now."

"Because I do," Ardie says, struggling to keep the

impatience from her voice.

Ardie hears something being dragged across the hardwood floor.

"The box — is it a metal box with a combination on the front?"

"That's it."

Ardie hears more scraping on the other end of the line; metal on metal this time.

"Ugh, it's heavy," Sandra complains. "This is probably going to cost a *fortune* to ship."

"I'll send you a check tomorrow," Ardie says. "I'll send plenty. All the rest of my stuff... well, sounds like you've already turned a profit off of some of it. You can keep it."

"You left in the middle of the night and didn't take anything with you," Sandra says, defensive. "Don't get mad at *me* just because I didn't want all your random crap cluttering up the house."

Ardie snorts. *That's* ironic. *Ardie's* things were cluttering up the house? Ardie's clean and owns very little — a minimalist. *Sandra's* the one who's the packrat. The woman never throws anything away. She's practically a hoarder.

But all she says is, "I understand. I just want the guns and my uniform. I'll send you a check tomorrow."

"I might not have time to send it this week," Sandra warns.

"Fine. Just send it when you can, okay?"

"I will."

"Thanks. And, uh, tell Omar her mama loves her."

"Whatever," Sandra says, and the line goes dead.

Ardie takes the phone from her ear, looks at it, not understanding at first that she's been hung up on. When she realizes she has been, she rolls her eyes and slides her phone back into her pocket.

And Sandra was surprised when Ardie left her?

She feels an urge to tune up her bike coming on. Everyone else can make fun of her bike all they want, but for Ardie, pouring her love into the old scrap heap is the only therapy that's ever really worked for her.

At least she gets to see Lucinda for the haircut. Maybe she'll be able to find out why she's been getting the cold shoulder lately. Maybe — she probably shouldn't get her hopes up, but she does anyway — maybe Lucinda will have checked her schedule, and they'll set up a time to do dinner.

Chapter 25

The bell jingles above Georgie's door as Ardie steps inside. It's Thursday, early afternoon, and she's been working all morning. She did her best to scrub the black streaks of motor oil off her hands and even used the nail brush to get the gunk out from underneath her fingernails. She has a smudge on her left cheek, though, and she only catches it when the glass door to the salon reflects it back to her.

She turns back around as soon as the door closes, embarrassed by the mark, angling in the doorway, trying to see her reflection and not the sun streaming in from the endless, cloudless summer sky outside. She's not completely sure she's gotten it all, but there's another customer coming in, so she hops back to get out of the way of the radius of the opening door.

She counts two stylists in the shop today. Kylah, the girl in her twenties who moved here from Greenville a couple years ago, and Rhonda, the stout black woman who only ever scowls at Ardie.

The stylist she doesn't see is Lucinda.

"She ain't here," Rhonda says when she sees Ardie looking around.

Ardie starts to quip sarcastically, *I can see that,* but

stops herself in time.

"I had an appointment with her at one?" she says instead.

"When she went home from lunch, she said she wasn't feeling good," Rhonda says. "She hasn't been feelin' good in general these last couple weeks."

"I know *that's* right," Kylah says without turning around.

"What's been wrong with her?" Ardie asks.

"Dunno," Kylah says, answering before Rhonda can. "She don't never talk about herself, so it's hard to tell with her. But she been *extra* quiet these last couple weeks. This is the first time she's canceled any appointments, though."

"Did she... am I canceled?" As much as Ardie has been looking forward to seeing Lucinda — or perhaps *because* she's been looking forward to seeing Lucinda — Ardie can't help but feel a little bit annoyed at the lack of advanced notice. "She didn't call me to cancel."

"Mmm," Rhonda says, pursing her lips.

Ardie stands there for a moment, uncertain about what to do. Finally, she heaves a sigh, shoulders slumping. "Well. I s'pose I may as well get on back to the shop." She turns towards the door to go.

"Ardith, hang on a sec," Rhonda says just as the bell above the door jingles again.

Ardie turns, hand still on the door.

"I got an opening this afternoon 'round three if you wanna come by then," Rhonda says. She crosses her arms against her chest, pops a hip out to the side, like Ardie was the one to make the suggestion and Rhonda's irritated about it.

It probably does *irritate her,* Ardie thinks.

Rhonda sighs. "I don't know if you wanted to wait specifically for Lucinda or not, but if you still wanna get your hair done today…"

Ardie nods. "Alright. I can come back at three. Thanks."

"Mmm-hmm," Rhonda says, but her attention is already off Ardie and back on the head of her client.

#

A couple hours later, Ardie is back and settling into the salon chair, lifting her chin as Rhonda sweeps the smock across her chest. Ardie's hair is still damp from the wash Rhonda just gave her — a completely silent wash, followed by a completely silent toweling off, ending with a completely silent trip back to the chair.

Ardie's always gotten the feeling that Rhonda doesn't like her very much, though she doesn't know exactly why. She can't remember ever crossing the woman, and she wonders as the smock snaps tightly around her neck if Rhonda's like this with everyone, or just her. It seems like just her. Because Ardie's come to Georgie's to get her hair cut since she moved back to Reverie two years ago, and the whole time that Kathy's been cutting her hair, Rhonda has hardly ever even so much as looked at Ardie, and until today, she never, ever talked to her. And that's despite the fact that Ardie's heard Rhonda chatter away about her sons, her husband, her church, her witchdoctor grandmother to just about anyone who will listen.

Which is why Ardie was surprised — shocked, even — that Rhonda offered to cut her hair at all.

Now, sitting in Rhonda's chair while the hairdresser combs and pins Ardie's hair out of the way, Ardie wonders if Rhonda finally talking to her was just a fluke, and now the whole haircut will go by in stony silence.

"So… how's your son?" Ardie ventures, eye catching on the wallet-sized photo of the handsome young man in a Reverie Rebels uniform taped to the bottom corner of Rhonda's mirror. It's a little odd to see a young African American man in the confederate grey jersey and leggings of the Reverie Rebels, but, well, that's Reverie for you. The school's integrated. The mascot isn't.

"Good."

Snip, snip, snip.

"He's on the football team, right?"

"Mmm-hmm," Rhonda says, and it seems like she won't say anything else, but then adds, almost reluctantly, "That's my older son, Brandt, in the high school uniform you're looking at. My younger boy, Michael, he doesn't like football. He's bookish. Much to his father's dismay."

Ardie smiles, feeling a connection with Michael immediately. A bookish young man in Reverie isn't all that different from a young woman who prefers fixing motorcycles to fixing her makeup.

Rhonda falls silent again. Ardie wracks her brain to think of something else to ask.

"What kinds of books does he like? Your younger son? I go through a lot of paperbacks, if he'd ever like any of my books."

"I doubt he reads what you do," Rhonda says curtly. A few seconds and a few scissor snips later, she adds, "When he bothers to pick up a chapter book instead of a comic book, it's usually some kind of fairy tale nonsense. He's already read all them *Harry Potter* books *twice.*"

Ardie chuckles. "Sounds like my kinda kid. I like *Harry Potter*. They're good books."

"Mmm," Rhonda says. Unimpressed.

Snip, snip, snip. A couple more minutes pass. Ardie thinks about how today was going to be the day she would try to pin Lucinda down for a dinner date.

Another minute passes as Ardie hesitates, debating whether or not to ask the question that's on her mind.

"About Lucinda," she says at last. "Do you think… is there something actually wrong with her — I mean, do you think she's sick? Or do you think she just wanted the afternoon off?"

Rhonda pauses, glances at Ardie briefly in the mirror before refocusing on Ardie's hair. "Oh, I think she's sick, alright." Rhonda lowers her voice, sliding her words in under the sound of the hairdryer on the other side of the room and Kylah's laughter, so that no one can hear them but Ardie. "But if you ask me, what's wrong with Lucinda Hamilton *isn't* gonna be fixed with a regular doctor."

Ardie doesn't understand. "What do you mean?"

Rhonda doesn't say anything for a minute, tips Ardie's head forward, combs the hair around her ears. She takes so long to respond that for a moment, Ardie thinks she's going to ignore the question altogether.

"How well you know Lucinda?" Rhonda asks at last.

"I don't know. A little, I s'pose. I mean, she's only been in Reverie for — what, two months now? Three? I've gone by her place a couple times before. Done some work on her house, since we all know Zeke Brinkmann isn't going to lift a finger to fix anything. We've spent a bit of time together. Had some nice conversations."

"Mmm," Rhonda says. "You ever know Lucinda to talk to herself?"

The question catches Ardie off-guard, and it takes her a second to recover before she says, "No. I haven't."

Ardie puzzles over Rhonda's question, contemplates how little she actually knows about Lucinda. She thinks back to the time she was at Lucinda's house, how she'd picked up the framed snapshot of Lucinda being hugged by the beautiful young woman. Lucinda's whole face had turned into a rigid mask of fear when Ardie asked about that photo, and it didn't escape Ardie that when Lucinda put it back on the table, it was face-down.

Ardie clears her throat. "I've never seen her talk to

herself, but… But I don't guess I've been around her enough to notice," she admits. "I don't guess many people around here have. Unless — you see her every day here, do you know her that well?"

"No. It's like Kylah said — she's quiet, most'a the time. And even quieter lately these last couple weeks."

Snip, snip, snip.

Ardie frowns in thought, wondering why they're talking about Lucinda at all, wondering why Rhonda is asking her these questions. "Why'd you ask me that? If I'd ever seen her talk to herself?"

Rhonda's scissors pause for just a moment, hovering over Ardie's head. "It's probably nothin.'"

"What's nothing?"

"Nothin.' Nothin's nothin.'"

"*Rhonda.* You can't just ask a question like that and then not explain why you're asking."

"Lean forward," Rhonda says, and Ardie does. A brush whisks across the back of her neck, over her ears, across her throat. It smells pleasantly of talc. Rhonda unbuttons the smock and pulls it off Ardie.

"What'd Lucinda charge you, last time you were here?"

"I can't remember," Ardie says. Her head is still spinning, and she's having trouble forgetting Rhonda's question, or ignoring the fact that Rhonda hasn't bothered to explain. "Eighteen or twenty or something."

"Mmm. Eighteen. Man's-style trim," Rhonda says with a sniff.

Ardie hands her twenty-five. "Keep the extra."

Rhonda takes the cash, but Ardie continues to stand there for a few moments longer, still disoriented by the incomplete conversation. It's not until Rhonda picks up the push broom that Ardie decides she's not going to get any answers to her questions. She sighs, feeling defeated. Nothing left for her to do but head back to the shop.

But she hasn't made it more than a few steps from Georgie's when she hears the bell above the door tinkle again.

"Ardith?" Rhonda calls.

Ardie turns around. "Yeah?"

Rhonda jogs a few steps towards her. Putting a hand on Ardie's elbow, she says, "Keep walking. We don't want to be in earshot of Georgie's or Linda's."

More confused than ever, but sure that this must be about Lucinda, Ardie obeys Rhonda's instructions, and the two of them march past the retirees taking up the patio furniture in front of Linda's and round the corner. The cross-street is empty, just a mangy stray dog and a dumpster that smells of fried chicken.

Rhonda looks left, looks right. Faces Ardie. "I'm worried 'bout Lucinda."

Ardie waits. "Go on," she prompts after a moment.

"Coupla weeks ago, I came by the shop after church because I'd left my cell phone here," Rhonda says. "I saw Lucinda walking through the graveyard down yonder" — she points across the street — "carrying on a conversation, happy as you please, with nobody who could be seen."

Ardie shrugs. "So? She was probably on the phone. You know how that is these days — everybody with their devices in their ears. Half the time, *everybody* looks like they're talking to themselves."

Rhonda shakes her head vigorously. "That's what I assumed at first. Then I looked again. And Ardith, I promise you she was *not* on the phone. Since then, I've seen her in town talkin' away with nobody who could be seen two more times."

"So you think she was… are you saying you think Lucinda has a mental problem? Even if she does, I don't know that it's any of your business. Or mine."

Rhonda puts a hand over her opposite wrist, fingering the glass beads of a rosary there that's interspersed with small shells. She gets a far-away look on her face.

"No, if Lucinda only had a mental problem, I'd be talkin' to Aggie Anderson instead'a you," she says at last. "I wish I thought Lucinda just had a mental problem. But I don't think that. I don't think that at all."

Ardie's brow crinkles in confusion. "If she's not talking to herself, or to… I don't know, hallucinations, and she's not talking on the phone… What exactly are you trying to say? And why are you telling *me?*"

Rhonda's face puckers into a disapproving frown. "You listen to me, Ardith. I don't approve of your… *lifestyle,* or sexual *preference,* or orientation, or whatever they're calling it these days. The Bible is perfectly clear that it's a sin."

"The Bible's perfectly clear that eating shellfish is a sin, too," Ardie grumbles. Her face is red with a combination of embarrassment and mounting irritation with this strange conversation.

Rhonda waves her hand in a *that's not the point* gesture. "Some laws of God can be interpreted. Others cannot."

"That's awfully convenient for — "

"I'm not here to talk about your lesbianism," Rhonda snaps.

You're the one who brought it up, Ardie wants to say, but she bites her tongue.

"I'm here because I've grown to care about Lucinda. As I know you have. And because I think she's…" Rhonda looks down, shakes her head with a sigh. "I think she shares the same sin that you do. It's not lost on me how she looks at you."

Ardie's blush grows hotter, but for an entirely different reason.

"I have reason to believe that, if anyone in this town can help Lucinda — if anyone can be her friend, and protect her — it's probably you," Rhonda says, ignoring Ardie's beet-red face. She lowers her voice, despite the fact that there's no one around to overhear them. "Ardith, I come from a long line of people who have a deeper sense for God's mysteries. A long line of people who can feel the presence of spirits — both good and bad. I *wish* Lucinda was just talkin' to herself. I do. But I don't think she is —

Lord have mercy, I *know* she's not. Do you understand what I'm sayin' to you?"

Ardie narrows her eyes. "No. I'm not sure that I do. Are you saying that Lucinda's talking to a… spirit?"

"Yes," Rhonda says, her voice barely above a whisper. "That is *exactly* what I'm saying."

Ardie scoffs, shakes her head. "Now *that's* crazy. I'm sorry, I want to respect your beliefs, Rhonda, but… I don't believe in 'spirits' anymore than I believe in your Holy Spirit. If you really did see Lucinda talking to herself, then she might need help — as in, professional help. Psychiatric help. You should talk to Dan and Aggie."

Rhonda shakes her head. "Aggie came in to get Lucinda to dye her roots the other day. I could tell just from lookin' at her she didn't know a *thing* was wrong."

"Well, you sure seem to know a lot about everybody just from lookin', don't you?" Ardie says sarcastically.

"Don't you smart-mouth me, Ardith Brown. You don't know the things I've seen, the things I know that most people don't."

"And apparently you don't know the things that I know, the things that I've seen," Ardie says, temper starting to flare. She hears the phantom whistling of mortar shells, the phantom sounds of explosions, the phantom rain of sand and dirt as someone yells *"Take cover!"*

Ardie shivers, squeezes her eyes shut for a moment before opening them again. She pushes back at the ghosts of her PTSD, ghosts that haven't made themselves known in daylight hours for a couple of years. It's clear this conversation is pushing her buttons in all the wrong ways.

Rhonda arches one eyebrow. "I don't know what you've seen? Like how I don't know about mortar shells exploding in the desert? Like how I don't know about Lucas?"

"What?" Ardie says, stunned.

"You heard me. Mortar shells, and the smell of blood, and — " The hand that's been fondling the beads around her wrist snakes out, grabs Ardie's forearm. Rhonda pulls it towards her and rotates it. "That's what this is, isn't it?" She taps one well-manicured nail on a crescent-shaped white scar. "A shrapnel scar?"

Ardie yanks her arm back. "How did you… Who've you been talking to?"

"Like I said," Rhonda says calmly. "You don't know the things I know that most people don't. And I am *telling* you that *you* need to help Lucinda. The more I hold it here" — she taps on her chest — "the more I'm sure. It *has* to be you."

"How do you… Why's it have to be me?"

"Spirits prey on us when we are weak," Rhonda says matter-of-factly, as if she's still sitting in the salon, discussing hair coloring techniques instead of the supernatural. "They prey on us when we're weak and when we're alone. And you know as well as I do — as well as anyone in this town with two working eyes — that Lucinda is both of those things right now. You can make her strong. You can make sure she's not alone. If she's going to open up about what's happening to her to anyone, it's going to be you."

"I can't help Lucinda," Ardie says. "She won't even…"

She stops herself. Wipes her hand down her face and grunts in frustration. Why is she even humoring this nonsense? Rhonda's nothing more than a superstitious woman who probably witnessed Lucinda reciting her grocery list to herself.

"She ain't ignoring you 'cause she don't have any feelings for you, Ardith. She's ignoring you because the spirit's stopping her. The spirit *knows* you're a threat."

"That's crazy," Ardie mutters. But a chill runs up her spine nonetheless. She shakes her head. "I need to get back to the shop, Rhonda. Thanks for the haircut."

"You know I'm right," Rhonda says as Ardie turns to walk away.

"Whatever you say," Ardie calls over her shoulder.

"Don't wait too long," Rhonda calls. "Lucinda needs you. And something tells me time is running out."

Chapter 26

In her dreams, Ardie sees what happened to Lucas Koch as if it were her own memory, as if she was the one who'd gone out on patrol that day.

He isn't a part of the rest of the platoon — that's the first thing that Lucas realizes about himself when he gets deployed to the lonesome base in Afghanistan a few clicks outside Kabul. As a dog handler, the nineteen year-old farm kid from southern Nebraska isn't a part of their brotherhood; he's a late addition, the new handler to replace the handler who'd gotten himself and his dog blown up beyond the wire a couple months before he arrived.

It's probably his outsider status that leads Lucas to bond with Staff Sergeant Ardie Brown, the mechanic who's an outsider herself. Yeah, whatever, she's the staff sergeant, the oldest and highest-ranking enlisted officer amongst the mechanics, but hell, she's still a woman — one of only, like, a dozen women on the whole base. And besides being a woman, she's clearly a *dyke*. This is November 2011, and Don't Ask, Don't Tell was repealed a few months before, but still, nobody really asks and nobody really tells.

Being a big ol' grease monkey dyke means that the handful of other women on base *respect* the sergeant, but it's not like they *include* her. She doesn't get to join in any reindeer games.

Which makes her a lot like Lucas, the mouthy farm kid whose only real friend on base is his dog.

Lucas can't remember exactly when he and Staff Sergeant Brown start buddying around together, swapping sci-fi novels and busting each others' chops. But by March, three months into his deployment, she's calling him Shrimp and he's calling her Sarge — much to her chagrin, because that's a big no-no in the Marines. It doesn't bother *him* to be called Shrimp. He's gotten called that, in one form or another, all his life. Five-five was good enough to get him into the service (barely), but shit, it's not like most IEDs are at the top of a goddamned basketball pole, right? He doesn't need to be Shaquille O'Neal to find them; they're on the fucking *ground* — buried in the road, planted in a pile of rubble, stuck to the side of some claptrap farmer's cart. He doesn't need to be tall to find what's under his fucking feet.

Lucas bets Sarge secretly wishes she was as small as he is. He bets her freakishly mannish sausage fingers get in her own way when she's trying to fix shit. But she's a good mechanic — the best. That's what everybody says. Lucas wants everyone to say the same thing about him:

"That Koch kid? He's the best goddamned dog-handler this base has seen in three deployments."

The first time Lucas gets a find in the field, it's Sarge he's running to first, Greco the bomb-sniffing dog loping alongside him, his long pink tongue lolling out of his mouth, every bit as pleased with himself as his handler is.

"We got one, we got one!" Lucas calls out. All he can see is Staff Sergeant Brown's boots sticking out from under the Humvee she's working on, but boots are enough to know it's her. She rolls out and sits up, gives him a lopsided grin and a fist bump.

"Well done, Shrimp. We had our doubts, but I guess the military managed to make something of you, after all," is what she says, but Lucas can see in her face that she's proud of him. Proud almost like a mother. Or at least — who the fuck knows — proud like a big gay aunt or something.

The day he gets blown to bits, Sarge acts like she doesn't want him to go out on patrol. She's squinting up into the sun right before he leaves, hands on her hips. It's motherfucking a hundred degrees already and it's not even nine in the morning, and she says to him,

"Just be careful. I've got a bad feeling about today. Something — I don't know. Call it a woman's intuition."

"Woman's intuition? They let you have that?" Lucas says with a snicker. He wraps Greco's leash around his fist. "But anyway, don't worry about us. We're careful. We're always careful."

She looks away from the sun, gazes down at him, searches his face in a way that gives him the fucking willies. Searches his face like she's trying to memorize it because she's never gonna see it again. He hates that shit, that "woman's intuition" or whatever the fuck it is she gets sometimes. He hates it, but he trusts it, because she's usually right when she gets "a feeling" about something. And so he *will* be extra careful today.

Emotion runs through the leash.

They beat that into your head in handling training. What you feel, the dog feels. What the dog feels, you feel. If Lucas starts getting anxious now, it's not just going to fuck with *his* head, it's going to fuck with Greco's head, too. And he wants Greco's head to be on straight. If it's not, well… that'll fuck both of them up real good.

An hour later, he and Greco are picking their way through a dry riverbed. He can feel the sweat trickling down the back of his neck, between his shoulder blades, into the small of his back. It's been two hours already; they haven't found anything. He pauses, glances over his shoulder. The rest of the unit is following behind him, relying on him and Greco to find a safe route through. He takes a sip of water, steps forward again, hears Greco whine.

And it's the last sound Specialist Lucas Koch ever hears before the IED he stepped on goes off.

#

Ardie wakes up at the same point in the nightmare she always wakes at — the explosion. The sounds of men screaming and the concussive blast of the bomb.

Something all the war movies in the world can't

prepare you for is the feeling of the blast itself ripping through space, like the very air around you has barreled into you, knocking you flat and stealing your breath. It's strange for something invisible to be so powerful.

Ardie sits up gasping, covered in a light sheen of sweat, reaches for the bottle of water on her bedside table.

Shrimp.

She'd known that day, hadn't she? Something about the taste of the high desert air in the morning. Something about the unforgiving sun and the way it baked her skin. She'd seen Lucas gearing up to go out, and her stomach just *dropped,* a black hole forming there from nowhere the moment she'd looked at him.

She'd *known.*

But that was impossible. You can't "know" someone's going to get themselves and their dog blown up on a patrol. What if...

She takes a sip of water, recaps it.

Emotion runs through the leash.

Lucas used to say that when he talked to Ardie about what it was like to be out there, him and Greco walking point, another couple dozen men putting their lives in his hands behind them. *Emotion runs through the leash.*

What if Ardie hadn't *sensed* what was going to happen that day; what if she'd *caused* what was going to happen? In her dreams, she passed the anxiety she'd felt to Lucas as easily as passing a beer or a book or a pack of cigarettes. And he'd taken that anxiety, and maybe he passed it to

Greco. And maybe Greco…

Ardie shakes her head at herself. No point. There's no point going down that rabbit hole again, that steep shell crater of survivor's guilt. Lucas was high-strung and reckless, eager to prove himself and always over-confident in his own and his dog's abilities.

What happened, happened. And going back over it now —

"Like how I don't know about Lucas?"

Rhonda *knows*. Somehow, she knows, too. She knows about Ardie's weird intuition that morning, she knows about the survivor's guilt, she knows about how Ardie has to keep her hands busy to keep her mind quiet.

"No, she doesn't," Ardie says out-loud to herself in the dark bedroom. "If she knows anything, it's because she's been talking to people. It's a small town. People talk. And…"

Ardie trails off, realizing that now *she's* the one talking to herself, albeit in the privacy of her own midnight bedroom.

Maybe the *spirits* are after her. They prey on us when we're alone and weak.

She laughs out-loud and puts the bottle of water back on the nightstand, lying back down.

"Go to sleep, Ardie," she tells herself. She figures that if she's gonna start talking to herself, she may as well give herself some useful advice.

#

Despite laughing it off in the middle of the night, Ardie wakes up troubled when the alarm goes off at six. Too many bad dreams swimming together with too many disturbing thoughts. Thoughts about Lucas. About Rhonda.

About Lucinda.

"Morning," she says to her mother as she wanders into the kitchen to pour a cup of coffee.

Her mother, eternally the household's earliest riser, is already sitting in her easy chair, watching the morning news.

"Hey there, sweet pea," her mom answers.

Ardie walks over in her undershirt and boxers, coffee mug in hand, and kisses her mother's forehead.

"What's the news got to say for itself this morning?"

"They caught that man in Florence who's been holding up all them convenience stores."

"That's good," Ardie says, blowing on her coffee before taking a sip.

"Your dad's not feeling right again this morning," her mother says. "Asked me to ask you to open up without him today. Says he'll be in after lunch if he gets to feelin' better."

"Alright," Ardie says.

Truth is, she doesn't really mind. With her dad's memory what it is these days, she sometimes finds herself going back and fixing his mistakes, anyway. It's not just the cars, either; she once discovered an invoice where her father had charged almost four hundred dollars less than what the work was worth. Luckily, she'd caught it and fixed it before the customer picked up their car, but Ardie wonders how many times it happens when she's not around to catch it. Ardie and her mother have both encouraged Daddy to retire and let management of the shop fall into Ardie's hands, but he's not ready to let go. Ardie can understand that, so she doesn't push.

"Oh — the weather's coming on," her mother says, pointing the remote at the screen and jabbing the plus sign on the volume control.

"She's been meandering around in the Atlantic the last few days," the weather man says, *"but now it looks like Hurricane Amber is swinging back towards the East Coast — and she's taking aim directly at our state."* A model of projected hurricane paths pops up, with a half-dozen spaghetti-like lines drawn from the blob of color in the ocean to the coast of South Carolina. *"You can see here the different paths she's forecasted to take, and all but a couple of them have her making landfall in South Carolina late next week. Now, so far, the governor has not issued a mandatory evacuation order for coastal South Carolina, but I know lots of residents are evacuating on their own anyway. At the moment, this storm's still a category three, but plenty can happen between now and next Thursday. Even if it doesn't hit us next weekend..."*

"Hear that? Sounds like Anna's gonna hit us," says Ardie's mom as the morning weather guy gives the weekend forecast.

"Amber," Ardie corrects automatically.

"Anna, Amber, whatever," her mother says. "One way or another, she's a big ol' girl, and she's headed our way."

Her mom sounds practically excited about the prospect of a horrific storm ripping through the low-country — something that Ardie can almost understand. Ever since the stroke that left her partially paralyzed on the left side three years ago, her mother's world has narrowed to her easy chair, her living room, and her kitchen. Now that Ardie's living at home, she hardly even leaves the house to go grocery shopping anymore. An impending hurricane is more excitement than she usually has a chance to see.

Ardie sips from her coffee. "Mmm," she says noncommittally, because they always predict big storms like this, but they rarely amount to anything. She half-listens to the weather report, and meanwhile she focuses on her more immediate concern — the checklist of things she'll need to do at the shop on her own today if her dad decides not to come in.

"Maybe we oughtta close Daddy's shop and take a weekend trip to Asheville," her mother says.

"Maybe," Ardie says. "But the storm might not hit us. And it's only a category three. This far in from the coast, we should be fine."

"You heard what the man said. She could strengthen.

Anything could happen between now and the end of the week."

"Exactly. Anything could happen, including it turning back out to sea," Ardie says. She walks into the kitchen, pours the last third of her coffee cup into the sink and rinses the mug out before putting it upside-down in the rack to dry. "I should get going, Mom."

"You and your father." Her mother's gotten up from the easy chair, shuffled the few yards to stand at the edge of the kitchen. "You'd think that the military woulda taught both y'all something about preparedness. Instead you're a coupla stubborn old mules who never take anyone's warning seriously unless it's your own."

Ardie smirks. "Storm'll probably give us a good hard rain," she says. "Some wind. Maybe a couple trees down in the yard. Nothing more. Not if it's just a cat-three or a cat-two when it hits the coast."

"It might work its way up to a category four. Or worse."

"Then we can cross that bridge when we come to it."

"Ya oughtta at least put some sand bags along the back end of the lot at the shop," her mother says. "You know how Miller's Creek tends to flood when it rains too much, even just an ordinary thunderstorm. And the shop's right up against the flood plain."

Ardie pauses, thinking for a moment. Miller's Creek *has* overflowed its banks before during big storms, and it's not unheard of for the downhill side of Reverie's Main

Street to flood. Including her father's shop. "Hmm. You make a good point."

Her mother grins. "See that? I get a good idea in me every now and again."

"You know if we've got any sacks to make sandbags?"

"Ask your father. I think there's some at the shop from the last time we had a hurricane predicted."

#

Ardie makes it to the shop just after seven-thirty, where a ragged looking Jim is sipping coffee in a folding chair in a garage, his feet propped on a tool chest in front of him. Tinny country music plays from the beat-up shop radio on the shelf behind him.

"Did ya hear?" are the first words out of his mouth when he sees Ardie.

"Hear what?"

"The hurricane. They're sayin' it's a category four now. And it's almost definitely comin' right on up towards us, through Charleston, then ripping right through the state."

"It's not a category four yet," Ardie says, getting tired of arguing with everyone about this stupid hurricane. You'd think they had nothing better to do than sit around talking about the weather. "They just said it *might* strengthen to a category four."

"Yes, it *is* a four," says Jim, his voice rising an octave. "That's what the man said just now!"

He points to the radio, as if "the man" must live somewhere within the confines of its circuit boards.

Ardie stops. "Are you messing with me? I was watching the news with my mama just fifteen minutes ago and they said it was still a three."

Jim grins triumphantly. "I shit you not, sister. This bitch is a four. And who knows, by the time it hits Charleston on Saturday, it could be a fucking *five.*"

"Fabulous," Ardie grumbles. "Hey, Jim. You know if we got any sacks leftover from Hurricane Matthew that we can use for sandbags?"

"Yup. Your daddy musta thought Matthew was gonna be the *rapture*. He prolly ordered a thousand of them sacks. I thought he'd done lost his damned mind."

"Good. Could you fish them out for me?"

Jim heaves a long-suffering sigh, unwinds his feet from the chair they're propped on, gradually stands with a grunt and a stretch. "Sure thing, Sarge."

Ardie walks around the garage, checking on the progress of the cars and trucks, making a mental to-do list for the day. There's a Civic getting picked up this morning that her father didn't quite finish the day before, along with a pickup truck whose radiator he was supposed to flush and drain but apparently didn't. And a jeep has been dropped off overnight, with the simple and rather unhelpful note *"Won't start"* wrapped around its key with a rubber band. Ardie sighs when she reads the note, balls it in her fist, and throws it in the nearest trash can.

But when she heads back into the office to unlock the front door, she's surprised to find someone waiting outside for her. And it's not the owner of the Civic, the pickup, or the jeep.

It's Lucinda.

Chapter 27

"Hey, Ardie," she says when Ardie opens the door. She's leaning back on the hood of her Pontiac, pocketbook held tightly across her stomach like it's shielding her from something.

"Well, hey there, Lu," Ardie says warmly, troubled thoughts quickly replaced by pleasant surprise. "Are you here about your car?"

"No," Lucinda says, straightening. "I'm here about your text. And about how I wasn't there yesterday for your appointment — sorry about that."

"It's okay," Ardie says, running her fingers through her hair self-consciously at the mention of the missed appointment. "Rhonda did an okay job, don't you think?"

"Rhonda?" Lucinda repeats, sounding surprised.

"Yeah. When you weren't there, she said she had an opening and could fit me in later in the afternoon."

"Oh." Lucinda takes a step forward, hesitates. "So about wanting to have dinner…"

"You got room for me on your busy social calendar?" Ardie asks with a wink.

"Lunch might actually be easier for me," Lucinda says, not meeting Ardie's eyes.

"Okay," Ardie says, swallowing her disappointment.

"Lunch is good. You wanna have lunch today? I could meet you up at Linda's around noon, if that works for you."

"I could, but... Before we make plans," Lucinda says, adjusting her pocketbook and finally looking Ardie square in the face, "there's something I have to tell you."

"Yeah?" Ardie asks, and she feels the uneasiness crawling up her spine. The "feeling" of something being wrong.

"I've started seeing someone," Lucinda says, the words coming out in a rush. "The girl who lives next door to me, as a matter of fact." She barks out a strained laugh. "Can you believe that? Didn't have to look any further than the other side of my duplex."

Ardie's uneasiness grows.

"So I want to have lunch with you," Lucinda continues. "I do. But you have to understand…" She reaches out, and a few of her fingertips fall lightly onto Ardie's forearm. "It's just going to be as friends. Okay?"

"Of course," Ardie says automatically, because what else is there to say but that? "Not a problem. Not a problem at all."

Lucinda nods, takes her hand off Ardie's arm.

"I hope I get to meet her sometime," Ardie says. "I'd like to see what kind of woman it is who sweeps Lucinda Hamilton off her feet."

An expression crosses Lucinda's face; it looks like a grimace.

"Maybe sometime," Lucinda says, and just like that,

Ardie's "feeling" comes back even stronger, coursing through her veins so suddenly and strongly that her skin practically vibrates with it. "So… I'll see you at noon? At Linda's?"

"Sure thing."

"I might be running a couple minutes late; I have a client at ten forty-five. So maybe we should make it twelve-fifteen. Does that work for you?"

"Absolutely," Ardie says. "Nice thing about being the boss is that I've got plenty of flexibility in my schedule."

"Alright, then," Lucinda says, smiling. "It's a date."

It's the smile that speaks to Ardie the most; the soft, beautiful smile is the reason she started to fall for Lucinda in the first place. When Lucinda smiles, it lights up her whole face, and it hints at something *more* to Lucinda than what most people ever have a chance to see. And Ardie really wants to see what more there is to this woman.

Ardie lifts a hand in a goodbye as Lucinda pulls out and turns up the road, headed for Georgie's. A lunch date today. Well, not a "date" so much as…

Before they meet for lunch, Ardie decides she wants to make a phone call. Her bad feeling is probably nothing. What Rhonda said to her is also probably nothing. But it never hurts to double-check, does it?

#

The phone rings twice before someone picks up, but

instead of a greeting, there's only the sound of fumbling and background noise.

"Hello?" Ardie says tentatively.

"Yeah?" says a gruff voice on the other end. "Who's this?"

"It's Ardie. Ardie Brown. Is this Zeke?"

"It is." A pause. "Who'd you say this is again?"

"Ardie Brown."

"Okay, right…" Zeke Brinkmann says uncertainly. "We went to high school together, right? Class of '91? Your daddy runs Brown Auto?"

"Yep, that's me," Ardie says.

"Somebody said you'd moved back to Reverie."

"Yep, I've been back a few years now," Ardie says. "Running Daddy's shop these days."

There's a hoarse coughing on the other end; Ardie pulls the phone a few inches away from her ear.

"So… what can I do for ya, Ardie?"

She clears her throat. "I have a question for you. And if it's — if you don't want to answer for confidentiality reasons or something, I'll understand."

"Yeah? What's the question?" Zeke asks cautiously. He probably thinks Ardie's going to ask him about something uncomfortable and potentially illegal, like the small marijuana operation he supposedly runs from his basement.

"I know you rented one of your duplexes to Lucinda Hamilton when she came to Reverie a couple months back."

There's a pause. "Yeah. I did."

"Is there anyone living in the other half of that duplex?"

"Nuh-uh. Just her." He lets out a short laugh. "I'm lucky I got even half it rented. Been standin' empty practically going on a year'n a half 'fore she came along."

"Is that right," Ardie says, a question that comes out as a statement. *Damn straight no one rented it for a year and a half,* is what she's thinking. The place is falling apart; a person would have to be desperate to rent it out.

Which leads Ardie to an obvious conclusion, a conclusion she really should have arrived at earlier: Lucinda Hamilton is desperate. Desperate, and since she came to the backwater of Reverie from the suburbs of Atlanta, she must be both desperate and running.

More hoarse coughing from Zeke. "Yup. Got me another property down on Culvert Road that's been sittin' empty fer a good six, seven months now. Know anybody who needs cheap rent? I'll cut'em a deal, if you can vouch that they won't trash the place."

Ardie almost laughs out-loud. How can a place be trashed when it's already trash in the best of conditions?

"If I think of anyone, I'll send 'em your way," Ardie says. A thought occurs to her. "Zeke. You don't think anyone could be squatting on the other half of Lucinda's duplex, do you?"

"Nah," he says. "Fact, I know for sure ain't nobody else over there. Couple weeks ago, Lory Wheeler came knocking on my door with some big-shot detective from up Sumter way, and I 'bout shit a brick thinkin' they'd done cooked my goose." He laughs; it transforms into more coughing. "But turns out, they wasn't there for me, they needed to get into Lucinda's place. Lookin' for some man. Lucinda's old man, I think. Anyhow, I walked the detective through the property, both sides of it. The other half of the place was as empty as I left it." Zeke falls silent for a moment, then asks Ardie, "Why'd you wanna know? Think Lucinda's hidin' somebody on the other side of her place? 'Cause if she's doin' something that's gonna get me in trouble, somebody'd better tell me."

I think Lucinda's hiding a lot of things, but it's only herself she's getting into trouble, Ardie thinks. Out-loud, she says, "Oh, no, nothing like that. I was just wondering. She'd mentioned hearing some noises on the other side of her duplex, and asked me if I'd look into it for her. I figure it's just coons or possums or something, but I thought I'd ask you first."

"You're prob'ly right," Zeke says. "The other half of that place has a hole up near the roof I've been meanin' to fix for a while now. Prob'ly whatever it is got in that way." He sighs, and as if it pains him, he says, "I'll go down there tomorrow and see if I can find anything. Tell her you let me know she was havin' a problem."

"No need," Ardie says quickly. "I'll go down there myself and see if I can figure out what the problem is. I'm sure it's no big deal; likely won't take me but an hour or so to sort out."

Zeke hesitates, as if not sure how to react to this unsolicited generosity freeing him from the landlord responsibilities he already does his best to ignore. "Alright then." He chuckles. "Just don't break nothin.'"

They say their goodbyes and Ardie ends the phone call.

She sits there in her father's office, surrounded by old filing cabinets, a worn-out desktop computer, and stacks of unopened mail, thinking. She can hear the clock on the wall, the tacky one whose face is set on a plastic wide-mouthed bass, ticking away.

Lucinda claims to be dating the girl on the other half of her duplex. Zeke claims there's no one living on that half of the duplex.

The only question Ardie has now is which one of them's lying. Her money's on Lucinda, because she doesn't think Zeke's creative enough to try to sell her on such an elaborate lie. Besides, what motivation would he have to lie?

Lucinda, on the other hand… She could be making things up because she doesn't know how to tell Ardie that she only wants to be friends.

Or is there something else at play here? And who were the police looking for?

Spirits prey on us when we're weak and alone, Rhonda's voice whispers to her over the ticking of the bass clock on the wall.

"No such thing," Ardie says to herself, shaking her

head. "I don't know what's happening with Lucinda, but it sure as hell isn't spirits."

Something *clangs!* loudly outside the office, making the glass windows vibrate and shiver. Before she realizes she's doing it, Ardie launches out of the chair she's sitting in and dives under the safety of her father's rusted old desk. It only takes her a second to recognize that the sound she heard was simply a wrench hitting the concrete floor of the work area, but by then, she's already under the desk with her hands laced over the back of her head — classic school tornado-drill pose — her heart racing, her palms sweating.

Feeling foolish, she climbs out from underneath the desk, glances briefly into the lobby and the work area of the shop to see if anyone noticed her.

Not this again, she thinks miserably. *Please, God, don't let it start all over.*

Chapter 28

"So," Ardie says carefully, mixing the caesar dressing into her salad with her fork. She doesn't lift her eyes to Lucinda's when she asks, "What's she like? The girl who lives on the other half of your duplex. She must really be something for you to start seeing her so soon after you came to town."

"Soon?" Lucinda says, brow furrowing. "It isn't *all* that soon. I've been in town a couple months already, and we only started seeing each other — officially, I guess — a few weeks ago."

Ardie shrugs. "I s'pose you're right," she says, wary of the defensiveness in Lucinda's voice.

"As for what she's like…" Lucinda turns her gaze to the ceiling, studying whatever she sees there for a few seconds before answering Ardie. "She's young." She giggles. "It's been something surprising to me, that someone so much younger than me would be interested at all."

Not that surprising, Ardie thinks. *You're still beautiful.* She'd like to say it out loud. She knows she shouldn't.

Ardie guesses that Lucinda must be in her late forties or early fifties somewhere, given conversations they've had in the past, but she doesn't look it. Maybe it's in how she keeps her hair cropped just below her chin, or the fact that she's stayed thin even in her middle age, or maybe Lucinda just has good genes. Whatever the reason, she's aged well. Much better than Ardie herself, who's going both thick and grey.

"She's a nurse," Lucinda continues. "Works down at the county hospital, in the emergency department. But she's second shift, so most of the time, by the time I get home in the evening, she's already gone to work. Sometimes, if I don't have a lot of clients and I get home early, we'll bump into each other. The rest of the time…" She shrugs. "I'm not much of a night owl and she's not much of an early bird, so we don't get to see a whole lot of each other unless one of us has a day off or gets home early."

A few tables over, a young waitress leans over to pick up the empty plates of the customers who just left. A fork gets away from her, though, sliding across the lip of the plate and dropping onto the table. Ardie sees what happens next coming before the waitress does: The girl leans over to pick up the fork she dropped, and all the other silverware spins across the surface of the empty dish, raining and bouncing down one by one onto the tabletop. The sound startles Lucinda; her shoulders clench as her head whips around to see where the noise is coming from. Even though Ardie sees it coming, her body goes rigid and she grips the edge of the table.

"That scared me," Lucinda says, and she laughs

insincerely, but when she catches the look in Ardie's eyes, her smile disappears and her brow creases with concern. "Are you alright? You look like you're going to be sick. Is it the salad?"

Ardie looks down at her hands, knuckles white against the table's edge. *Oh no,* she thinks. She wills herself to loosen her grip, wills herself into a smile.

"I'm alright," she says. She tries to have a laugh at her own expense, but her laugh is just as strained as Lucinda's. "Two tours in Afghanistan. One in Iraq. Sometimes I get spooked by the strangest of things. Earlier this morning, it was a wrench hitting the floor."

Lucinda's expression is sympathetic. "I know what that's like. I mean, you see how *I* jumped." She lowers her eyes to her plate, then lowers her voice. "A social worker said I might have PTSD."

"PTSD is my middle name," Ardie says. Then she sighs. "Or it was. It really hasn't bothered me in a couple of years. But now it's flaring back up again; I really don't know why." She looks down at her salad bowl, gets back to the business of mixing her dressing into it. "I've been having nightmares about the war. Again."

Lucinda sucks in a breath as if she's about to speak. Hesitates. Finally says, "I have nightmares, too."

Ardie nods slowly. As much as she doesn't want to talk about last night's bad dream, this might be her inroad to get Lucinda to open up.

"In mine, I'm not even me," Ardie says. "I'm this kid I

told you about, Lucas — not like I'm watching him; like I *am* him. Every time, it's the same dream. He and his dog are on their way out to go on patrol. He walks down this dry creek bed, thinking about what it's going to be like when he finds an IED, thinking about how the guys around him will start to see him as one of them. Then he steps on... and he..." Ardie stops, exhales hard. "I'm sorry. This is too dark for a lunchtime conversation, isn't it? I'm sure you don't want to hear it."

"No, no," Lucinda says, reaching out and putting her hand on Ardie's forearm. "I want to hear it. It's good to know I'm not the only one... Sometimes I wake myself up in the middle of the night because I'm screaming. Please. Tell me the rest."

Ardie gives her a doubtful look. "Are you sure?"

She gives Ardie an encouraging smile. "I am. Maybe it'll be good for both of us."

"Okay, well... Since it's like I'm experiencing everything Lucas is, it's not like I watch him when he steps on the IED. It's like *I* have to experience exactly what he feels when his body gets blown into a million pieces. The dreams feel almost like... I dunno, like a punishment or something. Like a penance I have to pay. For not being able to help him that day." Tears prick at her eyes, and she blinks rapidly, trying to bring both her eyes and her voice to heel. She doesn't want her voice cracking in front of Lucinda, as if she's some sort of scared little girl. "When the PTSD gets really bad," she says, after she feels like she's regained enough control to speak again, "I have to live through him getting blown up over and over again like that, night after night. It's gotten a lot better in the last couple years. When I dreamed about it last night, it was the first time in a long time."

The hand still on Ardie's forearm pats her. "I can understand that. My nightmares haven't gone away yet, but sometimes it does seem like they're getting a little bit better. And it's good to hear you say that eventually they go away."

"What do you dream about?"

"My ex-husband." Lucinda takes her hand off Ardie's forearm, looks away. She turns to the square of complimentary cornbread that she'd gotten buttered but never managed to take a bite of.

"And what's he do in your dreams?"

Lucinda shakes her head without looking up, takes a bite of the cornbread. She chews, swallows, still doesn't look up when she says. "I can't talk about it. If I do, I think it might just make it worse."

She takes another bite of cornbread; Ardie gives an understanding nod and eats her salad.

"You know what's making the nightmares better, though?" Lucinda says after a moment. Her expression changes into something lighter, more playful. "Having someone in the bed with me. Ever since the girl next door started sleeping over, they've been getting better. Shorter. Not as intense. And it's like every now and then, my brain forgets to have a nightmare at all — not often, now, mind you. But sometimes."

Ardie puts her fork down. "So... I guess we're back to where we started, huh? Back to your new girl. The young, head-turning nurse."

Lucinda giggles. "I didn't say she was head-turning."

"So you're saying she's not?"

"I didn't say that, either."

"What's she look like?" Ardie says.

"Brown hair — long and wavy, halfway to her waist. And brown eyes." She stops for a moment, smiling as if to herself, as if remembering something about the object of her affection. "Great sense of humor. Spontaneous, too, unlike me."

"And how long's she lived next door?" Ardie asks.

Will the right question catch Lucinda in her lie, reveal that there's no one living next door to her? Or will the right questions prove that she does in fact exist, and somehow, for some strange reason, she's tricking Lucinda into thinking that she lives on the other side of the duplex?

But Lucinda's response doesn't seem like she feels threatened by the line of questions. Nor does she look away when she answers, or touch her mouth, or change her voice — all signs of a liar.

"She moved in right after I did," Lucinda says. "And she's not from Reverie, either, so we sorta bonded over that. Came here from Florence for the job at the hospital. It's not her first job out of nursing school — her second,

~ 275 ~

though, I think. She can't be but twenty-seven, twenty-eight."

"Hmm," Ardie says, right as the waitress who dropped the silverware comes over to take away their first course dishes.

"Your order'll be right out, ladies," she says pleasantly.

Ardie and Lucinda both mumble their thank-yous.

Lucinda makes a face and shifts in her seat. "Ugh, my shoes are still damp."

"Damp?" Ardie glances under the table, notes that Lucinda's white Keds have taken on a greenish shade.

"Dionne — that's my girl's name — and I found an old train trestle over a river about a mile from our duplex. We jumped in. She took her shoes off, but I kept mine on, and they still haven't totally dried out."

"I think I know that trestle. It's a branch of Miller's Creek. My brothers and I used to go swimming there when we were kids. But a teenager hit his head on some rocks a few years ago and died, so nobody goes there much anymore. You should be careful… Uh, both of you should be careful." Ardie hesitates a moment. She sucks in a breath, rests her elbows on the table, laces her hands. "I called Zeke Brinkmann about your place earlier this morning."

She waits for Lucinda's face to change from easy to tight. But it doesn't.

"Oh, why's that?" Lucinda asks.

"I, uh, wanted to ask him about…" Ardie hesitates.

Should she really bring it up? What if Lucinda's just lying about the "girl next door" because she isn't interested in Ardie but can't bring herself to say so? What if telling her the real reason she called Zeke will make Ardie sound like a stalker?

What if she tells the truth, and Lucinda walks out of Linda's in sheer anger, and never speaks to Ardie again?

Ardie coughs a few times to stall for time, takes a sip of her water, smacks her fist against her chest a few times.

"You okay, Ardie?" Lucinda says, concerned.

"Yeah, 'course, I'm fine," Ardie answers, setting the water back down. "I guess I just had something caught in my craw for a second there."

Lucinda smiles. "Caught in your craw, huh? My mom used to say that."

"Maybe it's a Reverie thing," Ardie says.

"Maybe it is. What were you going to say? Something about calling Zeke Brinkmann?"

"Yeah. I was… uh, I was asking him if he thought your property would be prepared for the hurricane."

Lucinda's brow creases. "What hurricane?"

"Haven't you heard?" Ardie says. "Hurricane Amber. First hurricane of the season, aiming directly at Charleston. Some people think it might be as big and bad and ugly as Hugo was back in '89."

"Oh, right. I think I did hear about it. And I remember hearing about Hugo," Lucinda says, nodding. "My Aunt Sophie's place was hit pretty hard. Took them months to completely dry out their cellar, what with all the flooding."

"If a flooded cellar was all she had, she got off pretty light," Ardie says. "A big swath of Reverie — mobile homes, mostly — was pretty much just wiped off the map. Lots of folks never rebuilt."

"So what'd Zeke say? About my place?"

Ardie looks away, realizing that now that she's lied to Lucinda, she's going to have to figure out a way to cover her tracks. "Well, he said that there's a hole just under the roofline leading into the attic on your friend — what was your girl's name again?"

Lucinda smiles broadly. "Dionne," she says.

For some reason, the name sends spider leg-like tingles crawling up the back of Ardie's neck. She tries to shake it off.

"Yeah, so there's a hole on Dionne's side of the place, but other than that..." She pauses, asking herself if she thinks the old duplex will be strong enough to withstand a hurricane, if it actually comes roaring through Reverie the way that Hugo did. She's worried that the roof could potentially come off, and even if it doesn't, a crashing tree would make fast work of caving it in. Now that she thinks about it, she can't remember if there are any big trees close to the duplex. She'll have to check.

"I think it'll probably hold up okay," she says at last. "Y'all are on a bit of a rise there, plus you're a good mile from the flood plain. But Zeke said he wouldn't mind if I patched up the hole and did some other things to help y'all get ready for the storm."

"Oh, he 'wouldn't mind.' Isn't that just so generous of him," Lucinda says sarcastically.

Ardie agrees by rolling her eyes, only feeling mildly guilty for lying about her conversation with Zeke. Truth be told, he didn't sound like he had any immediate plans for fixing up the hole, and even if he did, he probably would've asked Ardie or someone like her to do it for him anyway.

"Storm's s'posed to hit this weekend," Ardie says. "Saturday night into Sunday morning. Jim told me it's up to a category four. If it goes back down to a category three, we'll probably be fine — get some strong winds, a whole lot of rain, maybe, and some parts of town will flood, but nothing too catastrophic. But if it stays a cat-four or becomes a cat-five, well… that could mean some serious trouble."

"What's the likelihood of it getting stronger?"

"Meteorologists don't seem to agree on that. Some say it will, some say it won't."

"What do *you* think?" Lucinda asks.

Ardie thinks about her mother's admonishment, saying she should've learned something about preparedness from her years in the service. She hates to admit it, but her mother's right.

"I think it's better to be safe than sorry," Ardie says after a moment. "If there's one lesson I learned from the military, it's redundancy, redundancy, redundancy."

Lucinda nods.

A plan begins to take shape in Ardie's mind. "I've gotta get the shop ready today and tomorrow. We'll probably close early for the week. I figure on headin' to the bigger hardware stores in Sumter maybe real early Friday morning — highways'll be clogged with evacuation traffic going towards Columbia. But maybe if I take the backroads… Sorry, I'm thinking out-loud."

Lucinda smiles sweetly. "It's okay. Go ahead."

"So then let's say I get back from Sumter on Friday around late morning… I could spend all day getting the shop ready, then work on Mama and Daddy's house Saturday morning… I could come by your place late Saturday afternoon, early evening, if that works for you. That should still give us a couple hours to get you buttoned down."

"That should work," Lucinda says. "I'm not sure if Georgie plans on keeping the salon open on Saturday or not — probably not — but I'm sure I'll be home by late afternoon one way or another."

"Perfect. Then Friday'll be my day for getting everything ready for the storm — especially the shop — then home and y'all's place."

"Ardie, you're like my guardian angel. You've been so kind to me," Lucinda says sincerely. "I really don't know what Reverie would be like for me without you always dropping by to fix things and keep me company."

Ardie smirks. "Sure, but sounds like I'm not the only

one who's been keeping you company lately. You're a sought-after lady, Miss Lucinda."

Lucinda says nothing for a moment. She pinks in the cheeks and allows herself a pleased smile. "I'm glad I can talk to you about Dionne," she says. "There aren't a whole lotta other people in Reverie — well, no one, actually — that I can really talk to about her."

"Hey," Ardie says, a new idea occurring to her. "Will your girl be around on Saturday evening? I'd love to meet her if she's gonna be home."

Lucinda's eyes widen slightly, as if the prospect of Ardie meeting her new girlfriend frightens her. It's a strange reaction, given that she just finished telling Ardie a second ago that she's glad she can talk to her about this "Dionne" person. Ardie's never heard of a woman being called "Dionne," either — the only Dionnes she can think of are ex-NFL players. Then again, there aren't a lot of women named Ardith, and she's encountered more than one surprised face from someone who'd been expecting an "Artie" instead of an "Ardie."

"I'll ask her if she's going to be around that afternoon," Lucinda says at last, still acting like she's uncomfortable. "But like I said, usually she works second shift."

"I'd love to meet her. Maybe the hospital will send her home early on account of the storm," Ardie says, and forces a smile.

Chapter 29

There's not much happening at the shop when Ardie gets back from lunch. Jim and another mechanic are working on cars. Two more mechanics are playing poker at a rickety card table in a shady back corner of the garage, conservative news radio crackling and echoing against the concrete beside them. Ardie interrupts their game to get them to start filling sandbags. Two more hours go by with so little business that Ardie's the only one working on cars. She sends the mechanics who'd been filling sandbags home early for the day, figuring they all probably have things to do to get their own places storm-ready.

By four o'clock, she sends Jim home, too, because there's no point paying him for doing nothing for the last hour of the day. Once he leaves, she changes the radio station to National Public Radio and decides to use the quiet time to work on organizing the tools in the garage. Despite the fact that her father was also a Marine mechanic, he didn't leave the service with the same appreciation for cleanliness and orderliness that Ardie has. His packrat tendencies drive Ardie crazy. She pulls over a garbage can and a stool, and sets to work on emptying out the first tool box.

"Forecasters say that Hurricane Amber might be the

biggest hurricane to hit the Carolinas in at least three decades," the announcer says when the news comes back after an update on local traffic. Ardie walks over to the radio, turns it up a few notches. *"The only problem is, they still aren't completely certain where and when it's going to hit. Some models show Charleston in its crosshairs; other models suggest Amber might still turn north and east, dealing only a glancing blow to South Carolina before making landfall around Wilmington, North Carolina. Adam Stafford is in Charleston with the latest."*

"With Hurricane Amber gaining power and strength today as she goes from a category three to a category four storm," says a male voice that Ardie assumes must be Adam Stafford, *"some residents in Charleston are preparing for a worst-case scenario."*

Ardie puts down the pliers she's been cleaning to listen as soundbites of Charlestonians play in the background.

"I'm gettin' out," an older woman says. *"And if it don't hit Charleston, then fine, it don't hit Charleston. But I sure ain't stickin' around find out what it hits or don't hit. I was here for Hugo. Anybody who remembers Hugo and has even a little bit of common sense is gonna get out, too."*

Two more interviewees say they aren't leaving the city for one reason or another; one is a business owner who says he worries about his store getting looted if he's not there to protect it, the other says that he doesn't have anywhere to evacuate to.

Ardie's mind wanders as the report continues to play.

She's forming a checklist in her mind of the things she's going to need to ride out the storm, along with the things the shop's going to need, if indeed it does hit coastal South Carolina and then continues to move north and west through the state.

And then there's Lucinda. Even though she'd had to think fast to come up with an excuse for why she'd been talking to Zeke Brinkmann, she really does worry about the rickety old duplex being able to withstand a strong hurricane. Hitting land will break Amber up, but with Reverie only an hour or so's drive from the coast, it would still be plenty strong by the time it came here.

Maybe even stronger than Hugo. The *I'm gettin' out* woman in Charleston has a point: If Ardie waits until forecasters finalize the storm's path, it might well be too late for her to do what she needs to do to prepare. The thought chills her, and she's just about to walk to the office to start writing down her to-do-list when a pickup truck pulls up to the back of the garage.

Ardie looks out through the open bay door, squinting into the late afternoon sun. A figure waves at her from behind the steering wheel, but given the backlighting, all Ardie can see is a silhouette. She walks around to the driver's side to see who's calling at such a late hour.

"Hey there, Ardie," says Dan Anderson cheerily.

"Hey, Dan, nice to see ya," Ardie says. "What can I do for you?"

"I know it's late in the day and all — I sure am sorry to

bother you with this," he says, briefly explaining the minor repairs he needs done on the truck.

"It's no problem."

"And I already asked Aggie to pick me up here — she should be here in a few minutes, and I'll just leave the truck with you for now, if it's alright, but it was easier for me to get the old girl in here tonight than in the morning before work."

"Sure thing. No problem at all. Why don't you go ahead and drive into this bay here and then meet me in the office with your keys while I lock up?"

#

Ardie enters the lobby a few minutes later, chats with Dan for a bit about his truck, then about his wife, his kids, his mom.

"Oh — I had lunch with your cousin Lucinda today," Ardie says casually, leaning her elbows onto the counter.

"That's good," Dan says, nodding. "She could really use a friend or two. I kinda worry 'bout her, spending all that time by herself way out at Zeke's place. That's not that far from where y'all live, right?"

"Yeah," Ardie says. "I've dropped by a few times. Done some work on the duplex."

Dan chuckles. "Now that's nice to hear. When Lory Wheeler and I moved her in, I thought the whole damn place might cave in on itself at any time. Made me almost feel guilty, getting her into that place."

"Speaking of Lory, somebody up at Georgie's mentioned that he served a search warrant on Lucinda's place not long ago. What's that all about?"

"Oh. That," Dan says with a heavy sigh. He hesitates, squints at Ardie. "Did Lu tell you why she moved to Reverie in the first place?"

"No. And I have to say I've definitely wondered why anyone would choose to move here who wasn't from here."

Dan holds Ardie's gaze for a minute, seems to consider something. Finally he says, "I don't know if she'd want me telling you this or not — "

"You don't have to tell me anything if you don't want."

"I know, but it's like I said — Lu could really use some friends here besides me and Aggie. We both worry about her. Aggie especially. And even more since her sister Harriet called us up the other day." Dan glances over his shoulder, even though the shop is quiet and contains only the two of them. He lowers his voice. "She's here because she's trying to start over after her husband…" Dan shakes his head. "Her husband's a bastard. Now don't get me wrong, if I ever caught Aggie cheating on me, maybe especially with a woman — no offense, Ardie — I'd be seeing red."

"No offense taken," Ardie says, even though it is mildly offensive.

"But no matter how mad I got at Aggie, I wouldn't *ever* go after her with a gun. Or anything else, for that matter."

Ardie gapes. "That's what happened? He went after Lucinda with a gun?"

"Oh, he did a hell of a lot more than that." Dan looks away, shakes his head. "But, I don't know, Ardie, maybe I really ought not be tellin' you all this. If you wanna know more about what happened, you should probably talk to Lucinda herself. But I'm not sure if she'll really want to talk about it. To be honest, she doesn't even talk about it to Aggie and me, and we're kin."

"What's his name?" Ardie asks. "Lucinda's husband?"

"Hart. Hart Hamilton, and may he fucking burn in hell," Dan says. "My pastor prob'ly wouldn't approve of me sayin' that. But if anyone deserves eternal damnation, it's men like Hart."

Ardie tries to smile. "I won't tell on ya."

"Yup. Anyhow." He pauses. "Y'all gettin' ready for the hurricane? What's your daddy have to say about it? I remember how when Hugo came through, he was one of the only businesses downtown that didn't get flooded."

Ardie nods. "Yeah, he had all his mechanics packing sandbags for days in advance. That was two, three years before I joined the service. Watching the good the National Guard did in the aftermath of everything — it inspired me a lot more than my daddy's stories about Vietnam ever did."

"You think it's gonna hit Charleston, like they say? Or are we gonna dodge the bullet?"

"I dunno," Ardie says, pushing herself up from the counter. "But you're making me think I'm gonna need a lot more sandbags than what the guys filled today. Whether it hits us or not, you know how Miller's Creek likes to flood down here."

Dan smiles. He pats his truck keys sitting on the counter. "Think you'll be able to get my baby fixed up by tomorrow?"

"Tomorrow… I hope so. If Amber's still headed our way, I'm gonna close the shop on Friday. But I'll call you tomorrow once I get a chance to look under the hood."

"Even if it's here over the weekend, I figure it'll be safer from the storm here than it will at my place," Dan says. "You're the best mechanic Reverie's ever had, ya know that? Don't tell your daddy I said so, though."

Ardie grins. "I won't. Talk to you tomorrow."

She locks the front door once Dan leaves, then heads back into the garage to close up all the bay doors before kicking her motorcycle to life and pointing towards home.

The grumbling roar of her bike isn't quite loud enough to drown out her thoughts.

Lucinda's mysterious girlfriend.

Finding sandbags before the storm comes.

"Spirits prey on us when we're weak."

Lucas.

And Hart Hamilton, going after Lucinda with a gun.

"May he fucking burn in hell."

Chapter 30

"Well?" Ardie says to her mother when she comes home that evening. "What's the latest on the storm?"

Her mother, who's tucked into an Afghan on her easy chair, pauses the television and looks up. "You're home early."

"Shop was quiet this afternoon." Ardie nods at the screen. "What are they saying?"

"Did you hear? It's a category five now. Just barely, but it is. They're 'bout positive it's gonna hit Charleston, too."

"Category five is worse than Hugo," Ardie says grimly. "Maybe we should go to Asheville after all."

"That's what I told your father this morning," her mom says, sitting higher in the easy chair and shifting to face Ardie. "I told him we'd better get on up outta here while there's still gas and such to be had. You know what he said?"

"We can't leave. We can't just leave the shop like that."

"That's *exactly* what he said."

"Sorry — I didn't mean that was what *Daddy* said," Ardie corrects. "I meant — well, if that's what he said, then he's right."

Her mother shakes her head and exhales a heavy breath.

"You two are just alike."

"But it's true. We have a lot of expensive equipment in that shop, and there are some unsavory types around here who'd love to get their hands on it if we leave the place alone for too long. Besides that, even if I manage to get enough sand bags over there by Saturday night, I still wouldn't be surprised if the creek comes up far enough to get a little standing water in the garage. I need to be there to dry everything out before it gets ruined."

"We talkin' 'bout the storm?" says Ardie's father, who's wandered in from another part of the house and stands at the living room's edge in his boxer shorts and a plain white tee. "What's its name, Crystal? Pearl?"

"Amber," the women both say simultaneously.

"I tol' yer mother we can't leave the shop." Like his daughter, Sylvester ("Sly") Brown possesses a broad, thick frame, the kind that evokes images of carnival strong men and football linebackers. As he delivers his proclamation, he sticks his barrel chest out, as if he's expecting a fight.

"Oh, simmer down, Sly," Ardie's mother says. "Your daughter already agrees with you. I can't imagine why, but she does."

Sly glances over at Ardie, nods curtly in approval. "I don't think it's gonna hit us anyhow," he says. "I still think it's gonna turn east like they said, bounce off-a North Carolina."

"And what makes you so sure?" Ardie's mom quips. "You a meteorologist now?"

He shrugs. "I just think it won't, is all. I'm going back to lay down. Call me when dinner's ready?"

"You been layin' down all day," his wife complains. "If you're gonna lay down, at least lay in here so someone'll keep me company."

Sly grunts his distaste for the idea, but hobbles towards the couch anyway, progressing in small, mincing steps.

"How's your hip, Daddy?" Ardie asks as she watches him.

"Oh, y'know," he says, lowering himself onto the couch with obvious pain and effort. "'Bout the same as it always is. Hurts." He looks over at her from his supine position on the couch. "Sorry I ain't been around the shop much lately."

"It's alright. Between Jim and me, everything's getting done alright."

Ardie's mother unmutes the television, and they all watch the ominous satellite footage of the mammoth category five storm as it inches closer to the coast of South Carolina.

"Oh, speaking of the storm," Ardie says. "We found some of the burlap sacks for sandbags today in a closet. You got more squirreled away anywhere?"

"Yup," her father answers. "There's some in one of the storage lockers in the garage, and I'm pretty sure I remember a whole bunch of sand still sitting in the woodshed from last time. I can help you haul it out tomorrow morning."

"Naw, you just rest," Ardie says. "I'll take care of it."

#

After dinner, Ardie excuses herself to her room, where she opens up the laptop that sits on the old desk in the corner. She opens the Internet browser and types

hart hamilton lucinda hamilton georgia

in the search field, and presses enter.

Georgia man accused of second-degree murder and attempted murder now missing

reads the first headline, dated only a few weeks ago. With mounting horror, Ardie scrolls through the other, similar headlines until she gets to the last one that looks relevant, dated several months earlier:

Man murders wife's lover, injures wife

Ardie clicks on it.

Calvin, Ga. — Calvin resident Hart Hamilton is accused of injuring his wife, Lucinda Hamilton, and then murdering her alleged lover, Dionne Summers.

Hamilton, who has an arrest record for previous domestic violence incidents but without any formal charges filed against him, allegedly attempted to kill his wife on Friday with a nine millimeter handgun. The bullet intended for Lucinda Hamilton, however, grazed off her side and struck the victim, Summers, in the stomach. Summers, who was a registered nurse at Calvin County Hospital, was pronounced dead at the scene by first responders.

Hamilton fled the scene on foot but was later apprehended by police two miles from the crime scene. He had discarded the handgun but later led police to its location.

According to official police reports, Summers and Lucinda Hamilton had been having an affair for some years. When Hamilton discovered their relationship, he became irate, then violent.

So far, Hamilton appears to be cooperating with authorities; his lawyer could not be reached for comment, but sources close to the investigation say that prosecutors have offered a plea deal of aggravated assault and voluntary manslaughter, which would make Hamilton eligible for parole in twenty to thirty years. It is unclear whether or not Hamilton has accepted the plea bargain.

The brother of victim Dionne Summers spoke out on Sunday at an emotional press conference.

"My family and I cannot begin to express our sorrow over Dionne's loss," Derrick Summers said, reading from a prepared statement. "Dionne was a ray of sunshine for everyone who knew her — for our family, for her friends, for all the people she helped as a nurse. There are no words to express how much we already miss her. We sincerely hope that the Calvin County Sheriff's Department and District Attorney's Office will bring justice to Hart Hamilton."

Lucinda Hamilton is recovering from her injuries at Calvin County Hospital and could not be reached for comment.

Dionne. That was what Lucinda had said the girl next door's name was at lunch, hadn't she? Lucinda must be so desperate to have her love back that she's hallucinated her back into her life. Hallucinated her, or…

Rhonda's words come back to Ardie, but she brushes them off.

No. "Hallucinated her" must be right. And if Rhonda saw her talking to herself, then Lucinda's psychological state is much more fragile than anyone realized.

Ardie lets out a breath she hadn't realized she'd been

holding when she reaches the article's conclusion. She hits the back button on the browser, returning to the list of articles and clicking on the most recent one.

> **Calvin, Ga.** — Georgia man Hart Hamilton, accused in May of voluntary manslaughter and aggravated assault after shooting his wife, Lucinda Hamilton, and killing her lover, nurse Dionne Summers, is officially missing.
>
> Despite refusing a plea bargain that would have reduced his sentence, Hamilton initially cooperated with authorities after Summers' death, even expressing remorse to the Summers family. Despite prior arrests for domestic violence, Hamilton's lawyer argued that his cooperation should earn him the right to bail. A judge released Hamilton on $100,000 bail, on the condition that he remain under house arrest and wear an ankle monitor at all times. When Hamilton missed a court-ordered check-in call, an officer went to his home, Hamilton was nowhere to be found. The remnants of what appeared to be the ankle monitor were found in the home's living room.
>
> As of the time of publication, police have been unable…

The article continues for several more paragraphs, but

Ardie can't read anymore. She feels sick to her stomach.

Zeke's story about Lory Wheeler and the detective from Sumter serving a search warrant on Lucinda's place is starting to make more sense. They're worried Hart Hamilton is trying to track Lucinda down. Track her down to kill her.

"Oh, Lucinda," she whispers. Her eyes well with tears.

#

Predictably, Ardie doesn't sleep well that night. She reads a little later than usual — her latest book is a Bible-sized, non-fiction tome by a Pulitzer Prize-winning author about the Salem Witch Trials. But despite reading for longer, she makes it through fewer pages, sometimes snagging on the same paragraph or two for several minutes, finding the words to be like a stubborn mouthful of dry cornbread that just refused to go down:

"Ghosts escaped their graves to flit in and out of the courtroom, unnerving more than did the witches themselves. Through the episode surge several questions that touch the third rail of our fears: Who was conspiring against you? Might you be a witch and not know it? Can an innocent person be guilty? Could anyone, wondered a group of men late in the summer, think himself safe?" (*)

She tosses and turns in the bed for at least an hour,

mind reeling between Lucinda's hallucination, Lucinda's safety, and the hurricane, before sleep finally takes her. But even sleep offers little rest; her subconscious mind immediately flings her into a nightmarish battlefield, where she's been tasked with fixing a Humvee to allow a unit of men to escape the Taliban, but she doesn't have the necessary parts.

"Sandbags!" one of the officers screams at her. *"What are you doing here without any sandbags?"*

She wakes from the dream feeling more exhausted than she was before, drags herself out of bed to pee and get a glass of water from the kitchen. She stands barefoot in the darkened living room with her water. Moonlight passes through clouds outside and casts speckled, undulating shadows across the worn area rug.

She picks up the remote control from the arm of her mother's chair, flips on the TV and mutes it before the noise can wake her parents. She presses buttons until she manages to find the guide, scrolls up and down until The Weather Channel finally appears. She selects it.

A muted anchorman wearing a serious, intense expression and bracing both hands on the desk in front of him talks while satellite maps show Hurricane Amber's progress in a sidebar to his right. She turns it back off after a few seconds, leaves the glass in the sink, and heads back to bed.

When she opens her bedroom door, a figure is seated in the desk chair.

She grips the door knob hard, heart hammering, sure that it's just a trick of the moonlight. She closes her eyes, opens them again — but the figure is still there. A man, she sees, profile facing her.

"I have a knife," Ardie says bravely. "If you want the laptop, just take it and go."

The figure turns, silver light of the moon illuminating him from behind, making his face a sea of shadows.

"Now is that any way to talk to an old friend, Sarge?"

Ardie's stomach does a backflip. "Shrimp?" she whispers.

"Why didn't you protect me?" Lucas asks. "Why'd you let me die out there?"

"I didn't… I couldn't…"

"You had a *feeling* that morning," he says, tone filled with bitter accusation. "You had a feeling, but you let me go anyway. You didn't lift a finger to protect me." He stands up, and it's only then that Ardie realizes he isn't whole. Dark blood drips from a watermelon-sized crater in his chest; below it, his entrails begin to spill out like long linked sausages. "You let me *die,* Sarge."

"Lucas… if I had known — if I had *really* known — I never would've let you go out there that day."

He shakes his head sadly. "You did really know. Just like you know about Lucinda now. Are you going to do something this time, or are you going to ignore that feeling again, like you did with me?" He gathers handfuls of his own intestines, walks towards Ardie. "Look what happened. Look at me."

Ardie takes a step back. "I can't, Lucas, please."

"Look," he says again, more insistent. Blood begins to trickle from the corner of his mouth; another trail of blood follows him across the carpet, spreading uneven dark dots like spilled motor oil. He's getting closer now, and the smell of death fills Ardie's nostrils. "Look at me."

"Please. No. Please." She takes another step back, bumps against a picture frame hanging in the hallway.

"Look at me!" he shouts. He charges her, guts leaking out between his fingers, and Ardie lifts her arms instinctively, shielding her face.

She wakes to the sound of her own screams.

Chapter 31

After the night of the awful nightmare-within-a-nightmare with Lucas, Ardie reverts to the best coping mechanism she knows — she stays busy and she tries not to think about it. It's not hard to stay busy, either; Thursday evening, Hurricane Amber makes a hard left, putting Charleston unquestionably in the center of her crosshairs. Local media becomes hysterical, warning South Carolinians from Columbia to the coast to be prepared for flooding, electrical outages, water outages, food shortages, gas shortages.

Every time she turns on the radio, all she hears is people comparing Amber to Hugo. They interview guests who recount what living through Hugo had been like, interviews that inevitably end with either the reporter or the interviewee asking the question,

"Could this storm be even worse than Hugo?"

State officials, meanwhile, frame the question differently, repeatedly calling for calm.

"We're much better prepared today than we were thirty years ago when Hugo came through," they say.

"We have multiple emergency resources already in place."

"We're urging everyone in the evacuation zone to take

the evacuation orders seriously. But people in the Midlands and even in the Upstate still need to understand that this storm will affect them, too. This storm will affect the entire state of South Carolina."

All day on Thursday, even before the hurricane's turn, Ardie and her father turn away customers from the shop and set the mechanics to work filling sand bags and nailing plywood over the lobby's outer windows, instead. Her dad tries to help, but after managing to fill a single sandbag, his back and hip have him in pain, so Ardie sits him down in a lawn chair so that he can help "supervise" some of the younger mechanics as they work.

When the news comes in around closing time about the hurricane's hard left, Ardie tapes a sign to the door that reads, "CLOSED UNTIL AFTER AMBER" and tries not to think about the amount of money the shop is going to lose over the next few days. At least not paying the mechanics for three or four days will help to offset the lost profit.

She hates closing, but she has to do it. Only two days remain before Amber is scheduled to hit, and in that time, Ardie has to finish preparing the shop, get her parents' home ready for the storm, plus she's promised Lucinda that she'd prepare the duplex, too, which means Friday will be taken up with a trip to Walmart and the big hardware store in Sumter or Florence — or maybe both, because she doesn't doubt that supplies are already low across the state.

There is, at least, one bright spot. A package awaits her on Thursday evening when she returns home from a long day of filling sandbags. There's no sender name on it, but Ardie recognizes the Tucson address. Inside, she finds her dress blues and her two handguns, still in their locked box, along with a note from Sandra:

"Had to pay a whole lot extra to ship the guns. Please reimburse immediately."

and the amount she wants to be reimbursed for. Ardie leaves one of the guns in the metal box. The other gun, probably due to PTSD-induced paranoia and nightmares about Lucas, she puts in the glove compartment of her father's pickup truck when she leaves for Sumter the next morning.

It's during the pre-dawn Friday morning drive to Sumter that Ardie turns off the radio and decides to keep it off at least until her hardware store trip is over. She's tired of hearing the frenetic tone of the reports, as if the four horsemen of the apocalypse will be descending upon South Carolina at any moment. Besides that, more nightmares Thursday night, combined with the mounting itch of jumpy anxiety, are enough to convince her that she doesn't need to do anything more to tempt the demons of her PTSD.

She lucks out and gets everything she needs in Sumter, despite the fact that even the backroads she uses to get there are already swamped with coastal refugees fleeing inland ahead of the storm. Her eastward trip home is much easier; she's home in time for a late lunch and finishes most of the preparation on the house by early evening. Her mom spends the day bustling around the kitchen, cooking nearly everything in the chest freezer in anticipation of impending power loss.

"If nothing else, we'll have fried chicken to last us a good while," she says as she bustles around the kitchen.

"I still say it ain't gonna be as bad as they're makin' it out to be," says Ardie's father, who's sitting on a kitchen stool, shucking corn. "I think the media's done hyped it all up just for ratings."

"Maybe so," Ardie's mom concedes, "but don't you think we'd better be safe than sorry?"

"As long as I ain't gotta shuck any more corn after this," he retorts.

"Oh, you hush. If you'd gone out there to help Ardie, like you said you were gonna, instead of just layin' on the couch watching Price is Right, I wouldn't have made you come in here to help me."

Ardie stays out of their squabbling, instead works on the mental checklist of things she still needs to do before the storm hits on Saturday night.

#

The air has been humid and heavy all day, despite a constant, restless breeze, and by the time Ardie gets to Lucinda's around four in the afternoon, it's started to drizzle. Lucinda must've heard the old truck headed her way a while back, because by the time Ardie pulls into the yard, she's standing on the front porch, hands braced on her hips, waiting. She heads down the stairs and towards Ardie while Ardie parks and turns the truck off.

"Thanks again for doing this," Lucinda says. "Dionne and I are grateful, especially since Zeke doesn't want to seem to lift a finger to take care of his own property himself."

Ardie inwardly winces at the name *"Dionne."* She's of half a mind to confront Lucinda about it, to say, *"You don't have a next door neighbor. Your husband shot and killed Dionne when he was trying to kill you,"* but she doesn't have the heart to say it. If she'd hallucinated Lucas after he'd died while she was still in Afghanistan, coming around with his floppy-eared dog to play cards or swap paperbacks, she probably wouldn't have wanted anyone pointing out that it was only in her head. She might've been happier living with the hallucination in blissful ignorance.

But maybe Lucinda's sick, and Ardie should say something.

On the other hand, sometimes what people call "sick" is just a person's way of slowly getting better. Like how PTSD nightmares are the brain's way of trying to process what it saw. Or how a fever is the body's way of trying to kill off an infection.

Except sometimes fever will kill you before the infection does, Ardie reminds herself.

"Ardie?" Lucinda says. "Are you alright? You look kind of... wound up today."

Ardie forces a smile. "I s'pose I *am* wound up. Spent all day Thursday getting the shop ready for the storm, yesterday went to Sumter and started my work on the house, been finishing our place til just an hour ago. But we can't really know if we did a good enough job or not until the storm blows through. And now I'm here — still got some more to do for… y'all."

Lucinda's face falls. "I'm sorry. I shouldn't've let you do all this for me. I coulda asked somebody else, like Dan."

"No, ma'am, don't start on that again. I told you before — it's not imposing if I'm the one who volunteered to do it."

Ardie opens up the pickup's tail gate and starts pulling out sheets of plywood and boxes of tools while Lucinda asks her questions about her trip to Sumter.

"I didn't think to go all the way to Sumter," she says. "Dionne and I got the last two cases of bottled water up at the Shop 'n Go. And we're gonna both fill up our bathtubs tonight to have something to flush toilets with."

Dionne and I. The phrase is like sandpaper against Ardie's heart.

"And… where's Dionne now?" Ardie ventures.

"At work," Lucinda answers without missing a beat. "She's got her normal shift tonight, essential personnel and all that, but if the roads get bad, she might end up having to spend the night there."

"Makes sense," Ardie says, noting how fully formed

Lucinda's hallucination is.

Once Ardie and Lucinda have covered all the windows with sheets of plywood, Ardie turns her attention to the yard, looking for trees with any overhanging branches that look like they might be dangerously close. A walk-around inspection leads her to an old oak tree at the back of the house, Spanish moss dripping from it like scraggly grey tentacles.

"This one worries me," she tells Lucinda. "It's big, and it's close to the house, and if it gets uprooted…"

Lucinda walks up to the old tree, places her palm on its rough trunk. "It's a really nice tree. I've always loved live oak trees, especially when they're all covered in Spanish moss like this one is. It's what I associate with South Carolina the most."

Ardie sighs. "Be that as it may…" She checks her watch. Almost seven o'clock already. No wonder the rain's started to pick up. "If I were going to cut this down, I should've done it three or four days ago."

"Cut it down?!" Lucinda exclaims. "Please don't talk about cutting this old girl down. It's not her fault she's so big."

Ardie halfway smiles. "That's what my mother used to say to me, you know. Back in my debutante ball days. 'It's not really you're fault you're so big-boned. It's just 'cause you're your father's daughter.'"

"Nothing wrong with being big-boned," Lucinda says. "There are lots of different ways to be beautiful, and that's one of them. *You're* one of them."

Now why'd she have to go and say a thing like that?

Every time Ardie's ready to brush off her feelings for Lucinda, either because she doesn't seem to return them, or because she has a girlfriend, or because she's so sick that she's hallucinating her dead girlfriend back to life, she's got to go and do something like call Ardie beautiful.

"Thanks," Ardie says lightly, trying to play it off as if it doesn't affect her at all. "But what would Dionne say if she heard you calling me beautiful?"

Lucinda looks away, casts her gaze at the ground. Wraps her arms around her midsection and kind of hugs herself. "I don't think she'd like it very much."

"Nothing wrong with saying someone's beautiful. Sounds like Dionne's just a little possessive."

Lucinda looks back up, smiles wanly. "I don't think it's possessiveness. I think she's just a little jealous of you."

"Jealous of me?" Ardie repeats. "Why?"

She's surprised again by the depth to which Lucinda has hallucinated her missing girlfriend. Right down to her jealous possessiveness.

"Well, because. If I hadn't... I mean, if Dionne hadn't been interested in me... There's only one other gay woman in all of Reverie, as far as I know." Lucinda meets Ardie's gaze, holds it with her own.

Ardie feels the blush creeping up her neck and into her face, and she turns away from Lucinda to hide it, pointing up at the live oak branches. "I'm thinking I should at least trim a few of those big ones, in case they try and break off and hit the house."

"Oh, please don't," Lucinda says. "I can't bear the idea of you taking a chainsaw to this tree."

Ardie considers the tree, considers Lucinda. "Lu, we really do need to cut this down. Trim it at the very least."

She shakes her head stubbornly. "No. You just wait and see, Ardie. It's going to be fine. In fact, you know what I think? I think the hype over the storm is overblown. I think the press sensationalizes this kind of thing and just runs with it because it makes a good story."

Ardie grins, shakes her head. "You and my dad, I tell you what. At least you have the excuse of not living here when Hugo came through. He, on the other hand, should know better."

"See that? Your dad did live through Hugo, and he agrees with me. Dionne and I were talking about this just last night. It's probably not even gonna still be a hurricane by the time it gets to us."

Dionne and I, Dionne and I. Ardie should say something. But — no. She shouldn't.

"I don't know about it all being hype," Ardie says after a moment's hesitation. "Amber's looking like a monster. And we aren't but forty-five minutes or an hour from Charleston."

Lucinda pushes Ardie's shoulder playfully. "You're buying into the consumeristic media conspiracy."

"Consumeristic…? What media conspiracy?"

Lucinda shrugs. "Oh, I don't know. It's something Dionne says all the time."

Something Dionne used *to say all the time,* Ardie almost says. She looks from Lucinda, to the tree, to the duplex. "You know what, Lu? If you won't let me take any of this tree down, then you should come stay with Mama and Daddy and me. Mama's been cooking up a storm since yesterday, so there's plenty of food for you and — " She chokes on the name before she manages to get it out. "Dionne."

Lucinda shakes her head stubbornly. "Consumeristic media conspiracy. We'll be fine. Thank you for getting it ready for us."

As if to signal the conversation's end, the rain begins in earnest. The wind gusts, ruffling Ardie's hair into a temperamental wave, sending Lucinda's finer, longer hair into her face. She struggles with it a moment, trying to comb it away from her eyes, and Ardie has to repress an affectionate urge to reach out, push the errant strands away.

"Lu... are you sure you won't change your mind?"

"Ardie. We'll be fine."

"If you change your mind before things get too bad on the roads, just come on over to our place, okay?" Ardie says. "You don't even have to call, just show up. Turn right onto the highway, drive a little less than a mile. Dark green house on top of a short hill, old wooden fence around it. On your left. You can't miss it."

Lucinda takes a short step forward, puts both her hands

on Ardie's shoulders, squeezes them reassuringly. She gives Ardie an indulgent smile. "We'll be fine here, I promise. Don't worry."

We. *We'll* be fine.

Lucinda is far from fine. And there's nothing Ardie can do about it.

Chapter 32

LUCINDA

Lucinda watches Ardie go, affection for the sturdy, motorcycle-loving woman surging in her heart. If Dionne hadn't come back to her...

She shakes her head briskly. No point thinking like that. Dionne *did* come back to her, against all odds, a miracle, a gift from heaven that makes her re-think her disavowal of a loving God. Dionne is back, and with Dionne back, there is no one else Lucinda would ever want to be with.

The rain picks up and the wind gusts hard, picking up leaves and dust and little sticks in the front yard, twirling them in the air before setting them back down, sending grit into Lucinda's eyes. She pushes the hair from her face. The storm will definitely be here soon — a few hours off, at most. Lucinda's excited for it, almost. Unlike Ardie, she doesn't worry that it'll still be a hurricane by the time it reaches here. Like Dionne pointed out, they're inland, with plenty of pine trees and swamps and rolling hills between them and the coast to break up the storm's momentum. They're calling it the "storm of the century," but Dionne says it's all hype. Every storm that comes ends up as the "storm of the century" because it's good for television ratings and viewership and allows the networks to charge more for commercials.

"A classic case of the tail wagging the dog," is what Dionne said.

Storm of the century or not, Lucinda thinks it's going to get pretty nasty soon. Nothing to do now but sit inside with her phone and wait for Dionne to check in. With a little luck, they'll send her home early, before the road gets bad, and she and Lucinda will have the perfect excuse to snuggle up in bed together for the rest of the night and, if they're really lucky, even into the next day.

She already has her hand on the door handle of the screened-in porch and is pulling it open when a sound from behind draws her attention. She glances over her shoulder. A nondescript pickup truck — not Ardie's — is pulling into the yard. She squints through the driving rain, through the rapidly dimming light, trying to see who it is.

Her breath catches in her throat.

Hart.

Adrenaline-fueled instinct drives her forward. She rips open the screen door, then the regular door, locking and bolting it behind her. It won't stop him, she knows, but it should slow him down.

She hears a pickup truck door slam closed just as her trembling fingers twist the deadbolt closed.

"Lucinda! Don't you walk away from me!"

It's strange, the power he has over her. The way she

almost, like a child, turns back to the door to obey him, to let him in. But the drive to survive is stronger than the urge to obey, and she sprints through the living room and into the kitchen. She throws the backdoor open and springs down the back stairs, not bothering to slow down long enough to close it behind her.

"*Luu-cinn-daaaa!*" he shouts again from the front of the house, his voice carried to her on the rushing wind. She can hear him pounding on the front door of the house. "*Running's only gonna make it worse for you!*"

Lucinda pauses, glances around the backyard briefly, wondering which way to go. *The woods,* she decides, and takes off running down a path into the pines, rain-slicked needles sliding beneath her tennis shoes.

"*Lucinda!*" comes Hart's voice again, but it sounds a little further this time, a little more muffled, and she takes this as a good sign. She runs hard down the trail, slowing only for a moment when the path forks. Which way does she normally go, when she's walking with Dionne? Everything that should be obvious is fuzzy and confused, and she chooses the path on the right, picking up speed again as she commits to the decision. She can't remember the last time she's run like this. Her lungs burn and the rain stings her eyes, but she presses on as hard as she can.

She reaches for her phone as she runs. Dionne will know what to do. Dionne always knows what to do.

#

ARDIE

Ardie kicks off wet boots in the mud room, walks into the kitchen in socks that are only somewhat drier.

Her mother hugs her, kisses her cheek, then slaps her arm playfully as she pushes her away. "Girl, get out of those wet clothes. You'll catch your death."

Ardie nods numbly and moves on wooden feet into her bedroom. A hurricane rages inside of her even as the storm outside grows louder, fiercer.

She let Lucas die.

She's tried to tell herself over the years that it isn't true, that there was nothing she could've done. That's what the Marines shrink said to her, too, on each of the four occasions that she met with him after her last deployment in Afghanistan ended. Survivor's guilt, that's how Ardie thinks of it. *"Moral injury"* was one of the phrases the shrink used. One of the official, clinical phrases for the guilt and shame that comes from being part of not one but two wars she'd never really thought were completely right in the first place, the knowledge that she spent more than three years participating — hell, *contributing* — to a situation that kept stealing the lives of innocents. Innocent Iraqis. Innocent Afghanis.

Innocent Nebraska farm kids like Lucas Koch.

She tries to reason her way out of it; she tries to remember she never shot anyone. All she did was to keep the machines running. But she'd still been a part of it... hadn't she? She'd kept the machines running, and that made her a part of the war machine that got Lucas killed.

Had she really known something was going to happen that day? Or did she rewrite the memory later out of guilt? That's what the Marines shrink told her. He said she'd never had any intuition about Lucas; she'd added that part in later because of her *moral injury,* her survivor's guilt.

It wasn't your responsibility to save him. That's what the shrink said. *You can let go.*

Maybe Ardie wants to "save" Lucinda because she couldn't save Lucas. Maybe she's confusing "responsibility" with "meddling," and the best thing to do is to let go.

Ardie flops onto her bed, grabs the book about the Salem witch trials sitting on the nightstand. She'll read for a few minutes to calm her mind, join her parents for supper, get the latest update on the storm.

But she can't focus on the book.

Does Lucinda understand that Dionne Summers is dead? Does she speak of her as living because, not unlike Ardie when it comes to Lucas, she cannot let go? Or has she actually lost her mind? Temporarily, perhaps? — the way Ardie did when the PTSD was at its peak.

Or she could go with Rhonda's theory, that there's something supernatural at play.

Ardie shakes her head. *"Spirits"* belong to the same class of fantasy as *"the tooth fairy."*

She wishes Lucinda would've let her trim that live oak tree in the backyard. It's much too close to the house for Ardie's comfort. The right gust in the right place at the right time could send one of the bigger branches crashing into the back or the roof of the duplex. Which would prove to be stronger — house, or tree?

And if the whole tree comes down?

Ardie sighs, puts the book down. Wanders into the living room. The television blares; a split screen shows two reporters standing in different locations, both visibly struggling against blasting wind and horizontal rain, both squinting and pressing their earpieces to their heads. Ardie's mother sits curled in the easy chair, her father lies in his normal spot on the couch. They watch the reports of the approaching hurricane with the same relaxed curiosity that they might watch football games and sitcoms. It occurs to Ardie that they probably watched news reports come in from Afghanistan or Iraq in much the same way, staring at a screen while a journalist reports that a drone killed seventy wedding guests by accident, or that three servicemen were lost in a helicopter crash in the mountains between Afghanistan and Pakistan.

Ardie stands beside her mother's easy chair. "What's the latest?"

"Images just comin' in now from Charleston," her dad says. "Lookin' pretty bad."

"Is it as bad as they said it was gonna be?" Ardie asks.

"Worse," her mother says solemnly. On the screen, the

reporter disappears and a cheery commercial advertising anti-depression drugs replaces him.

"Is it worse than Hugo?"

Her mom nods. "They're sayin' that practically the whole city's underwater already, and the worst of it hasn't even hit yet. It's gonna be here in an hour or two. I'm thinkin' it's a good thing y'all covered up most of the windows."

Ardie's dad grunts, probably because he knows he had very little to do with covering up the windows.

"So it's not hype? It's really gonna be the storm of the century?" Ardie says. She doesn't know why she has to ask twice; maybe because imminent disaster always seems too surreal to believe the first time you hear about it.

"Worse than Hugo, worse than Katrina, worse than Andrew," her mother says. "Maybe the worst hurricane to ever hit the continental United States."

"Aww, it ain't gonna be *that* bad," her dad argues. "But it *is* gonna be bad."

For her dad to admit that it would be bad at all suggests to Ardie that the truth is probably somewhere in between her mother's dire proclamations and her father's dismissiveness. Either way, it makes her mind return to the live oak in Lucinda's backyard.

"I'm gonna go get Lucinda," she tells her parents. "I'm bringing her over here."

Her mother looks up at her in surprise. "I thought you already prepped her place?"

Ardie shakes her head. "Keep in mind who's property it is. You know as well as I do that anything Zeke Brinkmann owns is begging to get swept halfway to Oz."

Her dad sits halfway up from the couch, studies Ardie with an expression that, at least for him, approaches concern. "Ardith, you can't go out there right now. The hurricane's not but an hour away. Nobody with a lick of sense would get out on them roads right now."

"It's less than a mile down the road," Ardie says. "I'll be fine."

Her dad clucks his tongue, shakes his head. "At least take the truck. Don't go out there on that deathtrap you call a bike."

Ardie grins. "I do have at least enough sense to do that, Dad."

"Ardie," her mother starts, "for once I agree with your father. I really don't think you should — "

"I'll be gone and back before you know it," Ardie says, already slipping wet boots back on her feet and grabbing the truck keys from the hook beside the door. She pulls the door open and sees immediately that her father's right. The wind isn't hurricane strength yet, but the pines in the yard are whipping back and forth at a speed no tree should ever move. The darkness is nearly complete, and even if it weren't, the driving rain renders the world next to invisible. Taking in the world beyond their front door, Ardie hesitates for the briefest of moments, wondering herself if she's a fool for venturing out in this weather.

Lucas Koch is dead, says a voice inside her head.

"You be careful out there," her father hollers from the living room. "Get yourself and that girl back here as soon as you can — otherwise your mother'll drive me crazy with her worryin.'"

"I'll be careful," Ardie calls over her shoulder.

And with that, she steps into the hurricane.

Chapter 33

Even with the old pickup truck's windshield wipers working as hard as they can, the road is barely visible beneath the beam of Ardie's headlights. She's glad she only has a mile to go, doubly glad she's been driving these exact roads for almost thirty years.

She sits forward on the bench seat, leaning so far in that her chin hovers a couple inches above the steering wheel as she squints into the darkness.

Swipe of rubber against glass.

Water sheeting off the side.

For a brief moment, the road appears — glistening asphalt and double yellow lines.

Swipe.

The road vanishes, opaque mask of water blinding her.

Swipe.

It appears again, just in time for her to brake hard before she hits the branch lying across the road. The truck shudders, threatening to fishtail before it stops. She's glad she was only going twenty in the first place.

The branch splays across both lanes of the highway, with tender, clean yellow wood at one end contrasting with tough grey bark, showing where it broke away from the rest of the tree. Green leaves and yellow wood chips scatter like a blood trail along one shoulder, and Ardie can't help but think of a severed arm, blown away from its body by an IED, lying lonesome and abandoned in the center of some dusty village street.

She puts the truck in park and climbs out, shielding her face from the driving rain with a forearm while she pushes hard against the wind to make it to the fallen branch. Already soaked from the short trip from the house and into the truck, the waves of rain pelt saturated clothes without soaking in, as if her body itself has become the site of a flood.

Ardie drags the branch aside as quickly as she can, but it's heavy and wet and there's little light apart from the truck's headlights, and she stumbles and nearly falls into a rain-engorged gully beyond the road's shoulder. The gully is already a raging river, muddy water likely at least a foot deep, poised to begin spilling out onto the highway at any moment. Low parts of the highway closer to town have probably flooded already.

She hopes they put enough sandbags around the shop.

She hustles back into the truck, realizing only as she climbs in that she shouldn't've left the door open, because now the rain has blown in and the windshield starts to fog as soon as she closes the door. She curses under her breath as she puts the truck back in gear and wipes the inside of the windshield clear with a wet palm.

Good enough, she decides. Halfway there.

Ardie's headlights meet Lucinda's yard a few short minutes later, unveiling a soggy landscape of crater-shaped lakes of water, each one starting to merge into the other as the rain continues to pummel the summer-parched landscape.

The truck's headlights catch something she didn't expect. A silhouette on the porch, black and featureless, arms moving up and down in a motion Ardie doesn't immediately understand. Adrenaline spikes; she throws the truck into park even as she's still rolling into the yard. The figure on the porch stops moving, its attention drawn by the light of the truck. It turns, lifting a forearm to shield its face from the light, and Ardie finally sees what it is.

A man.

A man holding a shotgun.

The up-and-down motion Ardie saw earlier now clicks into place: He had been slamming the butt of the gun against Lucinda's door knob, trying to break the door open.

He levels the shotgun, double barrels pointing at the truck's windshield.

Ardie dives across the bench seat of the truck, fumbling with the latch on the glove compartment. She pulls out the gun just as the windshield explodes. Shards of glass cascade down all around her, landing in wet, glittering slivers in her hair, sticking to her wet skin, her wet jacket. She chambers a round with trembling hands, rolls onto her back on the bench seat, gun clasped with both hands.

Wind whistles through the hole in the glass.

Every Marine is a rifleman first, she remembers her drill sergeant screaming in bootcamp.

The thought, *I've never shot at anything but a target,* flashes with bitter, hysterical irony through her mind. After three tours in active war zones, after watching men and women medevaced into her base, limbs nothing but bloody hamburger, after years of nightmares, years of every unexpected loud sound reminding her of mortars, the only thing Ardie's ever shot at are targets. She escaped violence in two foreign deserts only to be confronted with a man who apparently wants to kill her in her own sleepy hometown.

But where is he?

Heart beating with hummingbird intensity against her ribs, Ardie slowly begins to sit up, gun moving with her. The truck's windshield hasn't shattered completely; only a cantaloupe-sized chunk is missing in the center, jagged teeth of glass beading with raindrops.

Ardie sucks in a breath, sits up just high enough to peer over the dashboard.

BANG!

She sees the muzzle flash a nanosecond before she hears the report of the shotgun and the shattering of the truck's rear window, but it's time enough to throw herself back down below the dashboard.

Lying on her side on the bench seat, she reaches into the

dashboard, fishes out another magazine for the gun. She doesn't know if she'll need it or not; the one that's already in should give her at least a dozen shots, and she hopes she won't have to fire that many times, but it's better to be prepared.

She shoves the extra magazine in her pocket, steels herself.

"Gahhhhh!" she screams as she sits up, squeezing several rounds off through the hole in the windshield at the same time. She hears nothing once the handgun goes silent — no shouts of surprise or pain, no pumping of a shotgun or shells splashing against the wet earth. Cautiously, she climbs out of the ruined cab, her shifting weight sending glass tinkling to the floorboards. Despite being a sizable woman, Ardie lands in the mud beside the truck with a quiet, cat-like grace. She uses the open door as cover, extends the gun in front of her as if she's at the firing range.

"Where's Lucinda?" a man's voice calls through the darkness. It carries above the rain, above the ever-stronger wind, a gravely baritone of the type that Ardie imagines belonging to a man twice her size. The kind of man with a barrel chest and a rust-colored beard, meaty hands and biceps painted military tattoos. She knows the type from the voice alone. She's met a hundred men who own voices like that one, a thousand, maybe, when she was in the service.

"I don't know," Ardie answers honestly. She hesitates. *Keep him talking,* she thinks. "Why are you looking for her?"

She hears the shotgun pump. The hurricane makes it hard to tell for sure, but she thinks the sound comes from the other side of the truck, probably just opposite to where she stands, near the hood.

"Because I'm going to kill her," the disembodied voice says.

Yes. He's got to be close to the front of the truck.

"Why?" Ardie asks. She keeps the gun at the ready in front of her, but takes a few steps backward, staying in a low crouch. "What did she do to you?"

"She cheated on me," says the man. "With a goddamned *woman.*"

Ardie shuffles backward slowly, staying in a low crouch, headed for the tailgate. She'll make it around the back of the truck, charge the front, surprise Hart — because that must be who this man must be, the same Hart Hamilton who killed Dionne Summers by accident while trying to shoot his wife — from the other side. Her boots squelch slightly against the saturated ground, but she's counting on the hurricane to swallow up any errant noises.

It's not just her hands trembling now; her entire body shakes, vibrating with the fear of what she's about to do. Strangely, her cat Omar appears in her mind from nowhere. Does Omar sense the danger Ardie's in, all the way from whatever sunny spot on the floor she's lounging in in Tucson? If Hart kills Ardie tonight, will Omar ever know that her second mother's gone? Will she miss Ardie if she does?

She breathes in. Holds her breath.

Ardie charges, screaming obscenities as she fires blindly into the rain.

Chapter 34

It is a strange function of memory that sometimes the most important moments in our lives have the most nebulous of shapes when we look back and try to recall their exact details. What is remembered is sometimes not the specific shape of an event — the start point, the end point, the decisive turn in the middle — but rather the odd and inconsequential details that hover around the periphery. The smell of someone's skin in the quiet second before she says she's not in love with you anymore; the sight not of the helmet resting atop a rifle, but of the bright orange of a desert sunset the evening of another memorial service; the rhythmic rattle of an ancient electric fan as the only accompanying music to the hardest decision you'll ever make in your life.

When Ardie looks back on the night that she shoots Hart Hamilton, she won't remember the gun battle itself — she won't remember the way that Hart aims the shotgun at her chest and fires, or how the bullets from her own gun slam into one of his arms, then the other, just in time to force his shot to go wide. She won't remember the way that she kicks his gun aside as he collapses backwards.

She won't remember any of that, because that part all happens much too quickly.

What she remembers later is the way his blood mingles with mud, and the way the wind is so loud that it sounds like being inside a Humvee engine. She'll remember the rain in her eyes and the way she grips the gun so tightly that it bites into her palms painfully. She'll remember how she can hear pine trees groaning and snapping in the distance, and how she worries fleetingly that a tree will crash down on her at any moment.

Hart is strong — even downed with two bullets, he's still strong. He roars at Ardie like a wounded bear, lunging at her as she kicks the shotgun well out of reach. He tries to wrap a blood-slicked arm around her leg, but she brings her knee up sharply into his face. His nose explodes in a spray of blood; his head snaps backward so violently that at first Ardie's afraid she's broken his neck. His grip around her leg loosens, but not fast enough for Ardie to get free. She stumbles and falls on top of him, still somehow maintaining the presence of mind to pistol-whip him in the side of the head as they both collapse into a heap of tangled limbs.

"Fucking bitch," Hart curses wetly, blood and rain garbling his words to near indecipherability as he tries to wrestle Ardie off of him.

Hart is strong, but Ardie's strong, too, and she's heavy, and she doesn't have bullets lodged in her arms. Still holding the handgun, she punches him in the face — once, then twice. On the third punch, bones crack beneath her fist.

He lies still, unconscious.

Ardie's stomach hitches, and she vomits on his chest. She stands up, wiping her mouth with the back of her hand, then retrieves the shotgun.

"Lucinda!" she shouts into the storm. "It's me, Ardie! You can come out now."

But the only thing she can hear is the storm raging all around her.

She looks down at Hart. His mouth hangs open; a stream of blood covers his upper lip and runs down the side of his face. Both arms are covered in blood and mud.

"Goddammit," Ardie mutters, because she knows what she's going to do a moment before she does it. She puts the safety on her handgun and sticks it in the waistband of her pants, then jogs up the ill-defined driveway to the place where the yard meets the highway. She flings the shotgun across the road, listening to it crash against branches before landing wherever it lands.

She jogs back to Hart's unconscious body, shaking her head at herself even as she kneels in the mud beside him and rips off the sleeves of his shirt. She uses the rain to help her wash the blood away until she finds each bullet wound, then binds his arms with the torn shirtsleeves into a rough, improvised tourniquet. That will have to do for now. She still needs to find Lucinda.

It takes three tries before her 911 call goes through.

"911, state your emergency."

"Desiree? This is Ardie Brown. You need to get

Wheeler or the Sheriff over to Lucinda Hamilton's place, along with an ambulance… Say that again? I can't hear you over the storm… One of Zeke Brinkmann's duplexes up on Highway 74… No, I don't know the exact address… Yeah. Yeah, okay. No, I don't know where Lucinda is — I'm going to look for her. Okay… Thanks."

Ardie bangs on the front door after Desiree lets her go, calling Lucinda's name, but no one answers.

The front door's locked. The windows are all boarded else, otherwise she'd shatter a window. She runs around the house, expecting the back door to be locked, but it's not. It's ajar.

Two minutes later, she's gone through every room and closet twice without finding Lucinda. Two minutes after that, she's finished searching the dusty, empty other side of the duplex.

Where could Lucinda be?

Ardie leaves out the kitchen's backdoor, calling Lucinda's name periodically as she shines the light of her cell phone beneath the back stairs of the porch. Befuddled, she stands beneath the live oak tree, turning in circles as she scans the backyard.

Which is when she notices the gap between the trees. A trail leading back into the woods. She jogs towards it.

#

LUCINDA

Age catches up to Lucinda before adrenaline wears off, and she's forced to slow from a run to a brisk walk, her breath a ragged mix of oxygen-hungry gasping and panicked hyperventilation.

She glances over her shoulder. The trail, inasmuch as she can see it through the punishing sideways needles of rain, is empty. She has gotten away. She has escaped Hart, again.

"I'm weak," she'd told Dionne a year ago. *"He beats me and I tell myself that this is it, this time I'm leaving him, and then I don't. I stay."*

Dionne had cocked her head to the side and given her a shrewd look. *"What makes you stay?"*

"Because I can't leave on a whim," Lucinda answered. It surprised her when she said it. As usual, Dee had ways of drawing things out of her that she didn't even know she was holding inside. *"When I leave, it has to be careful. It has to be smart. I have to vanish in a way that he won't expect."*

"Where will you go?" Dionne asked. *"Harriet's? Edie's?"*

"No. That's exactly what he'd think I would do. I have to go further. Out of Georgia. Somewhere I can get on my feet easily again, but somewhere he's never been."

"Where?"

Lucinda looked up, an answer suddenly occurring to her. *"Reverie."*

"*A reverie...? You'll go into a trance?*"

"*A trance?*" Lucinda repeated, confused.

"*That's what a reverie is. A trance. A dream.*"

Lucinda shook her head, smiling. "*No, no. Not that kind of reverie. I mean Reverie the town — a little town in South Carolina about an hour north and west of Charleston. It's where my mother grew up.*"

Dionne nodded thoughtfully. She stepped closer, took Lucinda's hands in her own. "*Am I invited? When you go?*"

The question overwhelmed Lucinda with emotion. Without warning, her eyes welled with tears, her heart constricted inside her chest. "*You can't. You'd have to leave with me in the middle of the night without telling anyone. You wouldn't be able to tell your family where you were going, or your job. If you left so much as a hint behind, Hart would find it.*"

Still holding Lucinda's hands, Dionne tugged her forward, kissed her gently. Lucinda closed her eyes, wondering how she would ever be able to stop missing those tender, soft lips, once she left. She savored the feeling of Dionne's lips against her own, knowing it might be one of the last kisses they enjoyed together.

Dionne rested her forehead against Lucinda's. "*If I have to leave in the middle of the night, then I will leave in the middle of the night,*" she said. "*If I can't tell anyone where I'm going, then I won't tell anyone where I'm going.*"

"I won't let you do that," Lucinda said. *"You can't just leave your whole life — your mom, your brother, the job you love so much, all your friends — just because I'm such a coward that I have to run away."*

"You're not a coward, Lu," Dionne whispered. *"You're the bravest woman I've ever known."*

The puddle of tears that had been gathering at the bottom of Lucinda's eyes overflowed. *"I'm not. I'm a mouse."*

Dionne reached up, brushed Lucinda's tears away with her thumbs. *"No. Cowardly mice who live with cats don't survive. Neither do mice who live with monsters. Mice who live with cats and monsters have to be smart. And brave. And you're both."*

"No. I'm not."

"You are," Dionne insisted. Her face brightened momentarily with an idea, and it was one of those expressions Lucinda adored in her — the way her eyes would suddenly glow with some fresh inspiration as something new occurred to her. *"You know who you are, Lu? You're Scheherazade."*

"Share-uh… who's that?"

"The wife from Arabian Nights.*"*

Lucinda frowned, feeling ignorant compared to her clever girl. *"I don't know what that is, Dee. I don't read as much as you do."*

"My dad read some of Arabian Nights *to Derrick and me when we were little. It starts with this evil king, and

he's all bitter towards women, so he marries one virgin after the other, sleeps with her, and murders her the next morning," Dionne said, excitement speeding up her words. *"He meets Scheherazade, and he plans to do the same thing with her as he's done with all the others. But Scheherazade, she says, 'Let me tell you a story.' So she tells him a story, but leaves it on a cliffhanger. The king wants to find out what happens, so he lets her live for one more night, but she ends the story on a cliffhanger again, and again the next night, and so —"*

Lucinda almost smiled. *"And so he never kills her."*

Dionne nods. "That's right," she says. "She outsmarts him and he never kills her."

But it's not the Dionne of her memories speaking anymore, it's the Dionne of the present, the beautiful girl next door who has somehow appeared on the trail a few feet in front of Lucinda. She stands arm's-length away — luminous, as if she is her own light source. And she is untouched by the hurricane; her long brown hair hangs loosely around her shoulders as it always does, her pale blue nurse's scrubs remain dry.

Lucinda's breath catches in her throat, though whether it is out of surprise at seeing Dionne appear so suddenly in the empty woods, or whether it is a reaction to her otherworldly beauty, Lucinda can't say.

"A mouse who survives a cat has to be more cunning than the cat," Dionne says. "And a woman held captive by a brutal man has to be smarter and braver than he is.

You're Scheherazade, Lulu. You became the master of your own fate."

"Dionne? But... how are you here? I thought you were at the hospital."

Dionne shrugs. "They sent us home because of the storm," she says. "Turns out it really is going to be the storm of the century. Guess I was wrong." She smirks. "Just this once, though. Don't get used to it."

"Hart's here," Lucinda whispers, stepping into Dionne's welcoming embrace. She buries her face into Dionne's shoulder, breathes in the scent of her — the feminine musk of her skin mingled with the smell of laundry detergent and body wash. "He found me. Somehow I always knew he would."

Dionne kisses the top of her head, squeezes Lucinda close. "He's not here now, though. You can still be Scheherazade one last time. Outsmart him one last time."

Lucinda looks up, the rain stinging her eyes and blurring Dionne's face. "But how? There's nowhere left to run to. Reverie was my last hope."

"There's always hope, Lu." She puts her hands on Lucinda's shoulders and pushes her back a few inches. "Do you remember when we found the old train trestle?"

Lucinda nods.

"You must've been thinking about it, back where the trail forked. Because you've been running towards it this whole time. It's only a few hundred yards from here. Let's go see it again."

"Now?" Lucinda asks. "In the middle of a hurricane?"

Dionne smirks, brown eyes twinkling with mischief and humor. "Yes. In the middle of the storm of the century, my love."

Dionne heads a few steps down the trail, turns, and holds out a hand. "You coming?"

Lucinda walks forward, takes Dionne's outstretched hand. "I would follow you anywhere."

"Good," Dionne says, and they stroll down the trail together as the hurricane rages around them. Lucinda struggles to keep her feet sometimes as the wind threatens to toss her into the woods like a rag doll, but Dionne's step is sure and never falters. Every time a gust tries to stop her, or push her into the trees, Dionne puts her back in the center of the path.

She will anchor me, Lucinda thinks. *Always.*

Chapter 35

Ardie races down the path as fast as she can — which isn't as fast as she wants, given the gusts that keep trying to yank her off her feet. She lived through Hugo without much fanfare, it's true, but she'd been a teenager, safely hunkered down inside her parents' home, all their windows boarded up. She'd never had to venture outside. She'd never had to contend with category four winds, which is what the storm must be at this point, and it's like charging through a wind tunnel in which the speed and direction of the wind keep changing.

Trees crack and crash all around her, but the trail is clear enough, her cell phone's flashlight bouncing along the ground in front of her. She dodges the rocks and roots and branches she can see, splashing through mud, slipping on slick pine straw.

"Lucinda!" she calls periodically as she runs, but she doubts her voice can be heard more than a few feet in front of her. She keeps calling anyway.

Ardie slows to a stop when the trail forks in two, shining the feeble light of the phone down one path, then the other. Which direction would Lucinda have gone? And if Ardie chooses the wrong path, what will that mean?

"Sarge," a voice says behind her, sending her heart into

her throat.

She pulls the handgun from her waistband and spins around, pointing it and the phone instinctively in front of her.

But the trail behind her is as empty and black as the two trails in front of her.

"Sarge!" she hears again, louder this time, behind her.

She whips back around, safety off, finger on the trigger.

No one. Only woods and rain and wind and silent trails who won't reveal their secrets.

"What, you're gonna shoot me, Staff Sergeant?"

She recognizes the voice this time. "Lucas?"

"That's right." It comes from behind her again, and she swivels, facing the boiling black cauldron of trees on the opposite side of the trail.

But there's no one there. She lowers her gun, her phone. "I'm losing my mind," she tells the wind.

"No, you're not," says the disembodied voice of Lucas Koch. It comes from everywhere this time — from above her, from behind, from in front of her, from the wind, from the rain. *"But there's someone who sure is hoping Lucinda will lose hers."*

"What are you talking about?" Ardie asks.

"Remember that trestle you and your brothers used to jump off and swim under when you were kids?"

Ardie knows the one he's talking about. It's an old railroad trestle, abandoned long enough ago that not even the oldest residents of Reverie remember it holding live trains.

"*River below that trestle would be awfully swollen, in a hurricane,*" the Lucas-voice says. "*Probably if someone jumped from that trestle, they'd get swept away by that river, even if they were a good swimmer. And if they were a bad swimmer...*"

"Is that where Lucinda is?" Ardie shouts, her words carried by the screaming wind into the forest. "Is she going to jump? Why?"

But the wind carries no words back to her, only rain.

She looks again at the fork in the trail, then closes her eyes for a moment, thinking. She and her brothers didn't come this way to get to the trestle; they always approached from the opposite direction. They'd crawl under a barbed wire fence, cross the field on the edge of Gil McCalaster's land, then pick through the woods until they found the old train tracks. Ardie visualizes the route in her mind, following the tracks until they veered left to head across the river.

She's always been blessed with a good sense of direction.

She opens her eyes, puts the safety back on the gun, and tucks it back into her waistband before jogging down the right-hand side of the fork. The wind buffets her like it's encouraging her forward, and she picks up speed.

#

LUCINDA

It's not long before the trail merges into a set of old railroad tracks. Time has covered the tracks almost completely in some places; the worn iron rails occasionally peek through the pine straw here and there, the only hints of the railroad's presence.

As they walk, the tracks rise, and the trees around fall away, diminishing in size like retreating soldiers. Soon, Dionne and Lucinda are higher than the smallest and youngest of the trees, and the railroad tracks are clear.

Lucinda doesn't know how she would keep her feet without Dionne. In her haste to escape Hart, she's brought nothing with her on her mad dash into the woods, and so she marches forward into the darkness of the storm determined but almost blind, bits of dirt and grit and pine straw mixing with the rain and the wind to fling into her face.

"How much further to the trestle?" she asks Dionne.

"Not much further."

"Why are we going there?" Lucinda says, realizing she hadn't thought to ask the question earlier. A particularly strong gust of wind blows her sideways, and she stumbles, nearly tripping over the rail on her right.

Dionne pulls her hard to the left before Lucinda can lose her balance completely. "We're going because it's the one place where Hart will never follow you to."

The answer confuses Lucinda. Why would Hart be

reluctant to follow her onto a train trestle?

"He's not afraid of heights," she tells Dionne. "He could still follow me this way."

"That's not what I mean," Dionne says.

"What do you mean, then?"

But Dionne says nothing.

They hear the river below the trestle before they see the trestle itself. Even in the midst of a hurricane, the sound of the current is like a ghost train rushing towards them.

I don't remember the river being this loud before, Lucinda thinks to herself.

But wait. Dionne has never taken her to the trestle before, so how could she have any memory of the rushing water?

No. I have been here before, she thinks. *But... I was by myself, wasn't I?*

Yet she's never walked through these woods without Dionne nearby. She doesn't like venturing into the forest on her own. She's not fond of hiking; she's always afraid of getting lost.

An image flashes into Lucinda's mind — it's a hot, sunny day, so hot that when she rests a foot on the sun-baked iron rail, she can feel the heat radiate up through the rubber sole of her tennis shoe. She hears the rhythmic drone of cicadas in the background, and she leans forward a little, peering over the edge of the trestle and into the river below.

The river is broad, green, slow. Graffiti decorates the

pylons below her — declarations of love and ownership spray painted on the trestle's spindly rusted legs, names and dates and crude anatomical depictions of phalluses.

This is the kind of place that Dionne would like, Lucinda had thought to herself at the time, and she had imagined her young lover's delight at discovering such a place, the way her brown eyes might light up with mischief as a new plot occurred to her.

"Let's jump," she would've said. And before Lucinda could even protest, she would've started stripping down to her underwear, preparing to plunge into the river some twenty feet below.

When Lucinda was here before, she imagined the conversation that might have played out:

"What if the river's shallow?" she protested. *"You could get hurt."*

"I'm not going to get hurt, Lulu."

"People get hurt jumping into shallow water," Lucinda said. *"You could break your neck or something."*

Dionne scoffed. *"For someone who never had kids, you sure sound like my mother sometimes."* She grabbed Lucinda's fingers, tugged her towards the trestle's edge. *"Jump with me. It'll be fun."*

Lucinda shook her head, but she was laughing. *"Dee, no. It's not safe."*

"I'll go first," Dionne said, ignoring Lucinda's trepidation and kicking off her sandals. *"And if I don't die, you have to follow me."*

Lucinda thought about this proposal. *"Alright. But if you break your neck,"* she added, waggling an index finger at Dionne, *"don't say I didn't warn you."*

Dionne rolled her eyes. *"I'm not going to break my neck."*

Lucinda started to argue again, but Dionne had made her decision. One hand on the diagonal crossbeam, one hand reaching forward like a superhero, she launched herself from the trestle and splashed down feet-first into the green water below. She bobbed to the surface a second later, laughing and wiping water from her eyes.

"Look!" she shouted up to Lucinda. She moved her head from side to side. *"My neck's all in one piece. Now get in here! The water feels great!"*

"I think I'm going to regret this," Lucinda mumbled, but she unbuttoned her shorts and shimmied out of them, then pulled her tank top off and dropped it on the shorts. *"I'm keeping my shoes on!"* she called.

"Whatever you want, sweet cheeks," Dionne said with a chuckle.

Lucinda took a breath, closed her eyes, pinched her nose, and jumped. Free fall took over, and for a second, she was weightless. Then the cold slap of river water greeted her, and she plunged downward. Her feet hit a soft, sandy bottom, and she pushed herself up, treading water next to Dionne.

"See? That was fun, wasn't it?"

"I guess so."

Dionne threw her head back and laughed.

Or at least — she would've laughed, if she'd actually been there. If she had been more than imagination. If Hart hadn't killed her.

If Lucinda hadn't gotten Dionne killed.

Lucinda swims a few feet from the center of the river and wades to the sandy embankment. She sits there by herself, listening to the insects whine, waving the mosquitoes away from her face. Yes, this trestle is exactly the kind of spot that Dionne would've loved.

How she wishes she could share it with her.

The longing is so powerful that it's almost a physical thing, a malformed creature crawling inside the empty cavity of Lucinda's chest. She wants to see Dionne so badly that sometimes she swears she actually *does,* that the girl materializes in front of her, and they talk about their days, they share a couple beers, they retire to the bedroom for an hour or two of sweaty lovemaking before they both collapse into contented sleep.

The crack of a branch and the flicker of movement on the other side of the trestle brings Lucinda back into the present moment, and she realizes she is standing on the edge of the trestle in the middle of a hurricane, one foot on the iron railing, gazing down into the black, frothing water below.

"Remember last month, when we went skinny dipping?" Dionne says behind her.

Lucinda turns. "I was by myself. You were only here

in my imagination."

Dionne's face puckers into a frown. "What do you mean I wasn't here? I was the one who jumped first."

"You couldn't have been here," Lucinda says sadly. "You're *dead,* Dee. You've been dead this whole time, ever since that night at my house back in May. Ever since the night Hart shot you." She waits for Dionne to respond, but the girl only continues to frown at her. "He was trying to shoot me, but you got between us, and…" She takes a shaky breath. "I went to your funeral, Dionne."

"So maybe I *am* dead. That doesn't mean I haven't been here." Dionne puts her hands on Lucinda's arms, pulls her into a kiss. "I've been here with you. I never left," she says softly, and even though her voice is a whisper in a hurricane, Lucinda hears her clearly. As clearly as if it's a hot summer's day, and the two of them are about to go skinny dipping in the river below. "I'm real. That kiss I just gave you was real. I told you I would never leave you, and I meant it." Gently, she turns Lucinda around so that they both face the river and wraps an arm around Lucinda's waist. "Are you ready?"

"Ready for what?"

"To go with me. To go somewhere where Hart will never hurt you again."

Lucinda is silent; Dionne waits patiently. She squeezes Lucinda to her side, and she can't be just imagination, she can't be some kind of ghost, because Lucinda feels the shape of her hip, the warmth of her skin, even through her rain-soaked clothes.

"It will be sunny every day where we're going," Dionne says. "Hot and sticky and with all the time in the world for swimming and barbecues and late-night conversations on your porch. And we'll be together. Every day, we'll be together. Forever."

"You want me to jump," Lucinda says.

"I want you to go skinny dipping," Dionne answers, smiling. "You can keep your shoes on, if you want."

Lucinda weighs each option in her mind.

A lifetime without Dionne. Spending her days cutting hair, her afternoons gardening, her nights waiting for an imaginary nurse to come home. Going to bed every night alone, a few sweet memories her only comfort.

Memories that will fade with time, like old photographs left too long in the sun.

Or she can take this bridge, this river, to some other place. A place that might be black and empty, a Godless void of nothingness for eternity. Or a place that may have hope. A place where Dionne might still live, not as a memory or as imagination, but as something real, something substantial. Something Lucinda can hold onto, that will anchor her through every storm.

"Lucinda?" Dionne says, pulling Lucinda from her thoughts. "Are you coming?"

Lucinda nods once, and peels off the water-logged cotton t-shirt she's had on all day. She drops it to the railroad ties and begins to unbutton her shorts.

"Lucinda?!" shouts a voice from behind. "What are you doing?"

She looks over her shoulder.

Ardie Brown stands at the spot where the earth leaves the railroad suspended in air on its own, the river bluff falling sharply away into the water below. Ardie is soaked to the bone, her thick black hair flat and plastered back on her head. She holds a cell phone in one hand, its pale blue-white light aimlessly illuminating her jeans, her motorcycle boots.

Lucinda looks away. She has made her choice, and it's too late for Ardie to stop her, if that's what she's here to do.

Lucinda's wet shorts stick to her hips as she tries to pull them off, and she finds herself wiggling back and forth, trying to get them to slide down. She hears Ardie talking to her, and the words are getting louder, which means Ardie's yelling now.

Yelling, or else getting closer, or maybe both.

Finally the shorts obey, and they drop to the wooden ties below. Lucinda steps out of them, puts one foot on the rusted iron rail, and pushes off the trestle.

The wind aids her, the churning river greets her like an old friend. Something hard strikes her temple. Then water and blackness embrace her, the current pulls her down beneath the waves.

Chapter 36

"LUCINDA! NO!"

Ardie sheds her jacket, drops the gun and the phone on top of it, kicks off both boots for fear they might fill with water and slow her down. The wind seems determined to either stop her or push her from the side of the trestle before she's ready, but she puts her head down and rushes through it anyway, like a football player fighting through the line.

She jumps feet-first into the water below.

Like the wind, the river seems to have its own agenda. It rushes into her nose, her mouth, threatens to pour down her throat even as its greedy hands wrap around her legs and yank her towards the bottom.

Ardie fights the water, thrashing blind and disoriented until she finally remembers which way is up. She surfaces, coughing, only for another current to tug her downward for a moment. She paddles desperately, kicking in her sock feet, pushing with her hands until she rises above the water again.

"Lucinda!" she shouts, but the hurricane steals each syllable away.

Frantic, she scans the river for any sign of Lucinda. The water has already pulled Ardie almost fifty yards past the trestle, and she decides that Lucinda, who wouldn't be fighting the current at all, is probably even further downriver than she is.

Her left toe cracks against something hard, making Ardie yelp in pain. But then her right foot connects with something hard, too, and she realizes the water is shallower here, and her feet have found the boulders. The same boulders a teenager cracked his head open on a couple of years back.

But for Ardie, the boulders are welcome relief — they give her something to brace against, holding her more-or-less in place as she searches for Lucinda.

There.

An unnatural shape, awkwardly placed against an uneven arm of rocks extending out from the bank. Ardie wades in that direction, each step bringing new, searing pain to feet that are already raw and bruised. She slips, falling face-first into the water, and for a moment the river is taking advantage of her weakness again, pulling her away from her target.

Her fingertips struggle for purchase below her, groping for something she can grab onto, something that will slow her rapid trek downstream. It's the wrong direction, and the shape she had been trying to reach is far away now, too far away, and if it gets much further away, she'll never reach it.

"Staff Sergeant!" Ardie hears. It's Lucas. With her face half underwater, she can't see him, but she can hear

him. *"Failure is not an option, Staff Sergeant! Not this time!"*

Not this time. She won't collude with Death again to snuff out another innocent life.

No, she tells the river.

No, she tells herself.

She brings her feet down forcefully, meets the river bottom, pushes up until she's standing. The water is chest-deep, and at the rate the rain is coming down, it might be neck deep in a matter of minutes.

"This way, Sarge," she hears Lucas say. *"There's still time, if you hurry."*

She leans forward against the current, fighting hard for each inch of progress, following the voice of Lucas Koch. She calls Lucinda's name as she nears the shape, but the shape doesn't move, doesn't respond, and for a moment she worries that it isn't Lucinda at all, that Lucas has led her in the wrong direction and she shouldn't have trusted a ghost in the first place. But a few hard-won steps later, Ardie reaches the shape, and Lucas was right — it's Lucinda, face-down on the line of rocks that extend from the bank into the water.

Ardie doesn't call Lucinda's name again, doesn't check to see if she's breathing — she assumes she isn't — and instead heaves Lucinda's limp body over her shoulder and picks her way to shore.

Once she makes it to the bank, Ardie lays Lucinda's body on the sand, shakes her, calls her name. Checks her breathing.

But Lucinda is not breathing. And her color is already waxen and dull.

"Hope you remember your basic CPR training," Lucas says, materializing without warning to Lucinda's left. He squats next to Lucinda's head, forearms resting on his knees and hands laced casually in front of him. Despite the rain, his desert-colored fatigues remain dry, sleeves rolled up above his elbows. Large ears protrude from beneath his patrol cap.

Ardie knows she should be startled to see the dead marine sitting in living color three feet away from her, but there's no time to contemplate the significance of his sudden appearance. He is there; he is not translucent the way she's always supposed a ghost would be; he is not shimmering and indistinct the way a dream image might be.

Ardie spares Lucas only a glance before tilting Lucinda's head back, pinching her nostrils shut, and forcing the first breath of air into her mouth, down her throat.

Lucas chuckles. "You know this might be the only time you get to put your mouth on hers, right Sarge?"

Ardie doesn't look up to see his grin; she focuses on counting chest compressions, then breathes into Lucinda's mouth again.

"Sarge? Did you hear me?"

"It's 'Staff Sergeant' or just 'Sergeant,'" Ardie grunts. "'Sarge' is disrespectful. We've been over this before." She goes back to counting chest compressions. "Come on,

Lu. *Come on."*

Twenty-seven. Twenty-eight. Twenty-nine. Thirty.

Ardie sucks in a breath, pinches Lucinda's nose, transfers the air from her full lungs to Lucinda's empty lungs, waits a beat, gives Lucinda a second breath.

One. Two. Three. Four.

"Dammit, Lucinda, *breathe."*

Five. Six. Seven. Eight. Ni —

Lucinda gives a gurgling cough, river water bubbling from her mouth. Ardie turns Lucinda onto her side, whacking her back as she retches. Her eyes flutter open, feathery gaze finally making their way to Ardie.

"Ardie? Where's Dionne?"

"Dionne's…"

"How ya gonna answer that one, Staff Sergeant?" asks Lucas's disembodied voice. He no longer appears on the bank, but his voice comes from everywhere, permeating the winds of the hurricane as if he is the storm itself. *"You can't very well tell her Dionne's dead and she's making things up when you're hearing me clear as a bell, can you?"*

"I haven't seen Dionne," Ardie says, because it's the only true thing she can think of to say. "We need to get out of this storm," she says, sitting Lucinda up and then pulling her to her feet. "Can you walk?"

"I think I…" Lucinda takes a tentative forward, yelps in pain, crumples.

Ardie catches her before she can hit the ground. "I've

got you."

"My ankle," Lucinda says. "I think maybe I broke it."

Ardie glances down, sees a dark red streak on Lucinda's right leg she hadn't noticed before. She kneels, touches the cut gingerly, earns another yelp of pain.

A tree cracks and crashes sideways through its neighbors, its trajectory carrying it towards the riverbank. Ardie tugs Lucinda towards her, curling her body around Lucinda's protectively as the tree slams into the spot where Lucinda had been standing a moment before.

It isn't a huge tree, but it's big enough that it could've easily killed Lucinda. Or Ardie, for that matter.

Without asking permission, Ardie kneels on the sodden bank and pulls Lucinda onto her back. She stands with a grunt, adjusting Lucinda's bare legs around her middle.

"Ardie, you can't carry me. Not in the middle of a storm. Not all the way back — "

"We have to get out of these woods. That tree almost took us out."

She begins to trudge up the embankment towards the trestle's edge, sliding back every few steps as the earth sloughs off beneath her sock feet. Not for the first time, Ardie finds herself wishing she'd left her motorcycle boots on.

"Wait! I can't leave without Dionne!"

"Dionne isn't here, Lucinda."

"But she is. She was here just a…"

Ardie steps onto the trestle, fighting the storm as she

pushes forward. The wind has gotten stronger in the half hour it's taken her to find and retrieve Lucinda, and she struggles to keep her footing as she moves from railroad tie to railroad tie.

Lucinda squirms and twists on her back. "Dionne!" she shouts into the empty forest behind them. *"Dionne!"*

She twists further, and Ardie almost drops her. "Careful. You're going to make me fall."

"I don't see her anywhere," Lucinda says, panicked. "She might be downstream, looking for me. I have to go back for her. I have to — "

"She's *dead,* Lucinda! Your husband killed her four months ago!"

Lucinda goes rigid on Ardie's back. "No. No, she can't be. She was just... I saw her just a few minutes ago. She brought me here, to the trestle."

Ardie, already remorseful over her outburst, already fearing that she might've pushed the mentally fragile woman over the edge, shakes her head. "I'm sorry, Lu, but I'm telling you the truth. She's not here. Dionne's dead."

A hint of movement catches Ardie's eye, and she glances to the side with half-open eyes, trying to see what it is without being blinded by the rain.

It's Lucas Koch, walking carefully along the edge of the trestle. The hurricane's gusts should push him over and into the river, but he seems completely unaffected. He looks back at Ardie, grinning for a moment before returning his gaze to the slick ties ahead of him.

"Careful who you think of as mentally fragile," he says. "You wouldn't want Lucinda to know you're talking to a dead marine, now would you?"

Ardie makes no reply.

Lucinda seems to collapse down onto her back, and Ardie hears soft sobs against her neck. She puts Lucinda down long enough to put her boots back on, her gun back in her waistband, and although it probably won't help, she wraps her rain-sodden jacket around Lucinda's shoulders. She tries to get the cell phone to come back on, but apparently, it's dead.

Time to get home.

Chapter 37

Over the wind, Ardie hears nothing — not a single siren, not a single tire splashing through the ankle-deep water on the road. The constant roar of the storm creates a kind of impenetrable shell around them, putting Ardie, Lucinda, and the occasional appearance of Lucas Koch in a kind of self-contained snow globe.

Which means the first sign she gets of the sheriff's department taking her emergency call seriously are the strobing blue lights that greet her as she emerges from the woods with Lucinda still sobbing on her back. The hurricane is at its peak now, and every step is a mighty struggle to keep her feet as she picks her way through the black backyard and towards the blue lights of the squad cars.

Wheeler is the one to spot her first, and he takes off towards them at a run, stumbling a few times himself as the wind tries to beat him back.

"I got 'er, I got 'er," he says when he reaches Ardie, and peels the limp form of Lucinda from her back. He drapes her in his arms, holding her like she's an overgrown child.

"Hart Hamilton?" Ardie asks once she's been relieved of her burden.

"Medics are treatin' him now," Wheeler says. His lip

curls into an angry sneer. "Though why we waste the time and money trying to save assholes like him has always been beyond me. Are you the one who shot him?"

Ardie hesitates for a moment, her Miranda rights echoing in her head.

"Anything you say can and will be used against you in a court of law," Lucas supplies helpfully from behind her.

"Yeah," Ardie tells Wheeler. "He started firing at me before I even made it out of the truck. I didn't have any choice."

Wheeler nods grimly. "Don't worry, Ardie. We got your back. There's not a judge anywhere in this county or the next who'll blame you for what happened. 'Sides, I'm guessin' you're also the one who patched him up?"

Ardie nods.

"Then you saved his life. He woulda bled out before we got here, if you hadn't made him a tourniquet."

Ardie looks away. She doesn't feel like a lifesaver. She feels queasy, like she might lose whatever's left in her stomach at Wheeler's feet.

"Where'd you find Lucinda?" Wheeler asks, dipping his chin down to indicate Lucinda.

"Over by the old trestle. She jumped. I think… I s'pose she thought death was the only way she could get away from him."

Wheeler looks down at Lucinda in his arms, whose eyes are closed peacefully, as if in sleep. "I've known her since she was ten years old, y'know. Shame how things turned out for her." Wheeler purses his lips and shakes his head. "I'll take her over to the medics." He turns to go, pauses, and looks over his shoulder at Ardie. "If she jumped, am I correct that you jumped in after her?"

Ardie says nothing.

Wheeler lets out a low whistle. "This is gonna be the most excitin' police report I've ever written."

"Put me down, Wheeler." Lucinda's voice is so quiet that at first Ardie thinks it's only a trick of the wind, another Lucas-like hallucination. "Put me down. I can walk."

Wheeler does as he's asked, but the truth is, Lucinda can't walk — not quite. Her ankle definitely looks like it's broken, and she leans heavily on Wheeler as the two hobble towards the front yard. Ardie follows close behind them, prepared to catch her if she starts to fall.

There's less chaos than Ardie would've expected in the front yard. They couldn't have arrived much sooner than Ardie and Lucinda did, because the paramedics are still kneeling in the mud next to Hart, doing whatever they need to do before they can move him into the waiting ambulance. Another sheriff's deputy stands a few feet behind them, his hands on his hips, his head tilted not towards the outsider on the ground, but skyward, as if he might be in conversation with the hurricane.

Ardie, Wheeler, and a hobbling Lucinda approach the knot of paramedics and deputy just as they begin to lift Hart onto the gurney.

"One... two... three..." a paramedic says, and they lift Hart in one smooth motion onto the gurney.

The gurney isn't flat; it's the kind that folds upward towards the head, putting Hart in a halfway sitting-up position.

Which means he sees Lucinda almost immediately.

His face contorts, he rips the plastic oxygen mask from his nose and mouth. *"Lucinda!"* Hart screams, and not even the hurricane seems to mute the animalistic rage he puts into the three syllables of his ex-wife's name.

Lucinda freezes in front of Ardie, a doe caught in Hart's headlights.

It seems like it should happen in slow motion, but it doesn't. It happens in such a short blur of seconds that Ardie will wonder later how the injured Hart could've managed to do so much in such an abbreviated sliver of time.

The injuries don't slow him at all. He twists on the gurney, and in one fluid motion, somehow manages to snatch the skyward-facing deputy's gun from its holster behind him. The gun swings around, muzzle blazing before Ardie hears the crack of the shot's report.

Ardie doesn't know how she does it, but she yanks Lucinda towards her, out of the bullet's path. And with a speed that rivals Hart's, Lucinda pulls Ardie's gun from her waistband, holds it with both hands, and fires.

The first bullet strikes Hart in the chest. The second strikes him in the chest. The third strikes him in the chest.

The fourth grazes his arm. The fifth buries itself in the gurney's mattress. The sixth time, the gun just clicks, then clicks again, then keeps clicking as Lucinda continues to squeeze the trigger at the monster she's already vanquished.

Ardie puts her hand on the gun's barrel. "Stop, Lu. It's done."

But the trigger keeps clicking, and through tears, Lucinda trembles uncontrollably.

"Lucinda," Ardie says again. The view of Hart's bloody body is obscured by the three paramedics, all of them consumed by the desperate attempt to revive the monster. The deputy has his gun back, and he holds it in both palms before him, looking down at it like it's a small and easily frightened animal.

Lucinda keeps pulling the trigger.

Gently, Ardie takes the emptied gun away from her, switches the safety back on, and returns it to its place in her waistband.

"Lucinda," she says. "It's over now. He's gone."

The spell broken, Lucinda half turns and crumples to the ground, fingertips pressing into the saturated earth.

"Dionne!" she howls, moving her hands back and forth as if she might conjure something forth from the ground. "Not again... not again... Dionne... come back to me, baby. Come back. Dionne, *no.* No, no, no, no, no, *noooooooo!"*

Wheeler drops to a knee next to Lucinda, shakes her by the shoulder. "Lucinda! It's okay! He didn't hit you! He missed you, Lucinda!"

"He hit *her!* He shot her — *again!*"

Wheeler looks up, and the expression he gives to Ardie is a mixture of helplessness and confusion, a kind of puzzled pleading.

Ardie drops to both knees, wraps an arm around Lucinda's shoulders. "I know. He got her. I know. But she's okay now. She'll be at peace."

Lucinda lifts her head. *"There is no peace!"* she screams into Ardie's face. "There is *never* peace!"

"There will be," Ardie says calmly. "Her peace will come, Lu... *Your* peace will come. I promise. I've..." Ardie glances up, looks over her shoulder. But the only thing behind her are pine trees, thrashing against the storm. Lucas Koch is gone. "I've been here before," Ardie tells Lucinda in a whisper. "Peace will come. In time."

"Nooooo," Lucinda moans. "You've never been here before. He's taken her. He's taken *everything*... Everything is gone... Gone, she's gone, she's gone..."

She collapses then, but Ardie is there to catch her.

And that is the part of the night of the hurricane Ardie will remember most in the years to come — kneeling in the mud next to Lucinda Hamilton, cradling a broken woman to her chest, rocking her back and forth like a child, while two deputies and three paramedics look on.

Chapter 38

Three days later, Ardie wonders the same thing she wondered almost thirty years earlier, after Hurricane Hugo ripped through town: How is it that any of Reverie has been left standing?

Downtown flooded, of course, as she knew it would. Her father's shop took on water, but not too much, thanks to their last-minute effort of adding a sandbag perimeter to the back of the lot. Ardie, Jim, and her dad use squeegees and snow shovels a couple days later to push as much of the water out as they can. They've got a wet vac, but there's no power, and Ardie's dad sold his diesel-powered generator a couple years back.

No power anywhere except for the lucky few who *didn't* sell their generators. No land lines the first day after, and three days after, cell phone reception still comes and goes like a temperamental teenager. They say that most of the cell towers between Sumter and Charleston were damaged by the storm, which Ardie doesn't find surprising.

Spotty cell phone reception doesn't stop Ardie from texting Lucinda a few times anyway. Not that she gets a response. Lucinda's staying at Dan and Aggie's, and supposedly her sisters are both on their way. The duplex fared better in the storm than Ardie would've expected —

but storm damage doesn't have anything to do with why Lucinda isn't staying at home. She's with Dan and Aggie because, after what happened the night of the storm, nobody trusts her to be on her own.

Law enforcement didn't see fit to charge Lucinda with anything related to Hart's death. Self-defense, pure and simple, and good riddance to Hart Hamilton, anyway. It's the kind of small town nod-and-wink understanding that comes in helpful at a time like this — there's not even so much as an investigation into Hart's death.

On the fourth day after the storm, Ardie hasn't gotten a reply from Lucinda, and she doesn't know if it's because Lucinda's phone isn't working or if it's because Lucinda doesn't want to talk. Ardie decides to take a chance that it's the former, and shows up on Dan and Aggie's doorstep with a foil-covered plate in her hands.

"Hey, Dan," she says when Lucinda's cousin opens the door.

Dan glances from the foil-covered dinner plate to Ardie and back again, and he doesn't look at all happy to see Ardie. Suddenly she feels foolish, like she's been caught courting Lucinda by an overprotective father.

Ardie half-lifts the plate. "I brought some cookies. For Lucinda and… and the kids and everybody."

Dan steps out onto the porch and closes the door softly behind him. "Ardie…" he begins quietly, but cuts himself off with a sigh.

"I understand if she doesn't want visitors. Just make

sure she gets the cookies?"

Dan deliberates for a moment. "Hold on a second, okay?"

He disappears inside the house for a minute, closing the door on Ardie, and Ardie waits obediently on the porch, shifting the plate of cookies to one hand so she can wipe off the sweat beading on her brow. Now that the hurricane has cleared out, South Carolina has gotten back to its typical late August weather, and today has been particularly brutal.

The door opens again a minute later.

"Come inside," Dan says.

Ardie walks into the foyer of the old Victorian home, realizing that in all the years she's known Dan and Aggie — not to mention Dan's mother, Sophie, who was friends with Ardie's mother before she died — she's never actually set foot inside. She wipes her boots carefully on the entryway mat, trying not to openly gawk at the crystal chandelier above her head, the antique grandfather clock across from the coat rack, the Persian rug spread across the hardwood floor.

"When Lucinda stays with us, she likes to take the bedroom at the top of the stairs," Dan says. His eyes look misty. "Turn left at the top, and her door's the first one on the right."

Ardie follows his directions, knocks on the closed white door a moment later. "Lu?" she says, mouth close to the doorjamb. "Mind if I come in?"

"Come on in, Ardie."

Lucinda's sitting up on the bed, an open book resting on her chest. The ankle she hurt is wrapped in an ACE bandage, propped on two pillows.

"Sorry I didn't come down to greet you," Lucinda says. "Doctor wants me staying off my foot as much as possible for the next couple weeks."

"It's no problem," Ardie says. She lifts the plate. "Peanut butter and M&M cookies. Like the ones you served me the last time I visited you. Remember? I baked these myself."

Lucinda chuckles. "I didn't know you baked."

"I don't. Which means I'm not vouching for these cookies."

Lucinda moves an old alarm clock and a pair of reading glasses from her nightstand. "Set them down, let's try one."

Ardie removes the foil before setting the plate down on the nightstand and waits for Lucinda to take a cookie before she takes one for herself. She stands awkwardly next to Lucinda's bed, taking a bite.

"Mmmm," Lucinda says, wiping crumbs from her chin. "You *should* vouch for these cookies. I can't believe how good they are."

"I got a confession to make. They're just from the store-bought pre-mixed stuff at Shop 'n Go. And since we still don't have power, I had to use a camp stove to do the cooking. I'm not sure if they're even cooked in the middle."

"Well, I've got a confession of my own to make," Lucinda says. "I used the same pre-mix the last time I gave you cookies."

They share a laugh.

Ardie looks around the room, points at the foot of Lucinda's bed. "You mind if I sit?"

"Oh, where are my manners! There's a chair in the corner over there, why don't you pull it around?"

Ardie finds the chair in question, pulls it up next to Lucinda's side of the bed, positioning herself between Lucinda and the window that overlooks the street below.

Lucinda takes another bite of the peanut butter M&M cookie and her expression shifts, becomes pensive. She stares past Ardie and through the window beyond.

"When I made these cookies last time, they were for my next door neighbor. For Dionne."

A long moment passes, silence stretching like cobweb between them. Ardie can hear Dan and Aggie's voices wafting up from the ground floor of the house.

At last, Lucinda meets Ardie's gaze again. "You must think I'm crazy, talking about my dead girlfriend like that. I know you and everyone else think she's dead — heck, I went to her funeral myself. I know she died. I can tell you where she's buried. But I swear to you, Ardie, she came back to me, and she was flesh and blood. Some of my clothes... I can still smell her on them."

"I don't think you're crazy," Ardie says. She chooses her next words carefully, thinking of her own experiences with PTSD after she got back from Afghanistan for the last time. "But I know myself how, after something horrible happens, sometimes it's easy to get... confused."

Lucinda's eyes well with tears. "Please don't do that."

"Do what?"

"Treat me the way everyone else has been treating me. Like I belong in an institution. Like I've lost touch with reality. Like I'm fragile little Lucinda, the crazy spinster cousin, the one everybody has to take care of. Dionne was *here,* Ardie. I didn't make her up. She wasn't in my head."

Ardie nods slowly, leans her forearms onto her knees. She lets her gaze fall, studies the wood floor between her still-drying boots.

"I don't know how," Lucinda continues, "and I don't know why, but Dionne came back to me, Ardie. I swear she did. She came back to me, and I didn't want to admit it to myself at first, because I think I was afraid I was losing my mind, but I knew it was her all along. Even when she was just the girl next door who wouldn't tell me her name, I knew. And I don't care if nobody else ever saw her, if I was the only one, *I* know she was there. I know she came back to shield me from Hart, one last time."

At this, Ardie looks up again. "Maybe she wasn't there to be your shield. Maybe she came back for something else."

Lucinda seems surprised. Ardie figures she must've been prepared for an argument, and doesn't know how to react when Ardie doesn't try to contradict her.

"You believe me? That she was really here?"

Ardie starts to answer, stops herself. Sighs. "Honestly, Lu, I don't know what to believe these days."

I've been seeing some pretty strange things myself lately, she almost adds, but she doesn't want to turn the attention off Lucinda and onto herself. That doesn't seem right. Not now.

"I tell you what I do know," Ardie says. "I think you *needed* to see her. So in a way, it doesn't really matter if she was really there or not. She was there for you — *you* believed in her. I s'pose that's what mattered most."

Lucinda seems to think about this for a moment. "So why do you think I needed to see her? If she didn't come back to protect me?"

"There's different sorts of protection," Ardie says. "Maybe... maybe you had to see her again in order to do what you did. Maybe it was less about being your shield and more about giving you strength. The strength to... *end* things with Hart, once and for all."

Ardie can't quite bring herself to say *kill Hart;* it feels like the word would be too traumatic for Lucinda to hear. After all, Ardie's been having nightmares about shooting Hart herself, and she only injured the man.

Lucinda goes back to staring out the window, and another long moment of silence passes. "But Dionne showed up before I ever knew that the police had lost track of Hart. Before I ever knew he'd come for me. Before I knew I'd... do what I did."

"You didn't know what was going to happen," Ardie says. "But what if Dionne did?"

She hadn't expected to put it that way, and when the question escapes her mouth, it surprises her. Because Ardie might have been humoring Lucinda a bit, but deep down she knows Dionne had only been Lucinda's hallucination… doesn't she? She probably shouldn't be playing along like this, supporting Lucinda's delusion.

Lucinda sits up straighter in her bed, like she's finally warming to the conversation and Ardie's presence. "Ardie… do you think maybe… do you think it's possible that Dionne came back to me for reasons that don't even have to do with Hart? For reasons that are — well, that had more to do with her and me than with him?"

"I guess anything's possible," Ardie says. The sadness in Lucinda's eyes seems to dissipate just a little, and she smiles softly, relaxing back into the bed.

"I didn't get to hold her when she died, the first time," Lucinda says. She looks back out the window again, and her voice seems to come from far away, as if each word has to travel through a long tunnel to get to Ardie. "It's something I've always regretted. Hart fired at me, and the bullet only grazed my side, because Dionne was trying to pull me away. The bullet went through me and straight into her stomach. I ran; I thought she was right behind me. She wasn't. She bled to death on my kitchen floor while Hart chased me out of the house and into the yard." Lucinda pauses, takes a breath. "I was halfway across the street before I realized Dionne wasn't behind me. I turned around to head back to the house, but Hart was right there. He would've killed me, too, if not for the fact that one of my neighbors tackled him. A good Samaritan." She looks up at Ardie. "My neighbor saved my life, and I don't even know his name. Not even now."

Ardie nods to show that she's listening.

"And now *you're* the one who saved my life, Ardie." Lucinda shifts forward, touches one of Ardie's forearms. "And I know your name."

Lucinda's hand is warm and gentle on Ardie's arm, and Ardie stares at it for a moment before responding.

"Why'd you jump off that bridge, Lucinda? For a minute — " Ardie's voice cracks unexpectedly, and she stops to compose herself before continuing. "For a minute there, I thought we'd lost you. I thought…" Her voice cracks again. She clears her throat. "I thought *I'd* lost you. And I really don't want to lose you."

Lucinda takes her hand back, and even though she doesn't change her position on the bed, it seems to Ardie that she shrinks in on herself, withdraws back into the shell that had only just begun to crack open.

"I'm sorry," Ardie says. "I shouldn't have…"

But she trails off, unsure about how to complete the sentence. She chastises herself in silence. Ardie has had plenty of instances in her life when her feelings for a woman haven't been reciprocated, and whenever that's happened, she's been careful not to hint at how she really feels. She never wants to make anyone uncomfortable.

But now, at the worst possible time for Lucinda, she's done exactly that.

She should leave.

Ardie stands from the chair beside the window. "I'll see myself out."

"You don't have to leave."

"I should. Jim and Daddy are still working on dryin' out the shop this afternoon, and if I don't get over there soon, they'll be wondering what happened to me. And… I'm sure you'll be wanting to rest."

"I've been doing nothing but resting," Lucinda says. "That's all anybody thinks I want, apparently. To rest. But I think it's just an excuse to stay away. So they won't have to talk to me about what happened." She gazes up at Ardie, studying her face. "Sit back down, Ardie. Just for a minute."

Ardie struggles for a moment, glancing between Lucinda and the door. "Alright," she says, lowering herself back into the chair. "But only for a minute. And then I'll get going."

Lucinda sighs, looks at Ardie. "To answer your question, I jumped because Dionne asked me to. Because she said we could be together forever that way."

"And did you believe her?"

"Part of me did. Part of me still does. Part of me is just waiting for all of you to forget about me again, waiting for you to turn your back long enough for me to go back to her."

    Ardie stares at Lucinda and says nothing.

Chapter 39

The date was May 9, 2015, and Ardie had been home from Afghanistan for almost eight months, officially retired from the military for nearly five months, and living in Tucson for nearly two months. Sandra was the one who'd picked Tucson out, almost on a whim, and Ardie, eager to get away from Camp Pendleton and the suburban sprawl of Southern California, agreed to the move. They didn't know anyone in Tucson; they left California without so much as a place to live, but between Ardie's savings from her combat pay, plus her military pension, they'd have enough to set themselves up and live comfortably, if modestly, for at least a while before either of them would need to think about working again.

They would end up signing a lease on the first halfway decent apartment they found there, living out of the beat-up RV Ardie'd bought to fix up for a few weeks until the apartment was ready. Once they moved in, Ardie would sell the RV and replace it with an equally old Harley, while Sandra furnished their apartment off a series of yard sales and charity shops. A week into living in their new home together, they would stock their empty fridge from the grocery section at Walmart on their first big shopping trip after moving in, the same shopping trip that yielded Omar the transgender cat from a dumpster.

Ardie drank too much back then. *"Self-medication"* is what the military shrink would call it later on. *Self-medication for her moral injury.* But Ardie just called it getting trashed. And she got as trashed as she could as often as she could in those first few months in Tucson. Usually she'd wait until Sandra went to bed before breaking out a bottle from the kitchen and setting herself up in the living room, turning down the television until it was just white noise, both soundtrack and witness to her pain.

Ardie drank to chase the nightmares away. She drank to blot out the late-night echoes of mortar rounds, the screams of bleeding men, the haunting visage of Lucas Koch.

Just a dumb kid with an even dumber dog. The dog followed Lucas blithely into battle, as if the kid from Nebraska actually had any kind of right to land himself all the way in Afghanistan. And like the dog, Lucas had also followed someone blithely into battle — a handful of Washington politicians, as if they had any kind of right to decide his fate.

Ardie drank to push Lucas Koch as far from her heart as she could.

Ardie drank and Ardie drank, drank until she'd forgotten why she was drinking in the first place. Drank until she forgot how or when she'd started drinking.

And it was on one of those late nights that she found herself sitting in the empty living room, the dance of blue-white television images her only light, gazing down numbly at a handgun in her lap.

There are different ways to chase nightmares away. Alcohol is one way, but alcohol doesn't put an end to them; it only mutes them for a while. It turns the volume down on the nightmares, the flashbacks, until they are white noise in the background, a soundtrack of pain playing on repeat, images strobing out occasionally into the emptied room of the mind. Alcohol, in other words, doesn't work, and Ardie learned this lesson the hard way.

There was another way to silence nightmares, she thought that night, staring at the Glock. She'd cleaned it earlier that day, a ritual that, much like working on the old Harley parked outside their apartment, usually calmed her. But she'd had a strange thought when cleaning the gun, the smell of oil clinging to her fingertips.

She'd had a strange thought, and now that thought wouldn't go away. Now that thought was back, and she was sitting alone in the living room at two o'clock in the morning, drunk, holding a handgun in her lap.

She turned it over and over in her hands, and once, experimentally, she pressed the barrel into her temple, curious about how the cool metal would feel against her skin on a warm desert night.

Now, years later, Ardie can't recall how the gun made it back to its place on the top shelf in the hall closet that night. She can't remember if she finally stumbled into bed, or if she slept on the couch. She can't remember how bad the hangover was the next morning, or if she fought with Sandra again over her drinking. She only knows that she felt alone — so very, very alone — and that no one, not even Omar the cat, could penetrate that opaque black sphere of her loneliness.

And if Lucas had appeared to her back then, the way he did on the night of the storm? How much would Ardie have savored his every word, his every flop-eared grin?

Would she have followed him anywhere? Would she have taken a bridge for him?

Undone — that was how Ardie had felt that night, May 9, 2015. She felt undone.

Not just in the sense of having unraveled, of being the many pieces of Humpty Dumpty, the debris of her soul scattered helplessly across the living room floor. She felt *undone* in the sense of feeling *unfinished*, in the sense of a quest granted during a half-remembered dream that was somehow both vital for her continued existence and yet, in her waking state, completely unreachable.

Ardie had left something *unfinished*, and she had a feeling whatever it was, it was half a world away now, slowly being buried beneath the desert sand. If Lucas would've asked her to take a bridge for him in order to finally finish things, she would've. But more than that?

More than that, she wanted to go back to Afghanistan.

#

It only takes a week for the power to come back on, which is long enough for most people in Reverie to run through their supplies of candles and canned food, but shorter than what anyone expected or even hoped for. The people who fled to Columbia and Greenville and Augusta start to trickle home once word reaches them, and Reverie slowly comes back to life. Cell phone reception becomes consistent once more, except for those backwater parts of town where it was never good in the first place, and most of the main roads are clear, if still coated in a thin layer of silt. The Shop 'n Go opens its doors before anything else does; Main Street yawns and opens its eyes again a day or two later. Linda's suffered a couple broken windows, but they spray paint a friendly "Open for Business" on one of the pieces of plywood, sweep up the glass inside, and are back to serving coffee and soups and sandwiches by the eighth day after the storm.

Ardie and her dad follow suit, opening the shop back up the same day. But he's unusually tender about it.

"You sure you're ready for all this?" he asks, giving Ardie a squint-eye. "What with everything that happened?"

"'Course I am," Ardie answers, surprised. "Eight days of being cooped up with you and Mom? I'll run the shop by myself if you want me to."

He responds only with a gruff half-laugh, but it seems to Ardie that he still gives her the squint-eye now and again.

With all the branches and trees that came down on cars and trucks, one would think the shop would be packed with business. But apparently, folks have more important things on their minds than their cars and trucks. Besides that, a good portion of the damaged vehicles won't be seeing the inside of a shop but the inside of a junkyard.

So day eight is slow; day nine is only marginally better, but finally they have enough business that it requires more than Ardie, her dad, and Jim to run the shop. Jim, it seems, is just as determined as her dad to fix a squint-eye on her.

On a slow afternoon on the tenth day, tired of sitting around with little to do, and having heard from a customer that Georgie's is open for business again, Ardie decides she'll make the walk up the street to see if Lucinda might be at work. She doesn't expect her to be there, but she goes anyway.

In fact, she kind of hopes Lucinda won't be there, because she's hoping to have a conversation with Rhonda in private.

Chapter 40

Both Georgie and her salon manage to escape the hurricane unscathed. And when the bell above the door announces Ardie's arrival, Georgie is the first of the stylists to look up, assessing Ardie with a smile from the spot that Lucinda typically occupies. An industrial-sized fan roars in one corner, trained on a shrinking puddle of water. Georgie's, like most other places on Main Street, must've taken on a little water. But it couldn't have been that bad, because there is no stench of mildew, no brown stains ringing the tiles.

Rhonda glances over, catching Ardie's eye, and Ardie gives her a half-hearted wave in return as she tries to figure out how she might get Rhonda alone for a moment.

Rhonda saves her the trouble. She sets her scissors and comb down on the counter, and says something that looks like it might be *"Hold on just a sec"* to the woman in the chair, but Ardie can't hear over the fan.

"You don't need another haircut, Ardith," Rhonda says when she reaches Ardie.

"No. I know I don't. I was actually hoping I could talk with you for a minute."

"I'm with a client."

Ardie hesitates, looking from the client to Rhonda.

"It's time sensitive. It's about Lucinda."

At the mention of Lucinda, Rhonda's face changes. The guarded mask she'd seem to reserve especially for Ardie dissolves, and Ardie thinks she sees a mixture of sadness and anxiety take its place. Just for a moment. But she can't say for sure.

"Let's step outside a sec," Rhonda says.

Ardie follows her out the door and a few paces up the sidewalk, stopping at a small fallen tree that hasn't yet been cleared.

"You told me that I could help her a while back," Ardie says once they're alone. "I think I understand now. I think I know what Lucinda's going through, where others don't. Because I've been there before myself."

Rhonda frowns like Ardie's said something particularly distasteful. "What Lucinda's *going* through?"

"Yeah." Ardie double-checks that they're alone, and even though they are, she still lowers her voice before she speaks again. "She thinks her girlfriend — her *dead* girlfriend, the girl that Hart Hamilton shot back in Georgia — came back to her, wanted her to jump from that bridge so that they could be together once and for all. And I can understand that because… well, because after Iraq and Afghanistan, sometimes I'd get some funny ideas, too. Sometimes I'd see some funny things."

Rhonda is silent for a long moment. "When did Lucinda tell you all this?"

"Some of it I put together on my own, before she told

me. Some of it we talked about a few days ago, last time I saw her at Dan and Aggie's."

"And why you tellin' *me* all this? What you think *I've* got to do with any of it?"

"It's no secret who your grandmother was."

"Great-grandmother."

Ardie waves dismissively. "Great-grandmother, then. What matters is that I heard stories about her growing up — even here, in Reverie. My daddy even knew somebody who went and saw her once. Wanted her to put him in touch with his dead son, who'd died in Vietnam."

"Where you goin' with this, Ardith?"

"I know you're not your grandmother, but I thought maybe you could... help Lucinda move on, so to speak. Help her think her girlfriend's found peace in her death. So that Lucinda can get on with her life. Get back to living."

Rhonda's eyes narrow. "And just what are you suggesting I do?"

"A seance," Ardie says. "Or just — I don't even know if you believe in all that stuff, communicating with the dead and what-not, or if it was just something your kin folk did. Even if it's not really a seance, even if it's just staged up to look like one, where Lucinda can — well, you know, where Lucinda can feel like she's said a proper goodbye to Dionne, her girlfriend."

Rhonda nods slowly, like she's contemplating. She touches a rosary wrapped around her wrist, fondling the pewter cross for a moment before she speaks. "Do you believe the dead sometimes don't cross over, Ardith?"

"I don't think I believe there's any 'over' to cross to."

"Mmm," Rhonda says thoughtfully, her hands still on the beads. Her gaze goes somewhere faraway, and it feels to Ardie that nearly a minute passes before she speaks again. "Things tend to go more smoothly when the people involved have faith in what they're doing."

Ardie shakes her head. "No offense, Rhonda, but there's not a whole lot I have faith in. Gamecocks football, maybe, but even them only about half the time."

Rhonda hesitates. "Alright. I'll stage your seance for Lucinda."

"Great, I'll tell her that you —"

Rhonda interrupts her. "But there's something *you* gotta understand before I agree to this."

"What's that?"

"What you're expecting to happen might not happen."

Ardie's confused. "What do you mean, what I expect? I'm not the one expecting anything. I just wanted to set this up for Lucinda. To give her peace of mind."

Rhonda nods. "I understand that. And I'm lettin' you know right now — I'm warning you — that what you're hoping for and what's *actually* gonna happen might not be the same thing."

Ardie shrugs. "That's fine. I'm not really concerned about that. I just think Lucinda will rest easier at night if she feels like Dionne is somewhere safe and happy. And I want to give her that chance."

"Mmm," is all Rhonda says, and she raises an eyebrow like she's skeptical.

Rhonda's an odd bird, never been one to be particularly warm to Ardie. So Ardie makes a decision to ignore the raised eyebrow.

They spend another few minutes setting up the time and the place (*"It needs to be at Lucinda's duplex,"* Rhonda insists), and Ardie is pleasantly surprised when Lucinda texts her back almost right away to confirm that she's interested and that she can meet on the day and time Rhonda proposed. Rhonda leaves Ardie with a list of supplies she and Lucinda should bring, including a picture of Dionne, which Ardie knows must still be at the duplex, and, strangely, the gun Lucinda used to kill Hart. Ardie can't imagine what place her gun would have at a seance, but then again, she doesn't really know anything about seances at all, other than what she's seen on TV from time to time.

She leaves Rhonda at Georgie's and walks with a light step back down the hill towards the auto shop. She feels optimistic, she realizes, and that's something she hasn't felt much of since the night of the storm.

Chapter 41

Lucinda is still limping when she and Ardie prepare the duplex for the seance, but she seems to be in good spirits.

"I'm glad I still have a kitchen table left," she says as she places the snapshot of Dionne and her in the center of the table.

"You're lucky any of this place was left standing at all," Ardie says, lighting the three candles and placing them around the photograph.

Lucinda puts her hands on her hips, takes a look around. Thanks to the preparations Ardie made before the hurricane hit, the old duplex managed to survive the storm. Or at least half of it did, anyway. The old oak tree Ardie had worried about came down on the house after all, but it hit the other half of the house. The house Lucinda used to say was Dionne's. The roof is partially collapsed on that side, and Ardie wonders if they should really be on this side, even though it seems sound enough. Lucinda's bedroom, the room closest to where the roof caved in, did take on some water damage; most of what had been in Lucinda's closet is now ruined.

But that's okay, Ardie thinks, because clothes are something that can always be replaced. Clothes, roofs, cars, trees — none of them are really all that important.

What matters is that Lucinda's here. And Ardie's here. The thought makes Ardie's heart warm.

"It's awfully hot in here," Lucinda says. "That's the thing about all the windows being boarded up. No air circulation."

"You want me to…" Ardie starts to ask if Lucinda wants her to turn the air conditioner on, but remembers at the last moment that this old shack of a duplex is one of the few places in Reverie that still doesn't have power. In all likelihood, there's some power line or another that a tree downed that hasn't been discovered yet. "I could open the front door and the back door," Ardie says instead. "Start moving some air around in here."

Lucinda nods. "Yeah. That'd be nice. I'll get the back —"

"No, ma'am. I know you're not supposed to be putting much weight on that foot."

"It's been more than a week," Lucinda protests.

"Yes, it has been, and you're still limping, too. You sit down," Ardie says, pulling a chair out at the kitchen table and ushering Lucinda into it. "I can get the doors."

Lucinda sits as she's been told while Ardie opens the door that leads out of the kitchen and into the backyard. Sunlight immediately floods into the darkened kitchen, and Ardie blinks painfully. Sitting in the dark with only candles lit, she'd forgotten that this seance was to be held in broad daylight. She'd forgotten it was a cheerful, sunny Sunday afternoon outside.

She traverses the kitchen and living room, and opens the front door as well, only to find Rhonda standing on the front porch.

"Good timing," Ardie says, stepping out of Rhonda's way.

But Rhonda doesn't walk inside immediately. She stands on the front porch and peers into the small, stuffy duplex.

"Is Lucinda here already?" she asks Ardie.

"Yeah, of course," Ardie says, surprised that Rhonda didn't spot her, before she remembers how dark it is inside. Ardie gestures towards the kitchen table. "She's right there at the table."

Rhonda nods curtly and picks up a large basket from the front porch.

Ardie reaches for it. "Let me help you with — "

"No, it's okay," Rhonda says, holding the basket close to her. "I got it."

Rhonda crosses into the kitchen, walks in a slow circle around the table, pausing every so often to look up or down, or to cock her head as if she's listening for something.

"Ardith, close the doors please."

"It's been hot in here," Ardie says. "And Lucinda's power's still not up. We just opened them to circulate some air."

"We're gonna need the doors closed," Rhonda says. "And I need you to move this stuff off the table." She points to the three candles and the framed photo of Dionne and Lucinda.

"But you said we were supposed to have this stuff on the table."

"We'll put it all back."

Ardie exchanges a glance with Lucinda, who shrugs.

"Okay," Ardie says, and she closes the doors — first the one in the front, then the one in the back. The house goes dark again.

Since Rhonda's still wandering around the kitchen like she's lost, Ardie also gathers up everything on the table and puts it in the chair next to Lucinda.

"Good," Rhonda says when Ardie's finished. She walks over to the table, places her basket on the floor and reaches inside it. She's holding something in her hand when she stands again, and she sprinkles whatever it is onto the table's surface.

"Blessings be upon this salt," she says. Slowly and deliberately, Rhonda walks another circle around the table. "May this area be cleansed and blessed." She repeats the phrase several times, sprinkling salt until there's none left in her palm.

Lucinda and Ardie both watch her in silence. Ardie can't say exactly why, but the hairs on the back of her neck begin to rise.

Rhonda reaches into her basket again and pulls out a white tablecloth. "Help me with this, please," she says, directing the request to Ardie.

Ardie hurries over, grabs an edge of the tablecloth, and helps Rhonda spread it out over the table. Rhonda nods when she's satisfied, takes the rosary with the pewter cross from her wrist. Carefully, she lays the rosary on the table, spreading it into a wide oval.

"Mother Izzie," Rhonda says, apparently to the rosary, "help me, your child, to complete this ceremony for the departed. Help them to cross over. Help them to be at peace." She straightens up. "Put the candles and the picture inside the rosary."

Ardie responds automatically, arranging the three lit candles and the framed photo inside the oval formed by the rosary. She hesitates a moment, then faces the photograph towards Lucinda.

Lucinda's gaze drops to the photograph immediately, as if entranced.

Rhonda points to a chair across from her, the one on Lucinda's other side. "Sit," she says, and Ardie sits without a word.

Rhonda sits, too, and reaches back into her basket, this time producing a small brass bell. She rings it sharply, and in the dark and silent kitchen, the sound is impossibly loud. Ardie winces and resists the desire to clap her hands over her ears.

"Dionne Summers, we wish to communicate with you. Are you with us? Make yourself known."

"How did you know Dionne's last name?" Lucinda asks Rhonda, but Rhonda ignores her and rings the bell again.

"Dionne Summers, we wish to communicate with you. Are you with us? Make yourself known."

Lucinda gasps and puts her hand over her mouth. She points. "Ardie, do you see her? She's next to you."

Ardie frowns, turns her head slightly to the side, and sees nothing.

Rhonda rings the bell again. "Lucas Koch, we wish to communicate with you. Are you with us? Make yourself known."

Lucinda glances from Rhonda to Ardie. "Lucas? The Lucas from Afghanistan?"

Ardie whips towards Rhonda. "What are you doing? Why are you — "

But Rhonda only rings the bell. "Lucas Koch, we wish to communicate with you. Are you with us? Make yourself known."

"I'm here, I'm here," Lucas says from behind Ardie. "Quit ringing that damned bell before I rip it out of your hand and stick it somewhere you won't like."

Half-afraid of what she'll see behind her, half-afraid she won't see anything at all, Ardie turns in her seat. Sure enough, he's standing right there in his desert fatigues, patrol cap pulled low above his brow.

"Lucas?" Ardie says.

"In the flesh — or… whatever this is." He looks down at himself, and Ardie realizes he's not entirely there. He shimmers somewhat, the way heat shimmers up from asphalt in the desert. He's luminescent. But beautiful, somehow. It makes Ardie want to cry.

Lucinda watches Ardie, a sympathetic expression on her face.

"Can you see him?" Ardie asks her.

"No," Lucinda says. "But I can… *feel* him, I think. Do you think you can feel Dionne?"

Ardie closes her eyes for a moment, not sure what it is she's supposed to feel. *Dionne,* she thinks to herself, remembering the jolly, laughing face from Lucinda's photograph. But she doesn't feel anything.

She opens her eyes and shakes her head. "No," she says to Lucinda. "I don't feel…"

But she stops, because there's a woman standing beside Lucinda now — a young woman, with long dark hair and twinkling, mischief-filled eyes. She's luminescent, like Lucas is, and she drapes an arm casually and protectively around Lucinda.

Ardie's breath catches in her throat.

This isn't… this can't be… how is this happening?

"No," Ardie says, shaking her head hard, as if the force of the motion might clear her vision, might make her hallucinations of Lucas and Dionne disappear. "No, this isn't real. None of this is real."

"'Real' is relative, Staff Sergeant," Lucas says behind her. "Know who told me that? You did. You said that everyone's got their own reality, and we don't have to like it, we don't have to agree with it, but we gotta acknowledge that it's real for them."

"Subjective experience of reality is one thing; seeing people who aren't there is something else entirely," Ardie says. "It's madness."

"What's madness? What are you talking about, Ardie?" Lucinda asks, clearly confused. Apparently she can only hear Ardie's half of the conversation. "I thought you said you believed me when I saw Dionne. I thought you said you — "

Ardie looks at Rhonda for help, but Rhonda sits silently, holding the brass bell with both hands, staring at Ardie impassively.

"I see Dionne, too, Lu," Ardie says. "That's the problem. But she can't be here, which means…"

Which means I've lost my mind.

"We're here," Dionne says with a smile. "We're all here. One day you'll come to understand, like I have, that there are all different kinds of reality. Or *realities,* I should say. Like your friend Lucas is trying to tell you."

"Lucas isn't there," Ardie says stubbornly.

"I'm not?" Lucas says, exchanging glances with Dionne.

Rhonda rings the bell again, pulling Ardie's attention away from the beautiful young woman beside Lucinda. "Lucinda Hamilton, we wish to communicate with you. Are you with us? Make yourself known."

Ardie stares at Rhonda incredulously. "What are you doing? Lucinda's sitting right here." She points at Lucinda in the seat next to her.

Rhonda ignores Ardie and rings the bell a second time. "Lucinda Hamilton, we wish to communicate with you. Are you with us? Make yourself known."

Chapter 42

"Rhonda?" Lucinda asks. "What are you doing?" Her tone is on the edge of panic. "Answer me!"

But Rhonda doesn't answer. She stares straight ahead, straight at Ardie — but maybe through Ardie would be a better way of putting it, because it seems like Rhonda is seeing something else entirely.

Ardie expects Lucas to make a smart-aleck comment, or Dionne to speak up in defense of Lucinda, but both of them are still. Still as death.

Rhonda rings the bell. "Lucinda Hamilton, we wish to —"

Lucinda bangs her fist on the table. "Dammit, Rhonda, stop it! What are you trying to —"

Rhonda turns her gaze in the direction of the sound. "Lucinda, is that you?"

"She's sitting right there, Rhonda!" Ardie yells, gesturing at Lucinda and Dionne. "Stop playing games! This was supposed to be to give her peace!"

"I'm *trying* to give her peace, Ardith," Rhonda replies calmly. "I'm trying to give you peace, too."

"What's she talking about?" Lucinda says, directing her question at Ardie before looking up at Dionne.

Dionne stays silent, rubs Lucinda's shoulder

reassuringly.

"She told you before, Sergeant," Lucas says from his spot behind Ardie. "What you were hoping for this to be and what it actually is weren't necessarily going to be the same thing."

Something cold seizes Ardie's heart. "What do you mean," she says to Rhonda, "about giving me peace?"

"You don't understand your own strength," Rhonda says. "No one ever taught you to recognize it, and so you're using it without understanding it. You have two people you've been holding onto — one for several years, one for the past week and a half. And by holding onto them, you're keeping them here. Keeping them from crossing."

"No," Ardie says, shaking her head. "No, Lucinda's sitting right there. Please stop pretending like you can't see her." She looks at Lucinda for help, but Lucinda, eyes wide with confusion and fear, says nothing.

She's beautiful, Ardie thinks, even in her fear. The soft light cast by the three candles in the center of the table makes her even more radiant, makes her almost… luminescent.

"I will not argue that she's sitting right there," Rhonda says, pointing at Lucinda but still talking to Ardie. "I will not argue that she's been sitting there the whole time. But I…" She turns her head in Lucinda's direction. "I cannot see her. The Good Lord did not see fit to bless me with that kind of sight. But he did see fit to bless *you* with that, Ardith."

No one speaks. The silence is only broken several seconds later, when Lucinda lets out a soft sob.

"Shhhh, baby doll," Dionne says. "Everything's going to be alright. I promise."

"Ardith," Rhonda says quietly. "Tell me what happened the night of the storm. When you came here to find Lucinda."

Ardie remembers everything clearly, as clear as if it happened the night before. She takes a moment, swallows audibly before she begins to speak.

"He shot at me right away," she says. "Didn't even wait to find out who I was, just started firing. And that's how I knew it had to be him. Had to be Hart."

Lucinda begins to cry; Dionne strokes her hair.

"When I couldn't find Lucinda, I figured she'd gone into the woods to hide, so I went after her, and…"

"And I saw you out there, Sarge, worried some tree was gonna knock you on that pretty, Incredible Hulk head of yours," Lucas says.

Lucinda looks up at the sound of Lucas's voice. "I see him, Ardie. And I hear him. Does that mean I…"

"I saw Lucas Koch," Ardie says, continuing. "Who died four years ago when I was in Afghanistan. But somehow he knew, he… he…"

"He led you to Lucinda?" Rhonda asks.

"Yes. He did. I found her just before she jumped." Ardie gives Dionne an accusatory glare. "Just before someone convinced her to jump."

Dionne shakes her head. "You don't understand, Ardie. Not yet."

"And you fished her from the river," Rhonda says.

Ardie nods. "She wasn't breathing at first, but I brought her back."

"No," Rhonda says. "You didn't. The fall killed her. Hit her head on some rocks before she even had a chance to drown. Coroner said her neck was broke in three different places. She was a corpse by the time you got to her."

Ardie shakes her head slowly. "No. That's not what happened."

"It *is* what happened," Dionne says. "Lucinda's time in that life was up. I'd known it would be up for a long time before." She looks down at Lucinda. "That's why you've been able to see me, love," she says gently. "Because it was so close to your time. You were always meant to go that night, one way or another. Either from Hart, or from the storm, or from that fall."

"You made me jump," Lucinda says, voice small.

"Your life was going to end no matter what, Lu. And I wanted your last moment to be with me," Dionne says. "I'm sorry. I should've just told you the truth."

"But then... why am I still here?"

Dionne lifts the hand that's not resting on Lucinda's shoulder and points at Ardie. "Her. You stayed because of her."

"Do you remember what happened when you brought Lucinda back?" Rhonda asks Ardie. "Do you remember killing Hart Hamilton?"

Ardie looks up sharply. "I didn't kill Hart. I shot him before I went after Lucinda, but I only wounded him. He was alive when we got back."

Rhonda nods. "He was alive, yes, but then you…"

Rhonda becomes hazy before Ardie's eyes, like a camera lens out of focus. The room spins, and Ardie feels herself falling, falling, falling…

#

Ardie carries Lucinda's limp form out of the woods towards the blue patrol car lights pulsing against the night. Wind whistles all around her; the trees all seem to live, thrashing in a mad dance as if attempting to escape their earthly confines.

Wheeler sees her approaching first, jogs over to her.

"Where'd you find her?" he asks, dipping his chin down to indicate Lucinda.

"Over by the old trestle. She jumped. I think… I s'pose she thought death was the only way she could get away from him."

He looks at Lucinda's lifeless body with sadness in his eyes.

"I've known her since she was ten years old, y'know," he says quietly. "Shame how things turned out for her." Wheeler purses his lips and shakes his head. "The medics will see to her in a second. We can just lay her down here for now." He turns to go, pauses, and looks over his shoulder at Ardie. "If she jumped, am I correct that you jumped in after her?"

Ardie says nothing.

Wheeler lets out a low whistle. "This is gonna be the most excitin' police report I've ever written."

Ardie gently lowers Lucinda's body to the ground. She hates setting her down in the mud like that, but she's too tired to keep holding her.

A few yards away, the paramedics are moving Hart from the ground and into the gurney.

"One… two… three…" a paramedic says.

The gurney isn't flat; it's one of the kinds that folds upward towards the head, putting Hart in a halfway sitting-up position.

Which means he sees Lucinda's body almost immediately.

His face contorts, he rips the plastic oxygen mask from his nose and mouth. *"Lucinda!"* Hart screams, and not even the hurricane seems to mute the animalistic rage he puts into the three syllables of his ex-wife's name. "You killed her! She was mine to kill! Mine!"

Ardie freezes.

It seems like it should happen in slow motion, but it doesn't. It happens in such a short blur of seconds that Ardie will wonder later how the injured Hart could've managed to do so much in such an abbreviated sliver of time.

The injuries don't slow him at all. He twists on the gurney, and in one fluid motion, somehow manages to snatch the skyward-facing deputy's gun from its holster behind him. The gun swings around, muzzle blazing before Ardie hears the crack of the shot's report.

But Ardie, as if she's channeling an Old West gunslinger, moves even faster. She levels the gun without really aiming, flips the safety off without really realizing she's doing it, and fires three times in rapid succession — *pop, pop, pop!*

Hart falls back to the gurney, blood blooming from his chest.

Everyone stops, stares at Ardie.

Wheeler puts his hand on the muzzle of the gun, pushes it gently down. "Stop, Ardie. It's done."

"Lucinda," Ardie says miserably. "He killed her. He finally killed Lucinda." She looks up into the storm, letting the rain blind her, pelt her face, stream into her mouth and nose. *"You bastard!"* she shouts at the black sky. *"Why? Why do you keep doing this to me?!"*

"Ardie," Wheeler says, placing a soothing hand on her shoulder. "It's okay now. She'll be at peace."

"There is no peace!" Ardie shouts. "There's *never* peace!"

#

"...Ardith. Ardith, can you hear me? Ardith?"

Ardie opens her eyes, sees three candles in front of her, and a framed photograph of Dionne and Lucinda. Her head feels like it's buzzing, like a million cicadas are inside her skull, all of them clamoring for her attention at once.

"Yeah," she says to Rhonda. "Yeah, I can hear you."

"Did you remember?" Rhonda asks. "Did you see what happened?"

Ardie turns her head slowly towards Lucinda. "Do you remember…?"

Lucinda nods, tears streaming down her face. "I remember, too. But… How can it be? I shot him, Ardie," Lucinda says. "I remember shooting him. I remember taking the gun from you, I remember shouting, I remember…" She looks up at Dionne. "I remember holding you. I remember you died. You died again, right there with me."

Dionne kisses Lucinda's brow, then meets Ardie's eyes. "It's like I said. There are many realities. Not just one. You needed to put an end to your nightmare with Hart. Ardie needed for you not to die. And so you both got your way." She shakes her head, smiles with a thoughtful expression on her face. "I don't know how it all works. I just know that it does."

"Ardith," Rhonda says agin. "Do you remember now?"

Ardie nods. "I do. I remember. I remember everything."

Rhonda's posture relaxes. She sits up a little straighter. "Then it's time to end this. It's time to say goodbye."

Ardie's throat tightens. She's unable to speak. She looks at Lucinda, but Lucinda isn't looking at her. Her face tilts up towards Dionne, tears still streaming down both cheeks.

Dionne wipes the tears from Lucinda's face. "It will be like I said, Lu. Every day a summer day. Every night with each other. Together."

Lucas steps forward, puts a hand on Ardie's shoulder. "I just want you to know, Sarge, there wasn't anything you coulda done differently to stop it. It's like the long-haired girl said. When it's our time, it's our time."

"I know. I guess I've always known," Ardie says wetly. "But I never got to say goodbye to you. Or your stupid dog."

"I always knew you secretly hated him," Lucas says, chuckling. "But look at it this way — we can say goodbye now. Both of us. Okay? Goodbye, Staff Sergeant Brown. It was good knowing you." He holds out a hand.

She takes the hand, shakes it, eyes full to the brim with tears. "Goodbye, Private Koch."

"We'll see each other again," he says.

But then he's gone. He doesn't fade away. There's no whistling sound of wind, no flickering candles. He simply vanishes, as if he'd never been there in the first place.

Ardie turns to Lucinda. For a moment, she struggles to find the right words, struggles to know what you should say to someone you'll never see again.

"I would've loved you," she says at last. It is the one

thing she knows to be true about Lucinda Hamilton.

Lucinda rises from her chair, takes a step in Ardie's direction. She reaches down, wraps her hand around Ardie's. Ardie looks at the hand that's on hers, marvels at how warm it feels, for something that's not even there.

"And I would've loved you, too," she says. She glances over her shoulder at Dionne. "I don't claim to know much of anything, and I definitely don't know about other realities. But I think, Ardie, that in some other reality, maybe we *did* love each other. Maybe we still do."

She leans down, presses her lips to Ardie's cheek. Ardie closes her eyes.

"Goodbye, Lu."

"Goodbye, Ardie."

Ardie doesn't want to open her eyes, because she knows that when she does, Lucinda will be gone. Gone forever.

"Oh, and Ardie," Lucinda says, and Ardie feels the tickle of warm breath against her ear as Lucinda whispers a name into it. Startled, Ardie's eyes fly open, but Lucinda — and Dionne — are gone.

Rhonda is watching her, and says nothing for a long moment. "They've gone, haven't they?"

"Yes," Ardie says heavily.

Rhonda nods and stands up, walking around Ardie to open the kitchen's back door before returning to blow out the candles. Sunlight returns once again, chasing off the gloom that had enshrouded the kitchen a second before.

"Help me with this, will you?" Rhonda says, pointing to the candles and the picture. "Just don't touch the rosary."

Chapter 43

RHONDA

Weeks after the storm, the hurricane is still all anyone can talk about at Georgie's. Every customer who comes in has something to say about it — a story about which tree came crashing down in their yard, or how their neighbor's car got caved in, or how the carport cover got ripped clear off its foundation. Rhonda thinks she's about sick to death of talking about the storm, but she thinks it must be the Good Lord's way of teaching her patience, which is something she's always been in short supply of.

She's taken over most of Lucinda's client roster, may she rest in peace, and figures it'll probably be that way 'til Kathy gets back from maternity leave. She would've thought Georgie would help with the roster, but to be fair, the storm did do a fair bit of damage to her house, so she's been spending her days trying to get things sorted out at home.

Which is how Lucinda's cousin-in-law Aggie ends up in Rhonda's chair a good three weeks after the storm.

They exchange small talk and niceties; Aggie talks about her kids and Rhonda talks about how excited Brandt is for the football season to start.

By and by, Aggie says, "Rhonda, I can't thank you enough for doing that thing for Ardie."

"It was no trouble," Rhonda says, gooseflesh spreading up her arms at the mention of the seance. Without any doubt, it had been both one of the most chilling *and* most rewarding things Rhonda had ever been a part of.

"She hasn't come by our house looking for Lucinda again one time since you did it," Aggie says.

"Mmm," Rhonda says. "How's Dan holding up?"

Aggie sighs. "You know men. I can tell he's still real broke up about what happened to Lucinda, but he won't talk about it. Just sits on the couch, stares out the window like he's waiting for her to show up on our porch step, ringing the bell for dinner."

"I've been praying for him. Our whole church been praying." Rhonda pauses, meets Aggie's eye in the mirror. "Isn't it something," she says, "that in the middle of the worst storm this town's ever had, we only lost one single person? And not even 'cause of the storm itself."

"Well, two people," Aggie says. "If you count…" She lowers her voice. "That *man.*"

"I don't like to think about him," Rhonda says, shaking her head. "I'm not a violent person, but I'm glad Ardie did what she did."

Aggie, still speaking quietly, says, "Nobody's supposed to know about that, ya know. Wheeler and the other deputy, they made sure Ardie's name never went in the police report. And they swore the paramedics to secrecy, too."

Rhonda nods. "I'm glad for that. And you know I won't say nothing."

"Poor old Ardie. She's been through enough, hasn't she?"

"Mmm-hmm," Rhonda says. "That she has."

She might not approve of Ardith Brown's lifestyle — that will never change, because a sin is a sin is a sin — but Rhonda saw something in her the day of the seance. Saw a good soul in there, a heart nearly as big as she was. And she might be a sinner, but the Good Lord had blessed her with *the sight* nonetheless. If she'd grown up in Rhonda's family, she would've been the one to wear Mother Izzie's rosary. Rhonda's sure of it.

"Let's hope she's found her peace," Rhonda tells Aggie.

"Let's hope," Aggie agrees. Then she smiles at Rhonda in the mirror. "Your younger boy getting excited about Halloween yet? It's only September, but my kids are already *begging* me to make costumes."

Epilogue

ARDIE

The following June

It takes her a few months after the storm and its aftermath, but Ardie finally starts making more of an effort to go see old friends in Beaufort, Charleston, and Columbia. A sort of reawakening takes place, the type of thing she didn't even know she needed until she started doing it. It feels good to be around old friends, even if the fact that most of them were married or had serious relationships highlighted her lonesomeness each time she drove back home to Reverie.

"*You should move here,*" they'd tell her over and over. "*There's nothing in Reverie but rednecks and mosquitoes.*"

Ardie would just shrug at that. "*The mosquitoes really aren't that bad, once you get to know them.*"

When Pride weekend gets closer, Ardie gets invited to join her friends in Columbia. Two of them were in the service at the same time Ardie was, and they're representing an LGBTQ veterans' group in the Pride Parade. Ardie, who entered the military right before the advent of Don't Ask, Don't Tell, and exited a few years after it ended, still revels in watching active duty servicemen and women march under both the stars and stripes *and* the rainbow flag. Every year that she sees it, she gets choked up. This year, with the governor of South Carolina finally taking down that wretched Confederate flag in front of the statehouse, she figures she'll enjoy the parade even more.

After the parade that evening, she and her friends gather for drinks and dinner at a steakhouse in the Vista, not that far down the street from the statehouse itself. They're a big, rowdy crowd of about twenty — all of them gay, most of them veterans — and Ardie just soaks it all in for a few minutes, watching her friends appreciatively as they laugh and enjoy themselves.

A woman across from her, a friend of a friend, watches Ardie for a few moments, a smile growing on her face. "It's something, isn't it?" she says to Ardie.

Ardie looks over. The woman's about her age, maybe a couple years older, with shoulder-length blonde hair that's going grey and smile lines around her mouth.

"What's that?"

"Well, I don't know about you," the woman says, "but I never thought I'd see this in my lifetime. Not in South Carolina. Active duty and openly gay. Marching in the parade."

Ardie smiles. "You've got that right. I never would've guessed, either. Did you grow up here?"

"I did," the woman says. "Born 'n bred right here in

Columbia." She chuckles and looks around. "Most people around here don't remember it, but twenty-five years back, this place was a lesbian bar. The Alley Cafe."

"Lesbian bars," Ardie says with a laugh. "Whatever happened to those?"

The woman shrugs. "Online dating happened, I s'pose. Can't say I miss the Alley. A hotbed of drama, most of the time."

Ardie snaps her fingers. "You know what? I think I came here a few times when it was still a gay bar." She glances around. "Yeah — I did. Right before I joined the service. I think I got drunk with a fake ID that said I was twenty-five."

The other woman laughs heartily, and Ardie likes the sound. Likes the way she throws her head back and lets the laughter take over her whole body for a moment. "Oh, sweetie, how could you have forgotten? Getting drunk at the Alley Cafe was a rite of passage for most of the lesbians from around here."

"I'm not from here," Ardie says. "I'm from Reverie."

"Reverie?" the woman says. "I've got cousins down that way. Maybe we've crossed paths before. What's your name?"

"Ardie Brown."

"Nice to meet you, Artie."

"No — it's Ardie. With a 'D.' Short for 'Ardith.'"

The woman laughs again. "Ardith? I guess you really are from Reverie, aren't you?"

Ardie shrugs. "It's a family name."

"It must be," the woman says with a smile. She puts a hand on her chest. "I'm Holly Anne. Or just Holly, to most people."

For a moment, Ardie can't breathe. Time rewinds, and she's sitting in a darkened kitchen, the luminescent form of Lucinda Hamilton looming just above her.

"Oh, and Ardie," Lucinda says, leaning in. She puts her lips close to Ardie's ear. *"Holly Anne,"* she whispers. And then Lucinda disappears, as if she never was.

Ardie recovers herself, managing to hide the unexpected memory with a warm smile. "Holly Anne," she says, the name like honey on her tongue. "It's nice to meet you."

* * *

Thanks for reading.

Support independent authors — leave a review at Amazon.com.

Yes, my dear readers, you've arrived at that point in the book where I ask you, rather shamelessly, to take two minutes to leave a kind-hearted review. I recognize that *Reverie* is, well, "different" to say the least from other lesfic romances, but I'm hoping that you liked it well enough that you're willing to recommend it to other readers.

Your review makes a big difference. A *biiiiiiig* difference. Reviews are often the determining factor as to whether someone picks up a book or not. Knowing that, if you liked this book, won't you just take a moment to tell others about it? It will take you less time than you think.

Oh and hey — love them or hate them, be kind and **please don't post any spoilers!**

Okay, I'll leave you alone about it now. Thanks for considering it.

Would you like a free short story?

I'd like to invite you to read a free short story. It's something that I published many years ago — the first piece of lesbian fiction I ever wrote, published in an anthology of lesbian erotica that has long since gone out of print.

I wrote it when I was twenty-three, almost twenty-four, and when the friend of mine who found it took photos of the pages (the anthology doesn't exist as an ebook — it's *that* old!) and texted them to me, I had to smile. I honestly hadn't even remembered I'd written it, but thinking back, I realize it was the first time I'd ever gotten paid for something I'd written. It made me feel like a "real" writer.

I re-typed the entire story from those texted photos, updating it and editing it as I went. And you know what? Even though I wrote it almost twenty years ago, it's still really pretty fun.

So if you'd like a hot, quick little read, let me give it to you for free. It's all yours when you sign up for my Reader's Club here: http://authorelizaandrews.com/readersclub/

My Reader's Club is also the best way to connect with me. It's where I share snippets of my works in progress, let you know about any sales or events I'm having, give you opportunities to get my new books for free, and highlight discounts from other lesfic authors. I totally do *not* spam you, and if you like lesfic and/or my work, you'll appreciate being on my mailing list. Honest.

And then there's me.

[If this is the first book of mine you've read, then you don't know it yet, but I always include a personal essay of sorts at the end of each of my novels in lieu of an "About the Author" or "Acknowledgments" section. I find when I'm a reader, the typical "About the Author" / "Acknowledgments" bore me, so I'm trying to give you something a little different. I hope you don't mind. And on that note…]

The first girl I dated was from Columbia, South Carolina.

She resented growing up there, not unlike the way I resented growing up in small town Georgia. And so, like me, she'd developed a love-hate relationship with the South.

Maybe it's something you can understand. Maybe it's something I can't explain. I love the South because it formed me, because it was my third parent, teaching me about life. I love highway signs that read simply, "Y'all come eat," and I love toothless old men with gnarled hands who sit at McDonald's for hours at a time with the same cup of coffee before them. I love state fairs and funnel cakes, drinking straight from the hose and wading barefoot through streams searching for crawdads. I love southern accents, which are a sort of oral comfort food for me that I want to wrap around myself like a blanket.

But growing up as a butch dyke sticking out like a sore thumb amidst an ever-shifting sea of bigotry, the South never loved me back.

Homophobia is like a shadow you see out of the corner of your eye at night, playing tricks on your mind. You're never really sure if there's something there or if it's only your imagination. Murmured conversations and furtive, sideways glances that might not have anything to do with you.

But then again, they might.

When I would drive back home from college, all dyked-out in those days in my leather jacket, combat boots, and bandana atop my head, I'd know I was getting close to home when I felt the itchy feeling of stares against my back.

You turn around just as someone else looks away, and you think to yourself, *Was that real, what I just felt? Is that hostility that hangs in the air alongside the humidity? Or am I imagining things once again?*

But back to my first girlfriend.

#

She was (and still is) a strong and proud woman of color, a high femme lipstick lesbian with a "don't f*** with me" attitude who was Out and Proud as a bisexual by the time she was sixteen or seventeen.

And keep in mind that when I say she grew up in Columbia, South Carolina, I'm talking about the South Carolina of the early 1990s, which, while much more tolerant than it would've been a decade or two earlier, was still much more regressive than it is today. It was a sometimes scary place to be either a person of color or a queer. Still is, I imagine.

To be both at the same time… (low whistle).

This was the Columbia where the Confederate flag still flew from the top of the state capitol building, after all, right under the American flag. This was long before the flag controversy that ended in a compromise: Add an odd, stunted little monument to African American history off to the side of the capitol building, and move the flag from the top of the capitol to its front lawn.

Anyway.

#

The girl in question outed herself to me the day that we met, which was move-in day my junior year in college. I was a Resident Advisor in a freshman dorm; she was a sophomore tasked with helping my freshman girls adjust to college life.

I was on crutches that day; she would tell me later that the crutches made it easy for her to corner me (*"You couldn't get away,"* she said with a sly grin). I was twenty years old, barely even out to myself let alone others, but here was this stunningly beautiful woman who was boldly and obviously flirting with me.

Does it go without saying that I had no idea what to do with her?

It took me a long time, plus a few more chance encounters with her on campus (including the time I accidentally got myself locked out of a production of *Sweet Charity* during intermission; she was running the concession stand just outside those locked doors), but eventually I worked up the courage to ask her out.

The rest, as they say, is history. Herstory.

#

The first time I ever went to Columbia was to visit her. It was during the summer after my senior year in college, and I remember walking around the state capitol grounds with her after dinner one night, watching lightning bugs flit here and there while we walked hand-in-hand around statues of Confederate war heroes. We settled onto a bench eventually; we made out for a while in darkness, under the shadow of the Confederate flag.

Kissing her on the lawn of the South Carolina state capitol building felt like a rebellion's first victory, a southern secession that managed to actually gain and hold more territory than a flagpole. (And we were young, too, and when you're young, simply *living* feels like an ever-expanding rebellion.)

She broke up with me later that same summer, while I stood in the lobby of a small hotel in the Yukon, payphone pressed to my ear. I guess we weren't holding as much territory as I had thought.

I cried for a while, but I got over it: I'm happy to call her a good friend all these years later.

#

The next time I visited Columbia, it was to play in a rugby game. It was a sunny winter's day that hinted at spring — February 1, 2003. I know the date not because I specifically remember it, but because in the locker room after we lost, my teammates and I heard the news that the Space Shuttle Columbia disintegrated while reentering Earth's atmosphere. The Columbia destroyed while in Columbia.

I passed the South Carolina Capitol on my way out of town, and realized it looked far less romantic under the crisp winter sun, Confederate flag snapping in the wind, than it had on a balmy midsummer's eve three years earlier.

#

I moved to Columbia for work five years after the space shuttle exploded. Coincidentally, my Main Street apartment was a mere block from the state capitol grounds. I took walks through the grounds frequently, trying occasionally (and always failing) to remember which bench it was on where I'd once made out with a beautiful girl on a summer's night.

Occasionally, I also drove by the field where we'd played that rugby game, remembering how our drive home to Atlanta that day was accompanied by sad news about the space shuttle's explosion.

I lived in Columbia for almost seven years.

I walked those capitol grounds often as the years went by, and memories began to layer themselves one on top of the other. Memories superimposed themselves over each other like double-exposed film. Youthful, rebellious love, with a firefly's brief lifespan. The hard-to-define loneliness of middle age. Rugby. Proteges. Pride parades. Space shuttles.

Explosions.

#

Memories tend to fragment like shrapnel and re-form into odd shapes as time goes on. But perhaps that makes them less like roadside bombs and more like something that melts and then refreezes.

I never know what to do with my memories. I can never tell if they're truly fixed in the past, or if they are ever-present in the eternal now. In fiction, I tend to write the same characters over and over, characters who retread the same grounds they've walked before, characters trying to understand why their past won't stay in the past, why it keeps inserting itself misshapenly into the present, forming stilted futures.

One of my favorite passages in any novel comes from Kurt Vonnegut's *Slaughterhouse Five*:

> "Listen: Billy Pilgrim has come unstuck in time. Billy has gone to sleep a senile widower and awakened on his wedding day. He has walked through a door in 1955 and come out another one in 1941... Billy is spastic in time, has no control over where he is going next, and the trips aren't necessarily fun. He is in a constant state of stage fright, he says, because he never knows what part of his life he is going to have to act in next."

I love this passage because I think it is more truth than science fiction — because this is how we experience our lives, as out-of-control time travelers flitting from one scene to another on the various stages of our lives, filling in with memories what we lack in understanding.

#

I cried on the day that I moved away from Columbia, South Carolina, to Washington, DC. I drove down the main drag in town in front of the capitol building, where the Confederate flag still (at that time) stood in the front lawn, and I said to myself, "This leaving is a kind of death. I may visit here again one day, but this particular time is gone. Gone forever."

And I did visit Columbia again. And it wasn't the same. *I* wasn't the same.

And that was okay, because life is a continuous cycle of death and rebirth.

#

We are Billy Pilgrim but we aren't. We are moving forward boldly into our futures even while caught in the sticky molasses of our past. We may walk out one door in 2017 and emerge into 2000, but it's not the 2000 we remember, because *we* are no longer who we remember. The past we recall is not the past at all, but a phantom version of it, a whisper of something we once knew. Of someone we once knew.

Friends, the past never truly stays in the past. That's one of the open but unspoken secrets about our lives — we are all Billy Pilgrim, come unstuck in time, trying to stand our ground, on crutches, in the present, while we wrestle with the ghosts of our past.

#

What is a ghost? What is a memory?

Are they really so different? Isn't a memory a kind of

ghost?

And what is the difference between what we call hallucination and what we call reality, if both of them are just Plato's shadows playing out on the cave walls — projections of a particular mind at a particular moment in space and time?

These are the questions I wanted readers to wrestle with when they read *Reverie*. I wanted them to shiver a little when they realized "the girl next door" might not actually exist; I wanted them to wonder what the heck was going on with Ardie when Lucas first appears with his guts hanging out.

I wanted them — I want *you* — to reflect upon their / your own past, the way it forms you and informs you, the way it melts down and changes shape over time, never quite staying the same despite the fact that the narrative seems like it should be finished, and set in stone, because, after all, it is over.

Supposedly over.

And I wanted you to do all that thinking inside the balmy atrium that is the Deep South, a place that is both eerily dark and cheerily inviting at the same time. I wanted you to feel the South as I have felt it to be many times — as another main character, a personality in its own right, struggling with its past the way we all do as it moves forward, haltingly, towards an unknown future.

Did it work?

#

I would like to say that, like a restless soul, the past needs to be buried first before we can move on with our lives, but I don't think that's true. The South itself is proof that you can't simply bury things and expect them to go away; if you try, the ghosts of the past will harass you even more.

Instead of burial, perhaps what we need is to make peace. And in making peace, perhaps we need to excavate rather than bury.

#

Excavation:

I drove from Georgia to Virginia this past autumn, and made a stop in the "other" Carolina along the way. My West Coast girlfriend happened to be on the East Coast — coincidentally in North Carolina the same day I was driving through it. We made plans to meet for lunch near my *alma mater* of Duke University.

I walked her through the campus grounds I had walked for many years. I pointed out the dorm where I lived as a freshman, then the freshman dorm where I lived as a junior, when I was a Resident Advisor. I pointed up at the window of the room where my first girlfriend cornered me on crutches; I walked her to the student center and showed her the place where I got locked out of *Sweet Charity*.

Later we made out on a bench. Not in darkness, but in broad daylight — discretely, beneath an off-the-beaten-path gazebo in Duke Gardens. We took selfies together by the fountain. I took her to the coffeeshop where I used to study all the time, and bought her a green tea. We drank it outside on another bench, the same bench where I sat next to another girl once as a freshman and realized, to my horror, that I was falling head-over-heels in love with her.

Memory atop memory; double-exposed film. Walking through a coffeeshop door in 2017; walking outside into 1997.

"Am I stricken by memory or forgetfulness?
Is this the first half of the century or the last?
Is this my father's life or mine?"
— Li-Young Lee, "Ash, Snow, or Moonlight"

#

Anyway, my dear friends.

Just by reading these words, if you have stuck with me this far, you have made yourself a time traveler. Because I write this as I sit here comfortably in Atlanta, counting down the days until I move to the West Coast to pen a new chapter in the ongoing narrative of my life with the woman I love, and when you read this, I will be there already. Out of the South at last; today's future is tomorrow's past.

I will say goodbye to the South and leaving will be a

kind of death, a kind of burial service. I will come back to visit, but it will never be the same.

That is the cycle of death. But with every death, there is rebirth.

There is no such thing as a truly fresh start. There is only the unending process of recycling of what is, what has been, and what is yet to come.

And friends, there is no shame in that.

#

<<<< >>>>

* The poem fragment recited by "the girl" in Chapter 13 is by Ocean Vuong, from his book *Night Sky with Exit Wounds*. It is a lovely book that my girlfriend gifted to me when we first started dating.

* The book quoted in Chapter 28 comes from the beginning of Stacy Schiff's *The Witches: Salem, 1692* (published by Little & Brown, 2015). I picked up a dusty copy of this book from my friend's bookshelf while cat-sitting in southwestern Virginia. I didn't read much of it, but the topic and tone seemed relevant to this novel.

<<<◇>>>

Printed in Great Britain
by Amazon